FEARLESS

BOOK TWO: AGE OF CONQUEST

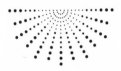

TAMARA LEIGH

WWW.TAMARALEIGH.COM

THE WULFRITHS. IT ALL BEGAN WITH A WOMAN.

A battle. A crown. The conqueror. The conquered. Medieval England—forever changed by the Battle of Hastings. And the rise of the formidable Wulfriths.

A CAPTIVE NORMAN

Sir Guarin D'Argent knew the danger of allowing a woman to turn him from his purpose, and yet he answered her cry across a bloody battlefield. Now he finds himself the lady's captive among vengeful Saxons, weeks becoming months while his liege, Duke William of Normandy, subdues his new English subjects. Biding his time, Guarin plots an escape dependent on captivating his captor, a formidable quest with one more a warrior than a lady. But when his compassion is roused by the suffering of her people under Norman rule, the question of escape is jeopardized by the answer to who, exactly, is captivated—and in a conquered country, what hope there is for enemies beyond a kiss.

A DEFIANT SAXON

Her husband and young son slain by invaders, Lady Hawisa lives only for protecting her people. And revenge. While outwardly bending the knee to the usurper, she amasses rebels to send the conquerors back across the sea, along with the silver-haired warrior she never intended to take captive. Now that Guarin D'Argent has cause to wreak vengeance of his own and knows his captor is a Wulfrith, she dare not release him—just as she dare not succumb to his efforts to turn her from her purpose. But all changes when she is betrayed by one of her own. Will the struggle between the English resistance and the Normans find the two on opposite sides of the battlefield? Or might the Lord have other plans for them?

From a fateful encounter on the battlefield of Hastings, to a rebel camp deep in the wood, to the threshold of the Harrying of the North, Sir Guarin and Lady Hawisa's tale unfolds in the second book in the AGE OF CONQUEST series revealing the origins of the Wulfriths of the bestselling AGE OF FAITH series. Watch for NAMELESS: Book Three releasing Autumn 2019.

For new releases and special promotions, subscribe to Tamara Leigh's mailing list: www.tamaraleigh.com

AUTHOR'S NOTE

Dear Reader,

Welcome to the second book in the *Age of Conquest* series. As with all series shouldering an overarching plot, there is some redundancy in storytelling. This is to orient readers who read the first books months earlier and to ground readers who enter the series out of sequence, allowing each story to stand alone. Of considerable benefit, pivotal events in successive books are experienced from different—often more informed—points of view.

In *Merciless*, the first book in this series, the story begins the morning after the Battle of Hastings when Sir Cyr D'Argent meets Aelfled on the battlefield. In *Fearless*, the story takes a step back to begin the night of the Battle of Hastings following the Normans' victory over the Saxons when Sir Guarin D'Argent encounters Lady Hawisa Wulfrithdotter searching for her young son. Enjoy!

I returned, and saw under the sun, that the race is not to the swift, nor the battle to the strong, neither yet bread to the wise, nor yet riches to men of understanding, nor yet favor to men of skill; but time and chance happeneth to them all. ~ Ecclesiastes 9:11 KJV

CHAPTER ONE

Sussex, England
14 October, 1066

*D*anger. With each drag of her hem over dirt, through blood and other things heretofore unimaginable, it seeped into this bodily vessel, filling eyes, nose, mouth.

Danger. It chilled, making her soul a quaking thing desperate to catch hold of the unsullied hem of the Lord.

Danger. It pressed in on all sides, sweeping over the silent dead in their heaps, the groaning dying soon to join those above and below.

"Not my boy," Isa Wulfrithdotter Fortier gasped as she veered away from a jumble of Saxons and Normans whose bodies were too great of size to include the one for whom she searched. "Lord, do I not find him, let it be he was never here, else returned to the wood…making his way back to safety…back to me."

She halted. Clasping her short mantle at the throat to prevent the hood from falling and making a beacon of her hair, she stared.

A body slight of stature and clothed in red lay face down on one of greater height and breadth. But before her breaking heart

1

could snatch back a soul straining to reach the Lord's hem, she saw here was a Norman. Rather than long hair, his was cropped, the red he wore not of cloth but chain mail coated in crimson. Much blood, but not her boy's.

"Praise You, Lord," she whispered and swept her gaze around this portion of the battlefield she had been searching since shortly after her arrival upon Senlac where the forces of Duke William of Normandy had defeated the army of England after slaying its king.

In the hours since, most of the victorious enemy had retreated from the carnage to celebrate, tend injuries, and rest. However, there were enough moving across the ravaged meadow, searching for their own or desecrating the fallen by relieving them of valuables, that she and other Saxons not yet granted permission to retrieve their dead were in great peril—as was her maid, who had gone opposite Isa when the two ventured out of the wood at twilight.

Might Aelfled have redeemed herself by finding Wulf alive and well? Or was he—?

"Nay, Lord," she beseeched. "If my most precious one is here, let him not number among the dead."

Telling herself she would not be ashamed of her fear even were her sire here, she continued forward, altering her course when it was blocked by bodies or she happened too near Norman scavengers who made her hand convulse on her dagger.

Once again, a figure more a boy than a man captured her regard. Pinned beneath a heavily-armored Norman, he had hair of a familiar length and color.

She ran and dropped to her knees. "Wulf!" His name left her lips a moment before her vision adjusted to the shadow across his face. These were not her boy's unseeing eyes, not his cheeks, nose, mouth, and chin. Just barely a man, this defeated Saxon was another woman's son.

"You served England well in putting down this animal," she

said, though she could not know it was true. It could have been a nearby Saxon who felled the Norman atop this warrior. "One less of his kind we must battle to hold what they would take from us. Be with God, faithful defender."

Fingers trembling, she closed his eyes, then dropped back on her heels, clasped hands against nose and mouth, and thanked the Lord it was possible her son lived.

She started to rise, but voices speaking in the Norman tongue stilled her. Looking around, she saw two men moved in her direction, a third following at a distance.

Certain retreat would bring her to notice, she hunkered low and placed her face near the dead Saxon's. Between sips of foul air, she swallowed to keep the contents of her stomach from climbing her throat, hoped she escaped the enemy's notice, and prayed she would find Wulf alive.

"I can bear no more loss, Lord," she whispered, "especially that of my son. If I am the last of the Wulfriths, I may break. If only for my departed sire, preserve his grandson."

Blessedly, the Normans turned aside, as evidenced by laughter in which only victors lacking heart would indulge in the midst of slaughter that included their own—men who whimpered, groaned, and cried out as death danced around them.

She shuddered, certain such men would try to make her their reward for having survived the battle, just as they would Aelfled who, seven years younger, of smaller frame, and having little training in defense, stood less chance of escape.

Despite how enraged Isa was with her maid for allowing Wulf and his friends to slip away from Trionne Castle, she ached over the possibility Aelfled might become a plaything for the Normans.

"Lord, keep her safe," she rasped. "Defend her life and virtue as you defend mine. Above all, protect Wulf."

She sat back and peered at the dozens of Normans moving over the battlefield. Confirming all were distant enough to allow her to resume her search, she stood and began forging a path among the slaughtered to the base of a hill atop which a skeletal tree reached gnarled fingers to the heavens.

More suffering here than other places she had passed, the ground alive with men struggling to rise or crawl.

Here a Norman. There a Saxon. Another Saxon. Yet another.

"Find your boy," she commanded and began ascending the hill. Halfway up, her trailing skirt so firmly snagged on something her forward motion could not free her. Dropping to her knees alongside a glistening stream of blood, she twisted around. And nearly cried out when she saw her skirt was caught by neither root nor rock.

She fell onto her backside and snatched at it, but the man held to the hem soaked in blood and other evidence of death that made her belly threaten to purge itself.

"Aid me," he said in her language.

She paused in drawing her dagger, looked to his head propped on the shoulder of an extended arm, face framed by long hair and short beard.

"Be merciful," he said. "I must die with my king. Pray...end it."

A royal housecarle. Even were it possible the Saxon would recover, he did not wish to suffer the indignity of surviving King Harold whose life he had failed to preserve.

She knew what he required of her. She knew her sire would not hesitate. And from all the blood, the pale of his face, and the absence of a physician, it would be merciful. But her heart and mind protested, splaying her hand off the dagger.

"Lady," he choked. "I would do it if I could."

She shook her head.

He snapped his teeth, said between them, "Show me your dagger."

"I do not—"

"You lie. Show me, Woman!"

She meant to refuse him but was moved by tears pooling alongside his nose and spilling over onto the dirt. Great his suffering, and greater if she left him like this, whether death circled for hours or the Normans made sport of their enemy while divesting him of mail tunic, gold necklace, rings, and leather boots.

He groaned, said more gently, "I am Edwin, Lady. Pray, your dagger."

Beneath her mantle, she touched the deadly weapon opposite the one used for cutting meat, moved her hand to the latter, and drew it from its scabbard.

"A keen little blade," he said, though were he to look upon her other dagger he would think this a dull thing. He released her skirt and moved his hand to his neck. "Here. The great vein."

He will die regardless, she assured herself. *It is not murder. It is mercy.*

But horror over bleeding him was stronger than reason. "Forgive me, Edwin. I cannot."

"Lady—"

"I cannot!" She took the hand with which he pointed the way to his demise, set the hilt in his palm, and folded his fingers over it. "It *is* keen, requiring less strength to do the deed than hold to my skirt."

As anger flashed in moist moonlit eyes, she surged upright and stepped back. "Forgive me," she repeated. "I…"

His lids closed, and the hand holding her dagger dropped.

Lest he merely lost consciousness he would regain and suffer more, Isa left the blade and turned away.

Feeling sticky grit on her fingers, she raised them before her face. Blood and dirt marked her, doubtless from when she placed the dagger in the housecarle's hand—and likely gained from her hem.

She dragged up her skirt and, wielding the deadly dagger, cut away two hands' width, baring ankles and lower calves. Thus, she would not be distracted by the horror of that bloodied material and other fallen warriors could not easily seize her.

Returning the dagger to its scabbard, she continued her ascent.

The nearer she drew to the tree, searching for a boy of good size though not yet eleven, the more quiet and still it became. The voices of the dying numbered fewer, movement of their pained bodies sluggish in places, absent in others. But that was due to greater blood and carnage here where the dead lay deeper. So deep her son might—

Feeling as if she walked the edge between everything and nothing, that slippery ridge threatening to tip her into inescapable darkness where one of Wulfrith blood did not belong, she gave her head a vicious shake.

Returned to this moment in which observation—not imagination—was required, she looked nearer on all. The fighting here had been momentous, as evidenced by the royal housecarle who wished to die with his king and other soldiers whose clothes, armor, and weaponry revealed neither were they ordinary housecarles who served thanes.

King Harold might have fallen here, but even had he not, this hill was too central to the battle for mere boys to reach it. Or so she prayed as she continued toward the tree past which she would begin her descent.

During her search, Isa had seen many horses sacrificed to carry riders through battle lines. Normans only she was certain, Saxon warriors not given to fighting astride though her sire had sought to persuade King Harold's predecessor, King Edward, to adopt mounted warfare. Among the fallen here were more steeds transported across the sea, and partway down the hill one that appeared merely at rest where it lay with forelegs tucked and head up, its rider slumped over its grey-black neck and pale mane.

Of a sudden, the horse turned its head in her direction, and it seemed all the light that could be found in this darkness shone from its eyes.

Realizing she had broken stride, Isa growled, "Wulf," and continued forward.

"Non, destrier," spoke one whose language and accent spun her around and up against one taller and broader than she.

Finding her palm empty, she jerked her elbow back and closed fingers around her dagger, but before she could draw it, the Norman gripped her arms beneath her mantle.

Unworthy! she silently denounced as her sire had done when he instructed the girl she had been in defending herself until finally he pronounced her otherwise. A dozen years later, now aged twenty and five, once more she proved unworthy. And might die when the plunder made of her was beyond tarnished.

Enough! she silently commanded. *You will not dishonor your sire nor his name. Fight!*

She wrenched backward. Glimpsing a clean-shaven face above hers, she slammed her knee up between her enemy's legs. And made contact in the absence of chain mail he must have shed following the battle.

The Norman lurched forward. If not for his chin clipping the top of her head, she might have escaped. Pain blurring her vision, she strained to free her arms. Then the ground was at her back, his great weight atop.

"Whore!" he spat.

As she translated his slur into her language, he turned his mouth to her ear. "After I have used you up, I shall give the husk of you to my men. Here you die, Saxon."

Unable to dislodge him, she heard her sire call across the years, *Know when to be still, Daughter of Wulfrith! Know when to wait and watch!*

"Aye, Father," she whispered.

Her assailant's head came up. "What say you?"

Guessing he was minimally conversant in her language, it occurred he might release her if she proved she knew his. "I am a lady, a Saxon wed to one of your own," she said in Norman-French. "Great ill you do my husband in attacking me. He will—"

He gripped her chin and raised himself slightly to peer into her face.

Bemoaning the arm he had released was not the side from which her remaining dagger could be had, she returned his scrutiny. Though his countenance was more shadowed than hers, he appeared two score aged.

"You are pretty and fairly young, Saxon. I shall enjoy this all the more."

Then it mattered not she was joined with one of his own? "My husband is Norman the same as you," she tried again.

He laughed. "*Not* the same as the companion of the great King William."

King. Already the invader named that as if all had been decided upon Senlac, Harold's death the only thing required to crown him.

Let it not be, Lord, Isa sent heavenward. *William may have carried the papal banner into battle, but it is for You to decide! Come back to us and we shall be more faithful!*

"Not the same," her assailant repeated. "That honor was lost when your husband sullied his line by wedding one of inferior race. And if he fought against William, what I shall have from you this night will be more due the traitor."

"He did not take up arms against your duke," she exclaimed and dared not reveal Roger had died in the North at Stamford Bridge while aiding King Harold in defeating the invading Norwegians. Nor that had he survived, he would have been obligated to fight Normans, having pledged himself to King Edward and his successors in exchange for the great demesne given him through marriage to the only surviving child of the thane of Wulfenshire.

"I care not what he did or did not do," her assailant said. "Though paltry your contribution toward a debt that can never be paid for those slain by your Saxon dogs, payment shall be made." He began dragging up her skirt.

"Nay!" Isa swept her hand over the ground in search of something to bring down on his skull. Finding only pebbles and dirt, she pried at his hand, but the calloused fingers continued upward, scraping over calf and knee.

She screamed, tried to bring her knee up again, but his legs pinned hers. Another scream, a failed attempt to sink her teeth into his jaw, a successful snap of the brow against his chin that pained her as much as when the top of her head struck that same bony prominence.

But though he released her leg, her triumph was fleeting. He slapped her, knocking her head to the side and cutting a lip that bled onto her tongue, then clamped his hand around her neck.

She hooked fingers over his and pried. To no avail. She dragged nails down his jaw and neck. To no avail.

I fail you! she silently called to her sire who had lived long enough to learn he was to be a grandfather and bestow the name *Wulfrith* on the unborn babe.

Dirt, she heard him bark as if he were here. *A woman's weapon, but effective.*

She remembered grumbling it was the sword and dagger she wished to learn, not the scramblings of weak women. Then he had dashed dirt in her eyes, incapacitating her as thoroughly as if he had stuck her with a blade.

Isa flung her arm out to the side. As lack of air caused bursts of black to obscure her vision, she scraped dirt into her palm, then brought her hand to her ear and cast that weapon of women.

Her assailant released her and reared back. While he cursed and ground palms against his eyes, she wheezed in breath. And found her right hand freed the same as her left.

The deadly dagger within reach.

CHAPTER TWO

*C*urse all, he had not time for this! Certainly not whilst he had three brothers, a cousin, and an uncle to account for, all of whom he had become separated from when day yet shone across a bloody battlefield. Then there were his injuries that needed tending, many of which pained though none would kill—providing infection did not set in.

His barely godly uncle would not approve of him being distracted from his purpose, and though his overly godly sire would understand his son's need to protect women, he would hesitate over the risk to life and loss of time spent seeking kin.

Still, the heir of the family D'Argent ran to answer the cry, doubtless of a Saxon who had cast wit to the wind to discover what was likely the remains of her loved one.

Another scream. As with the first, it drew the attention of others moving amongst the bodies. It was not fellow Normans searching for kin and friends who made Guarin stretch his legs long beneath the weight of chain mail, but those with whom he would not associate for the opportunity they made of the fallen—and the prey they would make of the woman where her king had died.

"Fool," he bit and swept his gaze up over the bodies he negotiated to the flat of the moonlit hill out of which grew an enormous tree that, had it boasted fruit this year, might never again were its roots poisoned by blood.

To its right, one of Guarin's own sought to defile the woman. The Norman had taken her to ground, even now might be violating her though she continued to fight.

What had she been thinking to venture to this place where likely the greatest battle fought on English soil had raged from mid-morning until dusk? Not only had night fallen, but Guarin's liege, Duke William, had yet to grant permission for the Saxons to retrieve their dead.

Reaching the base of the hill, he adjusted his course to avoid one of his countrymen who had died with the duke's pennon clutched to his chest, then drew his sword, began his ascent, and halfway up returned his gaze to the scene near the tree.

Abruptly, he halted, causing the links of his chain mail to ring more loudly. He was a seasoned warrior, and more so after putting down numerous Saxons who had sought to slay him and those he fought alongside, but that to which he now bore witness greatly disturbed.

Light shimmered across the silver wielded by the one with her back to the ground, and as she drove that blade into the neck of the man who clawed at his eyes where he had risen atop her, she cried in her tongue, "Die, Norman!"

As if following this command as he had not the others, her enemy collapsed to the side.

Yet another of Guarin's own cut down. Feeling the return of anger that had made him a formidable opponent as first he fought astride, then on foot when his destrier was slain, he watched the woman turn onto hands and knees. She stumbled upright, regained her balance, and reached down. When she straightened, she held the dagger drawn from her victim.

Guarin's anger surged—and receded with the reminder this

one's death was more warranted than those of Normans who had believed they fought to reform England's church which could be accomplished only by placing its rightful king on the throne.

The woman's assailant had used his greater strength to seize what she would not give. It was questionable whether Guarin's uncle would approve of his nephew's reasoning, but again his sire would understand. And approve.

Regardless of whether the Norman had gained what he sought, the Saxon had ensured he could not further harm her. Hence, Guarin could resume his search for those who might be in greater need of deliverance than one who would count him her enemy.

He turned, but too many bearing lanterns moved toward the hill, evidence he was not the only one to witness the death of a warrior outside of battle.

"Almighty!" No matter how quickly she moved, she had far less chance of leaving the battlefield alive than her defeated countrymen. And being a Saxon who had slain a Norman—more, a woman—no quick death would be afforded her.

Her only hope was this enemy whose sire had been forced to relinquish his sons' training at arms to their uncle but ensured Guarin and his brothers were instructed in faith to better guide the warriors made of them. And among Baron D'Argent's tenets was defenseless women and children must be protected. Not that this Saxon was defenseless, but she would fall to those coming for her if Guarin did not intervene.

Though a fatigued and battered body once more at swords could prove his undoing, he set his blade before him, its presence threat enough to persuade others approaching the hill to think better on trying to claim one about to be claimed by a chevalier prepared to defend his right to this spoil of war.

Despite whatever had happened to the woman, she had enough wits to note the Normans advancing on her, as evidenced by the single step she took opposite Guarin before whirling back around, dagger in hand.

Such golden hair she had, more visible across the distance than the face beyond unraveling braids. But before resuming negotiation of the hill, he glimpsed enough of her features to guess she was between twenty and thirty years—and of slender figure, the short mantle fallen back off her shoulders revealing the only swells of her body were a generous one above a narrow waist and a gentle one below.

Reaching the hill's crest, he slowed just enough to avoid trampling the bodies spread thicker and higher here. Though the woman would think he intended her harm, he would lose his lead over the other Normans if he approached more cautiously.

"Come no nearer!" she shouted in her language.

He glanced at where she had retreated to the other side of her assailant as if to make a barrier of his corpse, saw her sweep the bloody dagger before her. And noted it was not merely a desperate attempt to defend herself. Her stance and wielding of blade bespoke training. Also of note was her clothing. Though the gown was of simple design and its lower edge torn away, the bodice's neck and sleeves were edged in fur. Here a lady.

"I will cut your gullet!" She kicked the body at her feet. "The same as this vermin!"

Guarin was unable to interpret her every word, but he was familiar enough with the English language to understand her threat. And after witnessing her assailant's fate, he believed it. No ordinary lady, this.

Clearing the last great heap of bodies across which the barren tree cast clawed shadows, he lowered the point of his sword and raised his empty left hand. "I mean no harm."

Beyond braids draping shoulders that rose and fell with breaths that misted the air, blue eyes—perhaps grey—shone out of a battered face. "Out! Out!" she demanded the same as her menfolk had done in answer to the Norman battle cry *Dex Aie!*

Guarin stepped around the splayed body of another of his

13

own, causing the woman to jump back and look left and right for a way to escape.

He followed her gaze and saw all but two of the roused Normans had returned to scavenging. Injured though he was, the worst a wound to the side he bound at battle's end, he should be able to stave off attempts to take what others believed he wished for himself.

Returning his regard to the woman, he halted three strides distant. "Fear...not," he struggled for words in her language. "I—"

She lurched forward, jolting the body at her feet and slashing the air between them.

Though Guarin could arc his sword up, were she well enough trained, she might evade his attempt to knock the dagger from her hand. And if he succeeded, it could put her to flight, placing her in the path of one or both scavengers.

"I would...aid you," he said.

She slashed again. "Out! Out!"

"Others are coming, Woman!"

"Heathen! Barbarian!"

Assuring himself he could quickly return his sword to hand, he set the tip at the scabbard's throat. As he slid the blade in, he looked nearer on the man responsible for her belief Guarin was of the same ungodly bent.

That Norman's face was turned opposite, but it need not be seen to know he was no common soldier. Though his clothes were begrimed, ripped, and bloodstained, better they were named finery. Here was a wealthy chevalier at worst, a lord at best who ought to have been resting or celebrating were he not searching for those lost to him.

Guarin knew depravity came in all forms, ranks, and ages, but had he not witnessed this Norman's assault, he would have been inclined to believe murder his end rather than defense—or retaliation—against ravishment. Yet more reason to get the woman away and quickly.

Summoning words he hoped were in the proper order, he said, "I am...sorry for what he did to you. It is wrong."

"He did naught!"

"I saw him. Now we must—"

"Naught!" she spat, and he wondered if more she sought to convince herself than him. Regardless, she had suffered enough that she could be near emotional collapse.

"Hear me, Woman. We must get you away."

A thrust of the dagger. "He did naught!"

He glanced between the Normans who had begun their ascent —one to the right, the other the left—and was grateful they were slowed by heaps of enemy upon enemy.

As he took another stride forward, she jerked back and one of her braids lost the rest of its crossings. Like a curtain of the finest weave, the hair swept down over that side of her face. Though in moonlight she did not present as beautiful, that softening of what had appeared stern made him stare, then slam himself up against the reason he was here though he ought to be elsewhere.

He jutted his chin at the corpse dealt a blade to the throat. "You tell he did naught? For *naught* he is dead?"

"I..." She lowered her eyes, quickly returned them to his. "I slew him ere I could dishonor my...ere he could dishonor my..." She swallowed. "I did. Ere he could. I vow it."

Though her words were a swift-moving stream rerouted time and again by thoughts thrusting up through silt like jagged rocks, it provided time to make sense of them.

"You must permit me to see you away from here, Lady, else what this one began others will finish."

"You say you will not do to me what...?" She made a choked sound, then kicked the corpse again, causing its head to turn toward Guarin.

A wealthy chevalier and lord, indeed, but one thing more and of greater import—here a *companion* of the duke, so valued that even if Guarin bore witness the man sought to ravish this woman, William's wrath could prove deadly.

The time for persuasion past, Guarin lunged. An instant ahead of catching the wrist of her dagger-wielding hand and yanking her forward, he felt a sting across the underside of his jaw. Then her feet caught on the body between them, toppling her forward.

He let her drop to her knees. As hoped, the jolt loosened her grip on the hilt. She thrust upright, screamed when he tossed aside her keen weapon.

"The word of a D'Argent I give!" He caught hold of her other wrist. "I will not harm you. I will see you to the wood. That is all."

No reasoning with her. He saw it in her wide-flung eyes a moment before she became all teeth, hands, knees, and feet.

Releasing one wrist, Guarin drew back a fist. "Pardonne-moi," he said in his language. "C'est nécessaire."

She jerked when his knuckles struck her jaw, then her chin dropped, and he caught her up against him.

He had never had cause nor desire to strike a woman, it being an abhorrent act against the weaker sex, but it was the only way to keep her safe.

Feeling a trickle down the side of his neck, he swiped a hand across it and considered fingers bloodied by the dagger that sought to do to him what it had done to William's companion.

"No choice," he rasped and wiped his hand across the back of the woman's mantle that would better clean it than chain mail.

It was not easy to put her over his shoulder, though not because of her size and weight. The difficulty was the injury to his side that shot pain to his hip.

A moment later, her arms flopped against his armored back, and he knew were she conscious she would grab at his belted weapons. This was for the best, the bruise that would darken her jaw dealt to aid rather than harm.

"Chevalier!" called the Norman on his left who neared the top of the hill. "A good blow to the Saxon wench. When you are done with her, let your good friend, Guillaume, teach her further respect for her Norman betters."

"And your friend Joan," shouted the second Norman who was no more a friend or acquaintance. "A better lesson I shall teach her ere doing to her what she did to our countryman."

No choice at all, Guarin reaffirmed and called, "I share with no man." Anchoring her with his left arm around her upper thighs, he drew his sword lest these soldiers challenge him. "When I am done with her, *I* shall ensure she bleeds no more Normans."

He turned. Hoping when he came back around both would be in retreat, he thrust a booted foot and flipped William's companion onto his belly. And realized it was a waste of time to conceal his identity. The soldiers had only to search the area for the warmest body in the freshest pool of blood to see the man face up again. They would discover him, not only for curiosity's sake but because this place provided the best pickings for desecrators of the dead.

However, here was a means of ensuring these two did not challenge him. He turned back. "Better your efforts spent relieving our enemies of the gold around their necks and silver on their belts ere others sniff it out!"

Both halted, looked around.

"Many a woman's favors you can buy with such spoils," Guarin added and began his descent toward the horse earlier noted in the midst of slaughter, seemingly untouched by death beyond the rider collapsed over its neck.

The men did not continue their pursuit, and shortly Guarin had the unfortunate chevalier off a dark grey destrier that appeared too young to be battle-hardened and likely suffered from shock.

Getting astride took effort, not only because the animal was skittish, but the unconscious woman had to be steadied while Guarin mounted behind. Once done, he adjusted her seat between his thighs, causing her head to tip back and hair to fall away from a face exposed to moonlight.

It was scratched and bruised, but not so much it disguised her looks and age. Though her face was strong boned, it was pretty with large eyes and a mouth whose lower lip was full beneath the upper that would present as thin if not for high arches reaching toward a fine nose. She would live and…

He glanced at her hands in her lap, and seeing she wore a wedding band, hoped this day she was not made a widow and her children fatherless. But had she been, the lady should have little difficulty acquiring another husband, especially were she in possession of lands.

Not my concern, he told himself. *The sooner I deliver her from here, the sooner she will become another man's problem. And I can resume my search for kin.*

Cyr.

Dougray.

Theriot.

Maël.

Hugh.

CHAPTER THREE

*N*egotiation of the meadow was slow to avoid setting the horse to flight and trampling the fallen, but finally they entered the wood into which surviving Saxons had fled.

Having stayed far right of that section of Andredeswald that had swallowed the majority of the defeated and a great number of victors who gave chase and met their end at the bottom of a fosse known only to Saxons, he entered the trees.

There were Saxons here, though likely too seriously wounded to flee beyond the enemy's reach. Keeping one arm around the woman, Guarin released the reins and, continuing to guide the destrier with the press of his thighs, drew his sword.

He would take the lady only far enough to ensure she did not become easy prey to men who would do to her as William's companion had done, then send her and the horse opposite. That would be the end of it, allowing him to resume his duty and her to praise the Lord she had escaped far worse than already she had suffered—and return home to a world much changed now the duke's foot was firmly on England's throat.

Reaching his senses in all directions, Guarin urged the destrier deeper into the wood. When they passed beneath a gap in the leaved canopy that shone moonlight across their path, he caught movement and sounds not of nature but neither from a distance. The woman had regained consciousness, though she stilled as if gone under again.

Likely, she assessed her situation to determine what resistance to offer, and since he did not tighten his hold, when she reached for his dagger she was less cautious than she might otherwise have been.

"Lady," he growled, "do not."

She did not, though he sensed she would once she adjusted her plan and expectations of the Norman who had struck her senseless.

Readying his hand at her waist to intercept hers, he said, "I did not like doing it. I but wished to see you off the battlefield. Ahead, I shall…" He did not know the English word for *démonter.* "I shall get down, and you will ride home. That is all, Lady."

As evidenced by her grab for his dagger, no more did she believe him now than before.

He gripped her hand, but she was as prepared for his defense as he was for her offense, shooting the other hand past and seizing the hilt.

He released the first hand and captured the second before she could unsheathe the dagger. As he thrust the blade back to the scabbard's depths, she cursed him, twisted around, and drove an elbow into his injured side.

Pain, hesitation over further harming her, and determination to keep hold of his sword handed her the advantage—until the destrier protested the struggle on its back and swung to the side.

The yielding of his sword the only way to retain hold of the woman, Guarin tossed it away and grabbed the saddle's pommel as the destrier reared. Its return to the ground was so forceful both riders lurched over its neck and the woman cried out. Now the beast would run.

Guarin straightened, snatched up the reins and dragged on them.

With a toss of its head, the horse shuddered to a halt.

Seeing his sword lay ahead, its blade reflecting moonlight, Guarin decided it was time the woman and he part ways. He gripped her tighter, pinning her arms between their chests. "We are done," he growled. "Now you go your way, I go mine."

Straining backward, she raised her face.

If his life depended on knowing one thing about her character, he would say the rage there was directed more at herself than him. But it wavered when her eyes flicked left and right, and in them he saw the question to which he was accustomed the same as nearly all his kin—how was it possible one of relatively few years had so much silver in his hair?

She blinked. "I do not believe you, *savage*."

Reminding himself another gave her cause to name him that, he loosened his hold. "Turn forward, Lady." When argument widened her eyes, he snarled, "You have the word of Guarin D'Argent, and that is enough."

Further hesitation, then she turned, and he felt the press of her arms test the strength of his.

"Do you not move," he said, "all the sooner you shall be rid of this *savage*."

Defiantly, she jerked her shoulders.

"Be still!" he rumbled and released her. Retaining hold of the reins lest she attempt to trample him beneath hooves, he swung a leg over. The pain streaking his side portending he bled again, he dropped to the ground.

Warily, the Saxon watched as he moved to the destrier's head. Though he had meant to retrieve his sword and start back immediately, ever he had been good with horses, and this one that survived what its battle-hardened fellows had not, required reassurance were he to heed the commands of a woman rider.

Guarin smoothed its pale mane, caressed its great jaw, in his language said, "You will see her safely home, eh?"

The steed eyed him.

"You are Norman-bred, brave, true. It is your duty and privilege to aid this lady and prove what she will not believe of me." Feeling the animal's quivering ease, he looked to the woman and glimpsed uncertainty before she raised her chin to peer down her nose at him.

It was a show. Though she tried to make it appear her fear was overcome, it remained nearly as present as if there were a third person here.

Guarin gripped the bridle, led the horse to his sword, and turned his hand around the wire-wrapped hilt. "I leave you this destrier, Woman. You will return home, will you not?"

No answer.

He stepped nearer, causing her to shift opposite. "I did not delay my search for kin to have you return to where you are not welcome. For the kin that remains to *you,* await the duke's..." He fumbled for the word. "...permission to seek your dead."

"My son is my only family," she rasped.

"Then for him—"

"He is upon Senlac. Only ten winters aged."

Despite Guarin's limited proficiency with her language that confirmed her son was a boy, he did not believe he properly translated the rest that made it sound as if the youth was on the battlefield. He nearly asked for clarification, but he was too long in being reunited with kin.

He looped the reins over the saddle's pommel and drew his dagger, causing her to draw back. He hesitated over relinquishing something so cherished, but having cast aside her dagger, extended his. "Should you need it, Saxon. Now go home."

So forcefully she snatched it from him, she took his hand with it.

He pulled free, and she caught up the reins and put heels to the horse.

Here the end of it, Guarin thought. And discovered he was wrong on two fronts—the first when she turned her mount back the way they had come, the second when bearded and long-haired men came out of the trees.

For him.

~

ISA STAYED THE SADDLE, though not for long. Once the destrier rearing before short-haired, clean-shaven warriors returned to earth, she was pulled down. As soon as her feet were beneath her, she managed a swipe of the blade, causing her new assailant to shout before delivering a blow to her wrist that sent the dagger flying.

"Accursed woman!"

She knew the voice, and though he was not Saxon, neither was he the enemy. Or was he?

Hearing her panting breath over the shouts of men and ring of steel at her back, she looked up from the blood seeping through his sleeve.

Before her stood an aged Norman, the one to whom her husband had sent her weeks past to ensure her safety while he fought alongside King Harold in the North, unaware his own people had invaded the South—as ever Roger would remain unaware.

Pushing past hurt that should not have affected her so deeply she relinquished charge of her son to another, she returned her attention to Baron Pendery whose grown sons had taken to the battlefield off which she had been forced. Also of Norman stock, they had fought on the side of Duke William.

Was this man the enemy, then? She glanced past him to where his men stood unmoving as if awaiting orders. Meaning they were not responsible for the clash behind.

She started to look around, but Pendery barked, "As you are under my protection, you dishonor me and my house, Lady Hawisa. And memory of your husband."

Hating she appeared a witless, frightened female, she said, "My boy and others from the village were seen near Senlac. I must go back and find him."

"Non, you will return to Trionne with me, and should Duke William allow retrieval of the enemy—" He closed his mouth, but no more need be spoken.

Her people were the enemy to this Norman who had gained much favor under the rule of King Edward before the brief rule of King Harold. If this day she suffered a keener loss, severing her every tie with those of his race—no Norman husband, no half-Norman son—an enemy he would, indeed, be to her.

He cleared his throat. "Should the duke grant permission for the retrieval of fallen Saxons, your husband's men will search for Wulf."

My men, she silently corrected. Roger slain, those whose voices she now recognized at her back belonged to her as ever they should have.

Isa clung to that which, in this moment, seemed the only sanity in her world. It offered little distraction against fear for her son, but much distraction for what the vile Norman on the hill had tried to do to her—and failed. Because she was of Wulfrith. Because she had spilled his blood.

"It is good we are in agreement," Baron Pendery said. "Come."

"But my son—"

He yanked her around to face men who, unlike his own, were not unmoving. All six were upon the Norman at their center whose hair did not fit a face evidencing he was of an age near twenty and five.

Though ferocious in defense of his person, deftly swinging his sword, shouting, and snarling as he pushed back one Saxon after another, his chance of triumphing against so many was more impossible than those silvered strands.

"Stand down, Saxons!" the baron shouted.

As if deafened by hatred for one of those who had defeated their countrymen upon Senlac, they continued to strike at the Norman.

They played a game, Isa thought as she was pulled toward them. Her men being too versed in sword skill not to quickly end the man's life, they were the cruel predator to cornered prey.

"I say stand down!" Pendery bellowed.

They obeyed, but only after Jaxon—the one most esteemed by her departed sire—dropped the warrior to his knees then his face.

Isa gasped and wrenched backward, forcing Pendery to halt to keep hold of her. She stared at the one just visible beyond the legs of those who had ceased toying with their prey, he who had named himself...

What was it? No sooner did that which spoke of his hair slip in than she cast it out. Were he dead, it was one less Norman to beat back across the sea. Of course, were all like he who had given her his dagger...

Cease! she silently commanded. *They are all like the one you did not allow to take from you what is owed your husband only. And now owed no man ever again.*

"I commanded you not to harm him," the baron thundered, and tried to draw her forward again.

As she resisted, the long-haired, long-bearded Jaxon shouldered past men he had trained. "He would not yield," he said, halting before Pendery, "and so I did as commanded by my *Norman* lord, Roger Fortier. I defended his lady and avenged the ill done her—the same as required of you, her protector."

Isa shuddered at the crimson spray across Jaxon's beard and chest and the streak along his blade that would only bother him for it not being of greater quantity. Just as her husband had fallen at Stamford Bridge, so had the housecarle's only son. If Jaxon could not spill Norwegian blood, Norman would suffice.

"To ensure no further harm befalls my lady, she must be returned to Trionne," he said.

"I cannot go back whilst Wulf remains missing and Aelfled yet searches for him," Isa protested. "Unless... Have you seen her, Jaxon? Did she find my son?"

"I know not," he reverted to their language, eschewing her Norman husband's that had been forced on her household when she wed. "We have seen neither her nor Wulf and the village boys, but it is possible they have returned to Trionne."

She stepped forward, and Pendery released her.

"Or they are upon Senlac, Jaxon. I must—"

"My men and I will search for him, my lady."

The baron cleared his throat, and Wulfen's senior housecarle swallowed his Saxon pride and said, "Providing Baron Pendery agrees, and I do not doubt he shall since your boy was also under his protection."

She had always respected Jaxon's skill as a warrior but never cared for one who looked low on the fairer sex, voicing disapproval of his lord instructing his daughter at arms. But in this moment, she could embrace the man who provided the only way around Pendery whose warriors were of sufficient number that more Saxon lives could be lost were Isa's men not permitted to aid her.

Unfortunately, she would have to make her own way around the baron. But though she detested what that required of her, all the more believable it would be since she had never felt nearer the weak woman over whom he must withdraw his watch.

"I thank you, Jaxon. Pray, go for me. I am so very tired."

"Of course, my lady." He looked around. "Vitalis!"

She followed his gaze to the warrior half his age standing this side of the silver-haired Norman, noted as he strode forward the other four housecarles closed the gap the same as done with Jaxon. As if...

What? she demanded of a mind more fatigued than thought. As if to hide from Baron Pendery one of his own slain in his presence?

Vitalis stepped before her. "My lady."

She looked up at the big man whose long auburn hair was secured back off his brow. He should not be here, but as he had sustained an injury weeks before her husband departed for Stamford Bridge and not recovered sufficiently to accompany his lord, he had joined Jaxon in escorting her and her son south.

"You shall ride with me to Trionne," he said.

She swept her gaze around the wood. The only horse present was the one upon which the ill-fated Norman and she had entered Andredeswald.

"Our mounts are near and guarded," Vitalis said, "hidden well back from the wood's edge where we spied upon the battlefield and saw the Norman take you into the trees. We feared he meant to..."

He and the others had seen enough to know they were as wrong as she about the man of silvered black hair. And yet he was dead. Because that warrior had forced Jaxon to it? Or from her state did her men believe her savior responsible for what another had done beyond the blow to the jaw required to gain her cooperation?

Likely the latter. Feeling sorrow not due an invader no matter his noble behavior, she said loud so the baron heard, "Take me to Trionne. I shall sleep away these hours until my boy is returned alive and well."

Vitalis gripped her elbow, and as he led her toward the baron's men, she heard Jaxon tell Pendery he would take the rest of his Saxon warriors to the battlefield and search for Fortier's heir.

The baron murmured agreement, instructed him to send word

if he discovered the fate of his own sons, then followed his ward and her man.

"The dagger, Vitalis," Isa whispered when she saw where it had landed after being knocked from her hand. "Gain it for me when I stumble."

As instructed, he swept it up—along with her as he was not meant to do.

"Vitalis," she hissed as he settled her against his chest.

"More believable, my lady," he said, but she knew it went beyond that. He who should never have loved her had loved her too long and taken this opportunity to draw exceedingly close. Hating how much he hurt over feelings for her and fearing this would encourage him, she said, "Set me down."

"Nay, you will have to be angry with me. Now take the dagger."

She looked from his bearded jaw to the hand above the arm cradling her back and shoulder, noted how fine a weapon it was. A sapphire was set in the cross guard, and beneath that three letters inscribed in steel the better to ensure the dagger could be recovered were it parted from its owner.

Recalling when the warrior had given his word alongside his name, she shivered. He had been called Guarin D'Argent. Because of her, ever he would be parted from this keen weapon.

She swallowed hard, took it, and slid it in the larger of two empty scabbards.

"Why?" Vitalis asked, surely the same she asked of herself.

"I know he must have killed many of our people, but he only sought to deliver me from a fellow Norman who…" He had not, she assured herself. "…would have violated me. He wished me to return home to my boy." Her voice caught, and with pleading she said, "Tell me he did not wish in vain. Tell me the bloody duke will take neither my son nor my home."

Mouth grim, he said, "Rest, my lady."

She nearly demanded he set her down, but her body

concurred, rendering the return to Trionne a blur as she prayed for the Lord to grant what He had not with her husband.

A little thing to ask of the all-powerful creator that my boy be safe, she flattered Him in His heavens. *So little it requires no more than a nod to ensure I am not the lone Wulfrith whose line dies with me.*

Aye, a little thing to Him. All to her.

CHAPTER FOUR

Wulfen Castle, England
1 January, 1067

*G*rief. It emptied one of all that was good and bright and lovely. In the hours of greatest ache it turned thoughts to one's own demise, allowing to seep from dark places sympathetic counsel for hastening that event, be it days or decades ahead of its time. Sinful, and surely not the only means of escaping what felt like hot wax burning through the layers of one's soul, and yet...

"Yet not," Isa whispered. She must be done with this coward's cowering, must rise and show how great her strength and resolve as demanded of her in the missive delivered a sennight past. She would. Just not this day.

On the morrow, then. And this time she would keep the promise as she had not all the days of the past cold, cruel month that had seen the usurper crowned King of England on Christmas Day, while outside Westminster Abbey his men burned the homes of Londoners. Barely seventy-two days after King Harold fell upon Senlac, the devil's spawn had subjugated enough of her country to formally take the throne.

Throat tight with emotion she had refused to shed since the morn following the battle when she dragged her stiff, cold boy into her arms and wept what seemed enough tears to water the world, Isa swallowed. It hurt, like choking down something sharply edged, but it pulled her from that dawn to the one lurking outside the windows whose grey light squeezed through the shutters' seams.

Hoping to sleep away some of the day so she would be rested for the morrow, she closed her eyes, but there was no quieting memories ripe for the tasting.

She tossed off the covers, winced at the rustle that would awaken her maid, laughed when it did not. No Aelfled upon her pallet, the young woman consigned to Lillefarne Abbey so Isa would not have to look upon she who had left her lady—and four other mothers—grief-stricken.

Isa closed stinging eyes, opened them wide, and accepted she must rise. The needs of the body demanded it—as did the return of her menses she discovered upon straightening from the bed.

She suppressed a sob. She had begun to believe that woman's affliction gone forever, it being absent since the loss of her husband. As if to remind her she was yet young and there could be other children, it was back. But no matter the missive's warning, she would do all in her power to avoid wedding again.

She looked to the rolled parchment on the bedside table opposite that other thing over which Vitalis frowned each time he reported on the state of the demesne and the measures she ordered taken to protect it, its people, and those in need of sanctuary.

Only once had she read the words of King Harold's mother. Only once was needed to understand Wulfrith's daughter was expected to aid Gytha in avenging her son's death and ousting the usurper so her grandson could ascend the throne. And greater that aid if Isa agreed to wed a Saxon of the woman's choosing.

The Norman dog will give you to one of his own when he learns you are widowed, she had written, *and though your son is half Norman, ill will befall him so the issue of your new husband gains your lands.*

Isa knew that. Hence, few were aware ill of an irreversible nature had already befallen Wulf. Though more and more his absence was questioned, the answer remained the same. Beyond grieving his sire, he was being prepared to become Lord of these lands earlier than expected for one soon to attain eleven years of age.

Another slain sob, another painful swallow.

That Wulf was occupied with learning how to administer and defend his lands was a good explanation, but with every day that passed, it weakened. Since the one who styled himself King of England would be sending men to make demands of the Lady of Wulfen, her boy would have to show himself.

Hopefully, Vitalis's search for a Saxon orphan who could be presented as boasting Norman blood alongside that of Wulfrith would bear fruit. Were that boy accepted as her departed husband's heir, she should be able to evade marriage to another Norman—or Saxon—and keep hold of her lands. Rather, what remained of them if the rumor imparted by Gytha was true that already William le Bâtard had promised portions of this demesne to two of his followers, one of whom the old woman told was Sir Raymond Campagnon and suggested he was being positioned to take her to wife.

Anger, welcome reprieve from mourning, blew across Isa's smoldering center, lit embers, rose to flame. "My lands," she hissed. "Saxon lands."

Though a widow the Norwegian invaders had made her, the Normans had struck a greater blow in rendering her childless. She would not wed another of those people for whom she felt such hatred that never would she care for one as she had cared for...

Memories caused the flames licking up her insides to lower, crackle, return to embers.

Over the next quarter hour, amid the sounds of an awakening household beyond the curtain hung between solar and hall, she struggled to suppress those memories by busying herself. After opening the shutters of the high-set windows with a long pole, letting in dawn's light and chill air, she attended to her bodily needs.

Next, she cast off gown, chemise, and hose she could not recall having last changed. She soaked a towel in the basin's chill water and scrubbed herself head to heel. She cleaned her teeth and dragged a comb through hair so snarled she tore strands from her scalp. With jerks and more snapped strands, she fashioned her hair into a fat braid that fell to the small of her back. She dropped to her knees before the trunk at the foot of the bed, opened the lid, and...sank back on her heels.

Her garments, once neatly folded on the left side, were scattered both sides atop her husband's as had suited her the day this childless widow returned to Wulfen Castle. However, across the bodice of her blue gown was a dark green cuff, the sleeve above it the color of wine. Here the tunic her husband had worn the day they wed.

"Roger," she said and, swept by memories soaked in guilt and regret, saw again the man to whom she had been wed—her wishes proving no match for King Edward's desire to reward a Norman favorite and her sire's need to provide his line the best chance of survival following the loss of one son after another.

Isa had thought she hated the arrogant Norman who placed a ring on the finger of she who believed herself a woman though she was barely ten and four, but hate had been too strong a word. Dislike fueled by resentment was what she had felt.

Her husband had been fairly young and, though hardly

handsome, exceedingly fit. Mostly, he had been patient with his Saxon wife—moved to strike her to silence only thrice during their eleven years of marriage though often she tested him.

Each time, the Wulfrith in her had struck back, jolting an apology out of him. If not for his sincerity, never would she have grown fond of the man who came to love her despite her resistance to behaving in a manner of which he approved—one that did not embrace her belief she should be active in carrying on the Wulfrith legacy, a belief strengthened when her sire's heart failed days after he learned he was to be a grandfather.

Arguments had flown between husband and wife, the seeds often sown by Roger who did not like nor trust Jaxon who did not like nor trust his new Norman lord. Thus, Isa's husband had sought her counsel over practices and techniques for training up warriors, and ever that reminded her she was first Wulfrith's daughter, making her resent she was not allowed to stand alongside Roger as he acted on things with which she was more familiar.

Having donned the mantle of her sire's reputation, the only visible Wulfrith presence he wished was that of worthy sons born of their union. She had provided that in Wulf who became all the more precious to him when no more children were forthcoming —and that he returned Roger's love as Isa had not.

Remembering the tidings of her husband's death delivered to Trionne three months past, she lowered her chin. Such ache she had felt, and more when Wulf reverted to a little boy. As she held her weeping, sobbing son, that ache had further enlarged upon recall of the final parting of husband and wife.

Leaning down from his destrier, Roger had cupped her jaw and said he could better bear the battle ahead if he knew she loved him. Telling herself she must feel that for him no matter how slight, she had tried to speak it, but all she could summon was the truth—words of fondness and assurance she would pray for his safe return.

Roger had not masked his disappointment, and every day since being widowed she wished she had told the lie that might have made the difference in preserving his life.

At Trionne, guilt over the death of her husband and loss of her son's sire had so burdened she had struggled to eat, sleep, and keep company. Still, she had watched over her son as he moved between sorrow and anger, next anger and rage when tidings arrived more invaders had landed at nearby Pevensey—this time Normans.

Then came the day she took ill and allowed Aelfled to persuade her to remain abed with assurances she would stay near Wulf. A fine job the lady's maid had done. Until she had not...

What was worse than guilt over the deaths of Roger and Wulf? Regret from which guilt sprang—a rope that, hand over hand, ever returned her to the profession of love that might have saved her husband's life and, hence, their son's.

Had Roger survived Stamford Bridge and next fought at Senlac, regardless of whether he once more sided with Harold or broke faith with her and went the way of his own, Wulf would have had no reason to depart Trionne whilst the battle raged. And there would be no need for another to play Isa's heir.

If only she had said she loved her husband. Having failed that, if only she had arisen from guilt over his death rather than relinquish a mother's duty to protect her young. Having failed that, if only she could rise above guilt over Wulf's death and do her duty to her people rather than direct others to do it.

"If," she breathed, then once more told herself all would be different on the morrow. When next she awakened, she would slam the door on apathy that sought to persuade her she had naught to live for. For vengeance she would rise up and gird her sire's name. For her people, she would become the Wulfrith who led rather than grieved.

No longer would she entrust others to do as bid and themselves determine the course when she denied them an audience. She would oversee all being set in motion to protect her people and lands from Normans. She would stand strong, nevermore casting shadows over her family's reputation. As best she could, she would make restitution for severing their line.

Come the morrow.

Realizing the panting she heard was her own, she closed her eyes and breathed deep. Across that forced calm, a voice within whispered, *The morrow could be this day. Should be this day.*

"Just one more to set myself aright," she answered.

Ever one more. When finally the morrow comes, you will be the husk that Norman threatened to make of you. And if within that husk any remnant remains, the guilt of Roger that led to Wulf's death will become the guilt of Wulf that leads to your people's deaths because the enemy seized the day as you would not.

Isa dropped onto her backside, stared at the oaken trunk.

More regret. More guilt. Neither of which she could bear more than this day doing what she wished could await the morrow.

She got her bare legs beneath her, as she did so noted how thin they were, next her hips, belly, and chest. No surprise considering how tightly she laced herself into gowns to look presentable when she received villagers who came to request one relief or another or Jaxon and Vitalis ventured to the castle that was no longer their home.

Too sparingly she ate and too little exercise she took though, despite Roger's disapproval, previously she had strengthened her body with many of the exercises required of those trained into warriors. But this day...

"*This* day, I am no longer of Fortier," she said and started to remove the ring that proclaimed her the property of a man, but best it remain testament to her *son's* Norman blood—and ties to her husband's people. A deception, but only one among what would number many.

She crossed to the bedside table. Ignoring the dagger that

belonged to a dead man, she unrolled Gytha's missive, held it to the light, and lingered over the final words.

Remember and embrace who you are, Hawisa Wulfrithdotter. A Saxon strong of mind, body, and spirit.

"I remember," she said. "I am Lady of the Barony of Wulfen. Now its Lord."

That last drew her regard to the tapestry concealing the entrance to the castle's hidden passages. Though she had lost the argument with Roger against razing her wooden home and building a stone castle like those of Normandy, she had decided if she must live among the stones, she would make use of their strategic advantage. Her husband had thought hidden passages too great an expense in time and coin but yielded. However, he would not be moved to extend them underground into the wood. But now there was none to oppose her, work would begin to ensure Saxons resistant to Norman rule had another means of thwarting the enemy.

A half hour later, Isa was garbed as she deemed fitting, and many were the startles and stares when she thrust aside the curtain to reveal a body clothed as it had not been for more than eleven years. Though she strained seams that had fit the girl, better that than her husband's garments that would make her appear a child trying to be an adult. As soon as possible, new garments would be fashioned for the Lord of Wulfen.

Heartily, she partook of the morning meal alongside those of her household too disturbed by her appearance to give their own hunger its due. And though en route to the stables she had to go behind a shed to empty what she had stuffed in her belly, she resumed her plans for *this* day.

The stable lad met her just inside the doors, and when she instructed him to saddle three destriers rather than two and the palfrey which had been required riding for Roger's wife, looked to the accompanying housecarles.

"Three destriers," she repeated.

The lad inclined his head. "You wish your husband's, my lady?"

A fine beast recovered from Stamford Bridge. It was her right, and atop it she would sit higher than her men, but it would remind her of Roger and too much he would remind her of their son. "Nay, another."

"There are a half dozen palfreys, my lady, but only four destriers, and the fourth—"

"Only four?" she exclaimed.

"Aye, Jaxon and Vitalis took the others to…" He shrugged.

To where she intended to ride, a place not spoken of regardless of the degree of acquaintance. "Then saddle the fourth for me."

The lad called to another cleaning the tack and they hastened down the stall-lined aisle.

"I do not think Jaxon will like you riding to camp without notice, my lady," spoke the commander of what remained of her housecarles in residence.

She turned to Ordric of the village of Ravven from which her former maid had also been plucked. "I do not answer to Jaxon. He answers to me."

Ordric inclined his head.

The three destriers led forth were familiar, the last less so. Its coat was dark grey and mane flaxen, too striking a contrast not to notice even if one teetered toward shock as she had the night a Norman forced her off the battlefield.

This destrier had to be the one Guarin D'Argent had meant to send her home upon—and having yielded his only means of flight and his dagger, fallen to Saxon swords.

As ever, she salved guilt with the reminder he was one less Norman to send back across the channel. But there were more D'Argents, as learned when she escaped Pendery's watch over her the morn after the death of England's king and ridden toward Senlac with Vitalis. They had encountered Aelfled in the wood. With much weeping, she revealed they came too late, the only hope left to five mothers that of retrieving their boys' bodies.

Never had Isa thought to strike a lesser, but nearly she had. And again when Aelfled's grieving lady quieted enough to make sense of the answers Vitalis demanded of the young woman. And heard the D'Argent name again, this time attached to that of *Cyr*. Like his older brother whom he would not find upon Senlac, that D'Argent had aided a Saxon woman by conveying the bodies of Wulf and his friends to the wood to prevent their desecration.

Isa had gone light of head at the realization the Lord had answered her prayer to defend Aelfled's life and virtue as He defended her own, both by way of Norman brothers. But that He had not answered the greater prayer of protecting Wulf had kept praise from her lips, and Aelfled's answer to Vitalis's next question had dealt a backhand to any gratitude she might have felt toward the D'Argents. It appeared their uncle had slain the boys before himself expiring.

"My lady?" Ordric prompted.

She swung her gaze opposite the horse she had not been told was brought to Wulfen.

"'Tis a skittish beast and in need of training," her housecarle said. "Mayhap you would prefer to ride my destrier."

She nearly accepted, but it stank of weakness and fear. "Nay, this Norman will know the prick of my spurs and snap of my reins. The sooner he learns who is master, the less he will suffer this Saxon."

Concern lingering in his eyes, he said, "So he shall, my lady."

It boded ill the destrier's saddling required both stable lads, and further ill when the beast snorted and lurched as Isa gripped the saddle's pommel. Holding tighter, she fit a foot in the stirrup, swung a leg over, and accepted the reins.

The destrier tossed its head and stamped a hoof.

Isa tightened her thighs to secure her place atop a beast that wished her beneath it. Still, its wish might be granted, not because the last time she had ridden so fine a horse was before she wed but because of muscles so wasted they lacked the strength to keep her seat on a resistant mount.

Rethinking her determination to teach this Norman a lesson, she leaned forward and smoothed a hand down the pale mane, next the bristling dark grey coat to its jaw. "If you will be mine," she said low in the language it had not likely heard all these months, "I will be yours."

It whinnied.

"If you will keep me safe, I will keep you safe."

It turned its head and eyed her.

"Though Norman-bred, you are English now. More brave and true, you are..."

She stopped her breath, glanced left and right at where her housecarles stood alongside their mounts, loath to gain their saddles whilst her seat remained uncertain. And was grateful neither had been with Jaxon and Vitalis that night in Andredeswald. Had they, they might also realize she soothed her mount the same as the man who died there.

It was time to ride. Or nearly so.

Lowering her lids, she acknowledged she prayed more out of habit than sincere beseechings to the Lord—He who might never be persuaded His punishment of the Saxons was sufficient to return Him to their side. Certes, not without greater sincerity, but if that was required to move Him away from the Normans he had granted victory, He would have to await the morrow when she was stronger and fully in control of her birthright.

After a prayer for safe passage, she was pleased the stallion seemed less inclined to unseat her. Patting its jaw, she looked to her men. "For what do you wait? Mount up!"

CHAPTER FIVE

Wulfenshire Rebel Camp
England

They came for him. Again. More than sustenance to keep him alive, they provided routine.

Each time the one named Vitalis returned with a group of Saxons whose lives were uprooted by the conquering Normans, Jaxon welcomed them with a gift few resisted opening.

Guarin D'Argent was that gift. Barely recovered from beatings dealt by previous recruits, he was dragged from the dark of his stinking cave and staked on the outskirts of camp. There, each vengeful man—occasionally a woman—was allowed to land five blows with fists, knees, and feet.

Five blows was not enough to do great damage in the absence of cudgels and blades, but multiplied by several assailants one after the other, it could prove deadly. Thus, not only in preparation for escape did Guarin keep his body fit regardless the pain between beatings, but to ensure muscles of a strength to protect his innards. Did his organs tear and bleed, there would be no stitching them back together as had been done his side and other injuries that had taken him to ground when he delivered that accursed woman to the wood and been set upon by her countrymen.

As done often, he wondered what had become of the lady. Though Saxon the same as Guarin's assailants, that did not mean they had not done her ill. After all, she had been in the company of their enemy.

"More Saxons who wish to make your acquaintance, Norman!" called the camp commander. As ever, he entered with torchlight that flushed out the dim, causing the moist wall against which Guarin splayed his hands to shimmer. And accompanying Jaxon would be men capable of subduing their prisoner were he of a mood to resist.

Keeping his back to them where he leaned into the wall of rock into which were driven rings the chains fastened to his manacles were attached to, Guarin filled his lungs full. Then with arms whose muscles burned as he neared the two hundred count, he pushed his chest away. Before gaining full extension, once more he lowered. Slowly.

Am I of a mood to resist? he mulled as the scrape of boots grew louder and the anger pushed deep uncoiled alongside pride.

He was, and though they also proved of a mood and landed more blows than he, there was satisfaction in bruising an eye, breaking a tooth, and fracturing ribs.

Minutes later, he faced seven new recruits who were of less concern than the split flesh of his brow bleeding into an eye and obstructing his vision nearly as much as the direct sunlight denied him since the last beating.

Non, he corrected, the beating ere that. The last had been a day of clouds and rain.

As usual when he was *of a mood,* following the beating that subdued him, he had been dragged across the floor of the cave to a clearing in the wood where two posts were set ten feet apart. To these, the chains trailing his wrists were attached with so little slack that were he knocked unconscious as happened when dealt too many blows to the head, his knees would buckle, and that was all. Once he regained his senses, he would either be mostly upright facing another recruit or in a heap against the cave's back wall.

Make ready, he counseled as his vision cleared. *These recruits look worthier than usual. And angrier, especially the female.*

What crime would this sturdy, black-haired young woman level against a Norman who had never before looked upon her? Death of kin? Ravishment? Loss of home? Theft of food and possessions?

It mattered not. Like the many, she would make the most of her five blows. But they would not be as injurious as those dealt by the short, broad man whose tunic and chausses bulged with muscle.

If Guarin did not keep his own muscles taut throughout that beating, it could be his last. He held that one's gaze while his legs were secured to ensure they were as impotent as his fists. And was surprised by what the man made no attempt to mask.

Guarin had seen it before. Though most Saxons who joined the rebels were wrathful, not all were well with beating a man only because he was Norman. Here was one of those, but that did not mean he would not beat Guarin bloody. As upon Senlac, thirst for the enemy's blood by even a minority could become contagious, and those who might otherwise sip at it were more likely to drink with an unquenchable thirst.

Best this one first, Guarin determined. Across a tongue that tasted blood Jaxon's men had gained from a blow that cut inner lip against teeth, he said in the man's language, "You are not afraid of me, are you, Saxon? Come now, I can hardly fight back. Of course, were I loosed, far better cause I would give than already you have to want *this* Norman dead."

The man's lids narrowed. "You would slaughter more of my own?"

43

"Just as upon Senlac."

His mouth turned down as if a spoonful of something bitter were forced between his lips. Then the elbow at his side edged backward.

Guarin tightened his muscles.

"Hold, Zedekiah!"

Beyond the Saxon came Vitalis, the second in command who had delivered this new batch of rebels to a camp located well north of Senlac.

The exact location Guarin did not know, being unfamiliar with England and having been bound and concealed beneath slain Saxons in the back of a wagon during the long journey. However, on occasion he heard mention of shires in the midlands—Lincolnshire, Nottinghamshire, and Wulfenshire.

As ever, that last put him in mind of Wulfrith, the trainer of some of England's greatest defenders whom Duke William had esteemed. And Wulfrith put him in mind of Guarin's uncle whom William had also esteemed for raising up worthy warriors. Unlike his nephew, did Hugh reap the rewards of bringing England to its knees? Did he and the rest of the D'Argents think the one believed to be Hugh's greatest achievement dead?

"He wants it," Zedekiah declared. "'Tis my due."

Vitalis halted before Guarin. He was not as easy to read as most, but from his eyes shone disapproval and anger, though not directed at the Norman in their midst—rather, the camp commander.

A sennight past, while Guarin chewed bread whose inside was as crusted as its outside he had to choke it down with gulps of nearly soured wine, an argument between Jaxon and Vitalis had ensued. So ferocious was it that words not meant for their prisoner had made it to the rear of the cave.

The younger man did not approve of Jaxon's leadership and was certain neither would their lady when she learned what was withheld from her. Of interest. But of greater interest was the camp commander cursing the dirty, misbegotten Norman who had donned the crown that belonged to a man born of England.

Duke William was now King William, and it would take untold numbers of well-trained and equipped rebels to begin dethroning him. As usual, William had taken what he wanted, and he would defend his new possession with more vigor and venom than a starving dog with a joint of meat between its teeth.

"Vitalis." Guarin inclined his head as if in deference. "This warrior of yours speaks true. The fist he wishes to plant in my face is his due." He shifted his gaze to the Saxon he guessed was a smithy. "But it will take far more than five blows for one such as he to wreak vengeance. Time better spent beating steel into blades for other men to wield."

Zedekiah lunged. Vitalis snatched him back. And there was Jaxon, breaking the hold of the second in command.

The smithy landed a fist to the jaw that snapped Guarin's head so far to the side his neck cracked a warning. Not broken. Yet.

The next blow was dealt the gut. Though the flesh would bruise, the muscles held like a stone wall at the center of which perched a donjon that, were it breached, would prove the castle's downfall.

Three more blows amid shouts of encouragement from scores of rebels, and it would not have ended there if Vitalis had not shoved Zedekiah away.

The warrior thrust his bearded face near Guarin's. "That should be the worst of it. Now cease your taunting, and a fortnight hence we can do this again."

Guarin suppressed a groan over the ache in his side whose injury gained upon Senlac had yet to fully heal and might not until he escaped these savages. "I count you a true friend, Vitalis, but allow me to think on it."

The auburn-haired Saxon bared his teeth, swung away, and stalked opposite. His part in increasing the rebel ranks was done. *This* obscenity he left to its maker.

Honorable? Guarin gave it only a glancing thought, but a glance was something.

Jaxon swung to the side, causing the long hair bound at his nape and the beard bound halfway down his chest to swing. "You!" He pointed to the woman.

Her five blows felt like one, but she could scratch and spit, the latter of which she did in his face after cursing him for being a Norman the same as those who set her home afire, killing her family.

The third and fourth rebels were vicious, striking him about the head and neck, blurring his vision, bloodying nose and lip, pounding ear and chin, and nearly rendering him unconscious.

The next man was scrawny and of middle years. After a blow to the jaw, he cradled his hand against his chest and repeatedly drove his knee into Guarin's abdomen. The muscles standing barrier between those jabs and the organs screamed for ease, but he kept them taut as he suppressed groans and shouts.

How many more? he wondered, legs shuddering in response to his command they remain firm though he was tempted to unlock his knees and let his arms take his weight. But lax muscles would leave him vulnerable to internal bleeding.

Stand firm! he commanded as his uncle would. *Look each in the eye if they dare peer into yours whilst punishing you for another's sins.*

A fist to the cheek knocked his head back, and he saw black though he felt the sun on his face and was certain his eyes were open. The blows counted up, and when they ceased, he squeezed his lids tight and opened them wide to restore vision so he could look upon his next assailant.

Though that one now stood before him, the man was turned to the side, his expression a mix of fascination and alarm. And those gathered around were just as motionless.

Now Guarin heard the horses approaching at great speed, so near he should have caught the sound sooner. Was the camp under attack? If so, were they Normans?

A woman shouted, but she sounded angry rather than fearful.

Guarin tried to peer across his shoulder, but the movement shot pain up the sides of his neck and once more curtains began drawing across his eyes.

"Cease, Jaxon!" Her voice again, and in the language of the Saxons. "Now!"

To the left a flurry of movement, those who had not retreated springing apart to make an opening through which three horses came, at least one of their riders a woman though Guarin knew it only by her voice. Since he could either put his remaining strength into preventing his legs from buckling or keeping his head up, he let the latter drop and resented the bristling beard of a long-unshaven jaw scratching neck and collarbone.

"My lady!" Jaxon's voice sounded over the murmuring masses.

The salving of Guarin's curiosity was worth the strain to keep his legs firm and raise his chin, but it was wasted effort. His vision was too scattered to focus on those who dismounted war horses. But one of the destriers...

He dropped his chin, behind his lids recalled the glimpse afforded of a horse dark of grey across which a flaxen mane fell.

Could it be the same? He pushed back through days he had numbered as best he could, some lost to senselessness. Once again he saw the young destrier he had taken from the battlefield and relinquished to the woman before he was attacked by warriors.

Among those Saxons had been Vitalis and Jaxon, the latter having dealt the blow that dropped Guarin—one that might have taken off the top of his head were it not delivered by the flat of the blade. That vengeful Saxon had wanted this victorious Norman alive. For this.

"What goes?"

The woman's voice yanked him back to the present that must be the first of the new year of 1067 since it would take days for news of William's Christmas Day coronation to reach the midlands.

"What is this, Jaxon?"

Was that voice familiar the same as the destrier?

"What do you in my name upon my lands?"

Not shrill but growing louder as it spoke over the camp commander's curt responses. Louder because she neared, Guarin realized and tried to raise his head to look upon her and confirm her hair was golden.

The attempt made his legs give, but before the weight of his body could snap taut the chains running wrists to poles, he sank his chin to his chest, pushed up through the soles of his bare feet, and straightened.

"This, my lady, is the enemy."

"I care not he is Norman! We do not do this. We—"

"These people need it," Jaxon snarled, and Guarin knew the two were a half dozen strides distant. "They must taste vengeance, learn a Norman's weakness—"

"Weakness!" she shrilled. "He is chained, splayed, and of an age—"

"The hair is a lie, my lady."

Jaxon's booted feet kicked up dust where he halted before Guarin. "Look!" He dug into his captive's scalp, clenched a handful of strands as long absent a keen blade as the jaw beneath, and jerked up Guarin's head. "Recognize this foul Norman?"

The lady was near enough to confirm she was as familiar as the destrier, though never had Guarin seen either in daylight. And near enough to observe her color drain and body recoil so violently she stumbled back. She might have dropped if not for the reappearance of Vitalis who gripped her shoulders.

The shoulders of a woman clothed as a man. Visible between the edges of a long, dark blue mantle were a russet-colored tunic, belted chausses, and worn boots. They were not the garments of the woman upon Senlac, and too fitted to be those of the husband whose ring she yet wore. But she was the one responsible for these weeks of hell.

"Lady," he spoke across a cracked, bleeding lip with a tongue that felt large enough to choke upon. "I recognize you as well... will not forget your face nor voice until...you and yours suffer the same as I."

Unsurprised by the blow Jaxon landed, he hoped the knave was offended by the bark of laughter loosed ahead of the black come down over Guarin's eyes. Though that darkness stole sight of the Saxon lady, he would not forget her. Ever.

CHAPTER SIX

*Y*ou said naught! You let me believe him dead, and he has been here all this time. Treated like an animal—nay, worse!" Isa swung around, lunged across this damp, dark place requiring torchlight to ensure one's footing, and slapped a hand to Jaxon's chest. "Only the foulest of those who count themselves as bearing the likeness of God would torture even the meanest beast. And we are not that!"

She swept her gaze to Vitalis who stood alongside the camp commander. "Or is this what we have become?" Back to Jaxon. "Worse than those you claim made us thus?"

"They pillage and burn our homes," her sire's man tried again to reason with her as never would she be reasoned no matter how great her hatred of Normans. "They kill our men, ravish our women, starve our children—"

She thrust onto her toes. "Unlike you, I was where this began, on that meadow forever ruined, that place where I lost my son to a Norman and killed another who sought to violate me. But this..." She turned her head, using the excuse of looking upon the man who lay against the far wall to hide her struggle to swallow bile. "This is wrong, no matter how threadbare one's faith, no matter how desperate one is for revenge."

As is my faith, she silently acknowledged. *As I am desperate for revenge though my son's murderer is dead—and my assailant.*

Though less and less the latter came to mind and what he had done was distorted and missing pieces, at times she indulged in imagining him beaten bloody so she might combat horror over slaying him and bolster pride for defending herself as expected of a Wulfrith. However, to see those imaginings made reality, and that they were done to Guarin D'Argent...

Seeing resentment glitter in Jaxon's eyes, she demanded, "Why did you let me believe D'Argent died in the wood?"

"For the benefit of Baron Pendery."

So he could not save his fellow Norman, allowing Jaxon to do this to one who had slain his countrymen. More, to mete out revenge denied him against the Norwegian invaders who slew his son. "How long have you done this?"

"Since he was well enough recovered from Senlac to remain mostly conscious throughout."

Once more forcing down bile, she turned to Vitalis. "I am disappointed you kept this from me."

He remained silent, unwilling to defend himself though he could do so better than Jaxon to whom she had given charge of the establishment of a refuge for Saxons of a mind and ability to rebel.

Had she chosen wrong? Her sire would have placed his most highly regarded trainer in this position, but that would have been a different time when Jaxon answered to one he respected. Too, her father would have ensured those who acted in his name did as directed.

Hating the torture witnessed at too great a distance to sooner end made her aware of how alive she was and how great the need to arise from mourning, Isa stepped nearer Vitalis. "Why did you not tell me?"

"My orders," Jaxon answered for him. "He did as commanded, the same as all good soldiers. You may be of your sire's blood, but that of your mother made you a daughter incapable of understanding the world built and ruled by men—"

She whipped her chin around. "Go!"

"My lady—"

"Leave us!"

He spat on the ground, pivoted, and strode into sunlight.

Isa replenished her breath. "I know you, Vitalis, and unless much you have changed these months, you cannot approve of what he does."

Still he did not speak.

She slapped him. "Defend yourself! Prove I have not misplaced my trust."

He turned his face back. "As Jaxon told, I acted on orders given by one who, alongside your sire, trained me into a warrior and to whom I answer in your absence. And your absence has been long, my lady."

"Because I did not know he did this!"

"Of course you could not in the midst of great loss." It was said with understanding, not condemnation. "But now you are done with mourning, aye?"

The question tempted her to slap him again, but he meant well. "Never done with mourning, but I am done with hiding away."

"A good thing."

As evidenced by what she had ended this day. "I will have no more of this, and if Jaxon defies me—"

"You need him, my lady. Tread carefully."

"Or what?"

"To another he will give the protection his leadership affords you and your lands."

Her thoughts flew to Gytha, King Harold's mother who would

be pleased to gain Jaxon and might even attempt to wrest Wulfen from Isa.

"No better trainer of warriors is there," Vitalis continued.

"You did my sire proud."

He grunted. "Perhaps eventually I can replace him, but not now whilst I better my own skills and those of the men I train."

"Then in time, if need be." She nodded. "Henceforth, you are my eyes and ears. You shield me from naught."

"As you wish, but what of the Norman? If he is of no use to Jaxon, his life will be forfeit, whether by hidden or bold means."

Before this day, she might have questioned that, but no longer.

"He cannot be released now he knows your face is the one behind Jaxon's, my lady. Even were he released distant from here..." He sighed. "D'Argent knows enough it would require little effort to discover the area in which he was held. Thus, he would learn your identity."

She swallowed hard. "You suggest a merciful death?"

"Better than a cruel one."

More of what she had witnessed this day, though this time a decisive end to that torture. "I will not allow it, but neither can I..." Momentarily, she closed her eyes. "I hate him for the Norman he is and for who he is." The nephew of Wulf's murderer, she did not say. "But he meant me no harm—indeed, sought to save me."

"And yet something must be done with him."

"I shall think on it."

He inclined his head. "Come, there is much to show you of which I am certain your sire would approve."

She looked to the distant, unmoving figure. "What of D'Argent?"

"He will be provided a basin of water and towels to tend his injuries, food and drink as well."

"There is none to aid him?"

"No need. He keeps himself fit, doubtless to survive the

beatings and more quickly heal. Do not be fooled, my lady. He is very dangerous."

"He is chained, Vitalis, the same as when I happened upon this abomination."

"Not the same. Here, necessity warrants he be given much slack."

At her frown, he raised his eyebrows.

More imaginings, these making her neck and face warm. "How very humane he is not made to eat in the same place he relieves himself," she scorned.

"Other than that he yet lives, it is the greatest concession gained from Jaxon," Vitalis said. "Now come away."

Over the next hour, Isa struggled to show interest in those things of which she had been regularly apprised. The camp was well situated in this wooded area, sectioned into living spaces comprised of dozens of tents where scores of men and a handful of women slept at day's end. In a shallow cave distant from the deep one occupied by the Norman, the rebels ate and received tidings of their occupied country and instruction of the sort delivered by way of words rather than weapons.

The training yards in which they practiced at arms were not fenced as at Wulfen Castle, but great squares of forest had been cleared, their corners marked by posts hewn from thick branches. And all that had been empty upon her arrival were being put to good use now the ungodly exhibition had ended.

The voice and shouts above all others was that of Jaxon who coolly acknowledged her before relieving one of his trainers to himself instruct a young man in when to thrust rather than swing a sword. Nearby was a crudely constructed stable and several wattle and daub structures for the storage of food, drink, and weapons.

"Impressive," she said as her man walked her back to her escort.

"A good beginning, my lady."

She glanced at the cave and wondered if its occupant had regained consciousness. And what was to be done with one whose once handsome face bore bruises, cuts, and scrapes in various stages of healing.

"As for the boy we seek," Vitalis said, "once more the visit to Lincolnshire yielded none suitable."

That matter ought to occupy her, not her enemy. "One must be found, Vitalis. Do I not have a half-Norman heir to present when Le Bâtard's men come, all may be lost."

He thought long on something, said, "I have heard slavers from Bristol will pause in Lincolnshire a sennight hence to sell off some of their stock before sending the rest overseas." He raised a hand to stave off protest. "I know you do not approve, but as you say, do we not find a boy, all that belongs to you will be claimed by the usurper—and that may include your body."

She longed to upbraid him for suggesting she purchase another human, but he was right.

"My lady, among those offered for sale, many will be boys. If one is near the looks, age, and size of Wulf, you can save him from the terrible fate another's coin buys. And of good benefit, he is likely to have been taken from lands to the south and west. Thus, there will be none to reveal his true identity. He shall be..." Vitalis shrugged. "...a parchment scraped clean, ready for the words of a Wulfrith to be written upon it."

Distaste threatened to choke her, but the need to beat back the coming Normans handed him the victory. "You shall accompany me to Lincolnshire," she said.

"My lady, you need not be present."

"*I* shall choose the one to bear my son's name."

A muscle in his jaw jerking, he inclined his head.

She considered the cave again.

"I think I know what to do with the Norman," Vitalis said, and when she startled, added, "This past hour I have been nearly as absent as you."

55

He knew her well, that if half her mind had been on what he had shown her, it would be much. "Tell."

"Though I do not think you will like it any more than attending a slave auction, I believe it the best means of preserving the Norman's life, restoring his dignity, and making good use of him. Providing he cooperates." He led her to the posts where Guarin D'Argent had been chained.

Looking around, first at her, then the few who had not withdrawn to the training fields, he said, "Draw nearer, my lady. Should you agree to my proposal, it is best Jaxon believes 'tis yours alone."

When she halted alongside him, he laid a hand on a post with its large ring set in the side. "One post henceforth, my lady. Only one."

CHAPTER SEVEN

*T*he usual basin of water, cloths, viands, and drink had been placed on the rock slab to which he kept his back as was required—though no longer now the one who delivered them had departed.

He thirsted more than hungered and longed to clean the dried blood from his face. More, he ached to drag his blankets around him to ward off the cold of the cave—further reason for remaining fit, the intensity of exercise delivering him from body-quaking chills, even if only for a short time.

But having not heard the horses depart, he waited. Were the lady to return, providing an opportunity to make use of one whose appearance at the camp surprised as much as her anger over what was done him, it was best he continue to appear vulnerable.

How long since Vitalis and she left? An hour? And who was she? What brought her here now that had not before? Had she been as gaunt that night at Senlac? Had she found her son? Or lost him?

If only he had sooner regained his senses. It had taken the sound of a slap to pierce his darkness and her voice to reel him up out of it when she demanded Vitalis prove her trust was not misplaced. With what seemed reluctance, her man had acceded he but followed Jaxon's orders, then submitted her grief as his defense for leaving her ignorant of the treatment of their prisoner.

Grief for her son? Had the boy gone to Senlac as feared? Died there? Likely. But though Guarin was of those now her enemy, she remembered the good of the man forced to strike her to deliver her from harm. Hence, if there was a way out of Saxon captivity, she seemed the surest means. *If* she returned to this reeking cave that sought to become his tomb.

Staring at the wall of rock, drinking in the convulsing light of torches rarely afforded beyond brief visits to deliver his meals, Guarin shifted his thoughts to things with which they were best occupied following a beating.

First, prayer beseeching the Lord for deliverance, the importance of which his sire had impressed on him with as much passion as Guarin's uncle trained youths into warriors worthy of serving Duke William. Next, an inventory of new injuries—brow, eye, nose, mouth, jaw, ribs. Then the gathering of resolve needed to heal sufficiently before the next recruits arrived.

In the midst of that last, he heard footsteps, but they retreated and what sounded a whispered argument between that woman and Vitalis commenced. If the latter sought to dissuade the former from entering the cave, he failed. But the expectation the warrior would accompany the woman proved unfounded when only one pair of lightly burdened boots entered. Still, Vitalis would be near.

The lady advanced, negotiating the ground between the entrance and the rear wall and halting on the other side of the slab on which those things delivered him remained untouched. Doubtless, she had been warned about the reach of his chains and would remain distant enough he could not catch hold of her.

"I would speak with you, Norman," she said in his language

and with a fluency and accent so nearly true there was no doubt she was long acquainted with Norman-French.

"You are awake, oui?"

He could play at remaining unconscious in the hope she drew nearer, but if this battered body failed to capture her, he might not see her again, whether fear kept her away or Jaxon put an end to him.

"Of what would you speak to me, Saxon?" he said wearily. Naught feigned about that, but it was calculated to appeal to she who admitted to Vitalis this Norman had meant her no harm.

"Will you turn to me?"

"You wish to gloat?"

The silence was so drawn out he might have looked around to verify she had not departed were it possible to soundlessly traverse the cave.

"I cannot..." She cleared her throat. "I will not apologize for what was done you, but hate you though I do, never would I permit it had I known."

"Hate," he mused. "After what you beheld this day, you think you have more cause than I? The only ill I have done you is knocking you senseless to ensure no other man violated—"

"He did not violate me!"

With a clatter of chains to which Guarin had grown so accustomed they rarely awakened him in the night when aching places turned him side to side, he rolled onto his back. Making no attempt to mask his discomfort, he angled his face toward hers. "So you say now, Lady. So you said then."

Torchlight was at her back, making a silhouette of her mantled figure. Or mostly. Light reflected off the wall onto her face, allowing him to better see what earlier his wavering consciousness made him question—hollows beneath cheeks and fatigue about eyes that stared at his swollen, bloodied face. And where great offense must have shone from her moments before, horror, regret, perhaps even sympathy flitted across that canvas of grief.

Deserved grief, Guarin's anger pronounced judgment as if a sentence to be handed down though already it was carried out and still she served it.

Revolted by how depraved his anger, silently he appealed, *Dear Lord, forgive this beast who would savor her suffering. She may be responsible for my own, but never is grief deserved.* He breathed deep. *And if she is Your plan to release me from bondage, let me not ruin it by behaving the enemy.*

Now to make amends. However, before he could apologize for challenging her claim she had not been violated, she said, "Since many Saxon women are ill-used by Normans, it bears repeating I am not among their victims."

Perhaps not in that way, but in others. Hoping to move her to greater concern for him, he said, "I thirst. Would you bring the basin near?"

"So I might come within reach of your chains?" She shook her head. "I am sorry for what was done you, but not so much I would deliver to you that which is accessible."

He gave a grunt of laughter. "After the beating you witnessed, do I look capable of besting one who not only dons the garments and weapons of a man but commands rebels the same as that woman of old Britain—Boudica, is it not?"

"I will not be your prey, Guarin D'Argent. You are bruised, bloodied, and in pain. You may even be broken in places, but you are not wasting away. You have great strength, and for that you have survived every beating—thus far."

Thus far. Then the risk of leaving him alive was unacceptable? She had determined death the best option as Vitalis suggested?

Anger once more pressing in, he rasped, "Speak my fate, Saxon." He coughed to clear saliva that slid to the back of his throat. "Then leave me to it so you may sooner seek God's forgiveness."

He felt the straining of her conscience, then she pushed the mantle off her shoulders so it draped her back. He believed the threat of the dagger worn on her belt, having seen her put one through her Norman assailant, but the sword... Likely more for show than use.

He smiled, hardly felt the pain of cracked lips. "My very own Boudica."

The hand drawing the dagger from its scabbard faltered. "Do not call me that!"

Was she offended at being equated with the ancient one who failed to eject Romans from her country? Or his claim on her? "Then what, Lady? I gave my name at Senlac, but the one I aided and for whom I suffer did not give hers."

"It is enough for you to know me as the enemy."

He coughed again, turned toward her onto his side. "Reveal my fate, Boudica."

He heard her teeth grind, then grasping the dagger in one hand, she lifted the basin in the other as if to come around the rock. And within reach of his chains.

"Do you give your word you will remain unmoving," she said, "the same word that proved true upon Senlac, I shall bring this nearer."

"My lady!" Vitalis called. "What do you?"

She peered across her shoulder. "I but give a beaten, thirsting man water. Fear not, I am armed."

"But all is within his reach. You—"

"Your lady commands you to come no nearer!"

Vitalis's footsteps ceased.

Not a command Guarin would have followed were she his lady...

Returning her gaze to him, she said, "Your word, Guarin D'Argent."

"It is yours, my lady."

She came around the rock.

Were his body capable of responding to the demands made of it, he could be on his feet and, before attaining the full reach of his chains, upon her. But he was too beaten, she held a dagger she was capable of putting through a man, and this was a time of...

Wooing, he thrust the word down the gorge of one far from a mind and mood to charm this Saxon. However, were it possible to work her to his will, the effort could save him a violent death as well as a merciful one.

Was it possible? He was not yet wed or even betrothed, but it was not for lack of opportunities. Ever his esteem for and protectiveness toward the fairer sex had drawn girls and women to him. Though his ability to attract them had not been tested on an enemy, there could not be a better time to assess its effectiveness.

She took two more steps, lowered the basin to the floor, and pushed it forward with the tip of her blade. "I have brought it nearer," she said and withdrew the dagger which only then he looked near upon. There was no mistaking her unadorned weapon for the one given her before he was attacked in the wood. Did she yet possess that keen blade carried by all D'Argents who attained sword and spurs?

"You will have to come the rest of the way," she said and retreated to the end of the slab.

She made it sound a simple task, but it would hurt. Moving slowly, as much to prevent further damage as to avoid alarming her, he pressed to sitting and ground his teeth to keep them from clicking as chill air more deeply penetrated the rag of what remained of his tunic.

He considered the basin, glanced over his shoulder at the foul blankets bunched against the wall. He thirsted, but more he needed—

"You are cold," she said.

"That is the least of my afflictions," he muttered, "and of little concern if my fate is a merciful death or a violent one."

He caught the sound of her tongue coming off her palate. "You heard all of it—Jaxon, Vitalis, me?"

"Only Vitalis and you. Though much was unclear, I understood enough to know you risk much in keeping me alive. And I concur." He coughed again, this time against a dry throat.

"Pray, drink," she said.

He shifted forward a body that spoke with the voice of chains. Once the worst of his thirst was answered, he would use what remained of the water to soothe aches by pressing wet cloths to cuts and swellings, then clean away the blood and stench of a long unwashed body. Lastly, he would satisfy his hunger with bread and cheese. A simple life of mere survival…

The cold water refreshed and numbed his throat, but it further chilled a body across which hairs prickled. As he returned the basin to the floor, he was wracked by a shudder that snapped his teeth and slopped precious water over the rim.

"Almighty," he rasped and pressed his arms tight to his sides to suppress the next quake that sought to further unman him.

Something of good weight landed on his legs.

"You are in greater need than I," the lady said defensively.

Though pride demanded he toss back the thick, woolen mantle, he felt his sire's great hands on shoulders beginning to broaden, and heard him say, *Let not pride be so powerful as to be the death of you, Son.*

He lifted the mantle, suppressed a groan as ache tore through his side, and dragged the wool around his shoulders. Ahead of feeling the lady's warmth settle over him, he caught her scent above that of a long-stored garment. It was slight and in no way perfumed.

Containing the next shudder, he considered her figure clothed in close-fitting tunic and chausses. Too close, as if fashioned for a boy of good size, else a very young woman.

"A mantle for a dagger," he said. "Ere this day, I would have scorned such a trade." And had he yet his mail tunic and sword, of which he had been divested, he would be tempted to trade them as well.

"You will not be cold again," she ignored the opening given to reveal what had become of his dagger. "Henceforth, you will be afforded proper bedding, clothing, drink, and food."

He stared.

"And light," she exclaimed. "One cannot live in darkness."

"I have," he said more sharply than he should considering she provided confirmation of answered prayer—that she was the weak of the rebels, thereby his best chance of escape. "For near on three months."

"You are fortunate to have survived. But winter is upon us, and long it will be dark and cold."

"God is on my side," he spoke the same as Duke William had in rallying his troops. Words Guarin had questioned then. Words questioned since when he felt most abandoned.

"If that is so, how is it you are here?" she challenged.

Though he wished the answer simply that time and chance happened to all as found in scripture, he knew his decision to aid in conquering England was the beginning of this end. Still, he said, "I followed my God-given conscience in aiding you, rather than the flesh and heart urging me to sooner find kin. I trust eventually the Lord will make clear His reason and plan."

"That is the same expectation of Saxons yet capable of believing God will return to *their* side," she said, then almost to herself, "A pity He cannot stand both our sides."

Guarin had not considered that, but now he did and would have been tempted to hopelessness had not his sire imparted the belief God knew no limits, that whatever He deemed worthy was possible.

The woman started to return her dagger to its sheath, then once more set it before her. "Recall your word given me, and I shall bring your food and the cloths nearer. Then we can speak of the morrow."

"My word stands."

She tossed the cloths to him, then set the platter of food near and pushed it forward with her dagger.

Loath to lose any of the heat gained from the dark blue mantle whose return she would soon demand, he did not move. When she left the cave, he would eat and tend his injuries.

As she settled on the end of the slab and set the dagger across her lap, he said, "I think it time you reveal how long I am to be treated more a man than a beast and what is required in return—which, be assured, will not be betrayal of my own."

"What is required of you I do not think betrayal but, rather, instinct."

"Instinct?"

"No different from what has kept you alive these months, defending yourself with all means available, not the least of which is remaining strong. Vitalis believes it is how you protect your innards."

"Lady," he snapped, "cease your circling and tell what you and that knave have devised." He regretted his loss of patience, but he knew he would not like her solution.

"As you must know, I cannot release you. Thus, the only way to keep you alive is for you to remain useful to our cause."

He waited.

"By encouraging the recruits to beat you, Jaxon gave them a taste of revenge and the hope of righting wrongs. Thus, you proved useful, but I will not tolerate further treatment of that sort. Unfortunately, Jaxon answers to me only so far. And I need him."

Guarin longed to lie back, instead parted the mantle to let in a breath of cool air lest he yield to the seduction of wool.

"Thus, one post, one chain," she said. "And you will be armed with a dull sword."

She need tell no more. He was to aid in training her rebels, providing experience with how a Norman fought—and satisfaction in bettering one.

"I am guessing my Saxon opponent will not be chained to the other post," he snarled, "nor his blade dull."

She started to avert her gaze, firmed it. "Your opponents will not be chained, but I think it safest for all, regardless of skill, dull blades are used both sides."

It was more than a concern for safety, Guarin thought. He could do great damage with a sword whose blade was wanting, but far greater damage with a keen one he did not doubt he could wrest from many a rebel. "And should I decline to give my enemies an advantage over my people?"

"Then they will beat you unto death. But do you defend yourself, you will live."

"For how long, Lady? I may not know your name, but I know your face and your body. I know these are your rebels."

"Do you do as Vitalis proposes, you should survive long enough to be sent back across the sea with others of your kind."

He leaned forward as if to impart a secret. "That sea is now William's, as is his right now he wears England's crown." At her blink of surprise, he continued, "I am not entirely isolated. Joy of which your rebels have little and anger of which they have much loosen lips with such volume and speed words fly like bats to the back of this cave."

She stood, walked around the slab and, with it once more between them, returned her dagger to its scabbard.

"We are done?" he asked.

"I will come again. When I do, you will be alive, swinging a sword, and teaching my rebels how a Norman fights."

He knew he should not argue, but her words sounded a command. "I will not play your game."

"It is no game, D'Argent. It is instinct. It is life. And did you not already grasp that, I would be speaking with a corpse. You *will* fight." She turned and started toward Vitalis who was visible to Guarin now he had risen to sitting.

At the center of the cave, she turned and said with what sounded pleading, "As Jaxon seeks your death, I know not how else to keep you alive, Guarin D'Argent. Pray, defend yourself. And live."

Though angered that regardless of how dull the blade seeking his blood, she was right—instinct *would* drive him to do all in his power to preserve his life—he was moved by her determination he live. And her grieving over the one who did not. "Did you find your son upon Senlac, Lady?"

"I did."

No joy in her voice, only sorrow the same as Saxons who arrived at the camp to build on a foundation of grief the anger and vengeance of a rebel. Had Guarin to wager, it would be on a boy having died on that battlefield beneath the blades of men. Pity the one with the death of a child on his conscience—had he a conscience.

"I am sorry," he said.

"For what?" She was defensive again, as if he had lost the wager.

He did not think so. As she started to turn aside, he considered saying naught of what she left behind, but she would return for it, and he wished to be done with her—for now. "You forget your mantle."

"I do not."

Then he had her sympathy, a weakness to be exploited during the wooing. "Much appreciated, Boudica."

"Do not call me that!"

"A name, then. Or are you so uncertain of your ability to hold me you fear I shall use it to seek you out when I escape?"

"I will hold you. You will not depart without my leave." A long pause, then, "But I shall give you a name. I am Dotter."

He nearly called it a lie, but though it was not what he sought, there was some truth to it. Unlike the Normans who had begun taking surnames as Guarin's sire had done in choosing a reference to the silver hair by which he and his sire were known, beyond their Christian names the Saxons were mostly known by whose son or daughter they were.

Before freeing himself, he would learn exactly who had sired this woman who might not be a warrior but was nearer one than any of the fairer sex he had met.

He frowned. Was it possible...?

He narrowed his eyes at her, deemed it very possible that of the midland shires in contention for the camp's location, this was Wulfenshire. Were it, the lady might not merely be Dotter but Wulfrithdotter.

He smiled, called, "Come again, Dotter."

~

DOTTER.

She had not lied, though neither had she given him what he asked. Though she had spoken with confidence, were any capable of escaping Jaxon, she would guess it was Guarin D'Argent. And seriously she took his sideways threat to seek her out.

As evidenced by him learning the loathsome duke wore England's crown, it could prove impossible to hide behind the name of Dotter. And per orders Jaxon disliked as much as Vitalis being given charge of their Norman prisoner, now that D'Argent was to be more often amongst his enemies, he would have further opportunities to uproot her.

Though Isa had told Jaxon and Vitalis to instruct the rebels that in his presence they were not to speak of her nor the lands upon which they trained, so many could not long guard their tongues.

D'Argent would learn her name and that of her demesne, and for this Jaxon was right to protest him training rebels. But only this. She hated D'Argent as she must, but she could not allow the torture to continue nor grant even a merciful death.

If only she had come after Jaxon gained from the Norman the satisfaction he sought—

She gasped at so evil a wish D'Argent was gone from this world.

"All is well, my lady?"

She nearly startled over Ordric's presence at her side where she had turned her destrier to look back. Glancing first at the housecarle on her other side, she saw from his frown that neither had her reaction to so heinous a thought escaped him.

"All is well," she said, then once more considered the ravine to assure herself there was nothing to indicate the encampment lay at the opposite end beyond dense growth.

If one knew the path down through that rocky place, its every twist and turn and the light to be found at the end of long stretches of God-hewn tunnels, the troops of Normans reported upon Wulfenshire would uncover the resistance. And her rebels would die before they had the opportunity to add their strength to others across England.

Again she was struck by the thought that supported Jaxon's belief D'Argent was better dead. Again, horror over ending the life of one who was not the same as others subjugating her country— he who had sounded sincere rather than taunting when he sought confirmation of what he believed her son's death. And there another reason she could not release him, but providing care was taken to ensure she kept hold of D'Argent until the Normans were ousted, he could do her no harm.

But his duke could. To thwart the crown-wearing usurper, she must begin preparing mind and heart to bring into her home a boy for whom she would care naught but would call *son* when the Normans came.

CHAPTER EIGHT

Lillefarne Abbey
Wulfenshire, England

*I*nformed of the elderly abbess's passing, Isa had known there would be a new one at Lillefarne. But this surprised.

The woman who had stepped from the center of a long line of nuns, named herself Abbess Mary Sarah, and welcomed her patroness, appeared so young it was unlikely she matched Isa's twenty and five years. In looks only though, her pretty face and slim full-chested figure contrasting with a severe and proper demeanor befitting one aged two score.

Smile slight as if to appear serene, the woman said, "I would be honored, my lady, did you come out from beneath this foul sky and ease your thirst and hunger in my apartment."

Remaining astride in the courtyard to which she and the hooded Vitalis had been admitted, Isa glanced heavenward. The clouds' bellies were middling grey to dark grey. Hence, there could be no lingering.

"I thank you, Abbess, but we are for a long day of travel and can spare only a quarter hour. I shall return another day so we may become acquainted."

The woman arched an eyebrow toward hair that peaked lower on her brow than most. "I marvel you bothered to pause here, my lady. What small thing do you require of this humble house of God?"

Though loath to dismount for a short time that could stretch longer were the urgency imparted by staying the saddle lost, it was rude to continue talking down on the godly woman.

Isa swung a leg over and dropped to the ground.

Lids narrowing, the abbess considered what was revealed by the parting of Isa's fur-lined mantle. "You are dressed as a man, my lady, not as God would see you clothed."

Isa longed to say it was in the skin of a woman God had clothed her and she yet wore that beneath woven threads, but she said, "I find such garments best for hours in the saddle. Now, two matters bring me to Lillefarne."

The abbess tucked her hands into opposite sleeves. "The first, my lady?"

"Ere I tell, let us save time by preparing for the second. Pray, have one of your nuns summon my former maid, Aelfled."

"At this hour of morn, she is at prayer."

"She may return to her conversation with God once I have spoken with her," Isa said.

The abbess's nose twitched, but she ordered a middle-aged sister to collect Aelfled. "Now how may I serve you, my lady?"

"I would speak of the Saxon women who seek sanctuary here to escape the invaders' attentions."

"Though I have only recently arrived at Lillefarne," Abbess Mary Sarah said, "this past sennight we have taken in two—a lady and a commoner—adding to those who arrived following the great battle."

"Then within these walls is much to tempt men of ill repute."

"Aye, my lady. I have heard of the breaching of several abbeys across England, their occupants defiled and several ladies carried off and forced into marriage."

"I would not see that happen here, Abbess. Thus, the need for a stone wall like that which surrounds Wulfen Castle."

"Stone! But the cost—"

"I shall bear it. My grandsire funded this abbey, and I will not neglect his good work of providing women needed refuge."

"Generous, my lady. Such consideration I will not refuse."

Only a fool would, Isa thought, unsure whether this woman warranted like or dislike since something about her did not ring true. Hopefully, it was only her youth, which evidenced her position was gained by way of favors.

"When will construction begin?" the abbess asked.

"As soon as plans are drawn."

She inclined her head. "I will be pleased to offer suggestions on how best—"

"I thank you, but I would not take time from your charges. With the enemy upon us, more than ever they require godly guidance."

Hesitation, and was that a flicker of resentment?

Isa knew she trod on the woman's authority, but the wall had another purpose beyond keeping Lillefarne's occupants safe, and the fewer who knew of it the better. And here came one who would be entrusted with that knowledge.

Aelfled halted alongside the abbess and in her sweetly husky voice said, "My lady?"

Having not seen her since leaving her here en route to returning Wulf's body to the castle, Isa noted she looked older and thinner. Of course, the same could be said of her lady.

Aelfled suffered, and Isa wanted to be glad of it since it was due one whose failure had caused the death of five boys, but she hurt for the young woman who had been a friend and confidante.

Remember why you are here, she reminded herself. "Let us walk, Aelfled."

Unlike in the past, the young woman did not draw alongside. Once they were distant from the others, Isa turned to her.

"I am glad you have come, my lady," Aelfled said.

"Are you?"

"Aye, so I may see for myself you are well."

"And?"

She moistened her lips. "I know it is too soon to forgive, but…I ache for how much you hate me."

Isa was so vexed by how deeply she felt her maid's pain she nearly loosed words of cruel assurance hope was wasted on forgiveness. Instead, she said, "I have a use for you."

Aelfled's eyes widened. "Anything."

"Anything? You would kill for me?"

The young woman gasped. "My beloved lady would not ask that of me."

"But if she did?"

Her moist eyes sending a bolt through the heart, Isa determined to speak elsewhere, but before she could reveal the reason for her visit, Aelfled said, "I am sorry, my lady, but I could not kill for you. Pray, ask anything else of me."

"I wish you to aid the rebellion."

She blinked. "Me?"

"Once our numbers are sufficient and well trained, we shall strike at the Normans however we can. On occasion, that will require you hide rebels here where Normans will not think to look."

"We are all women within these walls, my lady! Allowing men to enter would not be borne."

"And need not be. These walls shall be replaced with stone and a passage built into them as at Wulfen. There you will harbor rebels until it is safe for them to depart." At the young woman's hesitation, Isa added, "That is the *anything* I require of you—and that you speak of it to none."

"Not even the abbess?"

"I shall deal with her." Isa frowned. "She is too young for so esteemed a position. What know you of her?"

"Very little, so few words have we exchanged."

"Is she well regarded by her flock?"

"Those who do not resent her youth are respectful."

"And those who resent it?"

"I speak of older sisters who believe her position should have been given to one of greater experience."

"One of them."

"There are several the old abbess would have been pleased to have replace her."

Aelfled's observations of little use, Isa said, "You may return to your prayers."

"Will you come again soon?"

"Doubtful. If I require anything, I shall send Vitalis or another."

Aelfled curtsied. "As you will, my lady."

When she went from sight, Isa returned to the abbess. "We must depart."

The woman inclined her head. "Godspeed, Child."

Spoken by one more a child than she! But it was as those of the Church addressed young and old, Isa reminded herself.

As she swung atop the destrier, she reflected women should not be restricted to gowns. So much easier it was in chausses and tunic to properly sit a saddle and move with the horse.

She patted the neck of the flaxen-maned mount she had made her own and wondered again what to name her Norman prize. But as she started to urge him after Vitalis, a hand touched her knee.

"Abbess?" she said, peering into the woman's upturned face, the angle of which emphasized a slightly cleft chin.

"I would offer words of encouragement, my lady. Words all require in these darkest of days."

Isa inclined her head.

"You, like many, feel God is punishing our people, aye?"

"What other explanation is there?"

The woman's shrug seemed an unholy response. "We cannot know the mind of our Lord. All we can do is remember and embrace who we are—Saxons strong of mind and body. And spirit."

Isa stiffened. Though not the exact words inscribed by Gytha, they were near enough fine hairs rose across her limbs.

"Godspeed, Child," the abbess said again and walked opposite.

When Isa drew alongside Vitalis, her man said low, "She unsettles you."

"Indeed. We must inquire after her."

"What do you fear?"

"That she is not as she appears, that she may be much more." She sighed. "But it will save until I have secured a son."

Lincolnshire
England

IN ONE THING, the Wulfriths could be likened to Normans—their attitude toward slavery. And did one know their history, they might understand that hatred.

Might. Just because one did not like something done to them was no guarantee they would not do it to another.

When Isa was not averting her gaze, holding her breath, and grinding her teeth, she was searching for one capable of fooling the Normans. But none of the boys led to the block and presented like wares to enthusiastic buyers and leering observers fit. Unfortunately, they neared the end of the offering, the last of the slaves having been herded from a tent to join the line to the left of the platform.

If not for the need to maintain anonymity, Isa and Vitalis would have joined other buyers in going tent to tent to examine the slaves to be auctioned. Instead, observance was limited to those who shuffled toward the block.

"What think you, my lady?" Vitalis nodded at the boy near the back of the line who had turned his profile toward them.

He was the right size and hair a similar color though shorn—likely due to lice infestation. From the side he was hardly familiar, but face on he might be near enough the look of the noble boy whose name he would take so those who had not seen her heir in some time could be persuaded the difference was due to maturation.

The boy turned forward again, and Isa looked to Vitalis whose face was in shadow the same as hers, both having remained beneath hoods as could hardly be thought strange in such cool weather that continued to threaten rain.

"Size and coloring." She nodded. "But his face is very angular, chin long. If only he had more the look of the smaller one ahead." She nodded at the boy who stood behind a young woman Isa guessed was his sister, the hand she reached to him clasped by his. It was good his accompaniment to the block meant they would be sold together. Otherwise, Isa would be tempted to choose this one who bore a good resemblance to her son but was shorter and slighter of build—two years younger, she guessed.

"Unless you resign yourself to returning to Wulfen empty-handed, the shorn one will have to suffice, my lady."

"Aye, soon the king's men come." She returned her regard to the boy she would have little time to shape into one who appeared worthy of the name Wulfrith and there fixed her attention to avoid looking nearer on the atrocity of humans sold like beasts—and in the case of pretty young women and girls, men's playthings.

Still, she felt their fear, pain, and shame as she had felt the agony and indignity of her own captive at a distance—and more so when she had recognized it was Guarin D'Argent chained to the posts.

Isa tried to return to the present and set her mind on transforming the hard-faced boy into one given the name of Wulfrith, but the Norman warrior was in her head again. Vitalis said D'Argent healed well and had been provided greater quality and quantity of food and drink, good bedding and clothing, and torchlight. A fortnight longer, her man assured her, and the most skilled of their rebels would begin testing their training against the enemy—if he cooperated.

Vitalis said he seemed not at all grateful for his improved circumstances, that he merely stared at those who came and went and refused to answer questions put to him.

Instinct, Isa had assured Vitalis. When it came time to prove he was worth keeping alive, the Norman would raise his dull sword and beat back those set at him. Since he was destined for Normandy rather than a shallow grave in English soil, he would fight.

A commotion yanked her back to the auction—cries, shouts, bodies surging forward and carrying her with them.

"What goes, Vitalis?" she demanded.

As he pulled her against his side, she followed his gaze to the block, and there was the young woman and her brother displayed for the buyers. Hands that had been joined in line reached to re-establish contact broken by two slavers, one who pinned the woman to his broad chest with an arm beneath her breasts, the other who hooked the flailing boy beneath a muscled arm.

"We were to be sold together!" the young woman cried. "It was agreed!"

It was terrible enough to witness the siblings' desperation and fear, but to feel and hear the excitement of the crowd as if they were presented a great feast...

"Dear Lord," Isa gasped.

"Look away, my lady."

She could not.

The struggling boy calling for his sister was carried to the far end near the steps the slaves climbed to be sold to others born into this world the same as they, while the young woman was hauled to the edge of the platform. As she looked wildly around with eyes that appeared of different colors, the bidding resumed.

Three voices rose above the others—one belonging to the auctioneer behind his stand, the other two of men who sought to outbid the other. Of note was one of the buyers Isa could not see over the crowd spoke with the accent of the invaders—a Norman whose people were opposed to slavery though, in this instance, surely only because it was abolished in his own country.

After fierce bidding that nearly muted the cries of brother and sister, it was the Norman who made the young woman his possession.

"The name of the one who has purchased the witchy-eyed wench?" the auctioneer called.

"Chevalier Raymond Campagnon!"

So disturbed was Isa that the man's name nearly slipped past. "Vitalis, he is the one—"

"Quiet, my lady. There is naught to be done."

"But he is—"

"I know."

Of course he did. She had shared the contents of Gytha's missive, among them the belief Le Bâtard had awarded a portion of her lands to one of that name. It had to be the same, and that he was so near Wulfenshire could mean he was set to claim his reward and introduce slavery to her lands.

"All the more reason your face remain hidden," Vitalis said.

"Em!" the boy cried, and Isa thought her heart would burst when he strained toward his sister who was being carried down the opposite steps. So much did his flushed, tear-streaked face resemble Wulf's when her son had learned of his sire's death, Isa's knees started to buckle.

Vitalis tightened his hold on her. "I see it too, my lady."

And now the boy would be sold to another who could take him so distant brother and sister might not meet again. And further yet if, like many who had not commanded the minimum bid, he was sold to slavers who would transport him across the sea to lands with a healthy appetite for trade in humans.

"I shall see you back to our escort and return here to purchase the shorn boy." Vitalis started to turn her from the spectacle.

"Nay, I want the younger one."

His frown was large enough to see its every line amid shadow. "He is too small—easily a hand in height and width."

"I want him! Do you not bid, I shall."

His nostrils dilated, but he nodded. "As my lady commands."

Certes, you are the fool he thinks, she silently rebuked, then said, "Draw near and pay what you must. I shall rejoin our escort." It was enough to know she had purchased another human without seeing it done. Though the boy would not suffer the life of a slave, the paper citing his sale to one of false name would list him as such. And she would burn it to the finest ash.

Lest Vitalis insist on escorting her back to her men, during which the boy could be sold to another, she said, "Go," and pulled free and began pushing her way through a crowd eager to close the gaps behind her.

Vitalis's concern for her choice of a son was well noted alongside her own. The boy was too small, but he would be well fed and, did he experience sudden growth as had her Wulf near that age, soon he would be nearer the right size. Her household retainers would know the truth, but not the Normans. As for the villagers who on occasion had looked upon her son, she would keep him isolated as long as possible to warp their memories lest they speak without thought in the presence of the enemy.

All will be well, she assured herself as she hurried toward her escort. *If Campagnon takes possession of my land ere the Normans are ousted and has he occasion to come into my presence, he will not recognize the urchin made to look a noble. And when I take back my lands, easier it will be to reunite brother and sister.*

"Worthy," she rasped and ignored the inner voice that once more named her a fool.

CHAPTER NINE

Wulfen Castle
England

*T*he last of the great Wulfriths had said that were one's anger justified it could be harnessed, mounted, and ridden such that its power was spent on worthy causes.

Isa's was worthy, but the boy in whose presence she had burned the parchment that made him her possession appeared unmoved.

He no longer cried, having shed his last tears days past when, no matter how hard he strained to see beyond Vitalis with whom he shared a saddle, no glimpse of his sister did he gain as the town receded.

Anger now ally and companion, the only one with whom he conversed behind eyes too blue to resemble the softly grey-blue of the boy he was to become, he stared into flames that had devoured proof he was a slave.

Isa looked to Vitalis, saw where he stood to the left of her bed he stared at the table where Gytha's missive no longer sat though the dagger did. She ought to hide it as well and did not understand why she did not now she knew its owner lived. What stayed her?

Drifting back to when her enemy had given it to her, she was swept by a sense of comfort and safety in a world lacking both—and awe it had been gifted by one worthy of great fear.

Feeling again the brief contact with the warrior's fingers as she had gripped the hilt and felt not cold steel but warmth imparted by his hand, she caught her breath. And slapped on an expression of frustration when Vitalis's head came around.

He shrugged, as much at a loss over the boy as she.

Isa looked back at the one recently turned nine who must become one nearer eleven. "Boy," she eschewed the name on the document by which he would no longer be known though she was not yet able to address him by his new name. "We are of the same language, you have heard all I have told, and I believe you are learned enough to grasp it. Now is the time to ask questions."

He glanced at her where she stood on the opposite side of the hearth behind a chair whose back she had folded her hands atop, immediately returned his gaze to the flames.

Annoyed, she gripped the chair's back. Were he reachable, how was she to draw near? The question turned her thoughts to Wulf. When he was being difficult, testing the bounds of her tolerance for rebellion—

She shook her head to scatter memories of her son, tensed as they scrambled to catch hold of something to arrest their flight.

How do I reach this boy? she silently demanded. *Think!*

Instead, she heard Wulf's voice, as angry now as last summer when the mother of her rather than the Wulfrith protested her ten-year-old son exchanging his dull sword for the keen one gifted by his sire.

If I am to become worthy of the name Wulfrith, he had shouted, *you must no longer see me first as a son but as one destined to bring glory to your sire and his sire before. Memory of your love for a boy I would have sustain me as I fight toward manhood, but a different love shown me now, one that passes my leash into Father's hand until I surpass its limits and myself unfasten it.*

His passion and depth of maturity had silenced Isa. When she could speak, she had apologized, taken his hand, and led him to her husband whom she had also offended. She had beseeched Roger's forgiveness and, seeing his anger recede, left the two with the killing sword and retreated to the solar. Alone with Aelfled, she had permitted herself only enough tears to soothe her burning eyes.

Husband and son had been right, but the answer she now sought was found in Wulf's words—*your love for a boy I would have sustain me as I fight toward manhood...*

She could not love this boy, but a semblance she must show to build a foundation to sustain him as he was forced toward manhood years earlier than expected of him.

She stepped out from behind the barrier made of the chair, crossed to him, and sank to her knees. "I know you are frightened."

"I am not!"

She moistened her lips. "I know you are confused."

"I am not!"

She blinked away flecks of spit. "I know what was done your sister and you was wrong."

His face contorted. "They lied to us!"

She took his hands in hers and they jerked, but he did not pull free. "Dear boy, tell how your sister and you fell to slavers."

More tears rimmed his eyes. "We gave ourselves to them. Had to."

She had heard of such. Faced with starvation or other cruelties that might end in one's demise, free men, women, and children sold themselves into slavery.

Instinct again, that of survival which required Guarin D'Argent provide a measure of training to his enemies. "You were very hungry, then?"

"Not yet, but winter is here, and…" He gripped her hands. "Our mother died last year, our sire in the great battle. Though our aunt took us into her home, there were too many to feed. She said the only way for all to survive the cold and Normans was for Em and me to be sold as slaves, that the coin would ensure our brother and sister lived. Though we thought we could bear it were we sold together, and it was as the slavers promised, the men who wanted my sister did not want me. They tore us apart." He sniffed hard, swallowed. "What will become of Em? What will that man do to her?"

Isa longed to tell him it was possible his sister would be near, to assure him Em was fortunate to have been sold to the Norman rather than the man whom Vitalis had learned sold the services of joy women across Northern England, to give him hope the Saxon rebellion would soon triumph over the Normans and reunite him with his sister. But she dare not.

He would know he was not a slave no matter the coin paid, but she needed him to need her. And that meant only enough hope to motivate him to become worthy of the name he would take and just enough hopelessness he did not go in search of his sister.

"I cannot guess Em's fate," she lied. "I can only provide the means to ensure if there is an opportunity to reunite you, you will be strong and capable enough to take it."

He bowed his head. "I am frightened, my lady, and ashamed I am so weak."

She released one of his hands, cupped his jaw, and raised his eyes to hers. "Let me make you brave. Let me make you strong."

She startled when he wrenched free. And again when he came off the chair, dropped to his knees, and flung his arms around her neck.

"I will be your Wulfrith." He nodded. "I will help you send the evil Normans back across the sea. I will do everything you ask. For our people. For Em."

She commanded her arms around him, as best she could

embraced him as she had last embraced Wulf. And ached even more for the one she would never again hold.

Hearing Vitalis cross the room, she composed her face and looked up. She did not hide her emotions well, as told by the hand he set on her shoulder.

Determining she would correct him later, she lowered her chin and breathed in the scent of this quaking boy who was as motherless as she was childless.

Lord help them both...

CHAPTER TEN

Wulfenshire Rebel Camp, England
February, 1067

I nstinct.

She had known it would give her what she required
of him. He had known it as well—that his desire to live and the
rebels' desire to thwart him would see the tip of his unworthy
sword rise from the dirt and beat back his enemies. And beat
them back he did despite his left wrist remaining manacled and
the chain between it and post providing only ten strained feet in
which to maneuver.

Dotter had known though he abhorred being made an
instrument that gave his enemy an advantage—one that might see
Normans dead—he could not resist. But had she guessed how
much satisfaction he would derive from remaining alive? How
exhilarating to strike back at those who had beaten a defenseless
man? How gratifying to make them shout, hurt, and bleed?

Though the Saxons he now faced were no mere recruits,
having been afforded training and wielding weapons of steel
rather than flesh and bone, very little satisfaction did he provide

them. Not so with Jaxon who liked to end *training* sessions by demonstrating techniques on his chained opponent—acts of vengeance against one who often bested his best.

Guarin ached to challenge the man unchained and with a keen blade. How long anticipation of that contest and his altered state of imprisonment would sustain him he did not know, but it was enough. For now.

He almost smiled over two seemingly benign words that had become his daily bread. But in their every stroke was a world of what came after. He would survive, escape, and justice would be his.

In the four weeks since Dotter discovered her savior lived and his reward had been torture, much he had healed as had often been impossible between beatings. To the detriment of those he was forced to train in order to mark another day, he grew stronger, quicker, and more focused.

When next she came, she would not find a man struggling to keep his pieces together but a warrior—albeit not yet of the strength of the one met on the battlefield.

When would she come? he pondered as he allowed himself once a day while being secured prior to his return to the cave.

Beyond healing, warmth, food, and drink, one basic need was denied him—to see her again. Not to express gratitude nor threaten her, though at times he longed to, so angry did he become as he had not when first they were reunited. To her benefit, he had been too beaten to further exhaust himself in expressing anger, but of greater benefit to him, his relatively passive demeanor had gained her sympathy as evidenced by the mantle around him day and night.

So for what did he need to see her? he asked himself as he had many times, lied as many times, and cursed himself many times when he glimpsed what lay beyond those lies. As he did now.

"Hold!" shouted the Saxon who supervised his transfer from post to cave, he whose sword Guarin would welcome against his own though the warrior showed no inclination to do to his prisoner what Jaxon did.

Standing akimbo throughout those demonstrations, Vitalis watched—excepting the one time he intervened when the camp commander landed a blow with his keen-edged blade that sliced open the chausses and flesh of Guarin's upper calf. Before the older man could gain another piece of the Norman whose loss of footing at the farthest reach of his chain presented the temptation of an exposed neck, Vitalis had lunged and shouted, "By command of Dotter, cease!"

Now again he spoke for her, Guarin guessed when he caught the sound of approaching horses he had not earlier for the ringing in his ears dealt by Jaxon's glancing sword.

He turned from observing Zedekiah who had begun securing his ankles.

Once more astride the Norman horse with a man on either side, he felt Dotter's eyes on him. And hoped she felt his on her. As she and her escort reined in, Zedekiah tested the chain once more run between Guarin's ankles and straightened.

"Leave him secured to the post," Vitalis called and strode forward to greet his lady.

Guarin expected him to aid in her dismount, but Dotter was out of the saddle a stride ahead of his arrival.

Distracted from searching for fault in the binding of his body that might later be exploited, Guarin stared at the woman whose gaze was now upon Vitalis.

Though once more garbed as a man, these clothes more visible now she wore a short, fur-lined mantle in place of the long one given him, she was more comely. She still appeared underfed, but her face was fuller, she had color in her cheeks, and hair that had been darkened by neglect was the gold he had first looked upon.

She exchanged words with Vitalis, then stepped past and returned her eyes to Guarin. They moved down him, up, and shoulder to shoulder before settling on his face.

"Leave us, faithful Saxon," she instructed Zedekiah as she halted out of reach of the chain.

The man moved in the direction nearly all had gone once Jaxon finished his demonstration—out of sight of Guarin where they partook of the nooning meal before venturing to a more distant place of training as evidenced by great sword song.

"By invitation I have come," she spoke Norman-French in a voice he had not known was so honeyed.

Guarin had no cause to smile, but mischief tugged at his mouth. He *had* told her to come again. Though he did not believe it was he who commanded her presence, he was certain he was among the reasons she was here.

He inclined his head. "Dotter," he named her, though great the temptation to speak *Wulfrithdotter* and savor her reaction. So certain was he this was Wulfenshire and it was Wulfen-trained warriors who afforded such excellent training that men born to the soil were quickly transformed into men who fought, he would almost wager his life on it. But better his enemy think he remained ignorant and powerless for not knowing south from north and east from west in this foreign country.

He did not believe deception—could this be called that—among his strengths, but under these circumstances it was necessary.

Though the lady's hands were beneath her mantle, from the jut of her upper arms he guessed she clasped them at her waist as if settling into a conversation. "You look much improved, Guarin D'Argent."

If she expected gratitude, she would be disappointed. It was due him, not her. Then there was the matter of an apology to which he did not believe she could ever do justice. "As do you, Dotter."

"I am eating better, sleeping better, thinking better. I am told it is the same for you."

Beginning to feel the cold as his perspiration-dampened

garments turned icy, he crossed his arms over his chest to conserve heat and save himself the indignity of shivering. "Much better now the torture has mostly ceased and the fighting dog made of me is not entirely lacking teeth and claws."

He nearly laughed triumphant when she averted her eyes, but a moment later they returned to his. "Vitalis says you are of good benefit in training our rebels, that you are as admired and respected for your skill at arms as you are detested for your Norman blood."

"If you think to swell me with pride, you think wrong, Lady. It is as you named it—instinct, the desire to survive all the more powerful for the desire to see justice done."

"In that we are the same," she said, "both of us staying this world to see it made right. Once England is Saxon again, I will return you to your country, and you will have to be content that, unlike those of your kind who burn and kill and ravage, your life remains yours to finish at your leisure. And my people..." She breathed deep. "Too great our losses to see us even halfway whole, but our children's children shall be."

After all Guarin had endured, he did not wish to feel for the plight of those who had lost their country to stronger swords, cunning, and resolve, but despite a heart much hardened these months, it yet boasted soft places where the torment of innocents slid through like blades into flesh.

Grudging though his sympathy, it prevented his faith from slipping through clasped hands. True, his prayers for escape remained unanswered and conversations with the Lord one-sided, but they suppressed rage on a scale that might move him toward madness and horrible acts that would render him unredeemable.

"I *will* release you, Guarin D'Argent."

"Generous," he said with so slight a taint of sarcasm it might slip past.

Her lids narrowed. "Is there anything you lack?"

"Much."

"I speak of necessities. More food, drink, blankets. Perhaps a razor since your kind prefer short hair and beardless faces."

He raised an eyebrow. "You would trust me with a sharp blade?"

"I see no risk whilst you are chained. One can be tossed to you and tossed back."

"Tempting, but I grow accustomed to the warmth hair and beard afford in this accursedly cold country."

"Then I shall see you returned to your cave."

Loath to let her go though there was naught more to be said, movement beyond the watchful Vitalis provided an excuse. "You have grown attached to one Norman."

"Attached?" she exclaimed. "What makes you believe I could become attached to one such as you? Just because I removed the noose from your neck and ordered you treated like the human you barely are does not mean—"

"I refer to the horse, Lady."

Her words dried up, and she loosed a breath that clouded the air, but not so much it masked her mortification.

Was there not some saying about how great the lies to be found behind unwarranted protestation? Guarin had not sought to rouse such a response, but it revealed she felt for him beyond pity, even were her emotions rooted in gratitude for what he had done for her and remorse for what she had done to him. Somehow he would make use of it.

The cold beginning to nip, he said, "It is your attachment to the destrier I speak of, not this vile Norman who gave him and a most precious dagger into your keeping."

He heard her swallow, was glad he discomfited her.

"I do grow attached to him," she said, "possible only because he is not Norman."

He grunted. "Norman-bred and trained is Norman, and for that a worthy mount he has proven no matter you deny his origin.

You are wise to once more entrust your well-being to one from across the sea."

As evidenced by the snap of her teeth and the back she turned on him, he offended when better his time and words were spent on wooing. But he was too weary and uncomfortable to think in a straight line.

Lord, I grow cold, he spoke heavenward as she stalked to Vitalis.

After ordering the warrior to have his men return Guarin to his cave, she directed her escort to water and feed her horse—a horse she loudly called *Anglicus.*

Latin for *English,* Guarin mused. He could not know if it was in that moment the Norman destrier was named, but he suspected it. And laughed.

CHAPTER ELEVEN

Wulfen Castle, England
March, 1067

A month since she left the boy's training to others to further her own at the camp. A month since being jolted by her encounter with Guarin D'Argent who had nearly looked the warrior first encountered on the battlefield. A month and still she heard his laughter that made her want to scoop it from the air, close her fingers around it, and sigh over its rumble against her palm as the girl of her had done the flutter of a butterfly's wings.

Witless, she named herself. But she wanted it.

Vitalis reported with each passing day their Norman captive became a more formidable opponent, that the strength returned to him had prompted inspection of the rings bolted into the cave wall whilst he trained Saxons. Upon discovering they were loose, possibly days from being wrenched free, the smithy Zedekiah had replaced them with ones twice as stout and sunk twice as deep.

D'Argent had not raged as expected, which Vitalis said would have been satisfying compared to the laughter he loosed.

In that Isa felt a kinship with her man, especially now that laughter returned to her when she ought to be focusing on something of greater import—Le Bâtard's men stepping past the porter, sullying her hall with the click and clop of their boots, many of which she would not be surprised to learn were taken from the stiffening feet of Saxons.

Face forward, she moved her gaze over her housecarles on both sides of the dais. Fifteen strong, they were fully armored and armed to defend her if needed. Next, she looked sidelong at the boy who stood to her right, his bottom lip becoming chapped as he scraped his teeth over it.

"Peace, Wulfrith," she whispered. "You have only to stand my side and say *oui* or nod when I tap the chair arm with one finger, say *non* or shake your head when I tap with two, smile at three, frown at four."

"Aye, my la—" He silenced himself as if remembering there were only two words he was to speak in the presence of the enemy. His lessons in Norman-French progressed well for the intelligence with which he was gifted, but it would be a year or more before he was sufficiently fluent to provide further proof he was sired by a Norman.

Isa returned her gaze to the dozen who neared the dais where the high table perched and from behind which she and her *son* would receive them.

Advancing slightly ahead of the others was a tall broad-shouldered chevalier. Like his companions, he had yet to remove his helmet, and his chain mail was so polished the light cast by a dozen torches licked its every link.

William's man halted two strides from the dais, and amid the helmet's shadow on either side of its nose guard, she caught the glitter of eyes.

She unstuck her tongue, spoke words rehearsed in the hope they sounded sincere. "I, Lady Hawisa Fortier, welcome to Wulfen Castle the representatives of King William."

She looked to the boy, smiled, returned her regard to the

enemy. "Here the son and heir of my Norman-born husband, Roger Fortier, who fell upon Stamford Bridge. He who bears the esteemed name Wulfrith also welcomes you." She tapped a single finger on the chair arm below the level of the table and out of the corner of her eye saw the boy nod stiffly. Wishing she had created a signal to let him know he did well so he would exude confidence, she said, "I pray you and your men are at ease in my home."

"Much gratitude." The chevalier unbuckled his helmet's chin strap, causing his men to do the same. Within moments, the visages of all were revealed.

Blessedly, the first thing that made Isa startle was good cover for the second. One side of the face of the man before her was terribly scarred, the more lightly disfigured side evidencing how great a loss he had suffered. The damage to his handsome features recent, she guessed it gained at Senlac.

Of greater note—and shock—was his hair. Short on the sides and longer on top in the style favored by the Normans, it presented as the black of the night sea beneath a moon casting silver light across cresting waves. Only once before had she seen a man below the age of thirty so silvered—the same whose laughter she wished to catch in her palm.

Cool green eyes going cold, Le Bâtard's man bowed. "Chevalier Maël D'Argent."

Of course he was. Heart hammering, she struggled to compose her face.

He smiled crookedly. "Pardon the fright, my lady. What can be done has been done to mend the injury dealt by your countrymen. I am assured when the flesh's ire cools, it will not be as unsightly."

She was almost ashamed by her reaction though it was not truly for what was done this Norman who had paid a great price for stealing a country—though not as high a price as that demanded of thousands of Saxons who had died from their injuries.

Grateful her horror could be blamed on his ruined face, she said, "It is I who must be pardoned. One would think never have I seen such grave misfortune, though I assure you I have, especially in recent months."

As she awaited his response, she wondered if it was coincidence the usurper had sent a D'Argent to collect her *tribute* —an unconscionable amount of coin to redeem her lands, in the absence of which they would be subject to forfeiture. Or was this man here because someone on the battlefield had recognized the lady with whom the silvered warrior shared a saddle? If so, surely one of her own had survived and been made to talk. Were that so, she was being baited.

"Understandable," Maël D'Argent finally said. "These are dark times for all."

And shall grow darker for you, she silently warned.

"As I am certain you are eager to resume your journey, Sir Maël, the tribute is here." She gestured to where the chest sat atop the table. "And drink and viands are on the sideboard." She nodded at the long table against one wall, a simple offering presented in unadorned vessels to downplay the wealth accumulated over scores of years, much from training the sons of monied men. Thus, she gave these Normans little reason to linger so her Saxons could sooner resume work on extending Wulfen's underground passage to the wood.

The chevalier settled into his boots. "Your king thanks you for honoring him with a great tribute and his men with a fine feast."

"I but do the same as would any loyal subject," Isa said, detesting the inference she was that to William of Normandy and fearing whatever held this chevalier unmoving.

"There are two other matters, one regarding your lands," he said.

Campagnon. As Gytha had told, he was to be awarded a portion of her holdings. It was good she was prepared. Still, she made no attempt to appear light of heart and face. "The lands of my Norman son, Wulfrith Fortier. Your—*my*—king would part them from the heir though the tribute is paid in full?" She tapped four fingers to elicit a frown from the boy.

"It is as our king decrees, my lady. As for the tribute, it covers just over half your lands."

The tensing of her legs and tightening of her hands on the chair arms keeping her in her seat, she said, "Then half my son's lands are to be given to one of William's men?"

"*Two* of our king's men." He drew a rolled parchment from the purse on his belt and stepped forward.

Immediately, the ring of chain mail and creak of boots left and right was answered front and center, evidencing her housecarles were prepared to defend their lady whilst the king's men prepared to defend themselves.

"Lady, I mean you no harm," Maël D'Argent growled, halting at the edge of the dais. "I wish only to present this." He raised the parchment.

As her men outnumbered those granted entrance, the greater number of the chevalier's entourage left outside in the cold of a day whose frost was just beginning to thaw, she beckoned Maël D'Argent forward.

He mounted the dais and set the parchment in her palm.

She unrolled it, and a crude rendering of her lands appeared, nearly down the center of which was a line dissected on the left by a horizontal one. Those two portions, one northwest of Wulfen Castle, the other southwest, were to be stolen from her. The only good of it was she would retain the slightly larger portion upon which Wulfen Castle sat—and more importantly, the far eastern corner where the rebel camp continued to expand.

As for the centrally located abbey, she was fairly certain it was this side of that vertical line. Regardless, her family had endowed it and would continue to do so—and reinforce it with the wall whose construction progressed well considering winter weather often turned the workers from setting stone to cutting the great blocks in preparation for days of sufficient warmth.

"How old are you, Wulfrith Fortier?" Maël D'Argent asked.

Isa snapped up her chin, gave a four-fingered tap. Hoping the boy frowned in a convincing show of anger over the theft of his inheritance, she said, "My son is—"

"Surely so fine a lad of Norman and Saxon breeding can answer for himself, my lady." The chevalier raised his eyebrows.

"He can, but well I know my son, and in this moment he exercises great restraint as trained to do." She slapped the backs of her fingers against the parchment. "To be expected since he has just learned the fealty gifted King William is of so little regard half his inheritance is lost."

She shifted around, inwardly winced at the confusion on the boy's face that portended a show of fear, and set a hand on his arm. When he looked to her, she smiled and continued in Norman-French, "It is as our king wills, Wulfrith. Loyal subjects that we are, we must accept he knows best." She tapped a single finger.

"Oui, Maman."

It was not that he spoke more than was required of him that made her heart shudder, but that he named her what had only ever passed Wulf's lips.

She was glad of their audience, else she might have snapped at him for being as bold a usurper as the Normans. It had to have been unintentional, for beyond deception, a mother to him she was not and could never be.

She turned back to the chevalier. "Quite mature, would you not say, for one who has barely attained his eleventh year?"

As expected, surprise shone from the eyes he swept over the boy who, at best, would be thought a runt.

"Now tell, Sir Maël, who am I to esteem as neighbors?"

He considered Wulfrith a moment longer, said, "The northern piece is given to Sir Raymond Campagnon who..." A pause as if he did not like the words he was instructed to speak. "… distinguished himself during the great battle."

Then the boy's sister *would* be near. Isa was relieved the one at her side did not exude emotion, evidence he had been too distraught at auction to attend to the Norman's name. Since she could do nothing to reunite brother and sister whilst the latter was the property of another, it was best he remain ignorant until the Normans left England.

"The southern piece," the chevalier continued, "is given my cousin, Cyr D'Argent, who greatly distinguished himself in battle."

Another blow, and it took all her control to remain unmoving.

Almighty, she sent heavenward, *not only do You make my neighbor the one who saved my maid from ravishment and saw the face of my real son whilst concealing his body, but You place him dangerously near the brother made my prisoner and let it not be revealed until I named another my heir—and to one who is likely the son of the D'Argent who slew my boy!*

"You know the name, my lady?" Sir Maël asked.

Easily he saw around the backside of her, meaning once more she failed her sire.

"I have heard it, albeit preceded by the word *Merciless,* and know it to be nearly as esteemed as the *Bloodlust Warrior of Hastings.*" He need not be told she had personal knowledge of the latter's Norman family from whose lands Wulf had fled to bleed out his life alongside men.

"Both well earned, my lady."

Was that a warning she not move against the man given a quarter of her holdings? "I look forward to receiving your cousin at Wulfen, Sir Maël."

"It is his younger brother, Theriot D'Argent, whose acquaintance you shall first make."

Another accursed D'Argent! How many were there? And what of the third matter the chevalier had yet to address? Also a blow?

Before she could move him to it, he said, "As my cousin, Cyr, has returned to Normandy, Theriot is to administer his English lands in his stead."

Reprieve then, time in which to find a way out of the hole she had dug herself in presenting to this cousin her only son whom Cyr D'Argent might realize had been substituted for the noble Wulf he had carried to the wood. If only Aelfled had not identified herself as being of Wulfenshire!

Isa frowned. Of all the lands in England...

This was not happenstance. Cyr D'Argent had chosen Wulfrith lands as his reward. Though Aelfled denied granting him favors for his aid, perhaps she lied. If not, then the Norman must have found something much to his liking in that lovely young woman.

Having taken little care to guard her expression, she said, "A very good piece of land your cousin shall hold—far worthier than that awarded Campagnon."

"As I determined at the king's request and for which it was given to my kin."

Then he had scouted Wulfenshire before approaching her walls? It seemed so—and furtively since neither her patrol nor the villagers had carried word to her. "When will your cousin return to England to take possession?"

"I cannot say. As it appears his oldest brother was lost upon Senlac, he may now be heir to his sire's Normandy lands, and with that comes great responsibility."

She longed to tell him that honor yet belonged to the man she hoped to restore to his family—and that it would leave Cyr D'Argent empty-handed when she had her lands back in their entirety.

"I am sorry for the loss of his brother," she said. "I hope all is quickly resolved the sooner to allow him to return to my country and administer his English holdings." That last was among the greatest lies she had ever told.

"If Cyr is his sire's heir," the chevalier said, "he may petition the king to pass Stern to his younger brother."

Until England was Saxon again and Guarin D'Argent returned to Normandy, that would serve her well.

The cousin sighed. "In the meantime, be assured Theriot will prove a good lord for his people upon Stern."

Never his people, she thought. *Mine. And I shall do all in my power to keep them safe no matter who they are made to answer to.*

"I pray you speak true." Isa extended the parchment.

"You may keep it, my lady."

"Generous, but I have more accurate renderings of my family's lands."

"Which must needs be altered to reflect the new boundaries of ownership."

Wasted time, she thought and set aside the map. "Now the third matter, Sir Maël. Pray, let us be done with it the sooner to see you and your men refreshed and my household at ease."

His lids narrowed, but though the reception of Le Bâtard's men would be considered inhospitable were they Saxons, it was beyond hospitable for Normans.

"As you have an heir and have given tribute," the chevalier said, "King William has allowed you to retain control of your lands—"

"Half my lands."

He inclined his head. "Beneficent since he was inclined to see you wed again to provide your son a firm hand as he moves toward manhood."

"*Was* inclined?"

"You are of the family Wulfrith, a name so respected in England it reached the ears of Duke William years past."

"As is our due, Sir Maël."

"Hence, King William would have Wulfen continue training up warriors—for him."

So grasping! It was not enough his warriors had proven their superiority upon Senlac, he wanted more—the better to slay the conquered.

Isa breathed deep. "He does my family much honor, but as he

knows, my husband died at Stamford Bridge. What he may not know is the greatest of Wulfen's trainers perished with him— Jaxon, Alfred, and others. Thus, I fear our reputation is a thing of the past, lost to the soil the same as the blood of Saxons who gave their lives in fighting back Norwegian and Norman invaders."

She knew her hatred leaked out, but the longer he stood before her in place of Le Bâtard, the looser the stopper.

"What of *your* knowledge of Wulfrith training, my lady?"

"Mine?" She spread her arms. "As you can see and men decree, I am but a woman learned in the sharp point of a needle rather than a sword. Little do I know of the means by which my sire and grandsire trained up warriors."

He set his head to the side. "Inquiries were made, and it was learned your sire taught you basic defense." Before she could concede, he continued, "However, after the last of your brothers passed, he determined to train his only remaining child in the ways of the warrior."

She laughed. "Would that were so. He tried for a time, but I had not the body nor mind. Thus, he made another son in wedding me to Roger Fortier and passed to my husband the wisdom and techniques for raising boys into men worthy of defending our country." Not entirely a lie, only that she had not the body nor mind to become a warrior. Given more time, greater patience, and much practice, she might have become a semblance of Boudica as Guarin D'Argent named her. But as if her sire had sensed his end, he had yielded to King Edward's wish to wed Hawisa to a Norman so sons would be born of their union.

"That was also told the king," Maël D'Argent said, "and that following your sire's death, often your husband consulted you to ensure Wulfen maintained its reputation."

Another laugh, another lie. "I was unaware I had so great an admirer he whispers flattery and exaggeration in William's ear. I am honored, but fie on him for raising hopes that must be dashed. Mostly it was Jaxon and Alfred who provided my husband direction." She sighed. "Pray, deliver to King William my regret I am unable to swell his army with worthy warriors. And convey my gratitude for acceptance of my tribute that permits me to administer Wulfen until my Norman son comes of age."

She raised a hand, gestured at the ladened chest. Now the chevalier and his men could take the tribute and drink and eat on their way out of the hall.

But Maël D'Argent gave the chest a dismissive look and shifted his regard to the boy. "You have undergone training, have you not, Wulfrith?"

Grinding her teeth, Isa tapped one finger.

"Oui."

"Of course he has," she bit, "but surely I need not tell you he is far from a warrior, the most intensive training coming between the ages of fourteen and twenty."

"You need not. Trained by my sire, my course was the same."

Isa shied away from thoughts of the man who had slain her child, but the question slipped in—had the murderer looked anything like his son? Might she be gazing at a much younger Hugh D'Argent?

"Well then, what is your motive for asking this of my son?" she asked.

"Only upon a strong foundation can a worthy warrior be raised. It is possible much can be learned of your sire's techniques from what was taught the boy." He looked around. "And your housecarles surely warranted Wulfen training."

"Indeed." Isa did not like the turn of conversation but was relieved the focus was off the imposter. "Many received training from my sire and their skills are exceptional, but the best either returned home to serve their own families or became the king's housecarles. Regardless, none advanced far enough to themselves obtain the position of trainer."

"Yet much could be learned from what was taught them."

"Doubtful. Now, pray, refresh yourself and your men for the ride ahead."

Though his smile lacked sincerity, the curve of his lips and show of teeth was of benefit to his disfigured face, allowing a glimpse of what once had set many a maiden's heart aflutter. "Lady Hawisa," he said, then to the boy, "Wulfrith."

She gave a three finger tap to indicate a smile was warranted.

Maël D'Argent stepped to the side, lifted the chest bound for Le Bâtard's treasury, and descended the dais. He and his men took drink and food whilst standing and, at last, the great doors closed behind them.

When the boy at Isa's side leaned heavily against her chair, she touched his arm. "You did well."

Pleading in his eyes, he said, "I was so afeared, I could understand little of what he spoke."

"In time, you will understand all."

"Then you will keep me?"

It was so desperate a question she ached that he thought he must ask it—and determined the need to speak to him about addressing her as *Maman* could wait. "Have no doubt, Wulfrith. Now go to the kitchen and tell Cook you are to have the pick of the pastries."

His eyes widened. "May I?"

"As many as you like."

He smiled so brightly she regretted anticipation of the sweets should bring him so much pleasure. Like many a commoner, his diet had been deficient, especially of meat. In the hope of strengthening and more quickly growing his body, he followed a strict regimen befitting a warrior, and that rarely included sweets her sire had called the food of women and children.

"Go," she said again, and the swing of his arms and reach of his legs brought to mind Wulf at that age. She looked away before he reached the kitchen entrance, turned her thoughts to Cyr D'Argent, and prayed ever he would remain absent.

CHAPTER TWELVE

Wulfen Castle, England
April, 1067

*T*he blood-thirsty thief was gone. But there was no relief
to be had. Le Bâtard, who departed Normandy a duke
and returned home a king, had left behind cruel men who
continued subjugating England in his name.

Also gone across the channel were high-ranking Englishmen
taken as hostages to deprive Saxons of leaders capable of
organizing rebellion in his absence.

"No reprieve," Isa murmured and looked to Vitalis who sat in
the chair opposite her in the solar.

"None," he agreed, then nodded at the missive in her lap.
"What is of such import Aelfled wrote it rather than have me
deliver it by word of mouth? *If* you can say."

He was offended the young woman was secretive though he
was Isa's most trusted man. Doubtless, Aelfled's terrible failing
made her overly cautious, and Isa did not begrudge her.

"'Tis of less import than your own tidings and those of Abbess

Mary Sarah." The first being Raymond Campagnon and Theriot D'Argent had arrived to take possession of their stolen lands and were accompanied by scores of Norman soldiers and craftsmen to begin raising castles. The second being an assault on two novices who had left the abbey for the pleasure of walking the wood on a spring day. They would not do so again.

They lived, but their virtue was lost, bodies bruised, and a final cruelty dealt in hair being shorn close to the head. The angry abbess entreated her patroness to quickly complete the work on the stone wall and see the surrounding lands more heavily patrolled—*by whatever means necessary,* she had spat at Vitalis who said it sounded as if she referred to the use of rebels.

It sounded the same to Isa, though how the woman thought it possible the Lady of Wulfen could honor such a request could only be guessed at. And her guess came back around to the discomfort felt in the abbess's presence. Unfortunately, answers to inquiries made of her were so vague as to be useless.

"Very well." Vitalis sighed. "I shall have to be content with being but the bearer of Aelfled's sealed words."

"Pardon, my mind drifted," Isa said. "Of course I will share her concerns. She has heard of the two in possession of half my lands and is shocked she knows the names of both. It comes as no surprise she recognized that of Cyr D'Argent since he aided with…"

She waved a hand as if it were possible to wipe away so great a loss, and in the breath she drew closed the door on her outward expression of grieving. "But what she knows of Campagnon surprises."

Vitalis clasped his hands between his knees. "What and how, my lady?"

"She says not only did Cyr D'Argent aid in concealing the boys in the wood, but he averted an attack on her by Campagnon and one of his companions."

Near unbelievable, Isa mused. Not only had a D'Argent removed both her and her maid from the dangers of the battlefield, but the brothers had sought to prevent their ravishment. Might that have been God speaking into the dark come upon them? Regardless, how fortunate Aelfled had not been violated before Cyr D'Argent appeared, whereas Wulfrith's daughter, who knew how to defend herself, had—

What? she demanded of elusive memories, then as done time and again determined she had been strong and worthy enough to sever the pig's life before he took what she would not give. Of course she had.

"My lady?"

She opened her eyes to find Vitalis standing over her.

"Are you ill?"

"Wh-why do you ask?"

"Your color returns, but 'twas as if all the blood went out through your feet. What troubles? Are you unwell? Or is it you are haunted by Senlac?"

She was ashamed, and yet she wanted to pull him to her and hold tight. But that he wished it as well for a different reason than the need to feel safe returned her to her senses. "How can I not be haunted by that horror when even the enemy must suffer great sweats and groaning in reliving memories of that battlefield?" She forced a smile. "Be glad you were not there."

It was the wrong thing to say, but effective, causing him to step back.

"I did not mean to offend, Vitalis. I know you would have been with Roger at Stamford if not for your injury and, surviving that battle, would have accompanied King Harold south and defended him well."

He strode to her bedside table, turned. "I wish it so, just as I wish I had been the one to deliver you from that battlefield, not..." He looked to the dagger. "...Guarin D'Argent."

Deciding it best they return to the place from which they had veered, she said, "It was from Campagnon Aelfled learned her savior is known amongst his own as *Merciless Cyr.* Strange, considering the aid he—"

"Why do you keep Guarin D'Argent's dagger at your bedside, my lady?"

She struggled against defensiveness, but he needed to be reminded of the boundaries. "Of what concern yours? You are not my husband."

"I could have been. Could yet become."

The first was true, so fond had they been of each other whilst he trained under her sire. But when Wulfrith wed her to another, she had put away the possibility of becoming more than friends. And now that possibility was packed so deep and the dirt of Senlac stamped down on it that all she wanted from her old friend was loyalty.

She stood and crossed to the bed. "If ever there was a time for us, it is long past. Pray, be my man and friend, thinking not on caresses and kisses. If you cannot, we must part ways, and I do not want that. But I shall accept whatever you decide."

After some moments, he said, "I shall remain your man and friend, but rid yourself of that dagger. Even if you filed off the initials, it would be too distinctive. Should a Norman discover it in your possession, and more likely that with D'Argents upon Wulfenshire..." He raised his eyebrows. "Much ill."

She closed a hand around the hilt, and as ever remembered when first she had done so. "It does present danger in my keeping, but not in the keeping of a housecarle turned rebel." She extended it. "Do with it as you will—wear it as a reminder of all the Norman blades you shall remove from our throats, destroy it, secrete it that it may be returned to D'Argent when he departs England. I care not."

He slid it beneath his belt alongside his own dagger and talk turned to the boy she yet struggled to call *Wulfrith* and his progress that was good but must be better, especially with his training at arms. Then in greater depth, they discussed the lessons to be imparted to Raymond Campagnon and Theriot D'Argent— regardless of who was responsible for assaulting the novices.

CHAPTER THIRTEEN

Wulfenshire Rebel Camp
England

*N*ay, Woman! Do you wish to die?"

The Saxon whose training was of no credit to her fellow rebels glared.

"Do you?" Guarin demanded in the language with which he was increasingly familiar.

"I am not afeared of death," snarled the black-haired woman of short stature and as many as thirty years. "It would be an honor to give my life to save my people from the devil's spawn." She stepped nearer than she ought and spat in his face the same as her first day here that had been his final day of torture.

Anger and pride clasping hands, Guarin was tempted to bring the hilt of his dull sword down on her head. But though it would take little force to crack her skull and reduce the rebels by one, for what? Retaliation for the spit running jaw and neck? To prove his superior skill over that of one nearly unskilled who boasted no care for remaining this side of death's door?

He drew a deep breath. "You will aid no one, not even yourself, standing as you do and holding a blade in that manner. Indeed, you will be a hindrance, endangering others."

Her upper lip curled. "What care you?"

"That my time and skill not be wasted." He looked past her to the men standing in the shade of a tree.

Leaning against the trunk and picking at his teeth, Jaxon watched this sorry contest, while beside him stood his weasel. Though the latter had no hope of proficiently wielding a sword, he possessed stealth, recently having entered the cave unheard though Guarin slept the half sleep of one surrounded by the enemy.

Only that once had Sigward dared trespass, and he would have achieved his end if not for what felt a tap on the shoulder that roused Guarin in time to knock from the man's hand a dagger destined for his throat. Worse than a blow to the nose would have been the Saxon's fate had he not snatched up his blade and scrambled over the rock.

Might Jaxon have ordered him to take Guarin's life? It would not surprise, there being two things the camp commander hated. One was Normans, the other women who aspired to learn the deadly power of sharp edges and how to make fists, elbows, knees, and feet into crippling weapons.

Here another reason Guarin would not take the life this woman seemed eager to sacrifice. Too much it would please Jaxon, ridding him of one of a handful of females and providing believable cause to slay the Norman. Since Jaxon had sent away all but Sigward before ordering this woman to test her skills against the chained enemy, only he and his weasel would bear witness and bemoan the mistake of granting her permission to feed the need for vengeance.

Guarin returned his regard to his opponent, swept up his manacled hand, and caught the wrist of hers gripping a sword somewhat keener than his own.

She cursed and strained opposite.

"Attend to what I tell," he said low, "and master what Jaxon does not believe you capable of learning."

She stilled, narrowed her eyes.

He glanced past her again. "Though I have hold of you, the mighty trainer of *men* but watches, cares not if I put through one far from prepared to face me."

She blinked.

"Aye, you belong here only insofar as you achieve what the men he sets at me cannot—cause to slay me."

A flicker of uncertainty.

"As I will not take the life you wish to sacrifice, here may be your only chance to learn from this Norman. Do you want it?"

Her eyes circled his face, then she nodded.

He dropped his dull sword alongside worn boots. "Then ease your hold on the hilt."

She tightened it. "Why?"

"So I may reposition it. As you grip too near the pommel, you lack the balance required to swing well and land true."

At her continued hesitation, he said, "Already you are defenseless and neither Jaxon nor Sigward come to your aid. What have you to lose?"

She did as told, and Guarin repositioned her fingers and stepped back.

Another glance at Jaxon, a slight smile for the woman. "He is not pleased either of us lives, will be even less so when I instruct you as he does not."

"He says women are best for baiting traps."

"He is right." Before the ire returning to her eyes birthed venomous words, he added, "But only as you stand now, not as you can stand."

She considered him. "Make good your boast, Norman."

"First, payment."

Her teeth began to bare.

"A name. Even if it is not your own, I would have one."

"For what purpose?"

"I do not mean to insult your sex, but it is unsettling to impart skills most often reserved men to one I can but name *Woman.*" Only partially true. More true was the hope of bridging her hatred so he might learn things he could not decipher nor discover no matter how many hours he mulled or strained to catch words spoken beyond his cave.

Dotter was the greatest of those things eluding him. Though he had no glimpse of her these two months, he was certain she visited. The sound of horses was no rare thing since Jaxon's rebels patrolled the area in four shifts, but once a sennight at earliest morn, Guarin heard hooves. In the afternoon, shortly after his return to the cave, he heard their departure. She had no wish to see him, but he wished to see her, and greater that desire these past days since the dagger worn by Vitalis came to notice.

"You do insult my sex, Norman," the woman said, "but Rosa is how I am called."

He inclined his head. Then keeping her in sight lest she try her blade against his exposed neck, he bent with a rattle of the chain fixing him to the post and retrieved his sword. "Let us begin, Rosa."

"WHAT IS THIS?" Isa demanded. "For what does D'Argent face one unequal to the challenge of a warrior?"

"I would know as well." Vitalis glanced at where she halted alongside him in the shade of an oak, next Jaxon and Sigward who had retreated toward the training yards upon realizing they were no longer alone in this portion of the wood. "As Jaxon only sets against the Norman those he believes skilled and angry enough to have a chance of taking his life, and this woman is among the least proficient, 'tis possible he wishes to rid himself of two undesirables."

Isa ground her teeth. Of course Jaxon wanted D'Argent dead, even at the cost of one of their own, and all the more acceptable were she one who dared believe she could be more than bait.

Even in an England ruled by Normans, the most esteemed of Wulfrith's trainers had not changed his view on the place of the fairer sex, one of the few things on which Roger and he mostly agreed. Thus, Jaxon seethed over women among the rebels and that Isa had resumed her own training—five days a week with her housecarles and the boy, one day a week at camp.

"You also think that his motive?" Vitalis asked.

"Aye, that grave injury or death to Rosa would justify slaying our captive. But he does not know D'Argent as…"

"As you know him, my lady?"

Her cheeks warmed. "He lives only because I am acquainted with his character beyond his ungodly place of birth and the one to whom he owes fealty." She nodded curtly and returned her attention to the man and woman at the posts.

For a quarter hour, Vitalis and she observed, during which D'Argent often interrupted swordplay to catch Rosa's arm and set her back, speak words of instruction, and demonstrate with his own blade. More than once, something nearly a smile appeared on her face. Rosa hated him but enjoyed herself, and not by way of vengeance as Jaxon intended. Likely, she felt empowered, even in awe of the Norman.

What a force you are, Guarin D'Argent, Isa mused. *If only you were born this side of the channel. Much my sire would—*

Thrusting aside such thoughts, she set herself to assessing his demonstration of the proper stance for a backhanded upward cut. A moment later, he stopped his dull blade near Rosa's throat which otherwise would have collapsed her airway.

Isa was not surprised he refused the bait Jaxon dangled. Had she thought he would harm Rosa, she would have put an end to this contest, but on Senlac he proved he was no animal. And even had he become one following months of torture, he had to know Rosa's death would warrant his own.

That woman drew a sharp breath as if to fill lungs emptied by surprise, then blurted, "Almighty, 'tis true what they say! Though you be bound, it is the sharply clawed paw of a wolf manacled and chained. A wolf out of Normandy."

Now it was Isa's lungs absent breath. Catching Vitalis's muttered curse, she rasped, "The rebels call him *wolf?*"

A muscle spasmed in his jaw. "At first in jest, but it begins to stick."

"He is not a wolf!"

"Neither does it sit well with me, but the more who challenge him, the more the truth of it. He is..." He did not want to continue, but as if to defend the rebels for equating the enemy with her family, he said, "He calls to mind your sire, my lady. Strong, fearless, cunning, and yet... Though he engages with our men to preserve his life, strengthen his own skills, and vent his anger by taunting those who taunt him, it is different with the women."

"How?"

"He does not exploit their weaknesses, instead corrects their errors, even to his own detriment."

She followed his nod and set eyes on the two a moment ahead of Rosa setting eyes on them.

The woman's smile fell, and she jumped back from D'Argent. "Lady Hawis—" She clapped a hand over her mouth.

And then Isa was staring into eyes too distant to see their green.

D'Argent did not smile, but she glimpsed a tug at his mouth and knew Vitalis and she did not only now come to notice. He had known they watched from beyond shafts of spring sunlight amid the shadows of trees beginning to pass from bud to leaf. A wolf, indeed.

In tunic, chausses, and boots begrimed by her training out of sight of D'Argent, Isa strode forward with what she hoped an air of disregard though she teemed with alarm and awareness of a gaze not felt in over two months.

Shoving her sword beneath her belt, Rosa hastened forward. "I am unworthy." She halted short of colliding with her lady. "Pray, forgive me."

It took effort, but it was a gentle hand Isa set on her shoulder rather than one given to shaking so hard the woman's teeth rattled. "Not unworthy, only loose of tongue. Go to the training yards and see it tightened."

Rosa ran, and Isa looked to D'Argent. As reported, he had healed well and appeared nearly as powerful as when first they met. But though his hair had grown longer and seemed more silvered, the beard he had deigned not to shave was closely trimmed—a dark, glittering shadow down the sides of face, across chin, above lips.

"Dotter," he said, then in Norman-French, "Or have my efforts to make your men and women of the soil into men and women of the sword earned me the right to more intimate address?"

"They have not."

"Then I shall reward myself, though I must decide which I like better—Hawise Wulfrithdotter or Hawisa Wulfrithdotter."

"Knave," Vitalis rumbled while she put much effort into an expression of indifference.

How long had D'Argent known he was held upon Wulfenshire? When had he guessed her lineage? Only now the woman he had charmed spoke nearly all her lady's name?

He tossed his sword distant as was required before his return to the cave. "Have you a preference, my lady?"

She considered the excess chain between post and manacled wrist and, deciding a distance of six feet provided ample safety, said across her shoulder, "I go alone, Vitalis."

"My lady—"

"Alone!"

Though legs fatigued by the day's training begged a short stride, she stretched them long and halted just this side of a small stone she visually marked as the right distance between her throat and D'Argent's hand.

Not only could she now see the green of his eyes but amusement there. "My preference is Dotter. But should a hundred years from now peace rise between your people and mine, I would not object to being addressed as Lady Hawisa."

His nostrils dilated as if he took in her scent, and once more she saw what his opponents saw—the wolf. "I like it better than Dotter, which is...impersonal."

"Considering our relationship, Dotter is more appropriate."

"I disagree, albeit on the same grounds—in consideration of our relationship. I am, after all, at your mercy though great the debt due me."

She crossed her arms over her chest. "It is questionable whether you saved my life in forcing me off the battlefield. It is not questionable I saved yours in providing a reason to keep my people from spilling every drop of your blood."

He laughed, and that rumble felt in her own chest was more disturbing for how many teeth he presented. He sighed. "Pardon, Lady Hawisa, but you will have to think me an ungrateful wretch."

"Then I am unworthy of being charmed the same as Rosa?"

His eyebrows rose, and she regretted not considering her words as often she advised Aelfled to do. "You wish *me* to charm *you*, Lady?"

She snorted. "I would but welcome the effort."

He moved his eyes over her. "Though methinks you far more resistant to smiles and kind words, you are worthy. You look in excellent health and of fewer years than two months past. Had I to guess, I would say your appetite returned, sleep more restful, and much time spent strengthening your body and skill at arms."

"I *am* of Wulfrith. Still, I doubt you approve of such pursuits, like Le Bâtard would see me fit with the yoke of another Norman husband."

The narrowing of his lids made her realize she had revealed already a marriage was made with one of his people and another could be made due to the end of that marriage.

He smiled. "It was not required I instruct Rosa in the basics of defense and offense which Jaxon neglects. Though on many an occasion I could have slain her, instead I added days, perhaps weeks to the life of my enemy who thinks to be a sacrifice for her people."

"In order to gain information," Isa retorted.

"Of some benefit, but more to give her a chance she has not as the bait of men. Unlike Jaxon, I am not threatened by women's instruction in defense of self and loved ones. Indeed, to my mother's distress, sire's discomfort, and uncle's disgust, I taught my sister to wield a dagger and loose arrows capable of finding their marks in living flesh."

Clearly, he was not done speaking, but his lips seamed.

Hating she had revealed her distress, Isa realigned her mouth and blinked eyes that had widened at mention of the one who slew Wulf.

"Speak, Lady," he said.

"Of what?"

"I believe mention of my uncle sucked the air from between us. What know you of him?"

She nearly turned away, but what harm in revealing that one's fate? Too, though she argued D'Argent was more indebted to her than she to him, she did not believe it. "I have made inquiries about your family who fought upon Senlac and learned your uncle..." She frowned. "Hugh D'Argent, is it not?"

He waited.

"He did not survive Senlac."

Though the sorrow rising on his face once more tempted her

to depart, she kept her feet planted. "More fortunate were your brothers, Cyr and Theriot, and your cousin. They live."

He lowered his lids and breathed so deep her palms longed to measure the breadth of his shoulders.

Shameful, Wulfrithdotter! she silently berated. *If you are not ill of mind, you are weak of character.*

His eyes opened. "Have you word of my brother, Dougray?"

Another D'Argent? Though tempted to demand how many they numbered, Isa said, "This is the first I have heard that name."

His jaw tightened. "Then perhaps he also fell and did not rise."

"I..." Stopping herself from offering to make further inquiries, she said, "I am due elsewhere. Before you return to the cave, is there anything you require?"

He shrugged. "I am as well provided for as a prisoner might hope, and more so now the weather has warmed such that if it did not offend, I would return your mantle."

"Offend?"

"Though long it smelled of you, now it smells of me—not nearly as pleasant."

Heat flushed her. Might he be as much a victim of wanting to touch what one should not? Or though he professed to believe her resistant to his charm, did he merely test that belief?

"Too, it makes an adequate pillow," he added.

"I am pleased you made good use of it."

"Still a poor trade, albeit held in higher regard than my gift to you." He looked to where Vitalis stood distant. "I would have to be blind not to recognize my dagger on your lover's belt. I wonder, is it for fear of your attraction to me he wears it? The hope of discouraging my attentions?"

She stepped forward. "Never could I be attracted to a Norman. And Vitalis is not my lover. Your dagger on his person symbolizes all the blades our rebels shall remove from Saxon throats and set upon Normans."

His eyebrows rose. "Had it come into his possession by way of the warrior, it might inspire. Non, it is but meant to taunt and discourage me." He glanced between them. "Lady, do you realize how near you are to one you have made your enemy?"

Only in this moment. If not that she remained just out of reach, she would have leapt backward.

"My lady," Vitalis called. "I know not why he gives warning, but you are too near."

Holding her gaze to D'Argent, she set a hand on her dagger's hilt. "Would you seek to harm me if I took another step?" Now *she* taunted to cover her unease.

"Harm you, Lady Hawisa?" he drawled. "I believe that answered long ago in a dark, dark wood."

So it was, but that was before manacles and chains, beatings, and being forced to train the enemy. "That does not mean you would not use threat to my person to gain your release."

"Under the right circumstances, oui. But if you do not yet know how useless such an attempt under *these* circumstances, soon you shall."

"You speak in riddles."

"I speak of Jaxon, and very little riddle is he. Though Vitalis would yield to my demands to preserve your life, not the balding one whose front is hardly different from his back."

He referred to Jaxon's hair bound at the nape, which was as long as her own, and a beard nearly the same length bound beneath his chin.

"If ever you had that man's loyalty, it is lost, Lady. When he determines the time is right, he will turn on you."

What he said was not entirely unbelievable.

"Did I take hold of you and threaten your life in the absence of my demands being met," he continued, "Jaxon would sacrifice you. For the good of the rebels, he would say, to protect the camp's location. Thus, a dead Saxon at my feet, I would be set upon and slain, and no longer would he answer to a woman." He shifted his stance, and she tensed lest he thought his chain long enough to reach her. "Be assured, as long as I am bound, the anger pushed deep shall remain below."

His choice of words chilled for their honesty, yet soothed for the compliment of not thinking her so gullible she was unaware that deadly emotion crouched in him.

"Even were you standing on my feet, Lady, you would be safe. Unlike Rosa, I wish to live—and well, all limbs and senses intact."

She felt a pang for the Saxon woman who had lost all— husband, infant son, friends, and home. To her village in Nottinghamshire, drunken Normans had come pillaging. Upon meeting resistance, they set all afire. The only survivor, Rosa now regarded death as but a thing delayed until she gathered about her a great number of the enemy to accompany her from this world.

"She lost even more than I," Isa said. "Still I have my home— rather, what remains of it. Le Bâtard has awarded nearly half to Normans." As soon as she said it, his brothers came to mind, both of whom she had yet to meet—the one returned to Normandy and the younger who served him by raising a castle upon Stern.

"I am sorry, my lady." Despite the anger Guarin D'Argent professed to have pushed down, he sounded sincere.

Feeling wearier than when she had departed the training field a half hour past, she said, "We shall send all of you back to Normandy or die trying."

"My lady!"

She startled, looked across her shoulder to Vitalis.

"Come away," he said. "We have matters to discuss ere your departure."

An excuse to end her audience with the Norman, but not without merit. "Collect my escort and horses," she ordered.

He glowered. "Surely you would not have me leave you alone with him?"

"I am safe. And armed."

He shifted his regard to D'Argent. "Does any harm befall her, I will be the one to kill you. And slowly." He strode opposite.

Guessing he would return within ten minutes, Isa faced her captive again.

"How long has he been in love with you?" D'Argent asked.

Denial rose to her lips, but it would make her sound foolish. "Far longer than I deserve," she said, then asked, "What makes you certain Jaxon will betray me?"

"I see and sense the same as you, but I am not loath to accept it. I know his kind. He does not like women beyond those eager to do his will. My uncle is—was—the same. If not that my sire esteems women, his brother who trained me into a warrior might have bent my character, making me of a like mind."

Did he think piquing her curiosity would draw her nearer? Likely, but his hope was rewarded only insofar as he claimed all her regard. "Why did your father not train you at arms?" she asked. "Was he not a warrior?"

"Very much a warrior, and a great one, but ere I was of an age to set mind and body to wielding blades, all changed."

"What happened?"

A corner of his mouth rose. "Why so curious, my lady? Do you truly wish to know me better? Here proof you *are* attracted to me as I am to you?"

Her eyes felt as if they might fly from their sockets. "I am not... You are not..."

"Indeed we are, and quite the problem that, Hawisa Wulfrithdotter. Though both of us unwed"—he raised his manacled wrist as if she needed reminding they were enemies —"what are we to do?"

He was not wed. Until that moment, she had not considered whether a wife awaited his return, and that one did not—

Appalled by such thoughts, she snapped, "You are arrogant! Mayhap not at all different from your uncle."

"Is it arrogant to speak in truth? Ever I have been told it is honesty and, as such, worthy of good regard."

Isa swung away and did not realize it was as he meant her to do until her head snapped back and body followed past the stone between safety and Guarin D'Argent. He had snatched hold of the end of her braid when it arced. As she stumbled back against him and her head struck his chest, he wound his manacled arm around her arms and waist.

Though her hand was on her dagger and nearly had it clear of its scabbard, Hawisa Wulfrithdotter was pinned.

CHAPTER FOURTEEN

*Y*ou lied!" Isa gasped though it was a scream upon which she ought to expel her breath.

Feeling his head lower down the side of hers, she was prepared for breath in her ear—or so she thought. "Though this wolf has sharp teeth, Lady Hawisa, he did not lie."

No surprise he liked being named a wolf by his enemies. No surprise he liked it offended the daughter of Wulfrith.

"As told," he continued, "under these circumstances you are safe with me."

"Then loose me!"

"And deny you a further kindness? Non, I shall impart your second lesson of the day."

She breathed in, more deeply smelled his perspiration that brought to mind taut muscles straining beneath glistening flesh. "Second lesson? What was the first?" Not that she did not know it had all to do with not drawing near the enemy without a blade going before her.

"The same lesson Jaxon has yet to learn though many a Saxon at Senlac did." His breath traveled down the side of her neck into the hollow of her throat, what remained of it swirling beneath the collar of her man's tunic.

"The first lesson?" she choked.

"The folly of long hair. Flying out behind one, it shortens the distance between your pursuer and you. But whereas unbound it might snap or slip through fingers, when it is braided or gathered into a great mass, it is as hard to tear from the head as an arm from the body. If not shorn, during battle or other times of danger it must be fastened close to the scalp."

Feeling the damp of the front of his tunic through the damp of the back of hers, she said, "The second lesson?"

"Another your sire did not well enough teach you, Hawisa."

It was disturbing enough he spoke her name with title, but without it... "Oui?"

"Never turn your back on your enemy until you are well out of reach. If then."

She swallowed. "I shall reflect well on your lessons to ensure I do not repeat my mistakes. Now are you done instructing me?"

He lowered his head further, and she startled when he lightly set his chin on her shoulder and his whiskers pricked her skin through her tunic—a reminder of the rough jaw that had scraped her cheek when her assailant on Senlac said he would use her up, leaving but a husk for his men. But she had stopped him, had she not? Aye, he was a husk, not she.

"Nearly done," this Norman said.

This one, not that one, she told herself lest fear quake her body. "Vitalis will return soon, D'Argent, and he will—"

"Look, Hawisa. Look down."

She lowered her chin, saw it was not the ground beneath her boots but his boots. And remembered he had said even were she standing on his feet she would be safe.

"Am I truly safe?" she said. "Trapped in the arms of the enemy, I am to believe you? Trust you?"

"I know my mind, Lady, that I speak true in telling under these circumstances you are safe with me. But were you my Norman sister and I her Saxon captive, I would advise against belief and trust, warn that until a man proves himself and his word, you exercise much doubt and caution."

"Is that your final lesson?"

The breath of his sigh traveled farther than the last. "For now." He raised his head.

She looked over her shoulder, marveled how attractive his face and wondered if he thought the same of her when his eyes moved to her mouth. "For now?" she whispered.

"You will come again. We will speak again. And perhaps like Rosa, I will instruct you in how a Norman wields a sword. Now, my lady, I shall loosen my arm. When your dagger returns to the bottom of its scabbard, I shall release you and you will step off my boots. Then you and your man may resume plotting against my people."

She looked forward again. "Loosen your hold."

He did, and though she had thought she believed him, it surprised when he released her after she seated her blade.

Feet returned to the ground, she pivoted.

He glanced at the hilt of her dagger. "I am pleased Hawisa Wulfrithdotter trusts me, though I would be disappointed were you Nicola."

His dagger and bow-wielding sister.

He could recapture her, but she did not retreat. "You are not much of an enemy," she said, then asked the question she hoped would not raise his suspicions, the answer to which might better prepare her for what lay ahead. "Are your brothers and cousin the same?"

Though she had met Maël D'Argent when he came for the tribute and much about him disturbed, further insight into the son of the man who killed Wulf was warranted. With kin upon Wulfenshire, eventually the cousin would return.

"I think very well of my brothers and cousin, but we are not the same—of different temperaments and passions. After Senlac, who can say how changed they are? I am, and the longer held captive, the more I shall be."

She averted her gaze. "Could I release you, I would. But Norman that you are, it is the duke who has your loyalty. Even did you give your word you would not lead the enemy to us, I will not risk lives beyond my own." She peered at him from beneath her lashes so he would not see how moist her eyes. "Would that the wolf amongst us were Saxon."

Did his green eyes soften? "Then what, Hawisa?"

What made her speak those words?

Before she could back her way out of it, he said, "You wish me born Saxon so, like Vitalis, I might fall in love with you—and far longer than you deserve? That I be yours to command?"

Had she made it sound a boast? It was not. It was... What? Guilt?

Forcing a laugh, she drew her braid over her shoulder. "I thank you for the lessons." She turned her back on him.

The timing was good, Vitalis reappearing as she distanced herself from the one who had done more than lay hands on her.

Her man commanded the three following him to return her captive to the cave, told Isa her escort were saddling the horses, and drew her away.

"That was a fool thing to do," he rebuked.

Blessedly, he knew not how foolish. "As told, I am armed. As you see, I am unharmed. And of a different mind with regard to the Norman."

His lids narrowed.

"He knows who I am. He knows where he is held."

"All the more dangerous, my lady, and still you will not grant him a merciful death?"

"Nay."

Vitalis inclined his head. "Of what different mind are you?"

"D'Argent is no animal. Dangerous, aye, but he does not sink his teeth into his prey's neck."

"You have not seen him fight the worthiest of our rebels."

"I have heard and 'tis surely a sight, yet he has slain none, though many an opportunity he must have to yield to vengeance."

"He does, and even to the worthiest he imparts lessons, though of course it is to taunt them—more, Jaxon and me."

"To prove his superiority," she acknowledged his Norman pride. "But I believe it goes beyond that. He *is* a wolf—strong, fearless, and cunning, as you say. And yet he is something more. My sire demanded those he trained into warriors learn to control their emotions. *Set the good example,* he commanded, *and men will follow you.*"

"I remember, my lady."

"Just as you remember though he himself had great self-control, he could be roused to a temper, railing against all—including God—whilst left and right he dropped those who offended even were they friends."

Vitalis smiled wryly. "Blessedly, only on rare occasion."

"True, but in circumstances similar to those of our captive, I believe he would have lost control long ere now and might even be dead for it. Guarin D'Argent is understandably angry, and yet he remains in control. Though no man or woman is perfect, all capable of being pushed or pushing themselves over a line they know not to cross, thus far his feet remain firm."

Even when one who numbers amongst his enemy stands on them, she silently added.

"Despite all, his cunning is intact," she continued. "Though forced to exhibit his skill against Saxons, he does not merely defend himself. He instructs the enemy, surely reasoning since eventually they will learn how best to fight him, it is to his advantage to sooner create worthy opponents against whom he can strengthen himself for the day he finds an opportunity to escape. Hence, I am of a different mind. To ensure he does not continue to move in a direction that betters his chance of escape, his circumstances must change."

"What are you thinking?"

"I believe Jaxon did hope to rid himself of an undesirable Saxon and Norman warrior. Thus, I shall make something better of Guarin D'Argent's instruction. Henceforth, only new recruits and the most unseasoned will train with him, of great benefit to women and others who struggle to become warriors—even our captive though he will be offended. Their skills will increase and less chance Jaxon will have to end D'Argent's life since you will choose his opponents."

"You know Jaxon will not approve."

"I do, just as I believe it is possible he will move against me." She tapped her teeth against her bottom lip. "I want a guard placed at D'Argent's cave at all times. Choose the worthiest of those you trust."

"As you command, my lady, but I must ask why you expend so much effort to keep the Norman alive."

Feeling herself move toward defensiveness, she shrugged. "You were in Andredeswald. You saw what he did. I hate it, but I am indebted."

"Only indebted?" Behind the question was the dagger she had kept on her bedside table and Guarin's claim she was attracted to its owner.

I am not, she told herself though still she felt his front against her back, his arm around her waist, his breath venturing down her neck. "Indebted," she repeated. "That is all."

He nodded. "How goes the underground passage?"

Grateful to leave Guarin D'Argent behind, she said, "Good progress since the ground is mostly soil, but that makes it dangerous, requiring the support of numerous timbers to prevent collapse."

"Still you anticipate a year before it reaches the wood?"

"Much depends on how much rock must be moved and

maintaining the passage's integrity to prevent the loss of life. Now let us discuss the trap to be laid for the Normans who offended God."

For a half hour, they spoke of the dozen rebels chosen by Jaxon and Vitalis and the two females to be used as bait—in this, a necessity, but they were the best of the women and now trained to defend their persons.

Hopefully, the rats who came sniffing for sweet morsels would not long keep rebel morsels waiting.

CHAPTER FIFTEEN

Lillefarne Abbey
Wulfenshire, England

*S*he believed herself prepared, thought she had an appetite for violence considering what those men would have done had this not been a trap, and yet...

"I warned this no place for a lady," Vitalis growled.

Lowering her gaze from the faces of the Normans slain within hearing of the bells of Lillefarne on the third successive day of lying in wait, Isa considered the purses on their belts. Surely, what was affixed to them had moved the rebels to such frenzy they would not heed her command to cease so the men could be judged in the rebel camp. Those present had themselves handed down the sentence. Doubtless, had the third Norman also sported the bundled hair of a ravished novice, neither could his death have been prevented.

Guessing Vitalis feared this sight returned her to Senlac, Isa said, "I am more than a lady. I am Wulfrithdotter. Though I must hide from our enemies the name and face behind these rebels, I will not sit by whilst others fight. I will be present wherever and whenever I can." She swung out of the saddle and was grateful her legs held despite ashamedly soft joints.

All eyes on her, excepting those of the face down Norman whom Zedekiah straddled, she strode forward and halted alongside the one denied the opportunity to affix hair to his purse. Unlike his companions, he would not die, but she had no fear of him looking on her with his face turned opposite and the big rebel pressing it into the dirt.

"Give the word, Dotter," Zedekiah spoke the name by which the rebel leader upon Wulfenshire was increasingly known. "'Tis time he join his friends and have his back scrubbed with the fires of hell."

She looked to the hard-eyed women who no longer appeared the godly prey of the godless. After their novice's gowns were torn, faces scratched, and the eye of one reddened, they had aided in dispatching their attackers.

"Filthy Saxons," the Norman spat.

Zedekiah backhanded his head, causing him to yelp.

Isa lowered to her haunches and considered his short hair that was several months beyond its last grooming—the same as his facial hair though the latter was mostly fuzz.

Guessing him a score aged, she bent near. In the rough, creaky voice of an old woman, she said in his language, "Filthy are Normans who take what does not belong to them, who claim it is the Church of England that must be reformed, who ravage women who have given hearts and lives to the Lord. But fear not death, boy."

Ignoring the murmur of dissent going around the wood, she continued, "Providing you give something in return, you shall live."

"What I will give is the point of my dagger, hag!"

Zedekiah struck him again. "Give the word, Dotter!" he beseeched as the man shrugged a shoulder up to his ear as if that little hunch would shield him.

"Boy, is your lord Raymond Campagnon?" she asked. "Or is it Theriot D'Argent? Another?"

He did not answer.

No matter. He had only to be followed to learn to whom he delivered her message. "When my men finish with you, tell your lord this—Two Norman sinners dead this day. Unless he leashes his dogs, that number shall rise."

"He will kill you!"

"Ah, but I am many. I am wrath. I am vengeance. And I have little to lose, whereas you…" She sank fingers into his hair, scraped nails over his scalp. "You are long without a shave, Norman. What would Le Bâtard say to see you thus?" She stood. "Fear not, we shall remedy your shame."

Pleased by the degradation to come—appropriate considering what hung from the purses of his companions—she said in Anglo-Saxon, "Apply a dagger to his hair, close to the scalp."

"That is all?" Zedekiah exclaimed.

As the Norman writhed and cursed—proof he was not entirely unversed in her language—Isa considered him. Though beaten and marked with blood drawn by blades he had survived, more could be suffered by one who had intended ravishment.

Noting how fine his garments, especially compared to those of the women rebels who had this day traded threadbare tunic and chausses for simple gowns, she said to Zedekiah. "Do you not think it unseemly a Norman dresses so well?"

Understanding shone from his eyes, but not satisfaction.

She motioned the women forward. "Here a reward well earned. When you have knocked him senseless, remove his clothes and divide them between you. Ere you leave him to the wood, deliver another blow to ensure he does not soon recover."

"Aye, Dotter," they grumbled, as displeased as the others.

As Isa returned to the destrier she had impulsively named, she heard the blows dealt, and her thoughts went to Guarin who no longer provided his enemy the satisfaction those behind surely felt at doing unto a Norman a small measure of what had been done them.

She mounted Anglicus, looked to Vitalis. "See the Norman followed to verify to whom he answers and know at whose walls to leave his dead."

Both were fairly certain it was Raymond Campagnon who would have turned ravisher had Cyr D'Argent not interceded with Aelfled. Unlike Theriot D'Argent, the slave-owning Norman was slack in raising his castle and allowed his men—mostly mercenaries—to wreak havoc across Wulfenshire.

"Aye, my lady."

"And commend the women. They made this easy for all."

"It is the men with whom you are not entirely pleased."

"With those *you* chose, I am mostly pleased. They did as instructed until Jaxon's men riled them beyond good sense." She reflected nearly all the latter had been recruited from other shires, those from Wulfenshire more inclined to draw near her man, Vitalis.

"Regardless, it is hard to regret the end result, my lady. The dead Normans would have slain ours did we not slay them."

"The manner in which it was done is what disturbs. I but bore witness to battle's end at Senlac, but I cannot believe the thirst for blood was as great as this whilst the fighting raged."

His brow grooved. "You fool yourself. I was not there to lend my sword arm to our king, but I have experience enough to assure you what you saw here keeps men alive when death takes measure of one's height and breadth to determine the place of eternal rest. It is bloodlust. Recall the state of the thousands of bodies amongst whom you walked on Senlac, and no further proof need you the thirst for blood was far greater there."

His rebuke offended, but it was his due. Just as she had heard her father warn if the savagery come over men fighting for their lives was not embraced, sooner they would be dead, she could not forget those whose blood had weighted the hem of her skirt.

Vitalis set a hand on her shoulder. "If you are to go forward in leading the rebels, you must accept this. And do not doubt your Norman accepted it upon Senlac though mercy he now shows those far beneath his abilities."

My Norman. She turned that over and accepted Guarin was that, though not as Vitalis made it sound. She raised her chin. "Put to the sword Normans who seek to put Saxons to the sword, but our rebels will not kill indiscriminately."

"Jaxon—"

"I care not what he wants, nor Harold's mother." That last was added in consideration of what Vitalis had informed her this morn. Jaxon had brought into the camp an aged housecarle. In the absence of introduction, by his garments and bearing it was surmised he was from the stable of a Saxon noble most high.

The man was shown the settlement, including D'Argent's cave, and the rebel guarding it overheard the housecarle say he expected great sport to be made of the prisoner before he was put down. Jaxon had held his tongue, but no word need pass it to know he was in accord.

Isa cleared her throat. "There is a difference between killing and murdering." As well she knew from what she had done on that hill, though exactly what her assailant had done continued to elude. "Both infect the soul, but methinks the latter more a plague with little hope for a cure. Once we rid our lands of Normans and the rebels return to their families, I will not have so deadly an infection spread amongst our own."

She thought he would argue, but she saw consideration in his eyes, then he said, "In defense only, for the preservation of life when death looks between us and them."

"That is as I command, and be assured I expect Jaxon to oppose me." She looked around, saw the senseless Norman had only his braies about him. To the left, a woman stepped into his chausses beneath a hitched skirt. To the right, the other drew the tunic over her gown, then lowered to her knees. A dagger in one hand, she caught up the Norman's hair.

And so the resistance moved a step nearer to ousting Normans from Wulfenshire. And all of England.

~

GAZE FIXED on riders who numbered eight, heart knocking at her breastbone, Isa said, "Who do you think 'tis?"

"Likely of Theriot D'Argent since we are on his lands." This from Ordric, one of four housecarles who had met her at the appointed place to escort her home whilst the rebels returned to camp.

He was wrong on two fronts. While England's crown sat William's head, the younger brother but administered lands awarded to the absent Cyr D'Argent. And they were *her* lands, which she would hold again in their entirety.

She looked sidelong at Ordric, knew from his grimace he sensed her anger over misspoken words. "We should have taken the long way back to Wulfen," she said, wishing she had not insisted on saving a quarter hour's ride. When the party ahead learned two Normans were slain in the wood near Lillefarne Abbey, she could become a suspect for having been in the vicinity.

Blessedly, she had donned a gown over tunic and chausses before departing the wood. Only her boots were amiss, visible since she sat astride rather than sidesaddle. But she *was* of Wulfrith.

"Aye, Theriot D'Argent and his men," Ordric confirmed, and she saw why he was certain. The black hair of the one at the fore was cast with silver. Once he boasted a handful more years, would he be as silvered as his eldest brother?

As the Normans closed the distance and the man's face became clearer, her heart beat harder. She had noted Maël D'Argent's resemblance to Guarin, but this was greater—so much she guessed here was her captive when he had five fewer years about him.

As Theriot D'Argent reined in twenty feet distant, his men fanned out left and right. "Your business upon Stern?" he said in her language.

She raised her eyebrows. "Habit only. I am—"

"Lady Hawisa. This I know. And I am—"

"Theriot D'Argent," she spared no sarcasm. "This I know."

He shifted in the saddle. "I wondered when we would meet."

"As did I. Were you not so occupied with raising a castle against people who were once mine, I am certain you would have behaved as befitting a nobleman by presenting yourself at Wulfen Castle weeks past."

His eyebrows rose. "I have been occupied, though not so much I would not have come had the Lady of Wulfen behaved as befitting a noblewoman and issued an invitation."

She gasped loudly, looked to Ordric. "What goes here? Might this be a first—a Norman who does not issue his own invitation?"

A corner of her man's mouth convulsed. "Had I not taken wax from ears this morn, I would not believe it, my lady. Might he be an imposter?"

Were Theriot D'Argent offended, he masked it with a chuckle. "My cousin did not prepare me for such good humor from those whose lands were awarded a D'Argent. It is good there are to be no bad feelings between our families."

"None at all!" Isa put her head to the side. "However, I must make complaint against your cousin for giving the impression the one to administer Stern is many years a man, not a... Forgive me, but you could not have been much more than a pup at Senlac. Did you squire for your brother?" Bold exaggeration. He was nowhere near the fuzzed boy-man recently shorn and soon to return to his lord attired in braies.

Seeing something flash in his eyes, she waved a hand. "Ah, but I see you have earned your spurs since. A fine beginning."

He gave what sounded a genuine laugh and sighed. "Oh Lady, I am... What is the word?" He searched the heavens, reverted to Norman-French. "Enchanted, oui. If it is true no invitation is required, I shall enjoy sitting beside you at hearth and speaking soft, sweet words sure to win your hand."

Lest he saw movement about her own eyes, she decided to end this—after one last insult. "You reach too high, Chevalier. Waste not soft, sweet words on one who will never take a Norman to husband."

"Never? Once you did."

"As King Edward ordered my sire's only remaining heir. But since now my son is Wulfen's heir, I am of no use to a landless Norman. You must look elsewhere—and for one of fewer years, I advise." Not that she was much older, but small though that barb, she liked it.

"I shall consider it, my lady. Now tell, what *habit* finds you upon D'Argent lands?"

"Surely you can guess." When he did not, she said, "Though Stern's people and those of Balduc are no longer mine, I am rightly concerned and seek assurance their needs are met."

"Admirable, but unnecessary. The Saxons upon Stern adjust well to their Norman lord and are in need of naught."

No lie as told by the reports come to her from rebels who occasionally slipped home to their families. Thus far, those of Stern had no great grievances against this Norman. Unfortunately, the same could not be said of those upon Balduc.

"What of the rebels?" she asked, deciding here a means of sowing further doubt should he suspect her a party to the ill heaped on Norman ravishers.

"They are about, my lady, but thus far their cowardly deeds are so minor as to be forgettable, even laughable."

He exaggerated, but once he learned of the two slain he would find naught over which to express mirth.

"Too," he continued, "they are more inclined to trouble Baron Campagnon."

"As they also trouble me."

He frowned. "I would think you suffer least from those who prowl Wulfenshire."

"Because I am Saxon?" She harrumphed. "Such consideration I might be given did I defy King William." How it pricked to name him that! "But having bent the knee, I am believed a traitor to my own and worthy of vengeance."

"What vengeance that?" His words dragged disbelief behind them.

"Theft of stores and livestock, an attempt to burn a village, and contamination of a well."

"I have heard Campagnon's lands suffer the same."

She sighed. "The rebels are my people, and I understand their anger, but they must be stopped."

"Indeed, especially if the mother of Harold directs them."

Certes, it was not Gytha, though she continued to make demands Isa continued to ignore lest the lives of her people were rendered disposable. Determining further talk would seem too much protestation, she said, "I am glad to have made your acquaintance. Now I would visit my people upon Stern and see for myself they fare well."

"I must ask, my lady, if you are truly concerned, why have you not visited sooner?"

She was glad to have an answer at hand, more that it presented another opportunity to make her less a suspect. "My health has been poor since the loss of my husband." *More, my son,* she did not say. "It seems grief is a disease unto itself, so terrible often I wonder if ever I will be whole again."

"I think you are right in naming it a disease," he said solemnly.

He did not elaborate, and she was glad. Had his thoughts not turned to the uncle who had murdered Wulf, then likely Guarin whom he must believe dead.

"Very well, Lady Hawisa, I grant you permission to ride upon these lands."

Bristling over his choice of words, she said, "Generous."

"Which village?"

"Ravven," she named the closest and in this direction.

"The day wanes. Allow me and my men to escort you."

She stiffened. "Even did I lack an adequate escort, I would not impose."

"No imposition." He motioned her forward.

"My lady?" Ordric said low.

This day Saxons had trapped Normans. Now Normans trapped Saxons—albeit in a less deadly manner.

"I think we must," she whispered, "and it would be good to show myself to the people and speak to their concerns." She urged her mount forward.

As she and her escort neared, Theriot D'Argent and his men turned their mounts toward Ravven. When Isa reined in behind them, Guarin's brother said, "I would be honored if you rode at my side, my lady."

And safer, she thought, though unless he intended her and her men harm, she would not work ill on him.

As she drew even with the young D'Argent, Ordric forced a place between her and a chevalier on her opposite side.

"Boots, my lady?" the keeper of Stern asked.

She looked full into his face. Though she had known he resembled Guarin, she winced over how much—and had to suppress the impulse to assure him his brother lived. "Oui, boots, and surely you have also noted this one born of the renowned Wulfrith rides astride the same as a man."

His bunched brow eased. "So she does, and that it is no palfrey."

Isa patted the destrier's muscled neck. "A worthy mount."

"Acquired from Normandy, I wager."

Hoping it too great a stretch he was acquainted with Anglicus before the beast was made Saxon, she said, "You have a high regard for those come out of Normandy, Theriot D'Argent."

"Rightfully so. As evidenced by our victory at Hastings, the use of horses in battle is essential to my people. Thus, we breed the finest, and your steed is quite fine. So I am right, hmm? Out of Normandy."

Lest he set a trap, she said, "I bought him from a traveling merchant months past. As Anglicus speaks neither Saxon nor Norman, I cannot know."

He chuckled. "Norman, likely taken from the battlefield."

"Regardless, he is Saxon now." She jutted her chin in the direction of Ravven. "Shall we?"

◄▷

Village of Ravven upon Stern
Wulfenshire, England

RAVVEN WAS A MISTAKE. Not because Theriot D'Argent hovered. He did not. He had escorted them only as far as the outskirts, then with a wink that made Isa long to blacken that green eye, said he would call on her at Wulfen and spurred away.

There was no way of knowing if the Normans watched from the wood as she moved among her people, but she had no sense of it and guessed the arrogant young man long gone.

The source of her unrest was another who cornered her following her audience with the villagers who did not like their Norman lord—mostly for his triumph over Saxons at Senlac.

Shrewd Bernia, grandmother of Aelfled, had little to no sight. The wind that had years past blown clouds across the skies of her eyes had gone still. For that, Isa could not comprehend how she came to be caught between the old woman and the chapel steps.

"I am sorry for the loss of your boy, my lady," Bernia said, "but my granddaughter is not all to blame."

Isa clenched her hands. Had Aelfled revealed to her Wulf's death? Or like so many happenings upon Wulfenshire, did the old woman simply feel it? Regardless, Isa knew she also bore blame—and even considered Wulf was not entirely innocent, though he had the excuse of youth from which he had been insufficiently protected.

"The sun sets," she said. "We must ride."

Bernia gripped her arm. "Pray, do not abandon her. She does not belong at the abbey. If you cannot take her back, send her home to me."

Isa stood taller. "She shall remain at Lillefarne. Now loose me."

A growl sounded from the woman, but she did as commanded, and Isa stepped around her.

"My lady!"

She halted.

"I think England lost," Bernia said. "Thus, better your time spent choosing the best of the Normans with whom to make a new life."

Isa swung around. "A Wulfrith does not lie down and roll over, exposing a belly to ignoble scratching. A Wulfrith fights."

"I know I offend, but I would save you time and further heartache."

"Both of which are well spent on removing Normans from our soil."

"So you think, but do you survive, I believe the end will be the same—a Norman-ruled England and another Norman husband. However, now you may choose the latter for yourself, whereas..." She shrugged. "The one I have heard is being called William the Great may force an alliance better suited to him than you."

Isa had heard him named that, and it sat no better with her now than the first time. "I have no intention of wedding again, but did I, it is to one of my own I would bind myself."

Bernia blinked opaque eyes. "There is a reason beyond

pleasing old King Edward your sire wed you to a Norman. He wished their blood to course with Wulfrith blood."

This Isa knew. When she had implored her father not to wed her to Roger, he had said it was necessary to strengthen his line that he saw weakening as one after another of his sons was lost to illness and the blades of lesser men.

"The Normans may be the most formidable warriors our age has seen," Bernia added.

As also her father had told, but Isa could tolerate no more. "You break faith with your own. Good day."

She was halfway to her escort when the old woman called, "I pray for you, Hawisa Wulfrithdotter, as does my Aelfled. Let not our prayers be misspent."

Isa had not known she was capable of so quickly gaining the saddle with skirts flapping about her legs, but she was soon astride and spurring Anglicus from Ravven ahead of her escort.

Bernia knows naught of what she speaks, she told herself as air buffeted her face. *She cannot know. England will be England again.*

CHAPTER SIXTEEN

Wulfenshire Rebel Camp, England
14 October, 1067

*O*ne year. Still no nearer to ridding Saxons of Normans.

One year. Still England's bloodied soil cried for justice.

One year. Still Wulf's mother mourned.

"One year," Isa whispered and wondered what two would bring. Head bowed, she blew out her breath, sipped another. "Return to us, Lord. Pour out Your justice. Avenge us. We are not idle. We do our part. And still they come, take, ravage, oppress. Lift Your punishment. Do *Your* part."

Sacrilegious? Likely. But if the Lord knew all, there was no hiding her resentment over His unwillingness to forgive her people for what brought the Normans down on them. And surely it was understandable why she, a mere mortal, could not herself absolve the enemy of their sins, especially as they continued to plague England.

Opening her eyes, she stared at her laced fingers pressed

against her chest and wondered what more could be done whilst waiting on Him.

Much had been accomplished since the first of the year when more fully she took control of the Wulfenshire rebellion. Scores of rebels, mostly commoners, had been trained in combat. Regular patrols under the command of Jaxon moved about the shire, keeping watch and interceding when the enemy made Saxons their prey.

Since the two Normans slain near the abbey, five more had fallen to rebel blades, three being Campagnon's men and two northern-bound mercenaries who should have taken the long way around Wulfenshire.

As for those beaten, shorn, and divested of coin and fine garments, they numbered nearly a score—and none was of Stern. They were of the Baron of Balduc whom thrice Isa had refused an audience due to a *lingering illness* that seemed the best means of providing cover for her role in the rebellion. As for the keeper of Stern, twice she had denied him entrance, though each time she hesitated before sending him away.

Like Guarin, he honored his family. Though months past he and Campagnon had lost crops of hay to a nighttime attack led by Vitalis—and Isa had reported hers also set afire—Theriot D'Argent had not retaliated by taking the villagers' crops. Not so the Baron of Balduc whose villagers Isa secretively supplied food to ensure their survival. Also unlike Campagnon, Guarin's brother had placed a heavy guard on his grain crops until they were harvested. Thus, nearly all harassment was dealt Campagnon. *Nearly,* since Jaxon's patrol did not always follow orders. Rather, not hers.

More reliable and trustworthy were those over whom Vitalis had charge. Trained and organized into what he called sorties, those select rebels set fires, seized supply wagons, and stole livestock. Though occasionally Isa accompanied Jaxon's men in patrolling Wulfenshire, more often she joined those of the sorties.

Careful to disguise her face and voice, she rode, crept, and wielded a blade alongside those who fought first for country, second for her. In addition to greater challenge, the sorties presented greater risk, but less so now the rebels had access to sanctuary when pursued.

Lillefarne's stone wall was not yet complete, but a sennight past it had become serviceable, allowing Isa and Vitalis to enact a plan they would not otherwise have dared. Last eve, a sortie set fire to the grain Campagnon had confiscated from villagers and evaded capture by fleeing to the abbey where Aelfled concealed the rebels inside the wall. Once Vitalis determined it was safe to bring them out, they would return to camp.

"My lady?"

She straightened so swiftly she nearly struck her head on the tree against which she sat. "What is it, Rosa?"

"Pardon." The woman who had cut her dark hair short, likely the result of being warned of the folly of long hair, dipped her chin. "'Tis D'Argent. He demands an audience."

It surprised he had not sooner. Often he had seen her come and go these six months, just as she had seen him training rebels, but that was all. Though mostly unexamined was the temptation to draw near him as she had when he pulled her onto his boots and into his arms, so great was that temptation she knew to fear it.

"You say D'Argent sent you?"

"Nay, my lady. I sent myself."

Too close this Norman hater had grown to Isa's captive, though never would Rosa admit it. As reported by Vitalis, Guarin was angered and frustrated at being denied the challenge of worthy opponents. For that, his instruction of women and new recruits who showed little promise had turned so intense several were now capable of trading blows with those trained by Jaxon and Vitalis. The latter was pleased, Jaxon not at all where the women were concerned.

He will turn on you, Guarin had predicted, and these past months had given her more cause to believe it. Her sire's greatest trainer did not hide how often he received Gytha's man in the camp. What he held close were their discussions.

When questioned, Jaxon said Harold's mother but kept herself apprised of their growing numbers and skills so when the time came to unite rebels across England, she could make good use of those of Wulfenshire. As for her contact with Isa, it was increasingly rare and mostly a reminder not to forget whose blood coursed her veins.

"Will you come, my lady?"

Isa returned Rosa to focus. "I have naught to say to him."

"But he is being difficult, and since Vitalis has departed to determine if it is safe to return the sortie to camp, I fear Jaxon will..." She shrugged. "It is a solemn day, anguish and anger running high. Though I care not what happens to the Norman, I know you value his training."

Isa rose, glanced down garments heavily creased, fouled, and snagged by this morning's practice at arms that was to have been a balm to a day steeped in memories. The only balm was proving herself equal to more of Jaxon's men than usual. Though those with whom she had crossed swords had not been the best of his rebels, they were far from the worst.

"How is D'Argent being difficult?" she asked.

"He makes the presence of the enemy sharply felt on the worst day possible—over and again shouting your name."

Isa raised a staying hand and listened, but she had ventured far from camp and could catch no more than the distant sounds of metal on metal. "He is in the cave?"

"Nay. As arranged by Vitalis, the women were to practice thrusts and parries with him, but he is unapproachable—could have taken off the top of Letha's head even had he struck it with the dull edge of his blade. Instead, he knocked her senseless with the flat, seized her sword, and began calling for you. Pray, my lady, come ere Jaxon quiets him."

Had he not already...

Isa ran, surging ahead of Rosa as the two negotiated the wooded, rock-strewn ravine. Before they reached the camp, she heard Guarin's voice above the clang of blades that was now of two rather than many—and another's voice, just as angry and demanding.

Isa pushed herself harder.

The rebels were gathered around the post to which Guarin was chained, providing Jaxon a wide berth to circle and counter blows dealt by the Norman's dull sword and the one taken from Letha.

"Hawisa Wulfrithdotter!" he shouted as he brought a blade down on his opponent's, turning aside a slice that could have opened his neck. "I would speak with you!"

"What you will do, Norman," Jaxon bellowed, "is what you should have done long ago."

Despite Isa's fear for her chained captive, when she thrust past two rebels she saw Wulfrith's greatest trainer was the one being bested. Though Guarin's tunic and chausses evidenced bloody slashes, Jaxon's boasted more though surely only because he wielded one sword.

"Hawisa Wulfrithdotter!" Guarin called again.

Jaxon swept his blade wide and nearly took the Norman's ear. "This time she will not save you!"

Isa sprang into the clearing. "I am here!"

As a great murmuring arose, Jaxon faltered. Guarin D'Argent did not, finishing his swing and causing his opponent to jump back from a slice to the calf.

"Cease!" she commanded as her sire's man moved to retaliate.

Jaxon stilled, and as his head came around, Isa looked to Guarin. Shoulders rising and falling, from behind perspiration-dampened hair now of a length from fingertips to wrist, he narrowed his eyes on her.

"'Tis past time, my lady," Jaxon said, striding toward her.

She knew what he meant but said, "For what?"

"One year since Hastings. One year too many. He must be put to ground."

"You have tried, you have failed," Guarin snarled and jerked his chain to emphasize his disadvantage. "You will try again, you will fail again—unless you enlist those *I* have trained."

Seeing the flush above Jaxon's beard spread toward his balding pate, Isa returned her regard to Guarin. "Hold your tongue, Norman!"

A moment later, a hand fastened around her arm and Jaxon thrust his face near. "Gytha wants him dead. Allow me to put him down!"

Staring into his bloodshot eyes, she longed for Vitalis. Together they were the balance to her sire's man, as much as possible keeping him in line with her wishes. But though rattled by fear, she spat, "Release Wulfrith's daughter."

His gaze wavered. "Did you not hear me? Gytha wants the Norman dead."

"Is she your lady? Is she of the house of Wulfrith to which you gave your oath thirty years past?"

His hand on her convulsed.

"*I* am your lady, your oath passed to me by my sire."

His eyes shifted and picked over rebels gone silent.

"Cease now ere thoroughly you dishonor my sire and yourself by challenging Wulfrithdotter's right to keep or dispose of *her* captive."

Was that hatred streaking across the eyes he returned to her? Had she made an enemy of him?

"Fool woman!" He thrust her away.

Isa kept her balance, then did the least of what her sire would have done. It was not a slap to the face she dealt but a fist to the nose. Pain burst across her knuckles and up her arm, but she bared her teeth and said loud, *"Never* lay hands on your lady. *Never* challenge your lady."

Jaxon's lips quivered beneath a trickle of blood running from one nostril, and she thought he gathered spit to scatter across her face, but he remained unmoving.

Isa looked around. Though surprise shone from most of the men's faces and what seemed admiration from the women's, some were as dark as Jaxon's—most notably his pet, Sigward.

"All answer first to me!" she called. "If ever the time comes for Gytha to lead, I shall command you to her side." She returned her regard to the camp's commander. "Are we of an understanding or must we part ways, Jaxon?"

There was threat in her words though she was not certain she could act on it, whether because she would be unable to bring herself to render him incapable of later exacting revenge, or the rebels who sided with him interceded.

"We understand each other well," he said, also with threat.

"Then we are done here." She considered the others. "There will be no further practice this day. Rest yourselves and reflect on what you can do to honor your living and dead and return England to its glory."

Though she knew were it possible to come near to matching Jaxon's sword skill it would be a day distant from this, she set a hand on her hilt and said, "Go, Jaxon."

He thrust past her, so near his shoulder bumped hers.

Isa started forward and saw Guarin's eyes shift between Jaxon and her as if to sound a warning should her man decide this was the day to turn on her.

The last time she had been here with Guarin, he had instructed her in watching her back, and for that she attended to a change in Jaxon's stride. Blessedly, it grew distant and became one with scores of others moving toward the camp's living area.

As she neared her captive and noted he retained both swords, she motioned forward the men who stood guard outside the cave.

Halting just beyond Guarin's reach, she heeded the hair loosed following practice. Since she had been careless with the pins and had no means of securing the braid close to her scalp, she drew it over her shoulder and tucked it beneath her loose tunic.

A slight smile moved Guarin's mouth, and he lowered his gaze down her. "It pains you," he said, and she knew his eyes were on the fist that struck Jaxon. "And yet it felt good, I am certain, the same as every piece of flesh I took from him. Much like the first sip of water across a tongue that has forgotten how sweet the taste of moisture, hmm?" His eyes returned to hers. "Are the bones intact?"

She peeled back her thumb she had long ago learned not to tuck into her palm and uncurled aching fingers. "I believe so."

"You surprised me, though not as much as you did him. Lessons in warfare are made of such. Do you push beyond yourself, you can do great, unexpected things—providing you are not rash."

His censure unmistakable, she said, "You do not approve of me striking him?"

"I liked it, but not only did you humiliate him on the heels of shame dealt by a Norman, you exposed strength it would have been better to reveal when the surprise of it matters."

"It mattered this day. He challenged me, and rather than slink away like a child, I affirmed my place, his place, and that of *my* rebels. More, that I am of—"

"Wulfrith," he said.

She raised her eyebrows. "The name carries much weight, and it is mine."

"Until he moves against you, Lady Hawisa, and now you have given him greater cause. Did not your sire teach you the advantage of holding close your feelings?"

Control of one's emotions, but did that apply here? she

questioned. "My father took pride in letting men know where they stood with him—did not temper words and actions, nor flatter where flattery was not due."

"With his lessers and equals," Guarin said. "But I wager he was more cautious with his betters. As for pride, I know much about that sin, just as I know ever it has been and ever it will be the downfall of many."

She crossed her arms over her chest. "Pride due my sire. He was—"

"Formidable, oui. But you are not your father."

Offense flew through her. "You say Jaxon is my better?"

"As England—and Wulfenshire—now stands, I do. His facility with weapons, ability to command, and reputation that finds him in the company of those determined to see one of King Harold's line take back the throne, are more valued than your claim to your sire's name. Do you not rid yourself of him, he will rid himself of you."

She longed to argue, nearly did, then sighed. "I fear you are right."

"You should have let me kill him."

Even chained, she believed it possible he could have done so and was not certain his victory would have been due to wielding two swords. This fearless Norman had survived Hastings where thousands had fallen, endured weeks of torture, was of muscled breadth and great height, and young relative to Jaxon.

"We should return him to the cave, my lady?"

She looked to those Vitalis trusted to keep watch over her captive, but before she could confirm they do their duty, Guarin said in their language, "Nay, Lady Hawisa and I have six months of silence to fill."

Though tempted to refuse him, she said, "I will speak with him."

"In the cave?" one of the men asked.

"Outside," Guarin answered again. When she shot her gaze to

him, he said, "The cave is better kept than when first you came to me there, but remains dim and foul."

"Very well. Unchain him."

"My lady!" Vitalis's men protested.

"Once he relinquishes his swords, I believe it sufficient to bind his hands behind his back," Isa said. And that belief was supported by their last visit when he could have done her great harm.

She glanced at his wrists, not for the first time noted the scraped and raw flesh above the manacles. Would he be scarred for life?

"Much appreciated, Lady Hawisa," he said and cast the swords at her feet and swept his arms behind his back.

Muttering beneath his breath, one of Vitalis's men uncoiled a length of rope. When he had bound Guarin's hands, his companion unfastened the manacle.

Isa led the way to the immense rocks scattered to the left of the cave's entrance, seated herself on one whose surface was warmed by the autumn sun, and gestured at another ahead and to the right.

As Guarin lowered, the men positioned themselves on either side of him.

"Return to the cave," Isa ordered.

"But my lady—"

"As long as you keep watch, he will not harm me," she said, though fairly certain even if she sent them away, she would be safe, especially since Vitalis was not here to prevent Jaxon from making much of aggression against her.

For further assurance, she slid her dagger from its sheath and set it across her thighs. "Leave us."

With glances over their shoulders, they retreated. Providing Isa and Guarin spoke low, their conversation would remain between them.

She waited for him to reveal the reason for his summons, but he closed his eyes and turned his face up, causing silvered hair to fall back and reveal a thick column of neck across which coursed the large vein Jaxon wished to sever.

"I thank you," he said. "As often I question my humanity—even God—it is good to feel more man than beast."

Pained by a heart that should be as empty of feeling as her life was empty of Wulf, Isa said, "I wish it could be different, that you had left me to my fate upon Senlac."

"I wish it as well." He continued to let the sun warm his face. "You know not how many times, especially during the beatings, I rued forcing my protection on you." He lowered his chin, met her gaze. "One year since first we met, Hawisa. One year since I sacrificed my freedom and dignity. One year since I became acquainted with manacle, chain, and gutted pride. One year since my family began to fear me dead and now surely believe it."

Knowing how near he was to one of his brothers, she averted her gaze.

"You think your loss greater than mine," he said, "and even if now I am absent a brother as well as an uncle, I would not argue you have more to mourn in losing a child. But it is time to right the wrong done me."

She looked up. "I cannot release you."

He shifted his jaw, and she felt the anger he contained as she did not believe her sire could have done. "The word of a D'Argent—"

"I cannot! Were I the only one at risk, I would chance it, but it would be unforgivable to endanger those I have been entrusted to protect. And so I ask that you bide with me."

His nostrils flared.

"I do not dispute your integrity nor good intentions, Guarin D'Argent, but we all have weaknesses that make us do things of which we would not have believed ourselves capable. My son was my weakness, as were—and are—my people. The same vulnerabilities afflict you, and I will not have innocents pay for the trust you would have me gift you."

He sat forward, causing the muscles of his shoulders to bunch as his bound hands strained against the movement. "It has been a year, and even in the absence of King William, England remains Norman."

Then he knew the usurper had yet to return from celebrating his victory in Normandy. He heard too much, though what did it matter as long as he had no means of escape?

"What chance has Gytha to place one of her grandsons on the throne?" he pressed.

"We thought the same of your kind," she retorted. "What chance had Normans of stealing the crown? But just as we underestimated your duke, you underestimate the Saxons' resolve. We will topple William."

"I do not believe it. I know him and that he is far more the wolf than I. Not only did he sink his teeth into your island kingdom, he swallowed it whole. Unless Gytha and her followers are able and willing to reach into his belly and risk being devoured, their cause—yours—is lost. The sooner Saxons accept Norman rule, the fewer will suffer and die."

She was tempted to yield to his argument, so hopeless did he make her cause sound, but she would be a traitor to her own if she freed him. And with a portion of her lands in the hands of his brother, how was she to keep hold of what remained with Guarin aware she was Dotter? Were the rest of her lands not taken, she would find herself on her face alongside a grasping Norman, his ring on her hand, a pall stretched over them as the wedding mass was intoned.

She stood. "I cannot give what you ask, and I believe my decision is the same you would wish your sister to make."

His eyes hardened. "Then we are done, Hawisa Wulfrithdotter," he said, but as she started to turn away, asked, "Have you further word of my family?"

She almost wished she had moved her one conversation with Theriot D'Argent to talk of his family so she might reveal the fate of Dougray to allow Guarin to be at peace or begin mourning. "I have made no further inquiries."

"And will not?"

"If I can without arousing suspicion, I shall."

He nodded. "As I am to remain your captive, benefitting your lesser rebels whilst ever watching for the day Jaxon turns on us both, I seek payment."

She startled. "Payment?"

"Rather, a favor."

Sensing the wolf before her, she said, "You look well enough clothed and fed. What do you require?"

"Once a week when you come to train, I would keep company with you."

"For what?"

"To know you better."

"To what end?"

"I may wish I had not aided you, but I believe I would do so again, just as I believe I shall do so again."

She snorted. "I do not foresee requiring further aid."

"You will if you stay the course."

"I will not!"

As if she had not spoken, he continued, "Do I yet live, I shall be there to keep you from King William's wrath and myself bring the Lady of Wulfen into the Norman fold."

She glowered. "You are becoming loose of mind, and I am sorry if I am responsible."

"Not loose of mind, but you *are* responsible for all this." He looked to the cave. "But in time I shall forgive you as the Lord would have me do—certes, all the more imperative if I am to prove a good husband."

HUSBAND.

156

A taunt to which there could be truth though Guarin had let her believe as she would. Once more manacled and back to the wall, he wondered what she had believed.

Emotions had lit her grey eyes and moved the muscles of her throat, but no further word had she spoken. When she strode opposite, he had called to her, reminding her of the payment that would find them together seven days hence. She had not answered, but he believed she would come.

The lady he wooed disliked him for a Norman, and that was all. Though her resistance to releasing him tempted him to rage, he understood. He had given her good reason to trust him with her life and mostly believed he could trust her with his, but neither would he risk his people were he captor and she captive.

Still, her guilt over his circumstances and the debt owed him made her vulnerable in a way he was not. Thus, given more time he might turn her from her course—hopefully well before this need to protect her saw him wed to a Saxon when it was a Norman lady with whom his sire wished him matched.

As the heir of a sizable demesne, the forging of his manhood fairly recent, and of attractive face and form, Guarin had many ladies to choose from. Of greatest consideration was one who stood apart from Hawisa—a lady of ten and seven who possessed childbearing years aplenty and was of great height to birth sons as tall as he. True, she was of many words and little thought, but their sons would be warriors of one mind rather than two were he to join with a Saxon. Providing another had not taken the Norman lady to wife during his captivity, he might.

Guarin picked another piece of cold venison from the wooden platter, followed it with coarse brown bread, and washed them down with ale.

"One year." He nodded. "Long ere the passing of another, I will be home."

~

Wulfen Castle
England

HUSBAND.

He taunted. Of course he did. And she would have it no other way. Never would another Norman's name replace Wulfrithdotter. As told the faith-breaking Bernia, it was a Saxon to whom she would bind herself, ensuring wife and husband were of one mind—*if* she wed again. And she would not.

Then your sire's line ends with you, spoke dissent which would see her bound to one of Gytha's choosing.

Isa read again the missive delivered to Wulfen whilst she was at camp. Harold's mother wished Wulfrith's heir to wed her nephew and planned to send him a month hence. Isa recognized the name of one a dozen years older than she who, for reasons unknown, had not been at his cousin's side upon Senlac. But just as she would refuse Guarin D'Argent did he not merely taunt, she would refuse Gytha's kin.

She heard boots and turned to Wulfrith.

The boy smiled, less shyly now. "I have completed my lesson," he said succinctly to demonstrate which one.

"Your accent improves daily," she answered in Norman-French. "And the written word?"

He halted before her where she stood with her back to the fire, wrinkled a nose longer than that of the one whose name he had taken. "I try, my lady, but it is difficult."

All the more so for having little exposure to reading and writing before arriving at Wulfen. "Then you must work harder, Wulfrith."

"I do not think I have the mind for it."

"Of course you do."

He sighed. "I prefer training at arms."

"As did Wulf." It was said without thought, and when thought followed, so did pain.

The boy was not oblivious, and she was both grateful and resentful for the sympathy in his eyes. He was kind, as of one yet too innocent to exercise caution in the casting of compassion, and he overstepped in feeling for her what only a son of the blood ought to feel.

"Forgive me," he said.

And another thing he was—too conciliatory. Was his sister the same? Rather, had she been? Doubtless, no longer now she served the vile Campagnon who abused the people of Balduc, though surely not as greatly as he made his slave suffer. One thing was certain—no matter what was done the young woman, no matter how apathetic she presented, she had fight in her.

Isa had been angered when Vitalis revealed he had enlisted a Saxon stable lad to recruit Em in passing information to the rebellion and persuasion was delivered with assurance her brother was safe amongst the rebels of England.

As the leader of the rebellion on Wulfenshire, Isa ought not care how information was obtained, but she feared Em would pay with her life were she caught. Determined to reunite brother and sister, she had instructed Vitalis to have the stable lad pass a message to Em that if it became too dangerous, she should send word and an attempt would be made extricate her. She had responded that for as long as possible she would aid her people. And much she had.

"If I have displeased my lady, forgive me."

She returned the boy to focus. "Do not apologize. I first misspoke, not you." She waved a hand. "Go to the training yard and practice at the quintain."

"I thank you, my lady." He turned and hastened across the hall.

A gift she had given him, since he liked going astride and tilting at the straw man attached to a post. Though Jaxon resisted adopting the practice of fighting on horseback at which Normans excelled, that training was underway at Wulfen Castle—and soon Vitalis would begin training those of his sorties though the technique was mostly unknown to the English. Even Roger, who should have been versed in such, had lacked proper training and not sought to rectify the deficiency. Thus, it fell to Isa.

When the doors closed behind Wulfrith, her thoughts moved to Guarin who would know how to fight on horseback. Unfortunately, it was too great a risk to enlist his aid. Astride and unbound, he would escape.

She slid her gaze to Gytha's missive. An answer was due, and she would ink it this day to ensure the woman's nephew did not venture anywhere near her walls.

CHAPTER SEVENTEEN

Wulfenshire Rebel Camp, England
Late Spring, 1068

Their routine was nearly unchanged these seven months. Had he a weapon to hand when she came prior to departing camp, he thrust it distant, swept his arms behind, and was bound. Though he had yet to turn her from her course, he had determined to make good use of the routine when time and circumstances were right.

Soon, he assured himself. He but required two things align— the presence of horses and the absence of Vitalis who kept watch over his lady's conversations with her captive when he was available.

During the weekly meetings with Hawisa, not once had either broached the subject of marriage his parting taunt had introduced. It was as if never spoken. Instead, she herded their discussion in the direction of the women and new recruits, but so conflicted was he over those he trained to battle his own, he did not long play the sheep.

When first the rebels had beaten a defenseless man whilst

listing their grievances, he had rebuked himself for feeling sympathy for them. But since he had begun instructing only women and men of so little promise their own lives would number among their losses were they not versed in defense, more and more he felt for them. Too near he was to their pain, whether they cast blame at him or but told of their losses as if in voicing them they might heal.

Since Guarin rarely rose to Hawisa's queries about those he trained, mostly the two discussed England, which he prompted by probing things overheard or revealed by rebels. Never did she stay beyond a half hour, and all the sooner she departed when she became aware of attempts to move their conversation to more personal matters. Thus, mostly he added to his knowledge and understanding of her when something slipped from others.

If not for the promise their routine held, lulling his captors into a state of vulnerability, Guarin did not think he could have continued to suppress his anger and suspected even were he able, the strain would crack his mind. Neither warrior nor wolf could long remain caged without becoming something more dangerous and ungodly—even if let out on occasion to vent restlessness and frustration.

Though he remained in control, at times his emotions threatened to break free, as nearly they had days past when he heard the name *Theriot D'Argent* spoken by Jaxon's men. As if feeling the sharp regard of the chained Norman, they had looked around. And hastened away.

Now as Guarin was led to the meeting place by a rebel on either side who would ensure a good distance between the Norman and their lady, he wondered how to entice Hawisa to reveal what she knew of his brother.

He considered her where she sat on her rock, noted her garments were fouled the same as his from practice over ground soaked by rainfall on the day past. But when she looked up from the dagger across her thighs, of greater note was how pale her face and shadowed her eyes.

When her men withdrew, he said, "You look tired."

"Appearances do not deceive." She pulled the pins securing the braid to her head. As that golden tail of many crossings uncoiled over her shoulder and slid down her breasts, he became aware of the beat of his heart and warmth beyond his exertions this spring day.

Leaving his own hair bound at the nape, now of a length that required a leather thong to keep it out of his eyes during practice, he said, "What has happened?"

The corners of her mouth pinched. "First tell what has reached your ears since last we met."

Deciding to wait on broaching the subject of his brother, he said, "Something terrible has occurred on Wulfenshire."

She nodded. "A Norman family passing through en route to lands awarded by William has been slain, including four children between infancy and ten."

"Was it your rebels?"

"Of course not!" She glared as if to impress on him how ridiculous the suggestion, then said, "Still, those of Wulfenshire will be blamed, and I fear your duke's eye will fall more heavily on us."

Which could be of benefit to Guarin. From previous conversations, he was well enough acquainted with what had transpired since the king's return to England to know what she feared.

At his Christmas court, William had awarded further grants of land to his followers, raising much concern—and ire—among Saxons not yet divested of their holdings. Then in the new year, William had summoned Saxon troops to aid in putting down a rebellion. Many had come, evidencing their acceptance of him as king, and in the depths of winter marched west to Exeter alongside Normans to prevent Harold's mother from making that city a base from which to dethrone the conqueror.

The king had blinded one of its citizens in full view of its defenders, but Gytha and her followers had not submitted, and a siege raged a fortnight. Though William's army suffered great losses, Harold's mother had escaped in the company of wives and widows of Saxon nobles.

Once more victorious, William declared her property and her followers' forfeit. If the murder of the Norman family did bring Hawisa Wulfrithdotter to his notice and it was believed she was involved—more likely if it was learned these rebels were in contact with Gytha—she would lose her lands. Or worse.

"You are right to be concerned," Guarin said. "And wrong to be certain your rebels did not commit the slaughter."

"It was not the work of our sorties."

That he believed, but there was a marked difference between those under Vitalis's command and those not. "It could have been the work of the patrol."

She lowered her gaze to the dagger. "I pray not. Jaxon…"

"What?"

"As increasingly I prove worthy of my sire's name, less he challenges me and more he follows my orders. He is adjusting to my leadership."

"In this, appearances deceive. Though Gytha's man has visited less often since the fall of Exeter, still he comes—indeed, not even a sennight past. And now a Norman family is dead."

She slid a hand back over her head, gripped her neck. And spoke elsewhere. "You will be pleased to hear Matilda was crowned at Westminster on the feast of Whitsun."

Since Hawisa rarely introduced events of which he had no knowledge, this surprised, especially as it portended ill for the Saxons that William was so confident of his kingship he had summoned his wife from Normandy. How much longer could this lady deny the Normans were here to stay?

"He is very certain of himself," she said, "but I believe he will be less certain soon."

"Then Gytha continues to plague him," he dangled what he hoped did not appear bait.

"Even if she remains on the island of Flat Holm where she fled, that I do not doubt," Hawisa said. "But it is another of whom I speak—Edwin Harwolfson, a royal housecarle who survived the great battle. He gathers rebels to him, and though they are as ghosts, it is believed Andredeswald is their base."

That great forest alongside Senlac in which Guarin had given all to protect this woman. "If Gytha could not draw to her side enough men of strength, what makes you think Harwolfson can?" he asked.

"It is told he seeks to right the wrongs against all Saxons, not merely against..."

"The house of Godwine," Guarin named that to which Gytha belonged. If Harwolfson truly sought to represent all, there was merit in his cause since still Harold's kin provided no relief to the people of this land. Saxons had to realize Gytha's only concern was that of returning her family to the throne—no matter the cost to the common man.

"The house of Godwine," Hawisa breathed and looked past him.

He followed her gaze to the three mounts led by her escort in readiness for her departure. At times they arrived here with her, other times in the midst of their meeting.

The former—and Vitalis's absence—must align for Guarin to set in motion his plan that would not be seen through this day, but perhaps seven days hence.

"It appears you have made Anglicus your own." He returned his gaze to hers and glimpsed suspicion that indicated soon she would depart. In the hope of holding her here and bringing her around to Theriot, he decided to answer a question several times she had put to him. "Though I wager your prize destrier did not wish to cross the channel, methinks he would remain with you given the chance to return home. Unlike *this* Norman."

Her eyes widened, and he knew she waited to learn his reason for joining William's invasion. As some truth would serve, he said, "So much your company refreshes, I would see you linger. Hence, I shall reveal why I aided in setting the duke over England though I will have lands aplenty when I come into my inheritance."

When she did not prompt, he continued, "As you know, I have three brothers—providing Dougray survived—and one cousin, all in want of land. I thought it wrong they should gain it by taking from others, but as I am the privileged first born, my argument carried little weight."

An ache in his right shoulder, he rolled it. This day's opponents had been worthy just as he had made them, the strength of their exchanged blows jarring his joints and making the strain on them more deeply felt now his hands were bound behind.

"Why did you join them?" Hawisa asked.

"The same reason as my uncle—to fight alongside them the better to ensure they did not fall. And that I did until we became separated amid the frenzy." He frowned. "Have you further word of my brothers or cousin?"

"I must be cautious with my inquiries, but though still I know naught of Dougray, I understand the others are well."

The knot in Guarin's chest eased. "Were any awarded the land they sought? Are they yet in England?"

She averted her eyes. "Only the whereabouts of Cyr is known to me. He is long returned to Normandy."

"As expected since it appears he is now our sire's heir. You are sure you know naught more of Theriot?"

Isa wished she could give a more convincing performance of ignorance, but she was fatigued and discouraged by the usurper's grip on England, so much she longed to be sitting at the hearth with Wulfrith discussing his lessons, even if it hurt each time his words and actions brought another to mind.

The boy who kept the Normans from her lands had yet to attain the build of Wulf, but he was a fine young man, and though it felt as if she betrayed her lost son, she grew fond of him. It was disconcerting, especially since recently she had called him *Wulf* and been sharp with him as if he were the one who trespassed on the affection reserved for the child of her body and heart.

"I wonder at your silence," Guarin pulled her back to him.

She looked up and thought how attractive he was, perspiration causing his mud-splattered garments to adhere to a form returned to the powerfully muscled state apparent at Senlac. What yet remained distant from their first meeting was his hair and beard. Though once a week he was provided a keen blade to keep the latter trimmed close, he did not apply it to silvered hair that had grown so long it had to be bound to keep it out of his eyes and the hands of opponents.

He raised his eyebrows, a reminder he awaited an answer.

"I search my memory," she said and shrugged, certain were she to reveal his brother dwelt at Stern, Guarin would refuse to train those who might raise a sword against his brother though, thus far, the younger D'Argent gave little cause to strike at him.

She recalled their recent encounter. Battling illness of the chest, she had admitted Sir Theriot to Wulfen to give credence to her claim of being mostly bedridden. Though Wulfrith had not been permitted to speak freely, he had presented well, answering D'Argent's seemingly innocent questions in Norman-French as he had been unable to do during Sir Maël's trespass upon Wulfen.

"You have remembered something?" Guarin asked.

Jolted back to the present, she nearly ended their meeting, but it occurred if she dangled him a bit longer, she might gain answers to other unanswered questions.

"Perhaps if I linger, I shall remember something. In the meantime, mayhap you would satisfy my curiosity over what caused you to risk your well-being to aid a stranger...your enemy...at Senlac."

He laughed, and though she knew it was at her expense, that rumble made her heart beat faster. "Be it ignorance or deception, I do not think you have anything to tell of Theriot. However, I will satisfy your curiosity if you satisfy mine, Hawisa."

Leave, she told herself. "What curiosity might *I* satisfy?"

"You have yet to enlighten me about those of Wulfrith." He held up a finger. "But I will speak first so you may earn my trust as I have earned yours. Agreed?"

Again she told herself to leave, then assured herself it would do her rebels no harm to tell of her family. "Agreed."

"I would think my reason for giving aid evident. You were in need."

She nearly argued that, but it would be childish. "I was, and yet I do not believe it was aid your fellow Normans sought to provide me. Why did *you?*"

"Ere Hastings, I thought my only great weakness was pride." He glanced at the cave. "To my detriment, also I suffer a weakness for women in distress."

"Whence comes such?"

"The weakness of pride—my uncle who believed a man could never be too prideful." Though her stiffening at mention of Wulf's murderer caused his lids to narrow, he continued, "The weakness of women—my godly sire."

"Godly..." She frowned. "You told your father was a great warrior."

"So he was."

"How could he be so different from his brother?"

Now he frowned, and she thought he would count his end of the bargain done, but he said, "Have you time, I shall begin at the beginning."

"Then begin."

"My sire and uncle were twins. To their sire's great displeasure, the midwife did not mark the one born first. Hence, it was decided once they earned swords and spurs, the heir would be determined by a contest of arms. Though it did not make for good brotherly relations, they had a care for each other. When it came time to secure the inheritance, so evenly matched were they and so fierce the blows dealt it was feared each might slay the other."

Guarin's sudden smile alerted Isa how far forward she leaned and how wide her eyes. She could not contain a laugh. "I am enraptured. Pray, continue."

"My sire prevailed without taking his brother's life though many believed he ought to have ensured never could Hugh present a threat to his lordship."

One moment she was warmed by how honorable his sire, the next wished he had not been. Had he put his brother to death, her son would yet live.

Or another would have slain the vengeful boy and his companions, an unwelcome voice whispered.

"My uncle departed to make his own fortune in service to Duke William. And many riches he gained—until great my sire's need for his aid."

"Aid?"

"Many were the private wars our young duke fought to retain hold of his duchy. Thus, my sire and his men provided military service. I was nearly three—Cyr half that—when my mother received tidings her husband was lost during one of William's campaigns, albeit no body was recovered. Months later, whilst traveling to visit family, her entourage was set upon. I remember my brother's wailing, the laughter of brigands, the screams of women, then the arrival of chevaliers on great horses who, I did not know then, prevented my mother and her maid from being ravished."

"Your weakness for women in distress," Isa mused.

"More, that it so greatly affected my sire, he impressed on his sons the importance of protecting women and children."

"Tell how he lived."

"A village priest found him on the battlefield, his legs rendered useless. For months, the man of God cared for the warrior, time and again prying him from death's arms, and it was months past that before my sire remembered who he was and his loved ones awaited his return. Or so he thought…"

Feeling almost a child, Isa pressed, "What happened?"

"He had instructed were he to die in battle, my mother should wed again to provide a protector for her and their sons. And nearly she did. My sire returned a fortnight ere she was to marry one of the chevaliers who saved her. As she had believed her husband dead, my sire forgave her. What surprised is he forgave her for sinful intimacy with her betrothed and gave his name to the babe in her womb and raised him as his own—my brother, Dougray."

Isa caught her breath.

"Though my mother counted him a good husband before, she says the one returned to her was more—that a godly man was made of the warrior lost to paralysis."

Swept by a longing to meet the one who fathered Guarin, Isa said, "I am glad to better understand you."

"The good of my sire but, as told, there is also my uncle, and not all bad."

"Your father recalled him."

"Not immediately. With the aid of his men, he undertook my early training, but eventually more was required for his heir and the sons coming up behind me. Thus, Hugh returned with his wife and son to make fierce and proud warriors of us all. Often, my sire and he clashed over our training, but I believe they found a good balance." He breathed deep. "Now the tale of your family, Hawisa."

Her hesitation caused his brow to furrow, but though she was tempted to break their agreement, she would give him some of what he had given her.

"Long the family Wulfrith has been esteemed for training up warriors. My grandsire and his brothers were formidable. My sire and his brothers were formidable. My brothers were formidable, and yet…" Seeing their bearded faces, hearing the growls, shouts, and laughter come out of them, she hurt over the loss of those who had tolerated the girl in their midst. "…all are dead. One to illness, the others to blades of lesser warriors—blow after blow dealt my sire who feared as his father had warned that—"

"That?" Guarin asked.

Though he had bared his family to her, she faltered. She was not ashamed—never that! However, this was not talk one shared with a mere acquaintance, let alone the enemy.

Neither of which he is, spoke that voice again. Still, there was no need to elaborate on the warning her sire had not heeded. "They feared our line weakened."

Guarin's eyes told he knew there was more, but he said, "And so you became your sire's heir. Tell, for what did he so esteem Normans he entrusted the last of the Wulfriths to one of my people?"

"He believed our union would strengthen the Wulfrith line."

"How did he come by that?"

She shrugged, stood, and motioned to the men at the cave. "It is past time I departed."

He sighed. "Though I feel cheated, I am grateful for the time afforded me. Until next week, my lady."

She slid the dagger in its sheath and strode opposite. Once astride Anglicus, she looked back and saw Guarin was being led to the cave. He did not look around, and she sensed he knew she wished him to.

Why do I? she wondered. *And why this ache?*

Because he does not belong here, she told herself, *because punishment rather than reward was given him for aiding me.*

Over a year and a half had passed since he was brought to Wulfenshire, chained, and abused. She had rectified the latter, but he remained a prisoner and only tight control and close watch ensured one who should never be caged remained thus.

When Vitalis had warned their meetings posed a greater risk of escape, she had argued her captive knew even if he overpowered her neither she nor Jaxon would allow threat to her person to secure his release. And did he forego threat, bound and on foot he would not get far before being recaptured. Regardless, she would be a fool to believe the wolf accepted his fate. When finally he attempted to free himself, it would end badly were it Jaxon's men who intercepted him.

She looked to the path that delivered those who traversed it to the training yard and living area. Seeing her sire's man at the farthest reach standing alongside the one named Sigward who lauded the camp commander as *a Saxon true to the bone, the blood, and the marrow,* she revisited this day's meeting with Jaxon.

He had shown no concern over the murder of the Norman family. Had he, less she would have believed his denial those under his command were responsible.

The work of other rebels, he had said and suggested the perpetrators were from northern shires who occasionally crossed onto Wulfenshire and, without regard for Saxons in their path, slew Normans caught out in the open.

On this day, Isa was less inclined to believe those perpetrators were his men. Ever he would dislike answering to a woman, but he had been fairly respectful and surprised her with the offer to instruct her at arms. It had occurred an *accident* might see her dead, but she had accepted.

Vitalis and scores of rebels had watched the match in the training yard, and greater respect Isa gained for Jaxon. Though he was far from young, no greater challenge had she been presented nor better lessons in placement of feet and swing of blade. Vitalis was formidable, but not as capable of passing along skills mastered. To ensure the rebels the best training, Vitalis was right not to seek to replace Jaxon. Hopefully, it would not be necessary, but *had* Jaxon ordered that family's slaughter...

Dear Lord, she sent heavenward, *help me see past the dark veils behind which murderers, usurpers, and deceivers hide. Help me keep my people safe as I did not keep my son safe. Help me hold to these lands and honor my sire's name.*

She looked again to the cave, and the words, *The wolf bides his time,* sounded through her, words she was not certain were her own. Were they answered prayer?

Regardless, to decrease the risk of escape that could see Guarin pay with his life or the rebels suffer discovery by William, it was best they meet in the cave henceforth, her captive manacled.

"A sennight hence," she murmured and urged her mount ahead of her escort.

CHAPTER EIGHTEEN

Wulfenshire Rebel Camp
England

*S*ix days rather than seven.

With urgency, Hawisa rode into camp, wearing her usual tunic and chausses and sparing her captive but a glance as he and the woman with whom he traded blows paused to ponder the unexpected.

"Trouble," Rosa said as she lowered her sword.

Normans, Guarin guessed and would not be surprised if they rode on Wulfenshire in response to the crime for which he believed Jaxon responsible.

Rather than continue out of sight to the stable, Hawisa and her men reined in and dismounted. After another glance at her captive, she and one of her escort strode to Jaxon and Vitalis who had surely been summoned by the sound of her arrival. Words were exchanged, then the four disappeared down the beaten path.

Guarin moved his regard to the escort left behind and the horses that were one of two things required, Vitalis's absence the second. But now there was a third—the meeting that was to have taken place on the morrow.

Silently, he cursed the loss of an opportunity greater than any hoped for. Were it Normans who roused Hawisa, better it would benefit him had they come a day hence. Much shortened his flight would be if he made for their ranks. However, were Vitalis otherwise occupied this day and Hawisa could be persuaded to speak with her captive...

"Rosa, I have a boon to ask of you."

She scowled, but he saw interest in eyes that no longer shone with hatred—at least, not of the strength that told she wished him dead. "I owe you naught," she said.

He tapped his dull blade against hers. "Only sword skill that rivals many a man's."

"As easily gained in setting my blade against a pel, Norman."

He grunted. "Mighty warriors those wooden posts, but they cannot better me."

"You flatter yourself."

"I speak true."

She sighed. "What errand would you send me upon?"

"I wish to speak with Lady Hawisa."

"You saw the same as I she is not long for here."

"I did, but I believe I know what delivered her in such a flurry, and what I know could be of use to her."

Her eyes narrowed. "You make it sound as if you would aid her."

"Then you hear me well."

"For what would you help her?"

He raised his eyebrows. "You do not suspect the same as others?"

Her flush of exertion deepened. "I do question your feelings for her, but I know how treacherous you Normans."

God willing, that last he would further prove ere long. "Pray, carry word to her. Let her decide whether to heed it."

"What of our practice? 'Tis barely begun."

He grinned. "As you say, the pel is a worthy opponent."

She made a sound of disgust.

Thinking she would refuse him, he decided to offer what thus far he withheld—and hoped he would not have to deliver on it since she was not ready. "Do this for me, and I will begin instructing you in wielding sword and dagger at once."

Her eyes widened. "Even if my lady refuses to come?"

"Even if."

She stepped to the side, as she secured her sword on her belt called to the men who kept watch, "I am not done with him. Let no one take my place." Then she hurried away.

Heart pumping with more vigor than when he sought to keep blades from it, Guarin withdrew to the post and set a shoulder against it.

If Hawisa came, here he would break with routine and, succeed or not, forever end it—no further meetings nor rebel training. All would change, and he would do everything in his power to ensure life rather than death was his end.

Either Rosa had difficulty locating her lady or had to wait on her, but when finally someone appeared on the path, it was Vitalis on horseback.

As Guarin watched the warrior spur past Hawisa's escort and their mounts and away from camp, he smiled. All aligned, and better than imagined. "Now come to me, Hawisa," he rasped. "Give your prisoner his long overdue reward for good behavior."

When finally she appeared, she was alone. That meant he must overpower only three—the two who would release him from the post and the distant housecarle who attended the horses. There was also Hawisa, but she would continue past to await him near the cave.

Providing he wasted no time putting down the three, he would be astride before she reached him and he had only to let run the swiftest horse who knew well the route out of this place.

When it was clear Hawisa approached her captive, signaling to Vitalis's men to prepare him for the meeting, Guarin straightened from the post. As required, he cast his sword distant and swept his arms behind with a ring of chain from which he would soon be released. By his own hand.

"No need for rope," Hawisa called as she neared. "I will speak with him in the cave."

Not routine, but though Guarin nearly cursed the hitch in his plan, it could be overcome. Just as he had intended to overpower the rebels before they bound him with rope ahead of removing the chain attached to the post, he would do so when they commanded him to his knees to manacle his ankles, between which would stretch a chain so short he could do little more than shuffle.

Hawisa continued past Guarin, next the rebels who were so assured of the usual routine they were far from alert.

Hoping he would not be forced to kill Vitalis's men, Guarin watched as one removed his sword from its sheath and the other veered to their prisoner's back, the latter leaving his sword on his belt while he readied manacles and chain to secure one they would curse no matter the outcome.

Horses present.

Vitalis absent.

Post behind.

Hawisa distant.

Lowering to his knees.

Before touching ground, thrusting upright.

Using the force in lengthening calves and thighs, Guarin swung around and drove an elbow into the face of the man who bent to manacle him. Then he unsheathed that one's sword before he fell onto his back.

With the rebel divested of blade clutching at his bloodied face, Guarin turned in time to deflect the other one's sword that sought to open his abdomen.

Having excess chain with which to maneuver, he countered with a backward stroke that sliced the man's sword arm.

As the rebel bellowed and stumbled back, Guarin took stock of the others—the housecarle running forward with drawn sword, the broken-nosed rebel struggling to rise, Hawisa shouting his name as she came at him from behind.

It was now or would never be.

He landed a booted foot to the head of the rebel who had made it to hands and knees, leapt back alongside the post, and thrust his manacled arm up, causing the chain to slap the wood. With the keen-edged blade, Guarin delivered two blows to links he had weakened these months with an occasional errant swing whilst engaged with the worthiest of those sent to him. Much they had enjoyed those displays that made them feel superior.

The links fell away, releasing him from the bulk of chain attached to the post, then once more he was forced to defend himself against the rebel whose sword arm he had injured. He knocked aside a thrust to his thigh, dealt a slice to the ribs, and brought the hilt down on the man's temple. As the rebel dropped, Guarin looked to Hawisa.

Eyes wild as she ran at him with sword before her, she ought to be next since she was nearer than her housecarle who had left the horses unattended, but Guarin had no intention of harming the woman once likened to Boudica who now looked as he imagined that warrior woman.

He snatched the dagger from the belt of the rebel at his feet, ran to engage Hawisa's last man standing to be all the nearer the Norman destrier who would carry him to his people.

Come, anger! he gave that dark emotion permission to rise and cast itself against the warrior he now faced.

The housecarle was swift and vicious, but Guarin's store of the same was greater as needed to ensure he did not have to turn his blade on Hawisa or others who were becoming aware something was amiss at the camp's edge.

"Stay down!" Guarin commanded the warrior who had dropped to a knee when dealt a blow to his back that sliced through tunic and muscle.

"Guarin!" Hawisa shouted.

She was too near. Rather than ensure her man did not come at him again, Guarin ran.

"Non!" she cried. "Do not do this!"

He launched himself onto Anglicus's saddle and snatched up the reins.

"Guarin!" Her feet nearly skidded out from under her as she slowed to draw back the sword she meant to use against him. But though she righted herself quickly, she did not swing to meet the blade with which he would counter.

For a moment they stared at each other, and Guarin thought how ironic now he was the one astride, she on the ground.

"Pray, do not do this," she beseeched. "My people—"

"It is done," he said and, catching the sound of those soon to appear on the path, drove his heels into the horse's sides.

As Anglicus prepared to burst forward, Hawisa screamed, "Non!" and grasped its halter.

She should have swung her sword, but again she hesitated, which would have cost her all were he of a mind to spill her blood. Instead, her defeat would be paid in the currency of humiliation and discomfort, but she gave him no choice with rebels running to aid her.

Guarin raised his booted foot and thrust it against her collarbone.

She cried out, lost her grip on the halter, and fell backward. As she hit the ground, he jabbed his heels into Anglicus's sides and let the destrier run.

The rebels would follow, but not far if Normans were on Hawisa's lands. Thus, soon he would be back among his own and would himself learn the fate of his kin. And Hawisa's fear for her people?

He would not think on that now. Now was for riding hard and evading capture. Now was for putting the rebellious Dotter behind him. Now was for becoming his own man again.

~

CHEST ACHING, vision blurred by tears of anger and fear, Isa pushed her mount hard and cursed Guarin D'Argent for making this day the one in which he was done biding his time.

He was well out of sight, as was she from whichever rebel had mounted the third destrier to aid in retrieving her captive.

If only it were Vitalis, she wished, but she had sent him to deliver tidings to Jaxon's men who patrolled the eastern reaches of Wulfen.

An hour earlier, one of her housecarles had overtaken her hunting party and told a sizable contingent tasked with rooting out those responsible for the murder of the Norman family had arrived at Balduc. After sending Wulfrith back to the castle with the majority of her men, she had ridden to alert Jaxon and Vitalis.

Since this day's patrol was distant from the abbey, it was decided to return the men to camp if possible. Jaxon was well with that. What he was not in accord with was her determination the rebels hunker down to await the departure of the trespassers. Jaxon wanted Vitalis to send out sorties to harass William's men, but Vitalis agreed that would add to the belief the murderers could be found on Wulfenshire and cause the Normans to extend their search to the shire's farthest and deepest reaches.

"Please, Lord," Isa prayed into the air rushing past as she left the ravine behind. "We have no time to decamp and hide. Give loving answer to this as You would not upon Senlac. Help me stop Guarin ere he reveals us."

She reined in, sent her gaze around the land bordered on one side by wood, the other by rolling hills, and in between a meadow whose grass swayed, causing small, brightly-colored flowers amid the green to disappear and reappear.

There—movement at the wood's distant edge. A lustrous dark grey coat and pale mane, atop the destrier a rider of silvered dark hair come unbound.

"Cur! Knave! Miscreant!" she named him—and nearly added *poltroon*. But no coward was Guarin. He was a man and warrior unlike any she had known. A wolf.

Let him go, a voice urged as she pressed her mount to pursue the one entering the wood.

I cannot. If he reveals us—and why would he not?—we are all finished. More blood. More loss. And Wulf yet to be reunited with his sister.

"Wulfrith," she corrected as she neared where Guarin had disappeared among the trees.

Slowing, she guided her mount over ground to which Anglicus had set hooves and peered over her shoulder.

She longed to wait on the rebel coming to aid her, but the greater lead her prey gained could be the difference between overtaking him and not. Thus, she entered the wood of long shadows, sparingly pierced by sunlight forcing its way through the leaved canopy.

Look, listen, smell, taste, she commanded her senses, and as she visually narrowed her search for sight of Anglicus's pale mane, remembered the gold of her hair and drew from beneath her belt a black cap and donned it.

Deeper into the wood she ventured, chest aching more from worry and desperation than the thrust of Guarin's boot that momentarily stole her breath.

Catching no glimpse of the destrier she had made her own, nor of the Norman whom Jaxon had made her captive, she beseeched again, "Lord, forsake me not. Deliver him so I may..."

Finding her hand on her sword, she shuddered. Were she

capable of besting Guarin in the absence of aid and trickery, she did not think she could slay him—even to save the lives of many.

Then for what are you here? That voice again.

She shook her head, halted her mount upon hearing a sound that did not belong—metal on metal. In other circumstances, she would think it chain mail or a sword exiting its scabbard, but as Guarin was somewhere near and yet wore a manacle and several links of chain, it must be him.

She urged the destrier onward, and knowing she had little chance of bringing her prey to ground, whispered, "Lord, if I could but speak with him, persuade him…"

She muffled a laugh, silently demanded, *What? Persuade him to return to camp, once more submit to chain and manacle and suffer punishment Jaxon and his followers will demand that could see him dead?*

Futile, and yet she swept her gaze all around in search of him.

"Halt, you!"

The command came from the right, the words and accent Norman-French, but not Guarin's, and when she peered over her shoulder, she saw a mail-clad warrior riding at her.

Her first concern for how near William's men were to the camp, she veered left and urged the destrier to greater speed, causing the trees and foliage to blur. She must draw him away, and if he overtook her, hope his discovery she was a woman rendered him vulnerable to her blade.

Though during Guarin's escape she had been unable to bring herself to wield her sword against his, this unknown Norman who had likely killed, ravaged, and pillaged was a different matter.

"Halt!" he called again, and she assured herself the Wulfrith in her who had slain William's *companion* could—and would—shed this enemy's blood.

She heard what sounded a whistle, gasped when pain tore through her shoulder.

Bereft of breath, she lowered her chin. She could not see what protruded above her collarbone, but she did not doubt an iron tip responsible for the glistening crimson spreading down her tunic.

First blood to the Norman. And more would go to him and others of his ilk if she did not escape. Were the Lady of Wulfen revealed as a traitor to the one who named himself King of England, her lands would be scoured, rebels discovered, all forfeited.

"Lord!" she beseeched, then demanded of her mount what Anglicus could have given—and had, carrying Guarin away from captivity. Away from her.

CHAPTER NINETEEN

*H*ow many times must he curse himself for being Hawisa Wulfrithdotter's fool before he let be what would be?

Once more and never again, he angrily vowed, then spurred Anglicus out from behind the trees where he had taken cover upon realizing he was not alone. He had prayed he shared the wood with Normans rather than Vitalis or the rebel patrol, but no sooner was that prayer answered than Hawisa appeared and drew the attention of the one who put an arrow through her.

Shortly, he drew alongside Hawisa whose chin was down, a white-knuckled hand on the saddle's pommel, the other shaking on the reins she gripped.

As the Norman once more commanded the quarry that had become two to halt, Guarin said, "I am here, Hawisa," and leaned to the side, hooked an arm around her, and dragged her onto his mount. If not for the arrow protruding from her back that forced him to position her sideways to avoid jostling the shaft, the transfer would have been almost effortless—and if not for Anglicus's protest.

The destrier whinnied and veered right, its skittishness

proving fortuitous when an arrow streaked to the left of Guarin and embedded in a tree. But as that turn decreased the distance between pursuer and pursued, which could see the next draw of the bow land an arrow to Guarin's back, the Norman would have to be slowed.

Guarin pulled the dagger from his boot, reined around, and as the soldier nocked another arrow, flung the blade. And prayed his fellow Norman stayed the course to ensure the dagger did not pierce his heart.

The blade landed true, causing their pursuer to reel backward. Dagger protruding from his upper arm, he stayed the saddle by releasing the bow and turning his efforts to bringing his mount under control.

"Pray," Hawisa choked, "do not let him see it is me."

"Silence!" Guarin growled and turned Anglicus forward and applied his heels. He knew what Hawisa feared. If she fell into Norman hands, she would be recognized and much would be made of her attire and attempt to outride the Norman. Were she not already suspected of supporting the rebels, she would be—and likely blamed for the deaths of the Norman family. At the least, she would lose whatever property she retained, at the worst, her life.

She lifted her head, and as she dropped it back, the cap slipped off, revealing a surfeit of golden hair and—blessedly—no spill of blood from her lips. "My people!"

"Still your tongue, else I will myself fit you with chains."

"I would not begrudge you," she rasped, then her head rolled and settled on his shoulder.

He had no time to determine her state of consciousness, a glance behind revealing more Normans who rode past the injured one.

Though Anglicus now carried two, the destrier outdistanced their pursuers, but as Guarin did not know the lay of Wulfenshire, it was no guarantee of escape. Hoping Hawisa had acquainted the beast with more than the ride between her home and camp, Guarin let it choose its path. And thanked the Lord each time he looked behind and saw the Normans fell farther behind. Then they went from sight.

It was a quarter hour before Guarin slowed Anglicus. Ribs heaving, the horse continued to a stream and halted to take water.

Knowing it would be difficult to dismount but must be done to determine how best to aid Hawisa, Guarin was relieved when she raised her head from his shoulder.

"You lost them?" she slurred.

Looking near on the arrowhead come through her tunic, so coated in blood little iron was visible, he said, "I did, as predicted once more keeping you from the king's wrath."

She moaned low. "Oui, but also you told you would...bring the Lady of Wulfen into the Norman fold. Never."

Very possible, but for her and her people's sake, he hoped she would accept William as her sovereign.

She forced up lowering lids. "I thank you for not abandoning me to my enemy. You are not the same as them. You are...one of us."

Her words should have offended like a slap, but something stopped them from leaving a mark on unsuspecting flesh. "I am not one of you," he growled. "I am Norman and shall ever be."

"Not Guarin D'Argent who wished the company of this Saxon."

For which he had motive, though that was not all. Each passing of six days had been more tolerable knowing at the end of the seventh they would speak outside the cave. He frowned. "Why no rope this day, Hawisa?"

"The last time we met, I sensed soon you would attempt an escape and thought to decrease the risk by...speaking with you inside the cave. But ever the greatest risk has been letting you off your chains."

Feeling the manacles' grip, hearing the links rattle, Guarin gnashed his teeth and set her hand on the saddle's pommel. "Hold while I dismount."

Once he was on the ground, he lifted her down. Though she had to be in great pain, a whimper was the only sound she made as he lowered her onto her side on the moss-covered bank.

He dropped to his haunches at her back, bent forward, and peered into her face. "I am no physician, so I dare not remove the arrow, but I will snap it near its entrance so the wound can be bound and more swift the ride to one capable of tending you."

She looked sidelong at him. "Wulfen Castle. My physician is there."

And further captivity, he thought. Still, he would risk it to save her, delivering her as near as possible, placing her on the ground, and alerting those on the wall. Then Anglicus would carry him away.

That was the plan. If it ended as well as the one which this day saw him freed, soon he would return to Normandy.

"I must raise your tunic, Hawisa."

"You may."

When he exposed skin that was smooth as if carved from ivory and of that same creamy color but for the streak of blood reaching to her chausses, she shuddered. And Guarin, struck by the impulse to press his lips to that lovely back and murmur assurances against quivering skin, wondered if he had been wooed more than she.

I will free myself of the hold she has on me, he told himself, then raised the tunic higher.

She lived only because the arrow had entered high to the right of her shoulder blade and exited above her collarbone. It did not mean she would survive, but greater the chance since it appeared nothing vital was pierced.

"Once I have fashioned bandages to bind the wound, I will snap the shaft," he said, then cut two strips from his tunic's hem and tied them together. As he washed the foul from them in the stream's chill water, he felt Hawisa's gaze.

"I do not know how near William's men, but long they will search for us," he said when he returned to her and presented the wet branch taken from the stream bed. "I will be as gentle as possible, but the pain you feel now will be worse."

She parted her teeth, and he fit the wood between them in the hope she would bite hard enough to crack a tooth were it required to keep her scream from alerting her enemy.

"Be Boudica for me," he said.

A weak laugh slipped from her, and he knelt at her back. Closing one hand low on the arrow's shaft, he curled the other directly above it.

She stiffened.

Knowing the more relaxed she was, the less possibility of a violent reaction that could cause further injury, he sought something with which to distract her. And could think of only what had often distracted him when the walls of the cave closed in.

He leaned down and put his mouth near her ear. "Never shall I forget how it felt to hold you, Hawisa Wulfrithdotter."

She drew a sharp breath.

"Your feet upon my feet."

She turned her face toward his.

"Your back to my chest."

Grey eyes searched green.

"Your heartbeat matching mine."

Her tension eased.

"Your scent filling me."

A soft breath slipped past the branch between her teeth.

"And neither would I have *you* forget how it felt to be held, Hawisa."

She made a mewl of surrender, and the muscles of her back softened.

Lest any sudden movement cause her to tense again, Guarin made do with the awkward leverage of bending near and snapped the shaft between his hands.

She convulsed, eyes slammed closed, teeth clenched on the branch, tears squeezed past her lids.

"The worst is over," he said, and though he knew he should not, pressed his lips to the outer corner of her eye. "Now all you must do is heal." A lie, since there remained the jarring ride to return her to wherever Wulfen Castle lay, and more the lie if she did not heal well. But it was all the comfort he could offer.

The salt of her pain on his lips, he drew back, and when he saw she was conscious, hoped soon she would succumb to darkness so she would not suffer the binding of the wound—worse, the ride.

Her eyes fluttered open and the branch tumbled from her mouth. "Guarin? Pray, bandage me and...take me home."

"Cease struggling to remain present," he said. "The sooner you give over, the less your suffering."

"You do not know the way to Wulfen."

"Does Anglicus?"

"He does."

"Then rest."

"Bandage me."

He began binding her. Though he was gentle, she shook and was panting when he finished.

"Give over, Hawisa," he growled.

"Get me astride."

Silently cursing, he slid an arm around the middle of her back, the other beneath her knees, and eased her toward him.

She cried out and muffled the sound by pressing her mouth to his chest.

Certain soon she would lose consciousness, Guarin determined it best to wait and, sitting back, settled her atop his thighs.

For some moments, her deep exhales heated his skin through his tunic, then she lifted her face. "Take me home."

"First rest."

"I must—"

"Tell me about the son and husband lost to you." Though he did wish to know of them, he asked in the hope of sealing her lips as done each time he had ventured there.

Her eyes closed, but in her own language she whispered, "Wulf. None can replace my boy. Roger. I did not want him...did not love him...as he loved me. But I grew fond. The Norwegian invaders..." She shook her head. "Roger feared for us, sent us to the Penderys, while he...joined King Harold at Stamford Bridge."

Never suspecting he sent his wife and son into greater danger, Guarin mulled.

"I hurt when word came of his death. And more for how it pained our son. I...should have lied."

"Lied?"

Her lids rose. "Told Roger I loved him. Mayhap that was needed to bring him back to us. Had he lived, our son would not have sought revenge against...other invaders. Would not be dead." She gasped. "Dear Lord, the bane of regret. The same as grief, it is a disease one cannot sleep away."

A sob escaped her, and once more she closed her eyes. "I blamed my maid, Aelfled, for not...keeping better watch over him. But it was for me to protect him. I should have been with him, not abed. Weak. Unworthy." She began to cry.

Though Guarin knew her emotional pain was greater than the physical, he guessed the latter more greatly moved her body, making her sharp draws of breath sound around the wood.

He turned her face to his chest and touched his lips to the crown of her head. "Give over, Hawisa, and all the sooner you will be home."

Her outpouring ebbed, and when it was barely a hiccough, he raised his head.

She peered at him through the glazed eyes of one descending into sleep from which they would not be roused easily. "Never have I hurt so much." She lowered her gaze to his mouth, shifted it to the side, then raised a hand and drew his hair through her fingers. "I wondered how silver would feel. This wolf's hair is not coarse. It is soft."

Feeling a stirring inappropriate at this time, this place, and with this woman, he said, "You must rest. All will be better when—"

"Tell me I am dying."

"You are not. Why would you wish to hear such?"

"So I might greatly err but one last time." She moved her hand to his jaw. "This time without regret."

"What say you?"

"Neither my head nor heart is right." Again, she looked to his mouth. "It is long since I was kissed, and also I wonder…" As he tensed further, she moved her thumb beneath his lower lip. "Tell me I am dying."

That he would not do even if she begged. Nor would he kiss her as she invited only in the hope she would not live long enough to regret that intimacy with him.

Her lids fluttered. "Too long, Guarin." She lifted her face, offering her mouth.

He came the rest of the way, so lightly touching his lips to hers it was possible he did not. But a moment later there was no doubt about it, whether she raised her face higher or he set his nearer.

He did not expect her to return his kiss, and she did not, but she murmured, "I wonder no more."

Guarin drew back and saw the glitter of her eyes between narrowed lids. "I *will* get you back to your people, Hawisa. You will not die. You will live again, smile again, your years many and blessed."

When her head lolled against his shoulder, he pressed a hand between her breasts to confirm her heart beat. Feeling it, he wondered if she would remember the joining of their mouths and how that intimacy came to be.

But what mattered now was delivering her to the castle, every minute saved or lost a step toward life or death. Careful not to disturb what remained of the shaft protruding from her back, he enfolded her and stood.

Anglicus raised his head from the grass and eyed their advance.

Guarin halted at the destrier's neck. "We have done this before, old friend. We can do it again."

The beast nickered.

As upon Senlac, it was difficult getting them both astride, and Guarin was grateful Hawisa remained oblivious the same as when he had been forced to land a fist to her jaw.

Once Anglicus resumed their journey, hopefully toward the castle, the sun too directly overhead to determine east from west and north from south, Guarin considered Hawisa. She looked as if she belonged in his arms. She did not, and yet he was struck by the thought that though he would leave her this day, never would he be shed of her.

More disturbing was the hope, fleeting though he rendered it, that thought would prove true. It was a Norman lady he was destined to wed, not a Saxon.

CHAPTER TWENTY

*O*nce more you deliver yourself into the hands of your enemy, Guarin rebuked as Jaxon's patrol sent out this morn sprang all around near the edge of the wood he had moments earlier realized bordered the ravine. The Norman-bred Anglicus had failed him. But then, it was to Hawisa he now bowed.

Guarin looked to Vitalis who had been sent to bring back the patrol, then the woman who had thrice regained and as many times lost consciousness as Anglicus negotiated the wood. "Captive again," he murmured and knew this time and this stand could be his last. "For you, my lady."

Regret served itself a generous portion of Guarin D'Argent. Hawisa had named regret a disease, but though he was afflicted with such, he knew he would feel more regret had his escape ended in her own capture or death. If only she had not pursued him…

He returned his gaze to the five circling him. From their expressions, there was no question fear of threat to their lady kept them from slaughtering him—as done the Norman family—and fear of Vitalis.

Wrathful eyes moving between Hawisa and the one once more

her captive, the warrior commanded the others to keep their distance and urged his mount forward.

Though Guarin's own anger and pride protested defending himself, the need to survive demanded it, citing that if there existed even a sliver of opportunity to escape, it was in this direction.

"It was not my arrow that pierced her." He nudged Anglicus around to keep Vitalis directly in front of him. "She was pursued by the king's men. Though I am at fault, having done what you yourself would have and causing her to pursue me, I return your lady to you. I tended her injury as best I could and believe she will live, but she is in need of a physician."

Vitalis halted his destrier before Anglicus, looked nearer on Hawisa, back at Guarin. Were he a dog, he would be frothing in anticipation of sinking his fangs into his enemy. "You know what is required of you, Norman!"

Keeping one arm around Hawisa, Guarin drew the sword from beneath his belt and tossed it on moldering leaves gathered amongst an ancient tree's roots. Next, he lifted Hawisa's scabbarded sword and dagger whose belt he had hung from the saddle and cast them down.

"I shall come alongside, and you will pass the lady to me," Vitalis said. "Speak wrong, breathe wrong, twitch wrong, and you are dead."

Unarmed, it was possible. Were his life's blood not spilt by this man, Jaxon's patrol would seize the opportunity and see it to its desired end.

The transfer of Hawisa was uneventful until Vitalis adjusted her seat between his thighs. She cried out, and her eyes flew open.

"Dullard!" Guarin named her man.

Vitalis showed teeth. "You are responsible for this."

"Guarin?" Hawisa's eyes searched the face above hers, swept around and landed on the one she sought.

"As promised, you are back among your own," he said. "Now rest, Lady."

Her lids lowered.

"Farewell, D'Argent," Vitalis said, and as he urged his destrier forward, called, "The Norman is yours to do with as you please!"

Immediately, Jaxon's men closed in on their prey who might soon breathe his last—but not alone.

Guarin looked to where he had tossed his sword, tensed in readiness to bring it to hand, and felt the destrier respond in kind.

"Do not, Vitalis!" Hawisa cried. "He is mine. To do with as *I* please."

Her man reined in. "My lady, he will try again and—"

"I have spoken. He is not to be harmed. Return him to camp."

Vitalis looked to Jaxon's men. "Does he resist, do what you must to subdue him, and that is all. Now I must deliver our lady to the physician."

Am I of a mood to resist? Guarin pondered as he had not since Hawisa discovered he was her captive and ended his beatings. Though reason told he should go peaceably, especially now a rebel had moved between him and his sword, what was left to one whose anger uncoiled at having once more sacrificed all for a woman? Too, at last here were worthy opponents upon whom to vent his wrath.

Once Vitalis went from sight, Jaxon's men showed they were also of a mood. But though provided opportunities to prove their fists superior to those of a warrior as fit as when he cut down Saxons upon Senlac, Guarin was subdued only when all united against him. Then he was bound, put over Anglicus's back, and returned to his prison.

~

Wulfenshire Rebel Camp
England

"YOU SHOULD NOT HAVE RESISTED," Vitalis said once Rosa departed the torch-lit cave.

Guarin shifted his single-eyed gaze from the entrance that had spit out the woman to the warrior who halted too near a chained man—providing the captive remained of a mind to resist.

He did not. On the first day of his second round of captivity, Guarin's anger and fists were fairly satisfied, but he hurt, blessedly not so much he needed to fit himself back together as when first this cave was his prison.

Settling against the cool rock wall where he had lowered to allow Rosa to tend him, he said, "You knew I would resist."

Vitalis raised his eyebrows. "I did."

Guarin lifted the cup of water Rosa had poured him, drank.

"For all your supposed concern," Vitalis said, "you do not ask after Lady Hawisa."

Guarin cracked open the swollen eye bruised and closed by Jaxon who would have landed more blows had not his men repeated Hawisa's command the Norman not be harmed. "Supposed... concern..." he tested the words, then considered the bruises on chest and arms to which Rosa had applied salve after cursing him for his betrayal and endangerment of those who sought to take back their country.

She was more hurt than angry, he was certain—that he had used her to gain his escape, resulting in injury to her lady. Some of her hatred had resurfaced, but it seemed forced. And proof of that was given when one of Vitalis's men appeared and demanded to know who had sent her. She had rounded on him, told she sent herself, and warned if he wished her gone, he would require another's aid.

The man had departed and not returned. Though Rosa had been rough in her ministrations, he did not think a single scratch, cut, or bruise had not been tended.

Vitalis stepped nearer. "Put the question to me."

"For what? I know your lady lives."

"How?"

The stretch of Guarin's smile stung, his lower lip split open above where Hawisa had pressed her thumb. "I am chained, of no great threat nor challenge. Your sword remains sheathed, as does *my* dagger." He looked to the latter. "That you have not cut my throat means she shall recover."

The Saxon warrior dropped to his haunches. "My lady would have me deliver a message."

Hating how muddled his mind, wondering how muddled hers —if she remembered what he had said to distract her from the arrow's snap, how long he had held and encouraged her to yield to senselessness, most of all their kiss—Guarin said, "I am in need of sleep."

Vitalis clasped his hands between his knees. "She regrets your captivity, says she would release you did she not fear for her people."

As already he knew.

"She regrets all you have suffered in service to her. She regrets, henceforth, you are to remain chained in the cave. She regrets it may be many months ere your people surrender the crown and take you back across the narrow sea."

Months, Guarin silently scorned. *Years, Hawisa. If ever. Though you refuse to accept how wily, tenacious, and brutal your new king, those who continue to test him will reap the most bitter harvest.*

"So many regrets they sound a disease," he said, then tipped his head back and peered at the man who, though his land was conquered, did as he willed in the absence of fetters.

Is this resentment? Guarin questioned. It was. *Is this jealousy?* It was. *Anger?* Undoubtedly. And all hungered.

Not caring what price he paid for feeding dark emotions, he said, "As your lady is not dying, do you think she also regrets asking me to kiss her?"

The man's face darkened, and the hands he clasped went white. "You lie."

"I do not believe she regrets it," Guarin said. "What was it she spoke when she refused your sentence of death? He is mine. To do with as *I* please."

Vitalis made one of his hands into a fist, moved his thumb across the knuckles. Then he straightened. "I would put to my lady whether she regrets asking that of you were it not cruel to speak of things done whilst one is too senseless to think right, be it from a great quantity of drink or loss of blood."

But would he dare ask what had come of her request? Guarin pondered. And decided he would not provide the answer. Though not proud of the resentment and jealousy gripping him, he was not ready to repent—did not know when he might sincerely beseech forgiveness for ungodly feelings and thoughts.

"Per my lady's instructions, you are to remain under watch of my men." Vitalis turned away, moments later stepped into the maw of night.

CHAPTER TWENTY-ONE

Wulfen Castle, England
Summer, 1068

She had named the boy Wulf again, then quickly turned aside so she not suffer his smile. He could not replace her son, but a great comfort he had been these weeks of confinement. Long hours he had sat by her bed, speaking of progress made in his training at arms, demonstrating growing proficiency with the written word while reading from her psalter, and telling of his life before this one.

Though that last made her yearn to reunite him with the sister whom he remained unaware was near and of aid to the rebels, she could not. But God willing, soon. Until then, he would become worthier of defending family and country—and this day accompany her across Wulfen.

Anxious for her people though Vitalis assured her all was well in the villages and camp, Isa was done heeding the physician's order to remain abed. Three weeks had passed since the arrival of William's men, and now a sennight since their departure. Only a single confrontation of any account could be reported to their king—that of one who was thought to be a man beneath cap, tunic, and chausses whose escape was aided by one most believed a fellow Saxon.

Most. Not Theriot D'Argent.

Long-haired and bearded though Isa's savior had been, the silvered hair of a man far from aged had been reported to the keeper of Stern. Believing it his lost brother, several times he and his men had searched Wulfenshire.

"My lady?"

She forced a smile to clear worry from the boy's brow. "That is all."

He hastened from the solar to deliver orders to her housecarles to prepare to ride.

As the curtains swung closed, her thoughts moved to Guarin who often filled them though ever she pushed him away with the reminder Vitalis would ensure he did not escape again—nor suffer Jaxon's men—but as usual, Guarin pushed back.

Just as when she had demanded the truth come out from behind Vitalis's eyes, she felt a stab that once more her savior paid more than the price of captivity for aiding her, this time in the Wulfenshire wood when left with the patrol so Vitalis could deliver her to the physician.

Because Guarin had resisted, her man had assured her, too that his injuries were dealt by fists and no more severe than those he dealt Jaxon's men. And just as the rebels soon recovered, so had he.

"Still, I do not know I can face him," she whispered. But she would. Determined to unburden her conscience, she swept open her clothes chest. And gasped, let the lid drop, and pressed a hand above her collarbone.

The physician told she healed well, but here evidence beyond what had become dull discomfort that it would be months before she regained what she had lost to an arrow.

A glance at the tousled bedclothes was the beginning and end of all consideration to suffer further idleness. Beyond her meeting with Guarin, matters long-neglected must be addressed—rallying the rebels, coordinating efforts to resume harassment of Campagnon who had resumed persecution of the people of Balduc with the departure of William's men, visiting villages to assure her people she had not abandoned them, establishing contact with agents in Lincolnshire and Nottinghamshire who would purchase Balduc hay and grain crops that appeared lost to the scythe of fire, and inspecting the passage believed to have reached the wood.

She must move slowly and carefully, that was all.

It was not all. But two hours later, she and a bright-eyed Wulfrith reined in ahead of their escort and dismounted.

As expected, Vitalis was not pleased to see her, eyes ablaze, a jerk in the stride carrying him down the path. "You ought to be abed, my lady."

The jostle of the ride having made her grateful for the pound of hooves masking groans and whimpers, there was no way to hide she hurt, only the extent. Fortunately, neither Wulfrith nor her escort knew how great her distress since she had led throughout.

Isa had yet to look to the cave, and she did not now, the man who halted before her having two days past questioned her feelings for Guarin after reporting on the rebels and state of the demesne.

He feared she was captivated by the Norman. As did she—and wished she had no cause. But throughout her days abed, something wonderfully calming yet fearfully exciting had teetered on the ledge between things remembered and things forgotten. Having thus far refused to pull it off the ledge for scrutiny, her heart beat faster in anticipation of doing so—and certainty Guarin had heard her arrival and awaited her appearance.

"My lady?" Vitalis said.

Though it hurt to press her shoulders back and stand taller, she forced a smile. "Fear not, I am much improved."

To ensure his next words did not reach her entourage nor the half dozen rebels present, he bent near, causing his bound auburn hair to shift across his shoulder. "For all your exertions, you are more grey than flushed, my lady. You may fool others, but I know how much the ride cost you."

"I thank you for your concern, but I am well enough recovered to resume the duties owed my people."

His nostrils dilated. "You risk undoing these weeks of healing. Do you worsen—"

"Better I know my body than you." Though not much, she silently acceded, certain already she had undone some healing. But she also knew she was needed here, and she knew her man. Thus, all was not as well as he told. "As there is much to do ere we ride on the villages, I give Wulfrith into your keeping." She nodded at the boy who toed the dirt. "Show him all that has been accomplished here to aid in taking back our country."

"Whilst you do what?"

He knew what, but she said, "I would see how our prisoner fares," and began unhooking the gown fashioned for ease of removal when she concealed men's garments beneath. Rather than loosen side or back laces to draw the garment off over her head, she had only to unfasten hooks running bodice to hem and exit it the same as a mantle.

"As told, my lady, D'Argent is long healed."

"Still, I shall meet with him."

"His mood is foul this day."

"Considering his state of captivity, that does not surprise." She folded the gown, shoved it in her saddlebag, and turned away. As she strode toward the cave, she called over her shoulder, "Inform Jaxon I shall meet with you both an hour hence."

Silence, then she heard Vitalis direct her escort to stable the horses and the boy to follow.

"Remain outside," she directed the men at the cave and stepped past them.

Isa was grateful the rocky interior was well lit by torches and daylight, requiring no adjustment to the dim to permit her to look upon Guarin where he stood facing her.

As she advanced, stepping lightly to keep discomfort from her face, that which perched on the ledge between remembering and forgetting caused her mouth to go dry. Fortunately—or perhaps not—she was distracted by the strength of the wolf's anger. But though the dark upon Guarin's face tempted her to stay this side of the rock, she continued forward and halted before him.

Foolish? She was, even if, in the absence of escape by way of threat to her, vengeance did not move him to harm her.

He looked well, no evidence of injury about the face nor neck, the muscles of his chest defined beneath a damp tunic. Since the cave was not warm enough to account for the material clinging to him and he lacked the cast of one taken with fever, she guessed her arrival had interrupted exercises that prepared him for his next escape.

Eyes further adjusting to the dim, she noted something else about his tunic. It was stained down the left side. Her blood.

She swallowed "I am sorry, Guarin."

"Yet more regret," he drawled. "Perhaps it is, indeed, the disease you named it in the wood."

Had she? Remembrance returning her to the stream, trees, scent of loam and that of the man she had pursued, she felt Guarin's arms around her, saw his face above hers, heard him urge her to give over. And in that same wood, she heard herself speak of the bane of regret, then feeling...

That ledge again, something she did not wish to remember but neither to forget. "Regret *can* become a disease," she said softly.

"Especially when it is as great and numbers as many as yours."

Which she had added to in tasking Vitalis with delivering her regrets to Guarin after the physician closed up her wound.

"And when it is as great and numbers as many as mine," he added.

She lowered her gaze. And hesitated over his mouth.

"Do you regret *that* as well, Hawisa Wulfrithdotter?"

The image that leapt to the side of things remembered was dim, but not the wonderfully calming and fearfully exciting sensation. She looked up. "You kissed me."

"As beseeched."

She swallowed denial. Though she could not recall all that had gone between them, he did not speak false.

"That you not regret my kiss, you wished assurance you were not long for this life," he shook her memory. "And when I told you were not dying, still you offered your mouth. So I ask again, do you regret it, Hawisa?"

She could not lie, but she could not be entirely truthful. Confirming Vitalis's men kept their backs to the cave, she stepped near and set her palm on Guarin's chest. "What I regret is you are Norman."

He raised his eyebrows as if amused, but there was no lightness about him. "A better answer than expected."

Too much of an answer. Not only did she acknowledge she liked his kiss but wanted more beyond the sharing of breath. A match with Roger she had not wished—to walk at his side in day and lie at his side in night—but were Guarin a Saxon...

"What is it you want, Hawisa?"

Feeling his perspiration against her palm, the powerful movement of his heart beneath muscle and bone, she said, "Though now you have less chance of escape, I fear still you will try and next time forfeit your life. What I want is time to free you without risk to my people." She breathed deep. "I do not want you gone from this world."

"I am a Norman. Why does it matter?"

"As told, you are different from your countrymen. Pity my people there are not more like you, that you stand alone."

"I do not stand alone."

"Then why is there no end to our suffering?"

Her question softened the steel in his eyes. Here another reason she wished more like him. He was not cold to the plight of others, even that of his enemy.

"Who else stands with you, Guarin? Who else is as honorable?"

"Many, including those of my family."

She was inclined to believe it of the brother who had aided Aelfled, as well as Theriot who was a far better lord than Campagnon. But the others?

Realizing she veered in a direction she was not prepared to go, she tried to turn back, but she recalled this day's ride when she had looked around half expecting to see Wulf and laid eyes on a boy purchased at auction—all because of the most dishonorable of Normans.

She drew a deep breath. "You refer only to the living of your family."

"I speak of all D'Argents, those living and those lost."

"Even your uncle?"

He frowned. "What have you not told, Hawisa?"

Again she could not turn back. "Hugh D'Argent's death was not one due an honorable man."

Guarin had gone so still that only when his hand turned around her upper arm did she become aware of his chains. "Speak," he commanded.

"It was Aelfled who found my son upon Senlac. Her arms who held Wulf as he slipped away the same as the village boys who accompanied him to work vengeance on the invaders. She who confronted the chevalier who came looking for kin and found an aged warrior felled by boys whom he also felled."

Seeing disbelief replace Guarin's anger, she said, "It is so. The chevalier was Cyr D'Argent, the aged warrior your uncle."

Guarin gripped her other arm and drew her to her toes. "Never would he—"

Lest her cry rouse Vitalis's men, she clamped her lips closed.

For all his anger, he noted her response, but though he did not release her, he eased his grip and set her back.

She pressed a hand to the injury that had protested the bunching of her shoulders when he raised her.

"I did not mean to harm you," he said, then demanded, "What blind fool allowed you to take to the saddle?"

"I am neither blind nor a fool. What I am is sore. That is all."

He released one of her arms, lifted her chin into the light. "You have not regained your strength. I saw it in your stride and felt it in the tremble of your hand. But your eyes and face... You are far from recovered, Hawisa. You ought to be abed."

She pulled her chin free. "I am better acquainted with my body than you," she said and winced at the realization it was less true with Guarin than Vitalis to whom she had also made that claim.

Guarin swept aside the neck of her tunic and peered at the bandage. "I do not think you are better acquainted. You bleed."

Looking down, she glimpsed darkness against pale linen. "I did not know."

He slid the material back over her shoulder, released her other arm. "Go home and do not rise from bed until you are fully healed."

"My physician says I heal well."

"And yet, I vow he is displeased over what you do this day—else unaware."

The latter, but the former as well once he returned from the village where he sought to save the leg of a young man who was not as proficient with a scythe as believed.

"Guarin, I would have your word you will make no further attempt to escape, that you will bide with me so I may see you returned to your family."

"Bide with you?"

"It should not be much longer."

"What is long to you?" He jerked so hard on the chains she was certain the men outside peered within. "Another year and a half? Two?"

She asked much of him, but there was naught for it. "I am certain it will not be—"

"You are hopeful, not certain! Whereas I *am* certain—of William. Go home. When you are healed, we will speak."

Were he still here, he did not say. Hoping desperation would not provide Jaxon an excuse to end him, she departed, not to return home but to seek out the camp commander and Vitalis ahead of all else that must be done this day. This eve, the physician would admonish her, tend her, and accept her days abed had come to a close.

When Hawisa went from sight, Guarin gave a scornful laugh. Bide with her? Like a tame dog sit at her feet hoping for scraps that might never fall from her hand?

Should he find another opportunity for escape, he would take it—of greater urgency since her slow recovery meant more than before his life was in the hands of Vitalis and Jaxon. Providing the former stayed true to his lady, the warrior presented little threat, but as long as Guarin's greatest finery remained chains, he was prey for Jaxon.

He would bide, but not with the Saxon woman who would not likely give her body adequate time to heal. Just as neither would he were his world upended.

"Were?" he scoffed and laughed again.

CHAPTER TWENTY-TWO

Wulfenshire
England

*H*e came, the dust of hooves gently billowing above the road's distant rise and the slight vibration felt through thin-soled boots suggesting one of two things. Either he numbered far fewer than the two score reported, else he advanced at a leisurely pace.

The latter, Isa guessed where she concealed herself amid trees. She had sensed no lies about the Norman messengers Vitalis questioned. Too, a shrewd man in unfamiliar lands would be attentive to the lay of the road, hills, leas, and bordering wood during his first pass. Then there was the advantage of a disciplined progress. The less commotion a sizable entourage made, the sooner it would become aware of and prepare for an attack.

Not that they were in danger this day, Isa mused as she glanced around at what remained of her party, three of whom distantly kept watch over the intercepted messengers. Six strong, they were but a shadow of those whose training had been interrupted. A pity that, good progress having been made since dawn.

As confirmed often these three days since she arose from her sickbed, all was not well among her rebels. The division between those drawn to Jaxon and those to Vitalis had grown during her recovery. In the hope of uniting the two, she had taken a dozen each of the patrol and sortie for training in stealth.

Such great numbers in one place made them vulnerable, but less in the absence of Theriot D'Argent who had departed Stern with a sizable host to continue the search for his brother across the border in Lincolnshire. Though he was now more distant from where Guarin could be found, not so the approaching brother who came to take possession of lands stolen from the Lady of Wulfen.

An hour earlier, a contingent of Vitalis's and Jaxon's men challenged to steal past one another had been distracted by two of the enemy on fine horses and, yielding to temptation, taken them to ground.

Beaten, bound, blindfolded, and gagged, the Normans were brought to Isa. The missive they were to have delivered to Campagnon told that Cyr D'Argent and an escort of the king's men would require a night's lodging at Balduc. Most curious this since they bypassed Stern which would sooner see William's baron assume his lordship and offered more comfortable accommodations.

Hoping whatever was afoot proved ill for Campagnon and Em would send word soon, Isa had ordered nearly all her rebels to return to camp in parties of six, each taking a different route, while she remained behind to observe the Normans' passing.

"There." Vitalis jutted his chin at the rise where the dust birthed pennants, spear points, the heads of men and horses. The entire entourage—of the numbers reported and unhurriedly advancing—was visible before Isa could identify the silvered black hair among those at the fore. However, that marker was not of one D'Argent but two—perhaps three, the last less liberally adorning a woman. Regardless, only two were heretofore unknown. Though they were too distant to see well their faces, the size and bearing of one was offensively familiar. Here came Maël D'Argent, doubtless in command of the king's men.

Movement to the left drew Isa's regard to Sigward, whom she had ordered to remain behind to speak with him about Jaxon's visits with Gytha's man. He had raised his bow toward the distant Normans. She hesitated, certain he would not defy her command to kill only for the preservation of Saxon lives, but he drew back the string of a nocked arrow and sighted its flight—surely on one of silvered black hair.

"Nay!" She sprang toward him.

The fingers holding the string taut at his cheek were beginning to open when she snatched the bow's upper limb. The arrow released, not in the midst of heavily armed Normans but the leaved canopy.

"Accursed woman!" Jaxon's man spewed.

Another wrench, and she had the bow from him. "What do you—?"

He lunged at her.

"Sigward!" Vitalis roared.

Isa could have let her man defend her, and perhaps she should have considering how much this day's training made her ache, but she growled, "He is mine!" and dropped the bow and drew her dagger ahead of Sigward drawing his.

It seemed irony her one instruction with Jaxon gave her the greatest advantage over the rebel whose skills were mostly exclusive to the bow and his ability to scout. Before he could fully pull his blade from its scabbard, she dodged the fist he swung and delivered her own knuckles to his gut and an elbow to his jaw.

He stumbled back and hit the ground, then she was astride, pinning his upper arms, dagger to his throat. "How dare you!" she hissed, not for fear of being heard by the entourage whose advance provided adequate cover, but lest her voice carry to the captured messengers. "Regardless of whether you hit your mark, you would have incited them to turn their forces into the wood, revealing us and putting our lives at risk!"

That *was* the greatest reason for averting the arrow's flight, but her first thought had been for its target. More than many, Sigward was capable of piercing the neck above chain mail at a good distance. The possibility she would be responsible for the death of Guarin's brother who had aided Aelfled was intolerable.

"A worthy risk," Sigward snarled. "Half a dozen I could have bled ere they were upon us, among them their leader."

"Half a dozen Normans for half a dozen Saxons—among them *your* leader," Isa snapped.

Mouth contorted, he glanced at where Vitalis had halted alongside her. "Release me!"

He was dangerous, defiance of her edict and the hatred pulsing from him further proof of how precarious her command and the necessity of being present among her rebels.

"Get off me, Woman!"

"You will not disrespect our lady!" Vitalis barked.

"This is between Sigward and me," Isa reproached, then bent near the rebel. "You are of Wulfenshire. Wulfenshire is of Hawisa Wulfrithdotter. Either you follow your lady's orders or you leave. Are we of an understanding?"

He closed his lips over his teeth.

"Answer me!"

"We are of an understanding…my lady."

Dangerous, she reminded herself and slowly withdrew her dagger and rose. "Return to camp."

He was cautious in rising, and when he moved toward his bow, she said, "Leave it. And your arrows."

He struggled several moments, then removed the quiver from his back and handed it to her.

She jutted her chin in the direction of the camp. "Go." As he set off, she swept up the bow and gasped as pain lanced her injury.

"My lady?"

"'Twas only a twinge, Vitalis."

"You should be abed."

"How can you say that after what you just witnessed?"

"Your presence among our ranks is critical. Given a few more days to ensure—"

"I am well!" She removed an arrow, then hung quiver and bow over her uninjured shoulder. After a glance at the approaching entourage, she said, "Come," and ran to where the remaining rebels guarded the messengers.

Standing over the kneeling and blindfolded Normans, in the voice of an old woman, she instructed them to deliver an arrow to the Baron of Stern and inform him its absence from the merciless one's heart wiped clean her debt. Then she directed her men to hasten their captives ahead and out of the wood.

Minutes later, astride her destrier alongside Vitalis, the multitude of Normans having passed, she caught her breath as the enemy halted their progress at the appearance of bound and bedraggled men ahead.

"I think it a mistake," Vitalis murmured.

She also questioned the wisdom of what she had done. It was one thing to relieve the messengers of thick-soled boots, exchange their fine garments for threadbare ones, and cut their hair close to the scalp as done the novices, quite another to deliver her own message.

Still, it was no impulsive act sending an arrow to Guarin's brother other than by way of a bowstring. It was an act of mercy, warning him to guard his back so he not suffer being pierced the same as she. But her words...

Unless there were other Saxon women indebted to Guarin's brother, it was to Aelfled his thoughts would travel and the mother of the noble boy slain upon Senlac.

Lord, just as my body is slow to heal, so is my mind, she sought to converse with Him who had abandoned England. *Pray, heal me that I not fail my people while we dwell in this darkness absent Your grace and forgiveness.*

Pain above her collarbone making her aware she pressed a hand to it, she lowered her arm. But Vitalis had seen.

Before he could admonish her again, she said, "'Twas not a mistake. It was a threat, one he would be a fool not to heed."

"Threat? It sounded more a warning, an attempt to protect Guarin D'Argent's brother."

Pressing her lips, she returned her attention to the Normans who had not grown so distant she was unable to pick the D'Argents from amongst them. As revealed when the woman passed near, she was young. Though her hair was not as silvered as the men's, ten years hence it might be.

Was she the D'Argents' sister? Another cousin? Regardless, what impelled that family to bring her to this unsettled country? It was the same Isa had pondered upon learning Maël D'Argent had escorted his widowed mother to Stern six months past.

Almighty, how bold and fierce these Normans! Though she did not wish to believe Guarin's warning they were here to stay, there was little evidence otherwise. Gytha might not have abandoned hope of reclaiming the throne for her family, but her failure was so great her influence withered. As for Edwin Harwolfson, it was said his numbers remained insufficient to seriously challenge the conquerors. Would they ever be sizable enough?

"Please, Lord," she breathed as Sir Maël and the Baron of Stern broke from the party, rode ahead, and dismounted.

"'Tis time you returned to Wulfen," Vitalis said as the disgraced messengers were loosed.

She preferred he escort her to the abbey to warn Aelfled her savior had finally followed her to Wulfenshire, giving the young woman greater reason to be cautious when she stole away to visit her grandmother as she was forbidden to do. However, Isa was so fatigued her limbs quivered. And she hurt. Had the strain of this day's exercises undone her healing? Or but worsened that undoing?

Her throbbing injury had awakened her several times throughout the night, but she had arisen before dawn with no thought of altering her plans. And easier it had been to stay the course in the absence of opposition, the physician having taken ill after tending villagers laid abed with fever.

Did she bleed again? Might the peculiar scent hovering about her be infection? Were Vitalis not present, she would check her bandage for seepage.

Determining the morrow was soon enough to journey to Lillefarne, and all the better were there more to tell by way of Em, she said, "Let us ride," and turned the surefooted Anglicus toward Wulfen Castle.

CHAPTER TWENTY-THREE

Wulfen Castle
England

*F*ever. Pained joints. Infection. But so slight were they, Isa saw no reason to reveal her state to Vitalis who had passed the night at Wulfen Castle and escorted her to Lillefarne this day. However, having often felt his watchful gaze during the ride to and from the abbey, she knew he suspected. As had her former maid.

Entering Wulfen's great hall alongside her man, Isa cast back to her meeting with Aelfled. She had seen the concern on the young woman's face even before it was revealed her savior had arrived upon Wulfenshire. Only once had Aelfled's disquiet eased —over Em's tidings that Campagnon's inability to end the rebellion afflicting his lands had caused him to forfeit Balduc, and that barony had been added to Cyr D'Argent's award of Stern.

The same as her lady, Aelfled's relief was dampened by the king's proviso Campagnon remain in the capacity of castellan, administering Balduc for its new lord. Since its people would remain subject to his cruelties, Isa had instructed Aelfled to prepare to hide rebels at the next full moon when Balduc's hay would be taken, its concealing hedge and inner stubble set afire to make it appear an act of complete ruination.

The young woman did not like the role she played, but she would participate, and all the more willingly for worry over her lady.

Isa halted before the dais and turned to Vitalis. "Much gratitude for accompanying me. I pray your return to camp is uneventful."

He inclined his head, then startled the same as she when the floor shook and a low rumble sounded through the castle.

"Nay!" she gasped. Following the death of a worker and injury to several during the first months of the underground passage's construction, further precautions had been taken against collapse. Though it slowed progress, there had been only minor incidents since. *This* was nothing minor.

Isa sprang onto the dais and around the table. Followed by Vitalis, she swept aside the curtain and ran to the corner of the solar where a mist of dust drifted to the floor. Another rumble as she ducked behind the tapestry, a great exhalation of dust and dirt when she opened the passage's door.

She dragged her tunic up over nose and mouth and through its weave beseeched, "Dear Lord, preserve them!" Then narrowing her lids against the sting of dirt, she began her descent amid the glow of torches and the shouts of men in the bowels between castle and wood.

"Turn back, my lady," Vitalis urged. "I shall—"

"As shall I!" A moment later, she stumbled and he caught her up.

Then they were moving again, negotiating the stone-laid passage to that of carved-out dirt and rocks supported by hundreds of timbers and immense boulders and slabs that often forced the miners off a straight course. The deeper they went, the less light due to the thickening cloud of dirt and the blast of air and debris that had extinguished many torches.

Isa was gasping and coughing when they reached the first of those aiding the workers fallen beneath buckled timber. "How many?" she asked the man who dragged a groaning worker past.

"Four, my lady. Certes, two dead."

She clenched her hands. *Will You forever withhold forgiveness, Lord?* she silently questioned. *Forever delight in punishing my people?*

"Delight," she whispered. It was sacrilegious to think He enjoyed the Saxons' suffering. And might she also wrong Him by insinuating the collapse was His doing? Perhaps it was hers. Other than when her injury laid her abed, once a day she ventured into the underground to survey the progress and ensure the workers' wellbeing. Had she done so more often and closely supervised construction…

She breathed in dust-tainted air, once more lowered her mouth into her tunic's material, and continued forward.

Over the next hour, Vitalis and she labored alongside workers and men-at-arms to recover the other three pinned beneath the rubble. Blessedly, the deaths numbered no greater than the two, though one of the injured would ever limp—could his leg be saved.

Isa had just begun to aid in clearing the debris when pain pierced her upper chest, her head lightened, and she collapsed.

Vitalis swept her up, carried her to the solar, and summoned the physician. After the two spoke distant and low, her man returned to the underground.

"Fool woman!" admonished the physician who had arisen from his sickbed to tend the injured. "Accursed martyr. Irresponsible. Selfish."

She gasped. "I sought to—"

"Deprive your people of a worthy leader? Aye, you did."

"I am a Wulfrith," she said as he turned her onto her side. "'Tis my duty…" She coughed with such force, she nearly cried out.

"Your duty, my lady?" He pushed aside the shoulder of her gown, probed her injury. "To die the same as your son? To extinguish the Wulfrith line? Aye, that would make your sire proud."

She wanted to rebuke him but set her teeth and tightly closed her eyes.

Shortly, he pronounced she had further undone her healing and gave her a choice. "Remain abed and leave your people to fend for themselves a fortnight, else stay the course and leave them to fend for themselves the remainder of their lives."

She swallowed hard. "I shall remain abed."

He jerked his chin, then left her to prayers for those dead and injured in her bid to provide the castle folk a means of escaping the enemy, a loss that could have been prevented.

Not so, according to Vitalis when he reappeared, so dusted with dirt the auburn of his hair looked brown.

Isa eased up the pillows, peered at him where he halted alongside the bed. "If not faulty construction, what?"

"An argument between the two who died. Before the others could intercede, their words became fists and their brawl knocked out several timbers."

"Dear Lord." She pushed a hand through her tangled hair. "What was their argument?"

"One tried to convince the other continued resistance was futile, that countless more lives would be lost if Saxons did not accept Norman rule. The other named him a coward and threatened to kill him."

Struggling against the comfort of tears, Isa said, "Now two Saxons dead, and no Norman in sight."

"And the hope of breaking into the wood a sennight hence lost," Vitalis said. "'Twill take days to remove the debris choking the passage, then the timbers must be set aright."

Wasted effort? she wondered. More lives lost to such arguments? "Of the men who died, who do you think right,

Vitalis? He who would have us stop resisting the conquerors or the one who would have us throw them off no matter the price paid in Saxon blood?"

He shook his head. "I have no doubt of Jaxon's answer, but I have none, my lady. Because it is too soon to determine? I am too stubborn to accept Norman rule? I am too ignorant to know?" He shrugged. "The only answer I can give is assurance I shall stay your side no matter *your* answer."

Isa wished it was his Saxon arms she wanted around her, his chest beneath her cheek, his words in her ear. But they were not. "I thank you, my friend. Now I shall sleep."

He bowed and started toward the curtains.

"Vitalis!"

"My lady?"

"Keep Guarin D'Argent safe."

"As ever, though much depends on how safe he wishes to be."

Following his departure, she tried to sleep, but her thoughts were too cluttered with memories of this day's losses and the losses of all the days stretching back to when a warrior of silvered hair forced his way into her life—the day she had feared her son would prove her greatest loss. And so he had...

Was Guarin D'Argent right? Was her fight for naught? Despite Saxon resistance, William had been making his formidable self known to England for nearly two years, and there looked to be no end to his rule beyond the hope Edwin Harwolfson could rally enough Saxons to send the invaders back to Normandy.

Should she cease resisting? Accept him as her sovereign? Other Saxons would not, among them Gytha and Jaxon. If Isa withdrew from the resistance, she would have to watch her back the same as Normans lest the next arrow or blade was delivered by one of her own. And if her report of Wulfen crops being burned became reality, more her people would suffer.

Staring at the solar's darkening ceiling, she pleaded, "What am I to do, Lord? What is England to do? Is our punishment

219

insufficient to end this terrible season? Or is the Norman way the only way forward? Joining with our enemy the only means of surviving?"

She waited, but when one hour passed into the next and she neither heard nor saw nor felt the answer, she determined to sleep away her pain.

As she began to drift, she heard a voice, glimpsed a face, felt a presence. "Guarin?" she breathed. He was only memory, but she wished he were here to further persuade her of the direction she should go. If any could, it was he who had a care for her as he ought not. As she had a care for him...

CHAPTER TWENTY-FOUR

*M*uch had transpired since she sent the arrow to Cyr D'Argent six days past. Or was it seven? Did it matter?

It did.

Seated in the high seat carried to the hearth to evidence the Lady of Wulfen was truly ill as long feigned, Isa fixed her gaze on the doors across the hall. As she waited for them to belch forth Cyr and Maël D'Argent, she recounted events to place herself in time over which a grey haze persisted.

Aye, seven days since the Baron of Stern's arrival. Six since the passage's collapse and the beginning of her confinement for healing. Three since Cyr D'Argent confronted Aelfled at the abbey and tried to return the arrow she rejected. One since he had overseen the harvesting of Balduc's hay before its time as if warned he would lose it.

That last had nearly incited Isa to climb out bed. Instead, she had sent Vitalis to collect Aelfled on the night past, though not until this morn had she felt well enough to grant the young woman an audience.

Aelfled had confessed to impulsively warning Cyr D'Argent to bring in his hay during their reunion, then told he had come to her a second time during that harvesting. It was then he voiced suspicion the Lady of Wulfen was Dotter and asked Aelfled to deliver terms of surrender to the rebels.

An air about the young woman and her defense of the Norman had caused Isa to ask if the two had been intimate. Aelfled had confessed to a kiss and assured her lady it would not happen again.

All of great concern, especially D'Argent's terms of surrender —if by summer's end the rebels disbanded and returned to their homes, all would be pardoned providing they surrendered those responsible for the murder of the Norman family. Nearly impossible were they not Jaxon's men, impossible were they.

Vitalis was less inclined to trust Aelfled, but he was no Jaxon. As angry as he was with Isa's former maid, he would accept the forgiveness his lady extended to one whose actions were born of a longing to end this soul-eating unrest.

At the end of their meeting, Isa had encouraged Aelfled the same as Gytha had in her first missive to remember and embrace who she was—a Saxon strong of mind, body, and spirit—then extracted a promise that for penance due Wulf, Aelfled would act the woman and not the fanciful girl who had allowed the enemy to seduce her.

As Isa had watched her depart, naming herself a hypocrite for allowing her own heart to be moved by a D'Argent, Vitalis appeared with tidings two of that family were outside her walls. Now they were minutes from being inside.

She glanced across her shoulder at where the boy who every day grew nearer a man stood erect. If not this day, soon she would be called to account for him. Regardless, both were prepared for the tale she would spin to prevent Normans from thieving what remained to her.

She drew close her robe's lapels, smoothed the coverlet tucked around hips and legs, reached to her hair. And dropped her hand back to her lap. That which Roger had loved was unsightly, long without benefit of soap and the ordering of a comb, but as with her feigned illness that had become reality, it would serve the encounter to come. She could not appear less the lady and leader of rebels had she set all her mind and resources to it.

Confirming her housecarles and servants were strategically positioned around the hall, she returned her regard to the doors.

Shortly, there came the sound of boots on the steps outside, and she raised a staying hand to the porter. When silence once more descended, she inclined her head. It was time to meet her fourth D'Argent and once more face the second.

Unlike when first her home was sullied by the usurper's men, the helmets of these warriors were removed in advance of their entrance. Thus, immediately she confirmed the only ones of import were two followed by an escort of greater number than she would have allowed if not for the need to lessen the chance Vitalis and Aelfled were seen stealing away from the castle.

Long of thick muscle, broad of shoulder, silvered of hair, the D'Argents halted at a respectable distance.

Out of a ruined face less unsightly than the last time he was at Wulfen when the scars were more prominent and the surrounding flesh the color of anger, the king's man considered her.

Did Maël D'Argent see what he was meant to see? A widow wasted away from grief? Or did he see beyond her loss to the rebel leader who had strained an insufficiently healed body lest Jaxon wrest from her control over the Wulfenshire resistance? Did he see she who had trained when she ought not? Did he see she who had descended into the underground passage to recover the fallen?

"I am pleased to once more be welcomed into your home and presence, Lady Hawisa." The chevalier bowed curtly. "Allow me to present my cousin and your neighbor, the long-awaited Baron of Stern, Cyr D'Argent."

Discomfited more for how Aelfled's savior looked at the boy than his resemblance to Guarin, Isa cracked a smile. "Neighbor. In another life, my *vassal* and *keeper* of Stern."

He stepped forward. "I am honored to meet you, Lady Hawisa Wulfrith*dotter* Fortier."

Were she not so unmistakably ill, his emphasis on *dotter* would have alarmed though Aelfled had warned he suspected she was the rebel leader.

His bow was as short-lived as his cousin's, and when his gaze returned to her, she said, "It would be false to say *I* am honored, but..." Pain piercing her shoulder to breastbone, she drew a slow breath to dissolve the black dancing before her eyes. "...I am grateful for the aid you gave my maid upon Senlac."

His eyebrows rose as if in amusement, but his regret sounded genuine when he said, "I am sorry for your loss, Lady Hawisa, and that of the other mothers whose boys died. A great tragedy."

"For you as well—more, your cousin." She looked to that one. "Oui, Sir Maël, when first we met and you gave your surname, I knew it was your sire slain by mere children, but I was fairly certain you were unaware my son was one of those boys. I was correct?"

"Quite so." His brow rippled. "And now I am curious, my lady."

Grateful to have had time to construct a tale to explain the boy given the name of Wulfrith, she raised her eyebrows. "Well I know how uncomfortable—near painful—curiosity's itch, so how might I salve yours, Sir Maël?"

"All those boys died, including the noble amongst them, and as it is told you had one son with your Norman husband, who is this boy at your side?"

That boy, now conversant in Norman-French, stepped forward.

"Non, Wulfrith." She caught his arm. "It is for me to correct what this Norman insinuates."

"But my lady mother—"

"For me!" As if to punish her for being so harsh, once more pain tore through her, requiring all her will not to fold over herself. Out of the corner of her eye seeing Ordric draw nearer, she raised a hand and shook her head.

"My lady," Cyr D'Argent said, "perhaps you ought to rest. If you would provide our party with drink and viands, we will wait until you are better able to discuss those things which brought us to Wulfen."

Thereby delaying their departure...

She eased back and looked to the boy. Seeing apology in his eyes, she released him and returned her attention to the Baron of Stern. "Let us finish this now. I have not the stomach nor heart to prolong it."

Though she offended, curiosity turned his expression. "May I ask what ails you?"

She nearly refused, but she had yet to answer Sir Maël and here seemed a good place to deliver her carefully woven tale. "The physician knows not, so perhaps it is grief—for my eldest son, my husband, my country."

Cyr D'Argent's gaze sharpened, and a glance at his cousin revealed she had his attention as well, both having noted her use of the word *eldest*.

"Will it kill me?" She shrugged. "Time will reveal what only the Lord knows."

And now to display the fine threads of her tale. Angling her head at the boy, she said, "This is Wulfrith—he who, until his brother's passing, was named Alfrith. As is custom in many a Saxon noble family, the eldest son is given the name of his sire from whom he gains his inheritance. As these lands belonged to my family rather than my Norman husband, our son was named for my sire. As is also custom with my family, should the heir die or prove unworthy, his name is passed to the next in line who sheds the one given him at birth. So it was with my sons."

Sir Maël's brow pinched. "Inquiries were made, my lady, and

though most are unwilling to speak of your family, a few told you gave your husband but one child. So who lies?"

She raised her chin higher. "None."

"Then?"

"It is the superstition of the—" As if she had dropped the shuttle with which she worked her tale's threads, her words fell away. She coughed to open her throat, pressed fingers to her lips, reached to Ordric. Moments later, she sipped wine passed to her.

Throat soothed, she lowered the goblet. "As told, none lie. Superstition of the ignorant is the reason many believe I birthed only one son. Tell, Sir Maël, is your king so intolerant—even fearful—of those things rare that the educated might name him uneducated?"

"Certes, he is not, Lady Hawisa. No heathen *your* king."

"Then I need not fear for my Wulfrith whom I birthed minutes after his brother." She smiled, nodded. "He is a twin."

He looked nearer on the boy, as did his cousin who surely compared him to the one slain upon Senlac, noting he was considerably slighter of form than he ought to be for his age. But thus it could be for those who had shared only a womb and, at most, resembled the other.

She raised her eyebrows. "Naught to say, Sir Maël? Or, unlike your *educated* king, do you believe twins are of the devil?"

"I do not."

"I am relieved, though still there is that other belief twins are proof of a woman's adultery—two children, different fathers. Would you accuse me of such, deny half my Wulfrith's blood was drawn from your own little Norman stream?"

His narrowing lids revealing her barb pricked, he said, "I would not, but there remains the question of how none knew you bore two sons."

She sighed and shifted her gaze to his cousin. "Is it really so different in Normandy, Baron D'Argent?"

He raised an eyebrow.

Attempting to disguise growing discomfort as dwindling patience, she rolled her eyes. "Only those trusted knew I bore two sons—including my husband who cared enough for his reputation and mine to ensure neither of us was besmirched by the superstitious. Thus, Alfrith was raised by a trusted Saxon family and reclaimed when my eldest son—yet a mere boy though now he would be a young man—was murdered by your cowardly uncle."

The son of that man lurched toward her, and his cousin caught his arm. "Maël!" he said, and well he ought to control the king's man with her housecarles readying to defend her.

Withholding the signal they awaited, she reached to the boy. When he set his hand in hers, she drew it to her shoulder. So comforting was his touch, for a moment it seemed her lost son was at her side.

She swallowed hard. "Now, what other business have I with my *neighbor?*"

"Loose me," the king's man growled.

Cyr D'Argent hesitated, then did as bid and looked to Isa. "It is more the king's business than my own, though I am to oversee it."

"Speak."

He reached to his sword, and when her men stirred, slowed.

Though not surprised by what shared his blade's scabbard, Isa fixed confusion on her face. "An arrow, Baron?"

"Would you do me the kindness of looking near upon it?"

"For what?"

"To determine if you recognize it. A great service you would do your king to whom you have given your allegiance by aiding in returning this to the rebel who sent it to me."

She gave a snort that triggered a cough, took another sip of wine. "How would I know one arrow from another? I am no archer. I am a lady."

"You are also Wulfrithdotter. If all that is told of your family is true, I cannot believe you ignorant of weapons. My own sister, young though she is, has enjoyed the benefit of many brothers trained at arms."

Isa handed the goblet to Ordric, then affecting an air of boredom, motioned Aelfled's savior forward.

He came, but only near enough she had to reach to take the arrow. As she examined it, he said, "The message delivered with it was that it was intended for me and its absence from my heart wiped clean a debt owed. Thus, I thought your Aelfled sent it, but no longer."

She frowned. "Your belief that little mouse could be responsible tempts me to question how fit you are to hold and defend Stern, Baron."

Once more she offended, but something else glimmered in his eyes. Suspicion? Had she gone too far in naming Aelfled a mouse? It *was* on the bloodiest of battlefields he had first encountered her.

Lest Isa make another mistake, it was time they departed. "Non," she said and held out the arrow. "It is far more believable I had this delivered to you since I am hardly pleased my son's inheritance was greatly reduced to reward Normans."

"Then you are the rebel leader known as Dotter?"

He was not one for prolonging a game—*if* he deigned to play.

Wistfully, she said, "Oh, that I were. Such would have made my sire proud. However, as much as I dislike your William, for the sake of my son and people, I am now his subject the same as I was King Harold's and King Edward's before him. Thus, you may be assured an enemy does not dwell within these walls." She raised the arrow higher, extended it further, but he refused it.

"Regardless, my lady, the rebellion upon these lands must cease. Do they not, at summer's end King William will send an army to root out the rebels and no mercy will he show."

It was as difficult to continue playing a part as it was to sit erect, but she feigned the surprise of one delivered terrible, unexpected tidings.

"It is decreed that should the rebels disband and hand up those responsible for the murder of the Norman family," he continued, "without fear of reprisal they may return to their homes and resume their lives."

"Resume," she murmured and, aching over all that was lost that could never be regained even were the Normans ousted, lowered the arrow to her lap. "A generous offer. I pray it reaches those desperate men so they may act upon it. Too much and too long the people of Wulfenshire have suffered." She set her head to the side. "Are we finished, Baron? I am exhausted."

"One more thing. Have you word of my brother, Guarin? It is believed he was sighted on these lands a month past."

Though she had thought herself prepared for that, it was a struggle to maintain a passive expression. "I know only that your youngest brother is so certain it was this...Guarin, he neglects Stern to search for him. But chances are that just as I lost a son upon Senlac, you lost a brother—a difficult thing to accept in the absence of a body." Not that it was much easier in the presence of one, she thought, struck by memories of dragging her boy out of his shallow grave. Blinking back tears, she said, "As told, I am grateful for the aid you gave Aelfled in ensuring I knew my son's fate. I wish you good day."

Cyr D'Argent nodded. "We shall meet again, Lady Hawisa."

"Your arrow." She offered it again.

"I believe it is where it belongs, my lady. Good day." He and his cousin pivoted and strode toward the doors, followed by their escort.

Once they exited the hall, Isa closed her eyes. She ought not regret refusing them offer of drink and food, but she did. Unfortunately, what time she had given them had nearly depleted her.

"My lady?"

Dropping her head back, she met the boy's gaze and patted his hand. "You did very well, Wulf."

If not that each time she thoughtlessly named him that, his

eyes widened and he had to suppress a smile, she might not have realized she did so.

"I thank you, my lady."

She inclined her head, started to call for Ordric, instead said, "May I have the aid of your arm in returning to the solar?"

This smile he did not suppress. "Of course, my lady."

"Lady *mother*," she corrected, then lest he think too much of it, added, "The more 'tis spoken, the less likely either of us will trip over it in the presence of our enemies."

He nodded, and when she rose, drew nearer and set her hand on his arm.

Aided by one incapable of bearing as much weight as Ordric, it seemed a long walk to the solar, but he kept her steady. Retaining her robe against the chill prickling her limbs, she sank onto the bed and slowly turned to set her back against the pillows.

Clumsily, the boy lifted her lower legs onto the mattress and swept the covers over her.

Though Isa hated being made to feel helpless, she thanked him and lowered her lids.

Silence. Guessing whatever he wished to say could not wait, she looked to him. "Pray, speak."

He bobbed his chin. "Mayhap 'tis not for me to know, but will you give the Normans what they want?"

"What is it you think they want?"

"What remains of your lands, mayhap even your death and that of the Wulfrith line."

She nearly protested his conclusion, her thoughts having flown to the D'Argents rather than the Normans from whom they sprang. "That I will not do."

"Then you will heal so you may keep your people safe and ensure ever there is a Wulfrith in England—a hundred years hence, two hundred, three?"

That last would require either she become an instrument of Gytha or the one increasingly known as William the Great, wedding another she did not want and birthing another who could easily be snatched from her regardless of whether the unrest in England boiled or simmered.

Though the thought of another husband and child wounded, the boy's sincerity soothed. She caught up his hand. "I am abed where I do not wish to be. Am I not, Wulfrith?"

"Aye, my"—he cleared his throat—"lady mother, but I overheard the physician tell the cook 'tis a miracle you have remained abed this long and you are as likely to undo your healing again as you are to breathe."

She could not fault the man. "Be assured, Wulf, in the absence of great danger, I will follow his instructions the sooner to heal and keep my people safe."

He grinned, and she thought how handsome he would be once he left behind the awkwardness of youth. "Then I shall see Em again, will I not?"

She wished she could make that promise, but as long as his sister belonged to Campagnon, she could not. Just as she dare not reveal how near she was. "You have my word I will do all in my power to reunite you."

He drew her hand to his lips and kissed her knuckles. "And I shall continue to pray for you every day and every night, my lady mother."

Even if she knew how to respond, her throat was too tight to breathe life into words. Inclining her head, she drew her hand from his.

I am coming to love him, she thought as he strode from the solar. And nearly choked, not because the silent admission stank of betrayal but that it hardly seemed such.

Isa pressed the heel of a palm between her breasts. Despite how worn she felt, the beat of her heart was strong.

Still I am here, it seemed to say. *Fill my empty places, Hawisa Wulfrithdotter, and I will fill yours.*

CHAPTER TWENTY-FIVE

Wulfenshire Rebel Camp
England

*S*peak, Rosa."

Though she sealed her lips, she would reveal what he asked of her—and what he was certain she had come to tell. As ever, she required coaxing to relieve her of guilt over confiding in a Norman.

"Ill has befallen your lady, aye?"

Her widening eyes confirmation, Guarin wished he was concerned only for how it would affect the good amongst the rebels. But he saw Hawisa again, felt how well she fit his arms, recalled her mouth beneath his, and was moved as only she had ever moved him.

Muscles tightening beyond the rigor to which he had recently subjected them, he prompted, "She is too long absent to be well, Rosa. It has been..." He feigned numbering the days since telling Hawisa to go home and heal. Was she gravely ill because she had not? Likely. Her leadership of the rebels on shifting sand, only the inability to rise from bed would keep her from doing so.

Hoping he did not know her as well as believed, he said, "It has been a fortnight since she was here, aye?"

Rosa's brow cramped. "I believe."

Fifteen days, he silently corrected. Feeling every tedious sunrise in this loathsome cave, he shifted on the folded mantle that had long lost the scent of its owner and eased back against the cool stone. "Tell, Rosa, else leave me to my own good company."

Her teeth plucked at her lower lip, then she stepped alongside and lowered to sitting. "I know not all, but what I do know took much effort to listen in on, and 'tis not good."

He shrugged, which often greased her tongue.

"That man came again," she hissed.

Gytha's man, as ever she referred to him. Counseling patience since pushing Rosa first in the direction of her lady's health could close her up, Guarin nodded for her to continue.

"He told Jaxon my lady met with the Norman warrior finally come to claim the barony given by your king—those Wulfrith lands known as Stern."

Anger over the theft of Hawisa's lands nearly made him curse. Certes, if Rosa knew his mind in this moment, she would more quickly spill her tale in the belief she did so to a fellow Saxon.

"Most curious," she said, "this new baron of England shares your name."

It was difficult not to react to that, but he maintained a passive enough expression she continued, "Either D'Argent is a common name in Normandy, else he is a relation of yours."

One *finally* come to claim his reward, meaning Hawisa knew all along one of his brothers—or cousin—was to become her neighbor. Another shrug to mask anger, then a lie. "A common name, though mayhap he is known to me."

Far more believable a lie, his uncle had instructed, *when truth is sprinkled on it.* Guarin had mostly eschewed such advice as his sire would have him do—until Hawisa Wulfrithdotter.

"Know you one named Cyr?" Rosa asked.

He drew a slow breath. "I have heard of one." Silently, he added, *Only one. And I know him well, indeed.* "You say this Cyr D'Argent met with your lady?"

She nodded. "And *that* man told Jaxon she does not look long for this world."

Of a sudden, seething over what Hawisa had withheld from him was replaced by concern. "Gytha's man was present when your lady received Cyr D'Argent?"

"I know not, but if 'tis true Harold's mother has eyes and ears in every corner of England, he need not have been present." She sighed. "But I take the long way around so you understand how serious this."

"How serious what?" Not that he could not guess since long he had expected what was now more possible with Hawisa gravely ill.

"Jaxon told *that* man the rebels who side with Vitalis are weak and must be dealt with else they will be the downfall of the Wulfenshire rebellion. Then *that* man said Lady Hawisa's son is the means of gaining control of Wulfen."

"Her son?" Guarin voiced his surprise.

Rosa blinked. "As often as the two of you meet, I assumed you knew she had one."

Had, the one upon Senlac lost to her. "Only one?"

She inclined her head. "That is my understanding."

Had he made an assumption he should not have? Been misinformed? Was it this woman who misunderstood? Or was something else at work here? "Continue, Rosa."

"Jaxon said with Lady Hawisa bedridden, now is the time."

"To do what?"

"He did not say."

Because it was told before she eavesdropped? Regardless, Jaxon readied to move against his lady.

"I believe 'twill be this eve when..." Her brow convulsed as if she questioned the wisdom of revealing more.

He gave a bitter laugh. "Unless you possess a key, Rosa"—he jerked at his chains—"or strength well beyond my own, I am of no threat to any but you. And as you must know by now, I would not harm you."

She inclined her head. "Nor my lady."

As evidenced by his present captivity. "Nor your lady."

"You would aid her if you could, aye?"

Considering the outcome of the last time he had done so, would he again? More averse to answering himself than her, he said, "I do not believe I need further prove myself. Now finish the tale."

"This eve, myself and others are to create a diversion, drawing Cyr D'Argent opposite a sortie Vitalis shall lead to take a great crop of hay in the North. 'Tis the usual order of things, and I would think little of it had I not overheard what went between Jaxon and *that* man—and what followed. Ere the sortie departed camp, Vitalis's scout took ill and Jaxon insisted on Sigward replacing him. Does it not smell foul, Norman?"

It reeked. "It does."

"And so I fear our diversion will be of no aid, that the sortie is not meant to return and 'twill be to Normans they fall."

Hearing tears in her voice, Guarin set a hand atop hers. "You warned Vitalis?"

"I tried but could not get past Jaxon, but Vitalis is no fool. He was displeased at Sigward being thrust on him, so surely he will watch him closely. Will he not?"

Guarin released her hand. "As you say, he is no fool. And neither are you. Now promise me something."

"Aye?"

"When you venture out this night, you will set aside your worry so it not prove your downfall."

Her eyes moistened. "Did I not know 'tis a lady who weighs upon your heart and mind, I might believe I did the same."

"Rosa—"

She held up a hand. "I may be simple, but I know people. Did I not, still I would wish you dead." She pushed upright. "And greatly I would err in seeing only the Norman, rather than the good man who made a wrong decision."

He stood and, looking down on her, thought how vulnerable she appeared and was glad it was an illusion. "This eve, think only on your safety and of those with you, Rosa. Do not—"

"—be a martyr," she spoke over him. "Do not yield my life without a fight. So you have said before, and as told before, I will make good use of your training in service to my people. If God wills, on the morrow you will enjoy my company again."

He believed her, and yet he sensed... What? Her death?

She started to turn away, came back around. "Are there other Normans like you, Guarin D'Argent?"

"I have no doubt, just as I have no doubt there are more like you. Indeed, there are many worthy Saxons in this camp."

"Do you think ever our two peoples will be at peace?"

Blessedly, ever was a very long time. "I do."

"I would like to see it."

"Then exercise much caution this eve so on the morrow you may thank me for all I have taught you."

Laughter clipped, once more she started to depart.

This time, Guarin halted her. "I do regret my decision, Rosa, especially if I am responsible for any of your losses."

She considered him, nodded. "Until the morrow, Norman."

CHAPTER TWENTY-SIX

Wulfen Castle
England

They were so near to breaking into the wood, it seemed impossible anything could dampen the joy of knowing that, despite the lives lost during the passage's construction, many would be saved in the event of an attack on Wulfen.

But now the first of two missives delivered this afternoon. It was expected, but not the contents, so lulled was Isa by the rebellion's success in harrying the enemy. Jaxon told that one of two diversions she had approved to ensure the rebels bettered Cyr D'Argent had suffered a casualty, that of a rebel of the sortie sent to Castle Balduc to burn a portion of the hay stored there following its early harvest.

Which rebel? Though she knew she should put the loss behind her, thinking forward as her sire would have her do, it mattered—be it a noble life or a common, a man's life or a woman's, a Saxon's life or a...

Norman's? She shook her head. That should not be a consideration. And it would not if not for—

237

"Cease," she rasped and tossed aside Jaxon's two-sentence message and snatched up the one from Lillefarne. As it followed on the heels of last eve's bid to take the great crop of hay in the North so it could be sold in Lincolnshire, likely it bore news of the large sortie whom Aelfled was to have hidden within the abbey's wall until pursuers abandoned the chase.

"Glad tidings," she entreated and broke the wax seal and unrolled the parchment.

I, Mary Sarah, by the grace of God the Abbess of Lillefarne Abbey, greet Lady Hawisa and beseech you to gird your faith for what I must tell of the events of last eve and this day.

Isa sought to do as asked, but that which she girded was so loose, its buckle so bent, she feared it would fall, entangle her feet, and drop her on her face.

She resumed reading.

Last eve, one no longer dear to you secreted Saxon rebels within our wall, unaware the Baron of Stern and Balduc watched from the wood. He and his host breeched God's house and captured the rebels, including your former housecarle. Blessedly, our residents suffered no harm, and it appears no rebels paid with their lives. All were bound and, I presume, marched to Stern Castle. Alas, there is more to tell.

Isa caught back a sob. More? Worse than the capture of Vitalis and his men? She read on.

Though it would be unseemly for the one from whom you have turned your face to remain at the abbey after endangering our women, I would not have had her depart as she did. Under threat of harm to her grandmother, whom Cyr D'Argent ordered taken from the village of Ravven this morn, he drew her out.

The capture of Aelfled, whom Isa had determined to return to her service at Wulfen, would have been a terrible blow had she been taken by a Norman other than the one whose aid on Senlac evidenced he was cut from the same cloth as his eldest brother.

Isa returned to the missive.

I believe she has also been delivered to Stern Castle to answer for acting against our king.

Our king. Did the staunch Saxon claim the usurper out of fear her missive would be intercepted by the enemy? Regardless, Mary Sarah ensured she but appeared a sympathetic bearer of tidings.

In closing, I thank you for your generous support of our abbey, Lady Hawisa, and I hope these events that bear witness to the Saxons' struggle to reclaim a place in a much-changed England end the persecution you and your people have endured for bending the knee. Let us pray the great one is not long in returning peace and glory to our lands. Amen and amen.

The great one—worded in such a way it could as easily apply to the Lord as to William or a Saxon, whether the latter sprang from the efforts of Gytha or Harwolfson in the South.

Isa dropped the missive alongside Jaxon's. Eyes falling on the other thing also sent by the abbess, of which no mention had been made in writing, she lifted the bundle and stood from the bed.

Experiencing no lightness of head, legs steady, and only mildly discomfited by her injury, it would be easy to persuade herself she was well enough to ride to camp and oversee preparations for the recovery of Vitalis and his men. But if she undid her healing again...

As she must trust Cyr D'Argent would do Aelfled no harm, so with his captive rebels. Just a few more days, and she could be the leader her people needed. And between now and then, Jaxon would come to Wulfen and they would devise a plan to recover the captured rebels.

Men Jaxon might prefer remain imprisoned, the unwelcome thought pierced her.

"He will come," she said aloud and stepped into the dust-stirred light slanting through an upper window. She unwound the string crossed a dozen times around the bundle and unrolled the cloth.

It was the dagger she had given to Vitalis to prove it meant nothing to her. Ignoring the flirtatious sapphire, she stared at the initials inscribed in steel, surprised her man had not filed them off —as if he had intended to reunite the weapon with its owner. That it was returned to Isa had to mean Vitalis, certain of capture by the brother of its owner, had left it behind. And somehow the abbess had known to send it to Isa.

"Who are you, Mary Sarah?" she murmured. "What is it you wish of me?"

~

Wulfenshire Rebel Camp
England

"AYE, SHE IS DEAD."

Guarin stared at the burly man who feigned no sorrow over the pronouncement.

"A pity since she had more courage than most of her sex—and some skill at arms," Jaxon continued. "But little good either did her when she fell into the enemy's hands."

Pierced by the passing of a Saxon for whom he had a care, Guarin rasped, "How did she give her life?"

Jaxon crossed his arms over his thickly muscled chest. "In service to her people. Saxon courage, Norman."

"How?" Guarin bit.

"'Tis believed she turned a dagger on herself so she not be made to betray us." He shrugged. "Certes, a better end for her than those she lost to your kind."

Nearly strangled by the longing to drive a fist into that smug face, Guarin said, "We are done."

Jaxon chortled. "Might you have been fond of her?"

Pushing off the stone wall he had settled against when the camp commander entered the cave as he had not in a year, Guarin knew the grind of his jaw and fists at his sides would be seen as a challenge. Chained though he was, he was well with being at so great a disadvantage should the miscreant draw nearer—even if, in the end, it provided Jaxon the excuse to end the life of one he had never intended to live beyond a few months of torture.

"I am tempted," the Saxon warrior drawled, "and mayhap I shall yield, but there is more you ought to know of last eve."

Now he would boast of the success of the diversions and the number of Normans felled.

Jaxon's lips curved at the center of a beard bound beneath his chin by a large gold bead. "Most unfortunate for the Normans, not only must we avenge the loss of Rosa but that of my pupil, Vitalis, and the men of his sortie who were captured whilst seeking refuge at Lillefarne Abbey."

Guarin's muscles tensed further. Like Rosa, Vitalis and those of the sortie were good men and women whose minds might be given to vengeance but not their souls. Not so those of the patrol who blindly followed this man's lead.

Once again responding as Jaxon wished, Guarin said, "They are also dead?"

"If not, ere long—providing the one holding them is as *merciless* as told."

Cyr. After what Rosa revealed, Guarin was not surprised already his brother moved to end the rebellion. And now better he understood the reason Jaxon was here. It was not merely to taunt him over Rosa's death. He sought assurance Cyr would show his captives no mercy, thereby taking responsibility for their deaths which Jaxon himself may have set in motion.

Guarin's thoughts shifted to Hawisa. Without Vitalis's support and protection, what would become of her, especially with illness making her more vulnerable to entirely losing control of the rebels?

Determining deception was in order, though it might not benefit her, Guarin gave a grunt of laughter. "If Vitalis and his men yet live, their breaths are numbered. Whether last eve, this day, or the morrow, all are dead to your cause."

Likely a lie, Guarin mused as the man's eyes narrowed. Cyr's greatest flaw was a competitive bent that often blinded him to grace due others even when the contest was clearly his. Unless Hastings had greatly changed the second-born D'Argent—and it was possible—the title of *merciless* earned at tournament and in battle was mostly exaggeration since it did not take into account the name of D'Argent by which Cyr was far longer known. Merciless, but not cruelly so.

Jaxon heaved a sigh. "As feared, but some good can come of nearly every bad does one look deep enough."

Guarin waited.

"The more Saxon blood spilled, the greater the rebellion's desire to oust the invaders. Then there is our Norman guest whose departure is long past due, do you not agree?" He smiled. "Soon you shall leave us."

Guarin flexed his hands. "If your lady wills it," he pushed in the thorn he hoped Jaxon would seek to remove by revealing his plans for Hawisa. "Or do you intend to betray the trust her sire placed in you to keep his line safe?"

His smile dropped, and he took a step forward. "I am not the betrayer. 'Tis she, the blood in her veins wasted on one who believes herself a man's equal. She who is good only for birthing a single Wulfrith. She who should never have had charge of her son. She who is responsible for his—"

His teeth snapped, but it was too late to hide how deep the thorn and how much blood it drew, just as it was too late to keep from confirming Hawisa had given her Norman husband only the one heir who died upon Senlac. Thus, the boy Jaxon wished to wrest control of was an imposter, doubtless enlisted to ensure Hawisa retained whatever lands William left to her and avoid another marriage.

Had there been any possibility Guarin would survive in the absence of Vitalis, it was gone. He knew too much.

Am I of a mood? he silently questioned as he had not had occasion to in a long time, then cited, *Rosa dead, Vitalis and his sortie captured, Hawisa the next victim.* He breathed deep, withheld his gaze from the weapons on the Saxon's belt. *If I can move him to recklessness...*

He took another step forward, inciting Jaxon to lower his arms and close his hands into fists. Now to taunt him. "So the mighty Wulfrith instructed that should his daughter be unable to withstand the losses incurred by an invasion, you should abandon her? Betray her?"

Jaxon bared his teeth. "She is willful, weak, unworthy."

"Willful? Aye. Weak? Unworthy? I do not see that in her. But in the betrayer before me..."

Jaxon stared his hatred at Guarin, then removed the belt from which dagger and sword hung. Not reckless enough, but there would be satisfaction in landing blows, proving even a chained Norman could pain an unchained Saxon.

"As told, your departure is past due, D'Argent, but with so much to be savored, let us not be hasty in parting ways." He cast the belt behind and lunged.

Prepared for the barrel of muscle and bone, Guarin ducked, drove a fist into Jaxon's side, swung up his other arm, and whipped a length of chain into his face.

Bloodied nose. Broken teeth. Not satisfaction enough, but though more was to be had as they grappled, testing the strength and range of the chains, Guarin's disadvantage served Jaxon well. Both were bloodied and bruised when the latter landed an elbow to his captive's ribs that allowed him to break free of the arm pressed hard to his neck.

Cursing himself for losing hold of Jaxon over a few broken ribs, Guarin lurched forward. The miscreant's tunic slipped through his fingers.

Once beyond reach, Jaxon swung around. Chest heaving, face and beard a crimson mess, he said, "I could kill you now, but that would be like quickly eating a fine meal."

Refusing to bend to the pain radiating from his lower ribs, Guarin glanced at the cave entrance where a dozen rebels had appeared to witness the clash, several among them Vitalis's men who had not participated in last eve's sortie. As the one to whom they were loyal had been captured and they were themselves outnumbered by men loyal to Jaxon, they would not challenge the camp commander even if he drew his sword to dispatch Guarin.

"We are not done, Norman," Jaxon said as he girded his belt. "I shall visit again." His grin was red-rimmed. "And savor again."

"As shall I, Saxon."

Jaxon swung away and, weaving slightly, exited the cave.

When all had departed, Guarin felt a hand across his ribs. At least one broken, several cracked. "And so it begins," he murmured. "Again."

CHAPTER TWENTY-SEVEN

Wulfen Castle
England

*I*t *was* Vitalis.

She had feared trickery when Ordric awakened her from an early night's sleep to which she had yielded after two days' worry over those taken prisoner by Cyr D'Argent—and this day's excitement over the assurance they were hours from completing the passage.

Isa ran, at the center of the hall flung her arms around the disheveled, begrimed man.

"My lady!" He returned her embrace and set her back.

"I..." She shook her head.

"We are all well," he said.

She peered past him at the empty space. "All?"

"I, alone, Cyr D'Argent released to strike a bargain with the rebels, but the others fare well."

She caught her breath. "He knows I am Dotter?"

"Great his suspicion, but be assured, I was not followed here."

She started to press for details of the bargain, but though it appeared those bedded down in the hall slept, she gestured for him and Ordric to accompany her.

When they had the fire-lit kitchen to themselves, Vitalis said, "First, I must tell who betrayed us. The one who rendered us vulnerable to capture was Sigward."

"Jaxon," she whispered.

"Aye, there is no doubt he moves against you—that you, the boy, and all of Wulfen are in danger."

Here further proof of what she had achingly accepted following two days of Jaxon ignoring her summons.

"I do not believe he is alone in betraying you, my lady."

"Gytha."

Vitalis inclined his head. "Still her man makes the rounds of England, inciting Saxons to rebel and rebellions to act."

"What of Edwin Harwolfson?"

"Rumor is he gains ground, and though likely he entertains Gytha's man, I do not believe he bows to Harold's mother."

She nodded. "Tell me of the bargain Cyr D'Argent wishes to make."

"Nineteen captives, twenty including the body of Sigward."

She caught her breath. "He is dead?"

"Not by the hands of Normans. By the hands of those imprisoned by his betrayal." He breathed deep. "It was a frenzy—one I led."

Feeling him tugged between assuring himself he was justified and judging himself a murderer, Isa said, "Surely it was not planned."

"It was not. All lost control—including Cyr D'Argent—when Sigward injured Aelfled." At Isa's gasp, he raised a hand. "I have been assured she will recover."

"Praise the Lord," she heard herself speak words that had become foreign to her, then assured him, "What happened to Jaxon's man cannot be changed and, perhaps, ought not be. Now tell what *can* be changed."

"Cyr D'Argent believes the sighting of Guarin is true and those of Dotter hold him. He says he will trade all the rebels for his brother—*if* he lives."

Just as no longer was there doubt Jaxon betrayed her, there was no doubt he would rid himself of her captive. Had he not already...

Heart clenching, Isa feared she would be ill, but she told herself Guarin lived and she would make good her promise to see him returned to his family.

"I agreed to his terms providing he release my men to me alone," Vitalis continued. "Are you in accord, my lady?"

Beyond seeing Aelfled released as well, there was naught to consider, only how it was to be done. "Of course."

"I shall have to steal into camp and bring out his brother," Vitalis said. "There is naught for it, even if I must..."

Take another Saxon life, he could not say.

"Providing you have adequate reinforcements," Isa said, "there should be no spillage of blood. Vitalis, refresh yourself. Ordric, choose eight men and instruct the master of horses to prepare enough mounts to also accommodate Cyr D'Argent's captives." She swung away. "We depart a half hour hence."

"We?" Vitalis demanded.

"*We,* Vitalis."

~

Wulfenshire Rebel Camp
England

ONE MORE BEATING? Non, two—perhaps three—he could endure, even if only to deny Jaxon the satisfaction of an easy kill the miscreant would attribute to Norman inferiority.

"Three," Guarin rasped, then laughed at himself. If he survived one more, it would be a miracle.

Would the Lord intercede? For what? So one who had lost nearly two years of his life suffer further? Again, for what? To test the utmost limit of Guarin's faith? To discover what was required for him to turn from it? Did the Lord truly wish to know?

Guarin did not.

Shallow breath after shallow he drew, occasionally a deep one, and less for need of a greater amount of air than to make the pain of smaller breaths tolerable. So tormented was he when he filled his chest as much as he could bear, for a short time afterward he was merely discomforted by the effort to sustain life.

He ought to be dead. Had he not kept fit, he would be. But that which protected his organs weakened with each beating. He would not be surprised if the blows last dealt had gone deep enough his innards bled amongst themselves.

Trying to distract himself from shallow breaths that must soon be fed an agonizing one, Guarin wondered how many men would accompany Jaxon to the cave come sunrise. As few as one, as many as three. Perhaps four for the final beating. But then sooner it would be done, in the end almost merciful.

"Lord," he breathed out. "Lord," he breathed in. And stilled.

A sound not of night opened his eyes, one eye more than the other. On his back, head and neck supported by the folded mantle of the lady lost to him and possibly herself, he looked to the side. Though the sudden movement made him hurt, he searched the dark.

Above the rock slab, only the upper portion of the cave's moonlit entrance could be seen. Hence, whoever entered absent a lantern or torch would have to draw near before the shadowed figure took form.

Not Jaxon nor any of his men, Guarin was fairly certain. With Vitalis gone and the majority of the rebels loyal to the camp commander, they had no need for stealth—indeed, enjoyed announcing their approach that foretold a beating.

Two pairs of feet, Guarin detected. And since his visitors

negotiated the dark cave without incident, they were familiar with the uneven floor and obstacles. Might one of these be Zedekiah who had led others aligned with Vitalis in protesting the loss of their watch over the Norman? The confrontation had not been visible to Guarin, but he had heard the argument. And the lies that ended it.

Jaxon had said Vitalis and all those of the sortie sent north were slain by the Baron of Stern and that the Lady of Wulfen was on her deathbed. Thus, henceforth they were accountable to he who answered only to the future Saxon king's grandmother. Might their silence since have been but a biding of time? Was it possible they defied Jaxon?

Or do I but fashion hope out of nothing? Guarin questioned his wits.

Two figures appeared, one tall and broad, the other the height of Zedekiah but not the width. Had Guarin to wager, he would say neither meant him harm, but he tensed in anticipation of wielding fists, manacles, and chains to prolong whatever remained of his life.

They came around the rock and halted. Though they knew where to find him, they would be able to see little—if any—of him where he lay against the wall. "D'Argent?"

Guarin stiffened. That one's voice he had not thought to hear again. What did it mean? As for the question asked, surely it was intended to give Guarin pause if he meant to attack before being attacked—else confirm Hawisa's man addressed empty space at best, a corpse at worst.

Of a sudden, exhaustion overtook pain that had denied him the comfort of sleep. As he began to drift, he pondered how Vitalis had escaped, next if Cyr had truly held Hawisa's man. More of Jaxon's lies?

"D'Argent?" the warrior repeated.

Respite slipping through his fingers like the water denied him two days, Guarin opened his eyes. "I live," he growled past a parched throat made raw as much by suppressing shouts of pain as loosing those impossible to keep down.

The slighter figure broke from the other and dropped to his knees beside Guarin. Rather, *her* knees. She who was not abed and dying. She who was not lost to him—though *he* might soon be lost to himself.

Such a potent mix of relief and anger burst behind his eyes, he careened toward unconsciousness.

The hand Hawisa set on his shoulder tugged at him, the scent of her when she bent near wrenched him back to her. "What has been done you, Guarin?"

He did not think it a question needing an answer, but he said, "Jaxon."

"Dear Lord, I prayed he had not yet moved against you. How badly are you beaten?" She moved her fingers to his face and began probing the cuts and swellings.

With a clatter of chain, Guarin caught hold of her hand—and nearly groaned over the movement. "You are healed?"

She hesitated. "Mostly I am myself again."

Far more than he was himself. "For what do you come on silent feet in the dark of night?"

Rather than seek her release, she closed her fingers over his thumb crossing her palm as if for fear he would escape her. "Those of Jaxon will name me a traitor, but it is time to return you to your family."

He narrowed his gaze on where he knew her face was, but no matter how he strained could not see past the shadows. "You are sending me back across the sea as ever you wished?"

"Did I?" she said so low he wondered if she knew she spoke aloud.

"Did you?" he clipped, anger beginning to surface.

She hesitated, then said, "The manacles, Vitalis."

Her man moved to Guarin's feet. As blindly he searched for

the keyhole of the iron plates fastened around the right ankle, Guarin released Hawisa's hand and coughed. Again. And again.

She slid a hand beneath his head and raised him. "Drink."

The spout seeking his lips trickling wine down his cheek, he turned his head and fit lips around it, gulped.

"Slowly, Guarin."

So great was his thirst, it was hard to be satisfied with less than his body demanded, but to ensure he kept it down, he drew back.

"This day's journey will not be long," she said. "When you are recovered you shall return to Normandy. And that...will be the end of us."

His attempt at laughter feeling like a blade to the side, he said, "You think it possible? To end us?"

He sensed her searching gaze, knew it would fail the same as his, and shuddered when the manacle parted and fell away.

"Soon you shall learn how entangled our lives have become," she said as Vitalis moved to the other ankle.

Already he knew, as revealed by Rosa and confirmed by Hawisa in assuring him the journey ahead would be brief relative to crossing the channel. Before the next setting of the sun, he would be reunited with Cyr.

"It is necessary to end us," she said. "Thus, I beseech you— embrace your freedom and go from my shores, live as ever you were meant to."

"Ever," he mused. "That is in the past."

She swallowed loudly. "You will avenge yourself?"

"Were I to confess such"—he winced at his slurred words, realized he drifted again—"would you leave what remains of me to Jaxon?"

"Non." No hesitation. "Once we have taken you away, never again will you set eye nor foot here."

Would he not? he questioned as the fog rising through his mind thickened. Were not demons best laid to rest where spawned?

"Move aside, my lady," Vitalis alerted her to the second manacle's removal.

Freedom, Guarin thought. *But not to live as once I was meant to. Hawisa Wulfrithdotter has changed all.*

"D'Argent?" Vitalis said, and Guarin realized his wrists were free of manacle and chain. "Can you stand?"

Ashamedly, that could prove beyond him, but not for want of trying. He rolled onto his side and closed his throat against a shout of pain. Teeth ground, he made it to his knees. And there remained, panting.

"He cannot," Hawisa said, then she was on one side of him, her man on the other. Gripping his arms, they raised him.

Keenly feeling an absence, Guarin rasped, "The mantle."

"You are cold?" she asked.

He was feverish. "Bring it," he growled, vexed as much by what it revealed of him as his inability to retrieve it himself.

Hawisa gave all his support to Vitalis, moments later draped the mantle over his shoulders and came around to fasten the ties.

Staring at her bent head, remembering when they were nearer in the wood, her lips beneath his, Guarin drew a breath of her. An end to them? Necessary perhaps, but possible?

Her hands lowered and head came up, and it seemed just the two of them—as if each sought to impress this moment alongside all those come before.

"It is done, Guarin," she said softly and gripped his arm.

For what seemed an ungodly distance, he supported enough of his weight to keep his feet moving, and that was all.

Exiting the cave unfettered for the first time in what seemed a lifetime, relief tempted him to hang his head. But there was light here, the great moon perched in a cloudless sky above a kingdom no longer Saxon. Though he longed to look near on Hawisa, he feared the effort would drop him to his knees and whatever bled inside would bleed more, perhaps so greatly he would not be reunited with his family.

"Jaxon's sentries?" he asked. "His patrol?"

"Bound and gagged," she said. "But they will not be long in regaining consciousness."

Meaning he must move faster. But he could not. Never had he felt less a warrior.

They continued forward and, after what seemed hours, Hawisa said, "We are here."

He raised his gaze from a ground mostly without form, saw what first he should have heard—three horses, all restless.

Praise You, Lord, he sent heavenward. Had they to traverse more ground on foot, he did not think they would make it out of the ravine before he collapsed.

Once he was astride, they began negotiating moonlit paths and deeply shadowed stone corridors. Vitalis ahead, Hawisa behind, Guarin hunched over his pain and tried to steel himself for the increased pace that would be required to distance them from those who might give chase.

However, when they emerged from the ravine, of greater concern was a score of horses ahead, only half of which carried riders.

"My men," Hawisa said, reining in alongside him as Vitalis spurred ahead.

Guarin looked to her, only then realized she rode Anglicus.

"Vitalis shall lead them," she said, moonlight on her profile evidencing though she was much improved, she gave little thought to her grooming and had yet to recover her proper weight. Lovely but careworn.

"Lead them where?" he asked, then what he was certain he should know but was too tired to make sense of, "Why so many horses absent riders?"

"They shall accompany you to your brother, the Baron of—"

"Stern."

She gasped.

He suffered for his chuckle. "Between the curious Rosa—God

rest her soul—and the venomous Jaxon, I know much of what goes upon Wulfenshire."

Isa stared, shocked less by his knowledge than his appearance that was more terrible in full moonlight.

The bend of his shoulders and pale of his face beneath dark bruises and livid cuts made her hurt. He had looked better the day she discovered he was being tortured. Might she be returning to his family one soon dead?

His eyebrows rose. "It is possible."

"What?"

"Jaxon will gain what he has long desired."

Had any man ever read her as well as he? "I pray not, that you—"

"Ah, I am slow of wit." Guarin rasped, his unswollen eye widening. "It is a trade you make, one brokered between Vitalis and Cyr—me for the rebels captured during the last sortie."

Feeling as if caught in a lie, she said, "Oui, but ever I have wished you returned to your family. You know this."

"Do I?" He looked to where Vitalis halted before the escort. "Would you have come for me had your rebels not been captured?"

"I would have."

"When?"

More accusation. "As Jaxon has ignored my summons since the sortie's capture, I now accept he answers to King Harold's mother ahead of me. Thus, I would have freed you. And soon."

"Not soon enough, Hawisa. Do I survive, it will be because you are here now—for your trade."

She hated he thought so ill of her, but she had no further defense. To ensure this was the end of them, better words were spent on dissuading him from vengeance.

She turned in the saddle to fully face him. Glimpsing past the mantle given him the stain on his tunic that was darker than the grime, she reached to evidence of the second time he had sacrificed himself for her.

"Your blood," he said, and when she started to draw back, closed a hand over hers.

She met his gaze. "Pray, Guarin, know I am sorry for what one noble beyond his birth has suffered. Know ever I am indebted for the aid given me. Know—"

"Do you think to soften me, Hawisa?"

She did, but that had not prompted these words.

"To render me the same as your lovesick Vitalis?"

She did not, and yet... Nay, an end to them was what she wanted. As if he had not challenged her, she continued, "Know I pray one day you can forgive me for all you have lost."

He flattened her hand against his chest. "Do you wish this to beat for you?"

The thud of his heart caused her own to make itself felt. Eyes tearing at the realization she did wish it to beat for her, she said, "I cannot begrudge you your anger. Nor the truth."

"Truth?" His voice was so graveled, she tugged her hand free and reached to the wineskin on her belt. As she unfastened it, moonlight coursed the jeweled hilt of its traveling companion. She looked up, saw he looked down.

When Guarin's gaze returned to hers, rather than ask after what he had last seen in Vitalis's possession, he said again, "Truth?"

As if to do penance, she had nearly confessed her feelings, but he would think it an attempt to soften him.

"Hawisa?"

She extended the skin. "You are dry, the ride ahead arduous." When he took it, she glanced at Vitalis and his men who awaited them. It was time to begin the journey that would take far longer than usual in Guarin's state.

"If you have something to tell," he said, "speak so sooner I may reunite with my brother."

She breathed deep. "The truth is never have I felt for a man what I feel for you." If her words affected him in any measure, his face did not reveal it. Suppressing the urge to put spurs to Anglicus, she continued, "These feelings are beyond my understanding. And unforgivable."

His uninjured eye narrowed. "Why unforgivable?"

"We are…"

"Enemies," he said.

Was that a statement or a question? she wondered, then asked, "You believe I lie?"

He drank sparingly, then hooked the skin on his saddle's pommel. "I know not what to believe. What I know is I *will* see you again."

"You speak of vengeance?"

He drew a breath so ragged she guessed great injury had been done his ribs. "Restitution is the better word. And few would deny it is owed me."

It *was* a better word, but not without threat. "Though neither would I deny it, I beseech you again—turn your efforts to life in Normandy."

"When I am done with Wulfenshire."

With *her*. Hence, all the more imperative the underground passage prove viable. God willing, this day. "First you will have to capture me," she said, "then you will have to hold me. For the sake of my people, no easy thing will I make it."

His lips curved. "I will capture the one who professes to feel for me. I will hold her. My word I give."

He was angry, his mind and body battered—perhaps even broken in places. Once he was where he belonged and healed, he would think right again, she assured herself. He would put Hastings behind him. He would put her behind him. He would cross the channel without a backward glance, grateful it was only two years lost to him rather than what could prove a lifetime for those he helped conquer.

As Isa started to urge her destrier forward, she remembered the dagger. Would he turn the blade on one of her men? Nay, even were he capable of setting himself at other warriors—and he was not this day—he had no cause. He had only to complete the ride to secure his freedom and be restored to his family.

She drew the dagger whose sapphire winked in moonlight, offered it.

His regard was cursory. "I shall collect it later."

Isa set her teeth, returned it to her belt, and gave Anglicus her heels.

After instructing Vitalis to ensure Aelfled was amongst those traded, she looked to the man who was no longer her captive. Though he remained upright, his head was down, portending he might have to be strapped over the back of his horse before he reached Stern.

Alive, Lord, she silently prayed, *even if he comes seeking restitution.*

She drew alongside and touched his hand that gripped the saddle's pommel. "Godspeed, Guarin D'Argent."

He turned his singular gaze on her, rumbled, "Until we meet again, Hawisa Wulfrithdotter."

She should have pulled back and reined around, but she moved her hand to his jaw and shivered at the rasp of whiskers against her palm. "Live," she whispered.

He stared, then dropped his chin.

Throat tight, Isa turned Anglicus aside and, accompanied by Ordric, spurred toward Wulfen Castle.

CHAPTER TWENTY-EIGHT

Wulfen Castle
England

*G*lorious tidings, as if the Lord deemed her and hers worthy of answered prayer. Now if He would answer another—that Guarin reach Stern alive. And another—that Guarin heal. Yet another—that Vitalis and his rebels encounter no resistance during the ride to Wulfen.

"My lady?"

Isa swung around to face the boy who had stolen upon her, hopefully a result he was becoming a master of stealth rather than she was terribly remiss in watching her back. "Wulf?"

"'Tis true? They have broken into the wood?"

Wiping dust from her tunic, she strode from the tapestry she had come out from behind. "Aye, near the waterfall." She halted, leaned in, and kissed his brow. When she drew back, he smiled broadly, likely more because of her show of affection than the passage's long-awaited completion. She erred in being so familiar with one not of her blood. And yet...

She allowed herself a small smile. "No longer can we be trapped inside these walls should the enemy lay siege."

"May I see?"

"'Tis yet too dangerous."

He frowned, but before she could explain, understanding cleared his brow. "When will the timbers be set?"

Supports that would greatly reduce the chance of collapse. "It is being done now. The master miner assures me it if is not completed this day, then the morrow."

"You think the Lord returned to us, my lady?"

She wished her feeling of abandonment had passed over him lest it shook his own faith and distanced him from God. But he was no longer a child more given to hope than despair. He saw and felt what those older than he strove to conceal.

"I believe He is with us." But would He stay? she silently questioned. Or did He but visit, dangling hope against which they could only brush fingers ere it was snatched away again?

"I believe it as well," the boy said.

The opening of the great doors beyond the curtain sounded, of no event if not for the urgency in the voice of the one who called to her. Had he word of Vitalis? Was it possible already he and his rebels had returned?

She skirted Wulfrith, tossed back the curtain, and stepped onto the dais as the doors across the hall closed behind the youngest of her housecarles and one who struggled to break his grip on her arm.

The woman cursed, stumbled, kicked at his legs.

"Witch!" He flung her ahead, dropping her to her hands and knees.

"What is this?" Isa demanded, motioning for the servants to resume their work as she advanced.

"She was discovered in the back of a cart behind sacks of grain, my lady. Doubtless, a Norman spy."

"Never!" the woman cried. "A hundred deaths I would die first!" She thrust back on her heels, started to rise. "A thousand!"

He gripped her shoulder and forced her back to her knees.

Certes, she was Saxon, but no matter her protest, that did not mean she was loyal to her own.

Isa halted before her. "At best I require a good defense for stealing into my home, at worst a confession and genuine contrition. So think well on your words. They shall determine how dire your fate."

The woman peered at Isa from behind a veil of tangled hair. "You are Lady Hawisa?"

"You know I am. Think better. Try again."

"Are you...?" She drew a shaky breath. "'Tis said you bend the knee to William, but rumored behind closed doors you stand upright."

Alarm sounded through Isa.

"Is it true you have not forsaken your people, my lady? That you merely bide your time?"

The same as had Guarin, Isa reflected "More ill-thought words that offend and prick my patience," she said and looked to her housecarle. Though she had threatened dire consequences were she not satisfied with the explanation, she ordered, "Set her outside my walls."

"Lady!" The woman snatched hold of Isa's skirt as it whipped around—just as once Guarin had caught hold of her braid. "Pray, hear me!"

Wishing herself back in tunic and chausses, Isa wrenched the material free.

As if to defend against a beating, the woman tossed up her hands. "Forgive me. I know not who is my side, only that *he* comes for me. And should he find—"

"Who comes for you?"

"My...beloved lord."

260

As it was angrily whispered and made no sense, Isa thought she heard wrong. "Say again."

The woman sank back on her heels. "I want him dead. A slow death. Very slow."

"Who?"

She dropped her chin and cradled her head in her hands. "My master. I have run from him. I am a…"

"Slave," Isa gasped, then fell to her knees before the one she had nearly sent away.

The housecarle touched her shoulder. "My lady!"

She glanced up at where he stood behind the woman. "She is Saxon the same as us. I am in no danger."

He loosed her but remained near.

Isa drew the woman's hands from her head and eased them into her lap, lifted her chin. She peered through the mess of hair, but her attempt to confirm that of which she was fairly certain was for naught. The woman's eyes were squeezed closed, lashes wet with tears.

Lest here was but another ill-treated slave, be her master Saxon or Norman, Isa prompted, "Em?" Receiving no response, she raised her voice. "Em?" And heard someone catch his breath.

Looking to the dais, she saw the forgotten boy there—unmoving, eyes wide as if he wished to believe but feared great disappointment.

Isa looked back at the woman, saw her shoulders convulse. This being far from how she had wished to reunite the siblings, she almost hoped it was not Em.

Gently, Isa parted her hair. As she hooked tresses over the woman's ears, she considered a lovely face beset with bruises, a swollen cheek, and scratched jaw. The visage of one who had firmly crossed the threshold into womanhood, it was youthful enough to belong to the sister carried from the auction block, desperately reaching to her brother.

"Pray, open your eyes, sweet one," Isa said.

The woman muffled a sob, drew her head back, once more dropped her chin.

Of a sudden it did not matter whether her eyes were mismatched. Foolish though Isa's sire would name her, unworthy though Jaxon would deem her, dispensable though Gytha would sentence her, all that mattered was solace for a tormented soul.

Isa slid her arms around her, and feeling her stiffen, murmured, "I will not set you out."

The young woman eased slightly.

"I will not forsake you."

She shuddered.

"I will not allow him to harm you again."

She sighed.

"You are safe."

She tucked her head beneath Isa's chin and sank into her.

Isa held her, rocked her, hoped this *was* Em so she could beckon forth her brother, giving the young woman what might greatly aid in her healing.

She stirred, said low, "This day, he discovered I pass information to the resistance."

Further proof this was Em.

"He attacked me…beat me." She gulped. "I cut him, though not deep. If he lives, you will help me kill him?"

Here the door to her identity that would either draw the boy from the dais or turn him away. Isa stroked her hair. "Of whom do you speak?"

Her laugh was venomous. "He who is no longer Baron of Balduc."

Even if Wulfrith heard her muffled words, he would not know it was confirmation of what he hoped for, oblivious to how near brother and sister had been.

Praying in time he would forgive her, Isa said loud, "You *are* Em."

As a cry sounded from the dais and boots hit the floor, the

young woman dropped her head back and opened mismatched eyes. "How know you my name?"

Isa smiled. "That tale will save. What will not is the one who longs for you." Though tempted to smooth the lines grooving the youthful brow, Isa set the young woman back, pushed upright, and stepped aside.

The air trembled as the boy rushed past and dropped beside his sister. "Em!" He reached to her, but the young woman recoiled so violently she fell onto her rear, slamming her back into the housecarle's legs and causing him to step back.

"Em?" He reached again.

She scrambled backward, once more found her escape barred by the warrior.

Isa touched the boy's shoulder. "Slowly, Wulf."

"What is wrong with her?" he demanded.

That which time and patience would remedy, she prayed, and hoped Em's inability to recognize her brother was due to the passage of time. Not only had his voice, body, and face matured, but his hair was of a length neither Saxon nor Norman, skimming his shoulders, and the garments he wore were those of a noble.

"As you no longer look the little brother—have become a young man just as she has become a woman," Isa said, "you must proceed with care."

He nodded and, seeing his sister gain her feet, also stood. "'Tis me, Em, your brother."

Her eyes searched him, then she said, "I want to believe you."

He stepped forward, halted when she flinched. "I have grown, as have you."

She looked to Isa. "Is it really him?"

"Aye, it is Wul—" Nay, Em did not know him by that name, just as Isa did not know him by the name given him at birth, having let it slip from memory after burning his papers.

"Eberhard," the boy spoke what *he* had not forgotten. "Your brother parted from you as he should not have been." He raised a hand, splayed it. "I could not reach you."

Her eyes widened, the contrasting brown and blue as intense beneath the sunlight come through the windows as those same colors on her skin which had incited her to stick Raymond Campagnon with a blade.

Did that poltroon live? If not and the young woman was captured, her sentence for slaying a Norman would be death.

"Ebbe?" Em said.

"Aye, Em. 'Tis your Ebbe. Then came Tristan, next wee Flora."

No surprise it took Isa longer than Em to realize he referred to the siblings whose survival had depended on the eldest selling themselves into slavery. No surprise it was that which persuaded the young woman he was of her blood.

She landed hard against him. They clung to each other as if oblivious to all others, and it was the boy—the young man—who drew back. "You are only recently arrived at Balduc?"

Isa wished the revelation requiring much explanation could wait. But her deception by omission was about to be laid bare, and there was naught she could do but hope they would understand.

Em cupped his face between her hands. "I was brought from the auction to Balduc and have resided there since."

"All this time? It has been a year and a half, Em."

Her frown was fleeting, as was her smile. "Is that all? It feels I should be an old woman."

The one who had long answered to the name *Wulfrith* glanced at Isa and she knew his sharp mind was traveling all paths possible to make sense of his sister's presence.

"Dear Ebbe," Em said. "Though I was told you are with the rebellion, and I need not fear for you, how is it you are here now? At Wulfen Castle?"

"I *am* with the rebellion. The same as you, I have been upon this shire since the Lady of Wulfen's coin purchased me."

Her glance at Isa brimmed with curiosity rather than malice.

She did not like that she and her brother had been reduced to slavery, but as with most Saxons, she accepted the trade in humans that was long abolished in Normandy—one of few things Isa admired about England's conquerors. And perhaps the only good thing William would bring to his reign should he survive attempts to oust him.

Em drew further back from her brother and considered his finery. "You are not clothed as a slave. You appear noble."

"I..." He frowned at the one who played his mother, and she was pleased he sought permission to reveal the truth.

"All will be explained," Isa said, "but first we must tend your injuries, Em."

It appeared she would protest, but she nodded. "I am tired and sore, my belly so empty it grinds."

Isa took her elbow. "Whilst a chamber is being prepared, let us slake your hunger and thirst."

"Ebbe as well?"

Isa was tempted to send him back to the training yard where he belonged at this time of day so she might first ease his sister into the explanation owed them, but the set of his jaw told he would argue. More, it was cruel to part them so soon.

"Ebbe as well."

CHAPTER TWENTY-NINE

Stern Castle
England

*C*onsciousness. It beckoned. It tugged. It pulled. Blessedly, a shake of the head freed him of the pain awaiting him on the surface.

Sinking back to benevolent depths, he wondered if the voices of his sister and aunt were imagined. If not, he was returned to France, and not only had he lost days of his life but...

He saw her face in moonlight, felt her hand on his jaw, heard her beseech him to live, longed to pull her to him—until anger once more drew him back from the edge of Hawisa with the reminder it was not mere days lost to him but months that numbered nearly two years.

"Is it not wondrous?" His sister again. "He is returned to us!"

Refusing to become pain's plaything, Guarin attempted to kick back from the surface, but he was thwarted by the one who answered Nicola.

"I will kill Vitalis."

That voice and those words did not beckon, tug, and pull. They wrenched. And cast Guarin on a jagged shore of pain.

"If you do not," Nicola said, "I will."

Cyr was here, meaning this had to be Stern. Hence, their sister and aunt who should be in Normandy were not.

Guarin groaned, rasped, "Beware Vitalis."

"I will kill him," Cyr repeated, boots sounding across the floor. "He will pay for every—"

"It was not him." Narrowly, Guarin opened his eyes, struggled to focus on the tall, broad figure striding toward the bed. "He did not do this."

"Not Vitalis?" their sister exclaimed. "Truly?"

He shifted his gaze from Cyr to the girl who sat on the mattress beside him. And remembered his arrival outside Stern—some of it clear, some merely smoke.

His cousin atop the wall revealing Cyr might not return until nightfall and assuring Vitalis he had the power to act on his behalf.

Vitalis's re-negotiation of the trade to include the release of Hawisa's maid.

Glimpsing Aelfled above, then below when she and the rebels passed over the drawbridge.

His mount carrying him beneath the portcullis.

Being eased out of the saddle in which he had struggled to remain upright lest he find himself delivered like a sack of grain over its back.

And what else?

Nicola, though only her voice. She had called to Vitalis, named him a pig, and said she would kill him if her brother died.

The Saxon warrior must have laughed, unaware she was not all threat. The girl—or was she a woman now?—had a good bite. And her brothers, foremost Guarin, had sharpened those pretty teeth as much as their parents allowed for one destined to become a wife and mother.

"It matters not if it was done by his hand," Cyr returned him to the present, "or he ordered another."

Shifting his regard to where the second born had halted alongside the bed, their aunt hovering near, Guarin was jolted by Cyr's appearance—exceedingly familiar for how long they had been brothers, exceedingly strange for how long since Guarin had looked close upon one of his own.

Though no longer was Cyr's silvered hair cropped on the sides as when they had crossed the channel, and his jaw was darkened by whiskers, he was groomed enough none would mistake him for a Saxon. Not so Guarin whose mirror all these months had been his reflection in others' eyes and basins of water on the rare occasion light entered the cave at the right angle.

The concern lining his brother's face deepening, Guarin recalled it was Vitalis of whom they spoke and his brother yet believed him responsible for these injuries. "Not by his orders," he croaked, throat so parched a swallow of saliva provided little relief.

A moment later, a cup was at his lips. "Drink," Cyr ordered.

Guarin gulped it dry—and more when it was refilled.

"God's sweet mercy," Cyr said, "I am glad you are returned to us. We feared you dead."

Slowly, Guarin filled his lungs. "Far from it, though had Vitalis not..." Ache crossing from one side of him to the other, he groaned and drew shallow breaths until the worst was past.

"If you can," Cyr said, "tell me what I ought know about the knave as quickly as possible, for I must pursue him whilst there is yet light."

Despite anger over his captivity this last beating had loosed from his depths, Guarin hesitated. *Am I a traitor to my own that I do not want that?* he mulled. *Is it not my purpose—my right—to see rebellious Saxons brought to heel and justice done?*

The answer was Hawisa who had lost a husband and child to

those who came into her country uninvited. The answer was Vitalis who must have lost loved ones but taken no part in tormenting Guarin. The answer was Rosa who lost all she loved and her own life. The answer was her fellow rebels who beat a Norman chained like a dog whilst accusing him of murder, destruction, hunger, and theft. The answer was all they cast at him was true, even if not dealt by *this* Norman.

"He is a knave," Guarin agreed, "but he is not the dangerous one. Rather, not as dangerous as..." He saw that one, still could not say if the light in those eyes was of evil or madness. "...Jaxon."

Cyr stepped nearer. "Jaxon?"

"The first in command ahead of Vitalis. I believe it was he who ordered the deaths of the Norman family passing over Wulfenshire."

"He answers to Dotter?"

Guarin stiffened. "Oui, but only if he determines Gytha would approve. If he thinks not, he answers to himself."

"You speak of King Harold's mother?"

He nodded. "She remains determined to return her family to power."

"Continue if you can."

"Long Jaxon has wished me dead, but ever Dotter and Vitalis stay his hand."

"For what if not ransom, a demand for which we never received?"

Gratitude and guilt, Guarin silently named Hawisa's motives. *And were I to believe her, that she feels the unforgivable for her enemy.*

"I cannot say."

Suspicion shone from Cyr's eyes. "What else can you tell?"

Though every breath made Guarin long for the numb place from which he had been wrenched, he said, "Jaxon seeks to come out from under the watch of Vitalis that Dotter sets over him, even if it means turning on her and sacrificing the lives of rebels."

"Lillefarne," Cyr said. "You heard Vitalis and his men were captured there?"

"Oui, and I saw the look on Jaxon's face that told he was not displeased. I am guessing it was his man, Sigward, who set all in motion."

"You guess right."

"Thus, he turned on Dotter, and sure of his success set to ridding himself of me. But no swift death, though I nearly wished it these past days when he and his followers beat a chained man unable to defend himself." Seeing Cyr's face darken, he reminded, "As told, Vitalis did not do this. Had he—" His throat closed, and the cough required to open it was so forceful he gave a shout of pain.

"Enough, Cyr," Aunt Chanson said. "Your brother must—"

"Non, I covet sleep," Guarin said, "but when I awaken it may be too late." He looked to Cyr. "Had Vitalis not stolen into the camp and brought me out, this eve would have been my last."

Cyr's eyes widened. "You are not saying he is your friend?"

"Non, but neither is he the murderer Jaxon is. Vitalis has a reason for what he does that I would act on were I in his place."

"And Dotter?"

"I believe her actions more justified than William's in gaining England's crown."

"You have met her?"

Were this not his brother, he would lie. Guarin nodded.

"You know whose face she hides behind?"

Even greater the temptation to lie...

"Do you protect your captor, Guarin?"

He did. But how far? Farther than he trusted Cyr?

"You know the woman who was traded for you is Lady Hawisa's maid?" his brother prompted.

Guarin drew another breath, felt his cracked and broken ribs shift. "I know."

"On the day past, I wed her."

Guarin jerked. Cyr wed? To a Saxon? To the one who had served Hawisa?

"She is Lady Aelfled D'Argent," his brother added.

And she had been traded for his brother. "I did not know. And I am guessing neither did Vitalis."

A muscle in Cyr's jaw convulsing, he said, "Where would he take her?"

"Not the camp from which he freed me."

"Where?" he demanded.

Guarin shook his head. "Methinks he will not harm her."

"Where, Guarin?"

He narrowed his lids. "You care for your Saxon wife?"

"I do, though I would have done the same as Maël to safely deliver you inside these walls." His shoulders rose with breath surely meant to calm him. "When there is time, I shall tell you how we came to be. Suffice to say, I want her back."

Was it possible he who loved the wielding of arms and his merciless reputation loved one not of steel and accolades but a woman forged of flesh? And so soon? Or was this desire that would run its course and leave Cyr bound to one he did not want? Regardless, the truth must be told.

"As you have guessed, Lady Hawisa is Dotter, and I believe she tasked Vitalis with retrieving her maid, but not to do her ill. As the lady does not know you, nor that Aelfled now has the protection of your name and position, she must fear for her."

"Then it is from Wulfen Castle I ought to retrieve my wife."

"I believe so, but be of great care, Brother." Guarin lowered his lids. "I would guess Jaxon and his men destined there seeking Vitalis who they likely believe stole me from them."

Cyr gripped a hand over Guarin's. "Ere I ride on Wulfen, I shall send word to Theriot and Dougray at Balduc you are returned to us. Rest well."

Mention of Dougray halted Guarin's descent into sleep. Here proof the third brother had also survived Senlac. Including Maël, they remained five. "Much praise," he breathed, then was struck that nearly all his family were in England. *As if we were born to this land,* he mused. *But were we, we would be the conquered. We would be the rebels. And I would not be Hawisa's enemy...*

Jolted by the sound of Cyr's boots in retreat and the realization Hawisa would soon face Normans and, likely, Jaxon, Guarin called, "I want your word!"

"Anything."

"Whatever happens, keep the Lady of Wulfen safe, whether it be her own come against her or ours."

His brother inclined his head. "I shall do all I can. We will speak more later." Then he was gone.

Lord, Guarin silently entreated as he returned to the depths, *keep safe Cyr's lady. Keep safe mine.*

~

Wulfen Castle
England

UNDER SIEGE. An offense—nay, abomination.

The enemy were not Normans. They were her own. *Her* rebels, led by *her* man. An abomination, and yet...

Light in the dark of this night, bright as if shone from the face of God—as if He were with the besieged. Was He?

Certes, much favor was shown Isa and her people that the betrayal came as no surprise...that they were prepared for the attack following her refusal to admit Jaxon...that as the rebels loosed flaming arrows into the outer bailey, Vitalis and his rebels returned from Stern as told by Aelfled who had stolen into the castle...that if the attackers took control of the outer bailey, there was food and drink to sustain all inside the donjon for weeks...

that were the inner bailey also lost, the underground passage would deliver them from the blades of those now more the enemy than Normans—and keep the young man longer known as Eberhard out of Jaxon's hands.

Aye, much favor shown them, Isa conceded as she led the way out of the passage revealed to Aelfled. It had to mean the Lord was with them.

Drawing a forearm across her brow, assuring herself it was moist from exertion rather than fever, she and her former maid stepped from behind the tapestry into the solar.

Those earlier gathered here to give counsel had been joined by another whose report shook her certainty the Lord was with them. Despite the efforts of Vitalis and his men, their numbers were insufficient against Jaxon's five score or more. The outer bailey was breached, and it was feared the inner would be taken as well.

Knowing the donjon's doors would not long resist the besiegers, Isa issued orders to prepare the castle folk for departure and the warriors defending the inner bailey to retreat the moment it was lost.

Her men hastened from the solar, as did Aelfled whom Isa, believing her in need of protection, had endangered by requiring her release with the rebels captured by the Baron of Stern. No safer place could she have been than beneath the roof of the Norman she revealed she had wed.

Rather than angered, Isa had been shocked by what was told her in the passage. And ashamed by envy.

Lady Aelfled was now of greater standing than the Saxon widow Lady Hawisa. More, she who no longer had cause to do Isa's bidding was much desired if not loved by a D'Argent—all the more enviable were Cyr as honorable as Guarin.

I am happy for her, she told herself and, determined to see Aelfled restored to her husband as soon as possible, crossed to the brother and sister who stood before the hearth. "Em?"

The young woman looked up from hands so tightly knit they brought to mind the slain warriors upon Senlac whose colorless flesh gripped weapons they would never again wield. But there was naught colorless nor lifeless about the eyes delving hers.

"My lady?"

"Take yourself to the hall and aid Aelfled."

Em blinked. "What of Eberhard?"

"He will aid me."

Seeing protest in the brown and blue, Isa said, "He is safe with me, as he has been since the day you parted." Then she addressed another of the young woman's concerns. "'Tis true those outside seeking to come inside are Saxon-born the same as we, but they are dangerous—in this moment, more than Normans. When there is time, I will explain. For now, trust me to do what is best for those within these walls."

Em looked to her brother.

"Lady Hawisa has been as a mother to me," he said. "I am well with this."

Not entirely, she knew, feeling his reluctance to be parted from his sister and sensing the turning of his mind that formed questions whose answers would be difficult to cast in a good light considering all Em had endured.

Will they forgive me? she wondered as his sister crossed the solar. In the dark ere dawn, she had pondered the same of Guarin. How many more had she wronged in defying William's rule to relieve her people's suffering? When all was done, would it be said she had hurt more than helped?

"Lady Hawisa?" Wulfrith—rather, Eberhard—said. "Are you afeared?"

She was, almost as much for what she had wrought as what Jaxon wreaked. Hearing the curtain drop closed behind his sister, she said, "I am, but though some would name it weakness, methinks this fear God-given."

He nodded. "Fear built the passage, did it not? And it will save us."

She nearly embraced him. "It will. Now come. There is wealth to be hidden and wealth to be taken to sustain us until our return."

And we will return, she silently affirmed. *Wulfen Castle is of Wulfrith—is Saxon, will never be Norman. I will reclaim it.*

CHAPTER THIRTY

early there, Isa assured herself as she peered past the housecarles leading the way. Though the one at the fore carried a torch whose flame lit the section hastily stabilized with timbers, there was no light beyond. But there would be little in the wood at night even were the moon full.

As she drew another breath that carried the waterfall's scent and moisture, she heard its sound. At this distance, it could be mistaken for a mother shushing her babe to sleep. Not so the creak of timbers, evidencing one of the castle folk had jostled a support. Not so the shower of dirt loosed on their heads. Not so the murmurs, whimpers, and muffled coughing.

Isa looked across her shoulder past Aelfled, Wulfrith, and Em to those no longer two abreast but single file, the soldiers amongst them ensuring an orderly progression and calming the ones who succumbed to panic.

At the center of the column, Ordric held a torch aloft, as did one of two housecarles bringing up the rear.

"Not much farther," Isa murmured and looked to the rope wrapped around the base of one timber and stretched to the base of the next. And so it went post to post, nearly all the way to the outlet ahead.

It was a sorry thing to undo so much work, but this farthest section must be collapsed lest too quickly their pursuers gained entrance to the donjon.

Jaxon was aware of what Wulfen's walls hid, and before Isa feared trusting him, she had revealed her plan to extend the passage to the wood. Since then, she had bemoaned the lack of progress, rued the collapse that cost lives, and agreed it was a waste of time, effort, and coin. But he would know where to begin his search for those who had disappeared, none of whom had been born with wings.

Lord, delay him long enough to see us aboveground, she silently prayed. And was punched by His answer—a shout from the bend in the passage they had minutes earlier come around, the voice frighteningly familiar, then another shower of dirt as the castle folk surged forward.

"Calm!" Ordric commanded. "Though pursued, we must consider each step. Move quickly, but remain center. And do not touch the timbers. As soon as all are clear, we shall collapse the passage atop those who follow. Go!"

How many did Jaxon bring against her housecarles? Isa wondered. How many would die?

Touching the hilt of her sword, she determined she would join those at the rear, but a moment later discovered it was too dangerous when she was shoved against the man in front of her.

"Fear not!" bellowed one of the housecarles. "The warriors at our backs will keep us from their blades."

A moment later, another shout from the opposite end. Though not of Jaxon, it made Aelfled bump her lady as she whipped around.

Isa turned. Seeing Eberhard had steadied the young woman and those behind pressed so hard they threatened to knock the two into a support, Isa pulled Aelfled close. "For what do you endanger all? Come!"

Aelfled resisted. "Pray, do not collapse the passage. My—"

Isa slapped her as she had never done, dropping Aelfled to her knees. "Get up!" She tried to drag her to her feet lest those pressing forward trample her, but the young woman broke free and lunged to the wall opposite the one whose lower posts were roped together. Pressing herself flat between the supports, she stared wide-eyed at Isa.

Regardless of what made her behave recklessly—likely panic—she was beyond Isa's reach, the castle folk carrying their lady forward.

"Dear Lord, keep her from Jaxon," Isa breathed.

Then from the rear came the sound of steel on steel and the shouts of Jaxon and her housecarles. And more distant, other shouts and the beating of blades.

Following her men up out of the passage, Isa heard Ordric command, "Collapse the passage!"

Then he deemed the castle folk clear of that section. But what of her housecarles at the rear? Were they to be sacrificed to hold back Jaxon and his men? Or had they prevailed against one who had been their instructor longer than their adversary?

Aided by a grip on her arm, Isa sprang into cool night air and heard Ordric again, this time Aelfled's name on his lips.

Guessing he sought to save her, fearing the attempt would take his life as well, Isa swung around to face the gaping hole out of which the castle folk hastened like ants from a flooded nest.

There her boy, Em, the physician, the cook, the porter—all yanked onto moist dirt excavated from the passage.

As Isa lurched forward to aid in assisting others from the underground, beyond their gasps and praise of the Lord, she heard Aelfled's name called again. But it did not sound of Ordric. Nor Jaxon. Then that same voice commanded the young woman to run and...

Collapse the passage? Surely not. Aelfled had not the strength.

Isa caught her breath at the loud creak of timbers, more shouts from those below, the groaning of supports.

"Please, Lord," she entreated as she pulled a chambermaid up out of the hole. Then she herself was yanked away. "Aelfled! Ordric!" she cried. A moment later, she was face down, the sound of crashing timbers paining her ears, dirt and rocks falling like cruel rain, the passage's foul, dusty breath billowing all around.

~

AELFLED LIVED, Ordric having carried her from the passage once sufficient debris was removed.

Thanking the Lord for answered prayer—*mostly* answered, the housecarles at the rear having been slain by Jaxon—Isa touched her former maid's shoulder.

A hand raised to shield her eyes against the light of torches, Aelfled looked from those gathered around to where Isa had dropped to her haunches. "Cyr?" she croaked, then coughed. "H-he made it out?"

Staring into the abraded, dirt-streaked face below hers, Isa wondered if the young woman was delirious. "What say you, Aelf?"

It was Ordric who answered. "D'Argent was in the passage, my lady."

She swept her gaze up him. "You say it was not Jaxon down there?"

"The traitor was there, my lady, but giving chase was the Norman who stole your lands."

Isa did not know how it was possible Cyr D'Argent had gained the underground—would have expected Vitalis long before the Baron of Stern—but here the cause of Aelfled's reckless behavior. She had heard her husband among their pursuers, knew he came for her.

279

"And it was the throw of his sword that slowed Jaxon enough for us to collapse the tunnel on both," Ordric added.

"Both!" Aelfled gasped and began to wail.

Aching for her loss, Isa pressed a hand over her mouth lest the enemy stalked the wood. "Aelfled aided in collapsing the passage?" she demanded of Ordric.

"Though I commanded her to it, she did not until D'Argent ordered the same. When I reached her to give aid, she..."

He shook his head, and she imagined Aelfled had grieved then for the sacrifice to be made as she did now for the sacrifice made.

She loved, Isa acknowledged. *Still, she did the bidding of one who may have returned her love, losing him to save the many.*

Catching sobs against her palm, Isa raised her other hand and brushed the hair from the new widow's eyes. "Brave Aelfled."

The young woman's chest convulsed.

"It seems we are not all the fools of men," Isa said. "You did what had to be done, Aelfled. I know there is pain in that, but there is joy in having saved so many—and of your own." She eased her hand from the young woman's mouth. "It is much to ask, but you must be strong again. Can you?"

Aelfled stared at her out of eyes so wet it was as if all the stars had come down out of the heavens to mourn her loss.

Isa looked at those gathered near. "We dare not return to Wulfen. Though Jaxon is dead, some—perhaps many—of his followers live. And of greater threat is the usurper. After what was wrought this eve, he will question my allegiance and if he does not remove me from Wulfen, shall take steps to better control me, forcing me to wed one of his own. And I will not..." She cleared her throat. "Never will I, the daughter of Wulfrith, be the prize of a Norman, valued only for bedding and making children to bear *his* name. Thus, elsewhere we shall gather our strength and prepare for the day we take back what belongs to us."

A foolish hope as Guarin believed? she questioned amid the still across which the sound of the waterfall traveled. Likely, especially as it was not only Normans they must guard against. But what else was there for them?

She straightened. "It is time to depart, Aelf."

Ordric raised the young woman. "I feared that," he said when she stumbled against him. "Your foot was pinned beneath a timber."

Guessing Aelfled's ankle was injured, Isa said, "You shall have to carry her through the wood, Ordric."

"Nay, I do not go with you," the young woman protested.

Isa ordered the others to prepare for departure, then said, "There is naught for you here, Aelfled."

"If Cyr is alive, there is much for me."

Isa grunted. "Tell her, Ordric."

When the young woman looked to him, he said, "You must know there is little chance he survived."

"Little, meaning not impossible."

"The passage is down, so filled with rubble that were there light on the other side one could not see it."

"That does not mean he is buried the same as Jaxon."

"Jaxon is not buried—not entirely. He was near us when the passage came down."

Aelfled caught her breath.

"Dead," Ordric assured her, "but as D'Argent was not far behind, I wager the Norman is well enough buried he could remain there were it consecrated ground."

"I wager against you!" Teeth chattering, Aelfled returned her gaze to Isa. "Even did I wish to go with you, I would slow you. Pray, leave me."

"Here?" Isa swept a hand around the wood sliced in two by the stream fed by the waterfall. "There is no time to deliver you nearer the castle, and I will risk no life for so distant a hope it will be safe for you there. Come with us."

"Nay. Find me a sturdy stick, and I can make my own way out of here."

Isa loathed leaving her, but furthering the argument would delay distancing the castle folk from any who pursued them. "Your path is your own. I will not stand in the middle of it nor force you onto mine. I…"

Was this farewell? Would they not see each other again? Would what had been broken by Wulf's death remain so? "It is hard to forgive, Aelf," Isa whispered, "but I try. I do."

Tears spilled onto the young woman's cheeks. "I thank you, my lady."

"See her sheltered upstream near the falls lest any venture here in search of us." Isa ordered Ordric, then glanced at the great veil falling from on high, the ridge of which many a warrior in training had negotiated since first Wulfen began supplying England's worthiest defenders.

Turning aside memories of time spent at the waterfall with her young son, often accompanied by her maid, she said, "Provide her a good stick and provisions, then we leave." She looked to Aelfled. "Do not risk the journey ere dawn. After all you have endured, you must rest, and regardless of the outcome of the attack on Wulfen, it will be better seen in daylight and aid in determining the way forward."

"I shall journey forth at dawn," Aelfled said as the housecarle lifted her into his arms. "Godspeed, my lady."

"My lady," Isa mused. "If you are still *Lady* Aelfled, and my fate lies beyond Wulfen's walls, I am no longer that to you."

More tears fell. *"Ever* you shall be my lady."

"Godspeed, Aelf." Isa pivoted. Head lightening, she firmed her footing and continued forward.

Though she wished to believe the sudden movement was responsible for nearly losing her balance, her people could not afford the lie. To lead them through and around whatever lay in wait, she would move only as fast as necessary to stay ahead of immediate danger. And God-willing, they would find their place in Norman-occupied England.

CHAPTER THIRTY-ONE

Wulfenshire, England
Late November, 1068

*T*he D'Argents were a hardy lot, else much loved by God. Likely both. And where these Normans were concerned, it was difficult to begrudge the Almighty His favorites.

He had answered Isa's prayers Guarin live and reclaim the warrior Jaxon sought to destroy. He had answered Aelfled's prayers Cyr survive the passage's collapse and reclaim his wife. And surely He had answered prayers the third brother recover from the loss of an arm at Hastings and the fourth depart that blood-soaked battlefield unscathed.

Aye, difficult to begrudge Him—even though what was hers was now theirs.

Cyr D'Argent first made Baron of Stern, next Balduc.

Theriot D'Argent made castellan of Balduc the day Em fled Campagnon, unaware her master would be arrested for acting against his liege.

And now Guarin D'Argent in possession of Wulfen which had been declared forfeit following the rebel-on-rebel clash that

283

proved too notable to escape Le Bâtard's notice and too great an excuse to relieve its heir of her property. In their entirety, the Wulfrith lands were now in Norman hands.

For the time being, Isa assured herself despite little evidence William's rule would be overturned.

Four months had passed since she and her faithful carved out a place for themselves in Nottinghamshire. Though Saxon uprisings were without cease across England, the few that gained footholds were not long in being unbalanced or toppled. Hence, the greatest hope for English rule seemed King Harold's former housecarle, Edwin Harwolfson—unless he was mostly rumor and, rather than patiently awaiting the right opportunity, had insufficient numbers and strength.

And inadequate funds, Isa considered, next the wealth she had been forced to leave behind. Were it possible to get it in Harwolfson's hands, allowing him to better equip his forces and attract worthier rebels, would it aid in dethroning William? Or would it become another foothold lost?

Isa tipped her face to the autumn sun, closed her eyes, and drifted.

Would Guarin come this day? If he did, would she dare as she had set out to do? Or would she falter?

She shivered and was more ashamed she did so out of anticipation than fear.

Her scouts sent out this past month reported there was little discernible pattern to his solitary outings other than he departed the castle on horseback, tethered his mount on the outskirts of his chosen hunting grounds, and stalked his prey on foot. She had hoped they would discover more of a pattern, but the warrior surely guarded against rendering himself inescapably vulnerable. Hence, this was Isa's fourth foray upon Wulfen's most distant hunting ground where he was not averse to venturing though it was that same portion of wood where she had taken an arrow.

Anglicus shifted beneath her, turning his head and stretching his neck toward another patch of grass.

"But an hour longer, and we shall start back," she murmured. Then rubbing her shoulder that often ached, she returned her gaze to what she should not have distanced it from.

Movement among the trees. Hooded and cloaked in a dark blue mantle, here was a pattern. Every scout had reported him attired thus, only the bow at his side and quiver of arrows on his back visible, other weapons concealed beneath that which she had given him. Rather, she assumed it was the same mantle. Perhaps she just wished it.

"Guarin," she whispered, and those sounds in her mouth, next her ear, nearly made her retreat.

Stay the course, she told herself. *Lead, and he will follow.*

She dropped her hood to her shoulders to expose unbound hair she had taken particular care to wash and brush to a shine the day before each of her forays. The one who kept Wulfen for William would recognize her mount, but here proof she had not been deprived of so fine a destrier.

She turned Anglicus's head and tapped him forward.

Counting on Guarin making her the quarry he was not to know she made him, she moved through the wood at a leisurely pace to accommodate his stride and stealth, occasionally peering around as expected of one who risked much returning to the place from which she had exiled herself.

Catching no further glimpse of Guarin, she paused at the stream to allow him to make up for ground lost to stealth. And remembered not far from this stretch he had kissed her as asked of him. And she—

A sound that might only be the patter of paws on fallen leaves warning he could be nearer than thought, she listened for further movement. Though she caught none, her senses told he was very near. As it was not the plan they face each other here and to ensure her return to Nottinghamshire, they must continue on.

Upon emerging from the wood onto the meadow, Isa set Anglicus to a gallop. Though she left Guarin behind, he would know where to find her. But would he come?

~

AND SO *I walk into her trap*, Guarin mused as her blade pricked the center of his back. *As she walks into mine.*

Like a hound with its nose to the ground, he had followed Hawisa across the meadow and into the ravine. And at the outskirts of the camp found her yet astride as if torn by the sight of what was abandoned the night Jaxon besieged Wulfen Castle.

As he had spied on the lady who had so thoroughly disappeared some believed her dead, he confirmed she appeared well.

She was fuller of face beyond lush golden hair he had never before seen completely unbound, fuller of figure as evidenced by curves above and below the sword-and-dagger weighted belt. And when she dismounted, it was no heedful endeavor but thoughtlessness born of confidence and vigor, the same as her stride. She had faltered as she neared the posts, either due to the missing rings and chains or remembrance of what was done there.

For that, she had set herself at his back when he followed her into the cave he had not expected her to enter. Why had she chosen this vile place, especially as it seemed she wanted something from him? But there the greater question—what she would ask of one from whom already she had taken much. To learn the answer and give warning, he had shown himself in the wood. But not recklessly.

Though the Hawisa he knew meant him no harm, it was possible she kept company with a Hawisa he did not know—one formed by a changed heart, mind, and resolve following Jaxon's betrayal, forfeiture of the last of her lands, and tidings her former captive had been given control of Wulfen.

The blade pricked deeper, and in her language she said, "I did not come alone."

Not a lie, but a threat? he pondered as he moved his gaze around the cave. Or warning only? he considered as he set to settling his soul as was only possible since venturing here alone and removing the greatest evidence of his captivity—manacles, chains, iron rings set in the wall.

Settled enough, he told himself and looked around.

Her dimly-lit face to the right of the cave's entrance was as familiar to him as his would have been to her when he entered with his hood down to allow her to sooner confirm his identity.

"How fitting you should catch me absent solitude, my lady," he said, "though I ought tell, this time I have the advantage. And a great one. Just as you set men around the camp in anticipation I would follow you here, hours earlier I set men around in anticipation you would lead me here."

Fear leapt from her. Watched by Guarin's men, no protection could they afford her. And none themselves.

"I do not believe you." Her words sounded more hopeful than firm.

"I saw you in the wood ere you saw me, Hawisa, to shepherd you onward made myself heard near the stream when you paused. And ere entering the cave, I ensured I was heard again, certain it was safer for all I not catch you unawares."

Silence.

Having left bow and quiver outside, sword and dagger on his belt, he opened empty hands to the sides. "My neck begins to stiffen, and much I desire to look close on you. Will you come around?"

She hesitated, then stepped wide to the side and in front of him.

Face and hair lit by sunlight angling between jagged stones, lovelier than ever he had seen her, she set the blade's tip beneath his sternum.

A glance confirming it was his dagger seen as she tethered Anglicus, he said, "I am glad you did not bestow my gift upon Vitalis a second time." Truth, though also a means of probing whether that warrior had survived Jaxon's attempt to slay him the night Guarin would have given much to be at his brother's side.

Though Cyr had ridden on Wulfen to retrieve the woman he loved, upon finding the two rebel forces clashing outside its walls, he and his men had allied with Vitalis and his *Rebels of the Pale,* as they were now known for the strips of material tied to their arms to differentiate them from Jaxon's rebels.

Vitalis had been the first to follow their common enemy into the donjon after the doors came down. When he fell to Jaxon's sword, it was left to Cyr to defeat the one who had not only dragged his brother to the edge of death but pursued Hawisa, Aelfled, and the castle folk through the underground. For it, Cyr had nearly been buried beneath the collapse.

But what of Hawisa's man who yet lived when the two parted ways, only to go missing with a dozen of his rebels when the injured and dead were numbered? As Vitalis had been left in the care of Zedekiah, it was believed the big man carried him from Wulfen. But for naught?

Though tempted to ask, and much he wished to know if one of those beyond the cave was the housecarle who loved his lady more than he ought, he said, "Do you intend to put the blade through me?"

"You know not how much I wish you were Le Bâtard," she said, then gave a huff of disgust. "Wishes—a fool's hope for light in a world bereft of sunshine, at times even wax and wicks." She took a step back, ran her eyes over him. "You are healed, look again the warrior first I met. Or nearly so. I expected your hair shorn and face shaven, but still you appear more a Saxon than a

Norman." Her mouth curved. "Have you found something about my countrymen you like?"

He lowered his hands to his sides. "I grew accustomed to the style and, particularly, less time spent submitting to the tug and scrape of blades."

"As also you grew accustomed to my mantle though it is worn and of Saxon cloth and cut?"

"It is comfortable. And keeps near memories of my captor."

Seeing her tense as if that last was threat rather than admission of feelings that distracted him beyond good sense, he rebuked himself for allowing one truth to embitter another. But then, she had chosen this place to face him.

Suppressing anger he did not intend to direct at her, he lowered his gaze over her garments whose wear evidenced her reduced state—likely the same tunic and chausses worn the night she and Vitalis released him. On the return to her face, he closed fingers into his palms to keep from reaching to her golden tresses.

"You look well yourself, though I did not know it proper for a Saxon no longer a maiden to wear her hair unbound and uncovered outside the marital chamber."

"'Tis not. I but wished you certain of whom you followed."

"Since I expected you on those hunting grounds, I had no cause to question it."

"Will you tell how you knew I would be there?"

"So you may find me unprepared the next time?"

"There will not be a next time—certes, not like this. I sought to meet with you because there is something I need, not for myself but…" She sighed. "It is for me, though now your king has taken all, I am no longer Lady of Wulfen."

"My curiosity is roused, but I am more curious about how you intend to charm a favor out of one against whom you hold a blade."

She lowered the dagger.

"So we might ease the minds of our men and ensure we are not interrupted," Guarin said, "let us show ourselves and speak outside." Beyond the cave as once they had done, their meetings keeping him from tilting into a place so dark it might have claimed him no matter how high and cloudless the sun.

At her hesitation, he said, "If Vitalis is among the six come out of the North with you, he will not long be content with your absence."

Something resembling satisfaction flickered in her eyes. "How were you not only aware I would be on those hunting grounds but whence I came with my men?"

"First we ease their minds, Hawisa, then I explain, and next we speak of what you want from me. And what I want from you." The latter spurred by recent events in the South.

Her eyebrows gathered. "I will not surrender myself nor my people."

"I would not ask it of you."

"Then?"

He motioned her to precede him.

She started to slide the dagger in its scabbard, paused, and extended it.

As done before, he said, "I will collect it later."

"Do you not take it now, you may not see it again."

"I believe I will."

She shrugged, sheathed the dagger, and exited ahead of him.

Imagining her men's relief, Guarin felt satisfaction that soon they would discover the Saxon rather than the Norman was prey —and the futility of attempting to defend their lady. Or so he hoped, yet troubled by what he might have seen in Hawisa's eyes.

Shortly, she settled on her rock and he on his, in sight of those who watched but distant enough their conversation could not be heard, providing it remained civil.

Clasping her hands, she lowered her gaze to them and slid one thumb over the other. Again and again.

More remembrance, he guessed and was also drawn there

though with less strength than during an earlier visit to the camp when he had flayed some memories and been flayed by others.

She swallowed loudly, and he saw now she looked at his hands. "I am glad you are no longer bound, Guarin. I wish you had never been."

He glanced at his scarred wrists. "Wishes, a fool's hope for light in a world bereft of sunshine, did you not say?"

Her lashes fluttered. "I hope you know how great my regret."

"I do."

She glanced at the wood. "Will my men and I be permitted to leave?"

Did she recall her pledge she would not make it easy for him to capture and hold her and his threat to do so for what he had named *restitution*—a threat fulfilled later than hoped, but with less effort than expected?

He inclined his head. "All will be permitted to leave."

"Unbound?"

"Unbound."

"It would be hard to begrudge you a lie."

He gripped his hands between his knees as had not been possible when last he sat here with her. "No lie. Providing your men do not aggress against mine, all may leave the same as you came."

"I thank you. Now will you tell how I failed my sire?"

"Your sire?"

"I thought I understood the training required to make men proficient in stealth, but that you knew my plan means it was executed poorly."

He smiled. "Fear not, Hawisa. Your men are admirably proficient."

"Then?"

"Dougray."

Color bloomed in her cheeks. "The third D'Argent brother you revealed is not of the same sire," she said with resentment for one who liked her no better, possibly as much for what one of her people had taken from him at Senlac as the captivity Guarin had suffered. "I understand he who is not of the silvered hair and lost an arm at Hastings is the same who disguised himself as a Saxon to insert himself in Vitalis's sortie, thereby allowing Cyr to capture all at Lillefarne."

Guarin nodded. "He is gifted with stealth beyond many a mortal. When weeks past I sensed I was watched and could not satisfy my suspicion, I had him follow me at a distance. That first day, Dougray rooted out the one tracking me and each day thereafter. As never did your scouts seek to engage me, he did not engage them though great our curiosity over the one for whom they sought a pattern. I hoped you sent them but also knew it could be Campagnon or—"

"Campagnon?" she exclaimed. "But he was arrested."

"And released, his men standing firm he was unaware of the attack on Stern. More unfortunate, weeks past those mercenaries were also released, their months of imprisonment deemed adequate punishment."

"Dear Lord…"

Was she thinking of the slave, Em, whose presence at Wulfen during Jaxon's siege Aelfled had mentioned?

"So this is how your *William the Great* rules England," Hawisa scorned, "punishing Saxons with death, Normans with—what?—a slap? A flick on the nose?"

"I like it no better than you."

"Not possible!"

He breathed deep. "In an England where Normans are the great minority, William makes good use of eager swords like those of Campagnon and his men."

She gasped. "Then that miscreant did not depart our shores with the mercenaries Le Bâtard released from his service."

He was not surprised she had heard that, following William's recent defeat of rebellions in the Southwest, the Midlands, and the North, the king had rewarded men eager to return home and sent them away. But whatever hope she found in fewer enemies roaming her country was surely trampled by despair over William's confidence he had a stranglehold on England.

"He remained behind," Guarin confirmed, "doubtless hopeful of earning another award of land and, in between, filling his purse with coin."

She gnawed at that in silence, then said, "No ill was intended in having you followed. I but wished us to meet alone. When a pattern to your solitary hunts could not be found, it was determined the best place to forge a meeting was the eastern wood since it is most distant from the castle. And safer yet could I draw you here."

"Where your men lay in wait."

"Only to defend me. I did not think it necessary, but they insisted. This is my fourth journey here."

"One every three days," he said, "the pattern Dougray found."

Her eyes widened. "How?"

"On days I did not depart the castle, he took it on himself to watch for your scouts and track their routes. He discovered no matter how many times they twisted back lest they were followed, always a mount awaited them in the eastern wood to carry them north. Hence, when a scout did not appear for two days, Dougray ventured there. And found a woman garbed in men's clothes, golden hair unbound, sitting atop a grey, flaxen-maned destrier."

Hawisa flushed as if ashamed of being oblivious to her own watcher.

"After wandering the wood for several hours," Guarin continued, "you departed, and he followed you here where you collected your men and rode north. As I believed you sought to meet with me, I joined Dougray the next day, but you did not come, nor the next. However, on the third day whilst I visited villages, my brother witnessed your return and saw you did as before—wandering the wood before retrieving your men and going north. He persuaded me to allow him to discover a pattern, and then we prepared for this day by seeding the camp with men before yours arrived."

She sat straighter. "Your murderous uncle taught you and your brothers well."

His first thought was to defend Hugh, his next he could not. Cyr having aided Aelfled in removing the bodies of five boys from the battlefield—including Hawisa's son—he had verified the likelihood their uncle slew the youths and told he believed the only way they could end Hugh's life alongside their own was if the warrior was seriously injured.

"Not the best of men," Guarin said, "and far from the worst, he gifted his son and nephews with unsurpassed training. I am sorry he took the lives of your son and the sons of others."

Her jaw convulsed.

"Though I cannot tell you it is in the past and to leave it there since I have not lost a child and pray never shall I, you are not without a future, Hawisa."

"Am I not?" she exclaimed. "Is not all that was Wulfrith now your brother's—and yours?"

Her tone offensive, Guarin said, "Despite my every warning of what you risked in raising rebel forces whilst bending the knee to William, you stayed the course."

"You say this is my due? Me and mine should suffer for defending our lives and homes?"

Her voice having risen enough to reach her men, Guarin raised a hand. "I do not say that, and I would make two things clear. First, no testimony had William from me that you led or conspired with the rebels, and only Jaxon and Sigward did I name as my captors. Nor did any of my family speak against you. Hence, your lands were forfeited because of the division between the rebels who set themselves at each other and information pried from Jaxon's injured men."

Her eyes widened. "What of Vitalis's injured men? I was told Cyr and you allowed them to return to their villages."

"We did—those upon Wulfenshire and the few from beyond our borders—possible only because Cyr had the injured who wore the pale taken to Stern where they recovered without the king's knowledge."

The relief softening her face was short-lived. "Does your cousin know this?"

Silent Maël, as changed by Hastings as Dougray, though not all because of the damage done the most handsome D'Argent. "He knows."

"And is the king's man!"

"We are all the king's men, Hawisa. But first, in between, and in the end we are D'Argents."

She parted her lips as if to contest that, then pressed them tight.

"I hope you do not think betrayal the reason those returned to their villages have not sought you out," he said. "They agreed to the terms of release—to live peaceably and raise arms only to defend family and home. Too, those upon Wulfenshire are watched closely."

"Then you do not trust them to keep their word."

"Mostly I do, but fear and desperation make oath breakers of many. Too, I am not the only D'Argent who risks much in sheltering those who defied William."

"I understand, as should you that never would I begrudge my people their safety. They are where I would have them be."

He believed her. "Now the second thing I would make clear. None of what was taken from you belongs to me."

She startled. "But you hold Wulfen."

"*Hold*. I remain in England only because the king commanded I administer this demesne until he awards it elsewhere."

Her breath caught.

"Hawisa?"

"I wish to take back my home, but should that prove impossible…" She shook her head. "I would be as well as I could knowing your Norman hands are the ones in which my people find themselves."

Her good regard caused his chest to tighten just as when he thought of her as he ought not—and spoke as he should not as done during Cyr's recent visit. Though he wanted to blame too much wine for his musing aloud England suited him and suggesting the second born remain their sire's heir as when it was believed the first was dead, he had done so before making it to the bottom of his first pour.

"I am honored, Hawisa, but the king will cast his gold, silver, and dirt where he wishes, and when he casts Wulfen upon a favorite, I shall return to Normandy and my inheritance."

"Of course," she murmured, then asked, "What of Cyr? William added Balduc to Stern. Will he not add Wulfen as well, making my lands whole beneath one D'Argent?"

"He will not, though it is possible he would have had not my brother angered him by wedding Aelfled."

Her lids narrowed. "Because she is Saxon."

"Because she is not you, daughter of Wulfrith."

No surprise leaping from her, she said, "I did consider a union with your brother would benefit my people."

Guarin tensed at imaginings of her as Cyr's wife and the mother of his children.

"But not seriously. A pity he should be punished for not wedding one who would have refused him."

Relief he should not feel eased the breath from him. "It sounds as though you would be well with Cyr possessing Wulfen."

"Again, as well as I could. Though he is not the D'Argent I would choose, thus far his dealings with the people of Stern and Balduc provide much to recommend him."

Wishing he was not so affected by her further admission she would choose him over another, he said, "Cyr is a good man, when I am gone he will do all he can for those of Wulfen should their new lord prove oppressive."

She looked away. Though when last they met she professed to have feelings for him, he had believed her sincere but questioned the depth of what she sought to convince him. Once more he questioned it—and wondered if it was possible she felt for him as Aelfled felt for Cyr.

She could not, he told himself. Nor could he feel for her what Cyr felt for his Saxon wife. Still, this was not mere attraction nor desire. What had been Christian duty, compassion, and impulse upon Senlac had become something more during captivity. He had said first, in between, and in the end, he and his family were D'Argents, but just as Aelfled was now covered by that unity, Guarin sought to cover Hawisa, risking not only his standing with William but that of his brothers.

Do I come to love her? he pondered.

"Guarin?"

Wondering what his face revealed, he moved his thoughts to what he awakened to every morn and struggled to cast off each night. "You heard Jaxon may have survived the passage's collapse?"

Once more, surprise. "My housecarle, Ordric, told he was dead!"

"Cyr believed it as well, but when the debris was removed, Jaxon's body was not found. Either someone removed it, else your man was mistaken."

"Nay."

"You must not be blind to the possibility he may be near, Hawisa. Though oft I go to the wood to hunt, it is not only to put meat on the table but to search for signs of him and his followers."

She thought on it, said, "If he survived, I believe he would seek vengeance against the usurper ahead of me and the D'Argents, that just as many of the surviving rebels loyal to him have joined Edwin Harwolfson, so would he."

Guarin recalled recent tidings from the South, then asked what she would not likely answer, "Where do you go when you ride north, Hawisa? And how many are you?"

As if pulled from a dream of Andredeswald where he had conveyed the senseless lady who searched a bloody battlefield—that same wood the Saxons' greatest hope now prowled—she blinked. "Dougray did not follow me from Wulfen?"

"He wished to, but I told him nay."

"You do not trust him to know where I go?"

"Though he struggles to find his way back to who he was before losing an arm to a Saxon, I trust him. What I guard against is drawing attention to you."

"Yet you would know where I go and how well defended I am."

"To warn you of danger, whether of Jaxon or the king."

She stared, then rose, closed the distance between them, and lowered beside him.

Though there was no contact between them, Guarin stiffened in anticipation her men would come out of hiding, but more for how much he wanted contact with her.

Almighty, he lamented, *I ought not have answered her siren's call.*

CHAPTER THIRTY-TWO

*I*sa delved Guarin's face. Seeing no cunning there, she said, "Still you protect me when *restitution* is your due. Why?"

Unease rose in his green eyes. Because this was not a conversation to be had before an audience? Or did he guess at what even she was not certain she asked of him—and recoil?

"I need not know where you make camp," he left her question unanswered, "but will you tell if it is upon Lincolnshire or Nottinghamshire?"

Fool, she rebuked. *What did you think? He welcomed what you professed when you thought you would not meet again? He would profess feelings for you beyond empathy, pity, and attraction—all of which are miracles in themselves? And look at you flying to his side, all hope now disappointment. Could you be more pitiful, daughter of Wulfrith?*

She shifted, increasing the distance between them. And decided there was no harm in answering *him* as he wished. Indeed, better it would sow the ground for what she had come to do.

"We are upon Nottinghamshire. As we are cautious in adding to our numbers lest we find ourselves betrayed again, nearly half consist of the castle folk who fled Wulfen with us. 'Tis for them I—"

"What of Vitalis?"

He probed again. Her man being of note not only in size but for the red of his hair and beard, his absence from those who thrice departed the camp to return north with her had been noted.

"Zedekiah brought him out of Wulfen, along with the able and injured loyal to him. Though we feared he would not recover, one would hardly know my physician wrested him from death."

"I am pleased."

His sincerity made her wish there were more like him and Vitalis on both sides so there would be no sides. Yet another wish bereft of sunlight. Was forgiveness bereft as well?

She glanced at the cave where she had meant to speak words yet unspoken, but had been too wary of the bitterness Guarin exuded.

"I interrupted you," he said. "You wish to speak of the castle folk?"

Likely, he knew what she sought, though not all. "Aye, and as you say, charm a favor from one who owes me none."

His mouth curved. "As I am no longer under threat of your blade, mayhap I can be charmed. Continue."

Certes, she was charmed, not only by what was nearly a smile, but his Norman accent running its tongue over Saxon words—drawing them out, giving them depth she had not known they lacked before she met him.

"The castle folk weary of exile, of being parted from family and friends," she said. "And now winter comes." She saw no reason to mention most of her fighting men and women pushed to journey south and join Harwolfson. Though thus far the castle folk gave her cause to resist, if Guarin granted her favor, still she would resist until it was verified Jaxon had not joined those rebels. She prayed for Harwolfson's success and knew his chances greater had his followers the benefit of Jaxon's training, but her sire's man had become to her and hers as dangerous as Le Bâtard.

"You wish them to return to their villages upon Wulfen the same as the injured to whom Cyr gave sanctuary," Guarin said.

"I do, and to regain their positions at the castle."

He arched an eyebrow.

"I am aware many have been filled these months, but if there are yet places, I ask you to consider ones who served me well. 'Tis how they earn their living and of great support to those with spouses and children."

Now he glanced at the cave. "You had to know in this I would have reservations."

"I did. Hence, I sought to give my word face-to-face that in no way will I enlist their aid in recovering Wulfen. They will not report anything that goes within its walls, and they will do the work given them the same as done ere William invaded. All they want is to resume their lives without fear of prejudice or reprisal."

"I will allow it. But hear me, Hawisa, if any give cause to suspect they act for you—with or without your consent—it would be best they leave Wulfenshire altogether."

"Be assured they will serve you alone."

"When should I expect them?"

"Two days hence I shall begin sending them in threes and fours."

He inclined his head. "Those who can be put to work shall be —and watched closely."

She nearly smiled. "Once more, I am in your debt."

"Once more." He lowered his gaze to her mouth.

Attraction only, she told herself and wondered if he was remembering their kiss—and forgot they were watched.

Lest she forget, she pushed upright. "I believe we are done."

He straightened and stepped in front of her. "Do you forget there is something I would have from you? Or do you hope to take without giving?"

She looked up. "What does this dispossessed lady have you could possibly want?"

"Assurance."

"I gave my word the castle folk will not aid me."

"Other assurance. For that, I would know what is to become of your rebels."

Fearing he would set conditions on the castle folk returning home, she said, "You ask if we will lie down, the bones of our submission paving the way for William to more easily roll his war machine across our country? We will not."

His nostrils flared. "What do you intend?"

"'Tis not decided."

Now *he* delved her face. "Though I accept your rebels will continue to bedevil those who oppress your people, I seek assurance you will not join Harwolfson."

"Joining him is desired by most, but now it is known Jaxon may live and has gone south..." She shrugged. "As we can be of no aid to the Saxon cause do our own slay us, I shall advise against it."

"And if your advice is not taken or it is learned Jaxon is dead?"

The censure in his tone scraping her emotions, she said, "If those who relentlessly train to defend their country are determined to stand with Harwolfson, I will not oppose them."

"That I do not contest. What I am against is *you* leading them."

Then he would have her cower, letting others bleed so she not bleed? "In Norman-ruled England, I may no longer be a lady, but I am a leader—theirs."

A muscle at his jaw spasmed. "The day I escaped and once more gave myself over to save you, you told your husband sent you and your son to the Penderys when the North was invaded."

Had she? She remembered him holding her, the pain of the arrow piercing her, their kiss... "Aye, Roger sent us to his Norman friends."

"Then you know the heir, Maxen Pendery, who earned the title Bloodlust Warrior of Hastings."

She nearly shuddered as when first she heard him called that. "Better I knew his father who, with my men, set out to retrieve me from Senlac and found me in Andredeswald." Where Jaxon, unbeknownst to Pendery the elder, made it appear he had killed the baron's fellow Norman.

"Weeks past," Guarin said, "I received tidings Maxen left the monastery where he had gone to atone for the numerous Saxons he slew in battle, and that he cast off his monk's robes to avenge the murder of his brother, possibly by Harwolfson. More recent tidings are he captured a great number of rebels in Andredeswald."

Isa had to remind herself to breathe. "And Harwolfson?"

"He eludes, but though his ranks were dealt a blow, the loss has caused pockets of resistance across England to flock to him."

Then still her people had hope.

"You think it a good thing, Hawisa, but more firmly it casts the king's eye on the threat of Harwolfson. And with one such as Maxen Pendery to do William's bidding, it portends slaughter. Even if Jaxon is not at Harwolfson's side, the danger is great if you go south. And I do not care to see you across a battlefield."

Was that last as it sounded? "You will fight for William again?"

With regret, he said, "Whether I reside in England or Normandy, he is my liege. When he decides to bring Harwolfson to ground, he may call on me. As I would not see you on the opposite side, I wish your assurance that if your rebels join Harwolfson, you will not."

Mere imaginings of looking past blades to his side stirred the contents of her belly—as did imaginings of not being alongside her warriors. "Nor would I wish to see you across a battlefield, but what you ask of me..." She shook her head. "You would have me abandon those who have suffered much to remain true to their lady?"

"I would have you live, Hawisa."

"For what?" Her voice rose. "I have lost all but my tattered name and what remains of my followers. Do I refuse to lead my people south, I have not even the tattered—naught for which to live."

Warning in his eyes, he said, "You tempt your men to leave cover, which will incite mine to prevent them from gaining your side. Though I told all may depart here unbound, I cannot guarantee they will do so uninjured—and alive."

Becoming aware of the rise and fall of her chest and the heat in her face, she said, "Is that a requirement? You will take back the castle folk only if I abandon my followers?"

His gaze wavered, then he sighed. "Much I am tempted to require that, but I will not."

Her tension eased, and further at the possibility of why he was so insistent she remain behind. If she did not matter beyond empathy, pity, and attraction, surely he would not have met with her nor sought assurance she would not go where Jaxon could have gone and where the usurper might soon take his forces.

Hope moved through her, and yet its coursing caused something inside to crack. Not a great shattering as when Wulf died, but sorrow in the same vicinity. Sorrow of the sort for what one could not have though it was yet of this earth. Or could one?

Nay, not Hawisa Wulfrithdotter who had provided the usurper cause to take Wulfen. Not she who could offer this heir to distant lands naught beyond yielding to attraction that would dishonor both. And apology that would never be adequate.

That last reminding her though she had sought advantage over Guarin lest restitution deliver him to her, for a greater reason she had led him to the cave, she said, "I would be alone with you."

He frowned. "Why?"

"I do not believe we will meet again." She moistened her lips. "Will you go again to the cave with me?"

His face hardened. "That is best consigned to the past."

"Not yet. Pray, grant me one more favor, Guarin."

Clearly he wanted to refuse, but he said, "Your men will not like it."

"They will not, but if I lead again, they ought to give your men no reason to act against them."

"Then I will follow."

The sun having gone aslant, there was more light in the cave when she entered. It lit the rocky walls and path among boulders and scattered rocks to where Guarin had spent every hour save those whilst chained to a post and when they sat and talked.

Halting before the wall, so aware of him she could almost feel his muscled chest against her back, she ran a hand down the rough stone, over ridges, and into smooth depressions until her fingers found a hole where there had been a ring.

"Dougray reported never did you enter the cave," Guarin said, "and yet you knew."

She did—that nearly all evidence of his captivity had been removed, not only from the posts outside but here, doubtless by Guarin though the night of his release she had said never again would he set eye nor foot here.

"My man Ordric told." She turned. "Did it quiet your demons?"

"Some. Do you think to quiet the others?"

She peered into his shadowed face. "I have apologized, but I know it is not enough. Thus, I thought if I did so here where—"

"I know what happened here. Now tell what you want."

"Forgiveness. If not now, then I shall try to be content knowing this is a good beginning."

The caress of his breath on her face ceased, and when it resumed, it did so across her name. "Hawisa," he said and pulled her to him and cupped her jaw. "Do you not understand what I have been saying? You wronged me, but I understand why it was necessary, just as I understand my suffering compares little to that of your people. The night we parted, anger made me threaten you, but I knew then as I know now there was some good in the beatings dealt me those first months—that to understand how great the injustice done your people, I needed to feel some of the pain of those like Rosa." His hand on her tensed. "You know it was for fear of endangering others she took her life?"

All of her straining toward him, she said, "I know, and that you were fond of her."

"She ought not have died," he growled, then cleared his throat. "Be assured, you and I are beyond good beginnings. When my anger rises, it *is* wont to look your direction, but ever it moves past in search of Jaxon. Once I am assured he is dead, methinks these other demons will be quieted, perhaps even slain."

"I want that for you, Guarin, for it to be as if you were never here."

He bent his head nearer. "You would have me ignorant of the suffering of Saxons—ignorant of you?"

Longing for his embrace, she said, "William is your liege. Thus, like Maxen Pendery, you must do his bidding."

"*Not* like Pendery. I shall defend what belongs to me—my life and the lives of those entrusted to me—be it by sword, negotiation, even trickery, but God be with me that never do I injure innocents."

Dear Lord, this truly is love I feel for him, Isa sent heavenward. *Swift and hard it beats inside me, tempting me to forsake my own though he is bound for Normandy. And I make it worse standing so near his every breath matches mine, the meeting and parting of our chests an intimacy I can bear now but not the memory of it when he is gone from me.*

When she stepped back and came up against the rock, he moved his hand to her shoulder. "Do you believe me, Hawisa?"

"That you are not and will not become the same as Maxen Pendery? I do."

"And that the forgiveness you seek is given?"

"That is hardest to believe."

"Believe it, and be at peace knowing I seek no revenge."

"What of restitution?"

His smile was sorrowful. "Do you not go south, that will be restitution enough."

She pressed her palms to the rock, thought how wonderfully cool it would be in summer, how terribly chill in winter. As well he knew. "Those men and women are all I have. Where they go, I go."

"They are all you have now, but you could have more. You could wed again, become a mother again."

To a man she did not want. To children she might fail as she had failed Wulf—and Eberhard who had reverted to his birth name when the future she had begun to think she could give him was stolen by Jaxon and William.

"A wife and mother again," she said. "Under Norman rule."

"As I do not believe there will be an end to it, aye, Norman rule."

Tears threatening, she said, "Whilst there is a chance to take back what is ours, only a coward would yield, and I will not be that. Harwolfson—"

"He may be a great warrior and leader, Hawisa, but he is not William who has put down every challenge to his crown these two years, who wearies of the uprisings, who believes too long he has been conciliatory, who will soon reveal what lies farther beneath his surface than ever the English have seen. Hence, for the sake of your people if not yourself, accept him. If you cannot, go nowhere near Harwolfson."

She trembled, as much for fear of what further terror William would unleash as the effort to contain emotions threatening to wet her face. "I hate him," she hissed.

"I understand, but hate him from a great distance and live as once you entreated me to do."

She had, and so he had done. And forgiven her. "I can promise only I shall do all I can to persuade my people to remain in Nottinghamshire."

She sensed further argument, then his grip on her shoulder

eased. "You will come to me if you need anything? Even if only word of how the castle folk and villagers fare?"

"You would have me risk making it appear you conspire with the enemy?"

"By way of the underground passage," Guarin said. "Though it is being rerouted, the first of several gates to be installed along its course has been placed at its current outlet near the falls."

"As told by my scouts."

He showed no surprise. "Leave word there, and I will come to you here."

Until he returned to Normandy...

"I am grateful," she said, and thinking it time to depart, pushed off the wall. But he eased her back against it.

"What is it, Guarin?"

"You." He slid his hand from her shoulder to her neck, hooked his thumb beneath her jaw. Might he kiss her?

"Have you ceased breathing, my lady?"

She had.

Now his other hand was in her hair, cupping the back of her head. Now he was pulling her to him, settling her chest against his. Now his mouth was on hers, nothing gentle about his kiss. As if...

He hungers, she thought, *as do I.* Seeking to fill hands she could not remember ever feeling so empty, she gripped his waist and rose to her toes, drew palms up over muscled ribs and sighed into him, slid her hands around his back and whispered his name, pushed fingers into his hair and pressed their tips to his scalp.

Not until Guarin groaned, "Hawisa," did she realize how close the fit of their bodies and she was as responsible as he—if not more.

Then he was easing her arms from around him and setting her back against the wall. But rather than follow her there, he kept his arms extended, hands on her shoulders.

Though she knew he was right to do so, she did not feel her

usual awakening self. This was how she felt coming up out of a rare, welcome dream that made her question what harm in returning to it for a short while.

"Hawisa, we ought not—"

"Isa," she said. "That is as my familiars call me."

He drew a shaky breath. "I am honored to be that to you, but you are not Isa to me."

Then he did not wish her to be his familiar? She was wrong to think he felt more than attraction? "Why, Guarin?"

"As ever you have been Hawisa to me, regardless whether my eyes are open or closed, ever you shall be."

She wanted to ask what he meant, but she was awake now and moving beyond reach of that rare dream. As long as Guarin was the side of William, it was of no consequence what she was and was not to him whether in the light or the dark. Thus, he was right to pull away before there was more to regret than the impassable narrow sea.

He released her and turned. "We are too long out of sight," he said as he strode opposite. "If your men do not come out of hiding, soon they shall."

Grateful he was more firm of mind than she, Isa followed and they exited side by side. "Stand down, Dougray!" he shouted.

"Stand down, Ordric!" she called.

In neither instance was there evidence they were heard—no sound or movement, as if they commanded ghosts.

"Show yourself, Dougray!" Guarin commanded.

Far ahead, a figure dropped out of a tree and straightened to a good height. Unlike his brother, he was blond of hair and carried no bow—a weapon useless to one who had but a single hand with which to wield the weapons on his belt.

However, the others ordered to show themselves held bows fit with arrows. In all, a half dozen Normans to match her half dozen Saxons. Or nearly so...

Though fairly certain Guarin did not know what she knew,

she shivered at how great the danger to her men were harm intended them.

"Hawisa," he urged.

She cleared her throat. "Show yourself, Ordric!"

He and his five appeared. Nearer than the Normans, all were vulnerable to attack from behind, and from their wary—albeit combative—stances, knew it. Just as they knew they were not entirely without recourse.

Guarin looked to Isa. "Now we know where each of us stands—"

"Do we?"

His frown was fleeting. "Vitalis," he said gruffly.

She returned her regard to the wood. "Vitalis!"

The big man who dropped from well behind Guarin's brother straightened to his full height, a bow in hand. As he tossed back the hood that had ensured neither his hair nor beard betrayed him, Isa noted now Guarin's men had turned wary—except Dougray. He looked angry. But then, the master of stealth had been bettered by the man he had bettered in infiltrating the sortie at the abbey. She did not have to look close upon Vitalis to know how much he enjoyed being at Dougray's back.

"*Now* we know where each of us stands," she said and was surprised by what seemed pride shining from Guarin's eyes.

"So we do, Wulfrithdotter. I wonder you tolerated Jaxon as long as you did."

His acknowledgment the ousted Lady of Wulfen did not need her sire's man to best the invaders was a balm.

"I am thinking Vitalis rode to the camp ahead of the others," he said. "He came a way known to few and, lest any lay in wait, used the distraction of your other men to ascend the tree unseen to watch their backs. And yours."

"You think right."

"You are more worthy than you believe, Hawisa."

Was she? These past months it was that toward which she

aspired more than ever. Her time no longer divided between administration of Wulfen and the rebel army, she had sought to prove those she trained in the ways of Wulfrith could flourish as well beneath her instruction as they had with Jaxon—and Vitalis, though for a time he had kept all guessing if he would emerge from the tent where the physician tended him.

"William was wise to seek a union between you and my brother," Guarin said. "Your sire's training of warriors paired with my uncle's might have proven unmatched in all of Christendom."

"Were I willing to betray my own," she reminded.

"I do not doubt there are bad—even worse—days ahead, Hawisa, but if your country's destiny is to become Anglo-Norman, there will be no betrayal in raising up warriors to defend a reborn England. As already begun, Normans and Saxons will fight side by side to protect their families and homes."

Her belly clenched. More and more, William demanded military service from Saxons. Grudgingly or otherwise, most came when called lest they lose what remained of their possessions. Hence, it was not only Normans who put down rebel uprisings.

As Guarin intended, she questioned what she did and if, in the end, all she would have to show for her efforts was more spent Saxon lives.

Doubt, she silently rebuked, *also a disease,* then said, "Since we cannot know what the ages will tell of these days, each of us must do as we believe right."

"Then this is where we part, Hawisa. For now."

Though it would be better were it evermore, she lightened at the prospect of seeing him again. "My men and I will leave peaceably," she said, "and I think it best ahead of you."

"I am well with that."

She adjusted her belt, tugged at the tunic bunched above it, and hoped their audience had not noticed its disarray by hands that should not have strayed where they had. "To me!" she called to her men.

"One thing ere you go," Guarin said. "As Dougray will not ask it of you, I shall."

She raised her eyebrows. "If I can answer, I will."

"Aelfled mentioned Campagnon's slave was at Wulfen the night of Jaxon's attack."

"She was."

"Cyr tells Dougray was moved by the young woman's plight when he witnessed Campagnon's ill treatment of her at Balduc."

Swept with guilt over what Em had suffered—and never spoke of—Isa said tautly, "Continue."

"I would know if she is with you still, and if not, whether you can get word to her."

"Of what?"

"As told, Campagnon has sold his sword arm and those of his fellow mercenaries to William. It is said when he is not earning coin, he searches for his slave and that her unusual eyes will prove her undoing. I would but see her warned so she may take herself far from these lands."

"She will be warned, but do not expect her to allow Campagnon to dictate where she goes, nor for her to fall victim to him again. Better than when she found herself on an auction block separated from her brother for the pleasure of that knave, she knows how to defend herself. Now is there anything else Dougray wishes me to pass to her?"

He shook his head. "I will inform my brother."

"Godspeed, Guarin." She strode past the posts she did not doubt would be removed the same as their fittings.

As she swung atop Anglicus, six of her men drew around her.

"He has agreed to allow the castle folk to return to Wulfen," she told them.

Ordric glanced at where Guarin stood unmoving. "Then we go south."

"We shall speak of that later." She looked past him, saw Vitalis slow as he drew even with Dougray.

The two exchanged words obviously of a hostile nature, then Vitalis laughed and lengthened his stride. To ensure the way he had entered the camp was not easily discovered, he would depart with her and the others.

As he neared, he called, "D'Argent!" acknowledging the Norman no longer the captive over whom he had charge. With the exception of Dougray whose offense was too great to forgive, Isa's man had little cause to dislike the D'Argents beyond their Norman blood.

"Vitalis!" Guarin answered, and added, "I trust you will give your lady good counsel."

"Ever I do." He gripped Anglicus's bridle and led Isa and the others from the camp toward the horses tethered beyond the ravine.

"We will meet again," Guarin said as Hawisa went from sight.

Out of the corner of his eye seeing Dougray approach, he turned. His brother paused before the posts, considered them, then Guarin. Had there been any doubt he understood their purpose and that of the cave despite little evidence of fettering, there was none when he halted before Guarin.

"And yet you want that viper," he said with less accusation than expected. "Careful, big brother. Our king might suffer Cyr taking a profitless Saxon to wife, but she who set against him Rebels of the Pale? Never."

"Careful, *little* brother," Guarin growled. "You offend in treading ground absent foundation."

"Then it was just a kiss of gratitude? *Thank you, Dotter, for releasing me when I had little hope of returning to this side of death's door?*"

He was only guessing—another thing at which he excelled— but Guarin was tempted to reverse the curve of his mouth.

313

Fortunate for Dougray, there was a less painful means than a fist to be rid of that smile.

"She *is* most comely," Guarin admitted, "and you must concede there is something exciting about one of the fairer sex possessing a facility with weapons." He nodded. "Fire there, and of the sort only a man of foolish pride would put out were it even possible."

Dougray's lids narrowed.

"From what the lady tells, you should expect the same of..." Guarin feigned searching. "...Em, I believe Campagnon's slave is called."

Dougray's mouth flattened and teeth parted as if to respond, but he did not. He now knew the young woman lived, remained with Hawisa, and was being trained in the art of weaponry.

He pivoted and stalked toward the others, a moment later, turned back. "Dotter is aware Campagnon paid no price for his treachery, that once more he and his men are loosed on the Saxons?"

"I told her. She will inform her people of the danger."

Dougray resumed his stride.

"I think you will see her again," Guarin murmured. "Then better you will understand Cyr and me. And if that is where you wish to go, perhaps you shall gain what I cannot."

CHAPTER THIRTY-THREE

Nottinghamshire, England
Late Spring, 1069

*Y*our blood, Woman! My blade laps it up!"

Back slammed to the chest of the man who required no sword to slay her, Em kept her chin up while lowering her gaze to the flat of the sword whose length jutted from beneath her jaw and tapered to a point past her left shoulder. No blood on its edges, though there ought to be—and would be were she once more a warrior's plaything.

"Tell, Saxon"—his breath in her ear made her throat close —"what will you do?"

What twice now she had failed at, she determined and slowly slid her left hand over her abdomen and between her breasts. Then she exhaled and shot her fingers up and around the blade alongside her jaw. Feeling no pain, she thrust the blade forward while driving her right elbow back into muscle-clad ribs. As her assailant grunted and jerked, she lunged forward, released the blade, and ducked beneath its sweep.

Her shout of triumph doused by their audience's boisterous

response to a contest that had seemed no contest at all, Em whirled around to ensure her opponent did not set himself at her again.

Never before had she seen Vitalis smile so large it could be known his lower teeth were crowded unlike the upper. He was handsome in a way other men were not, features so hard-boned and rugged she imagined Goliath of the David story had looked the same, though likely the one felled by a perfectly slung stone had lacked red hair.

"Better a bandaged hand than a slit throat," he said and tossed aside the sword that was unmarked by her blood only because it was wooden, its edges rounded.

Glancing at her fingers and palm, she acknowledged the pain would be great were they sliced. But he was right—still she would live.

She might have returned his smile if not that she yet felt his body against hers and it required effort to keep from retching water and bread that was all she had allowed herself in anticipation of this lesson. That humiliation she would not suffer again.

"Well done, Em."

Those words spoken above the commotion of the others returning to their training, brought her around. "I thank you," she said as Lady Hawisa halted before her. "Have you decided if I should join Vitalis's sorties or your patrols?"

The former, she hoped. Though the daughter of Wulfrith was formidable, her skill at arms surpassed by only a handful of male rebels, Em's respect waned with each refusal to lead the Rebels of the Pale in joining Edwin Harwolfson now the castle folk were no longer a consideration.

Month after month, Hawisa reminded those who tired of waiting that not only were they needed here, but they must increase their ranks and skills for what lay ahead. However, most believed the same as Em it was past time they went south.

As for Jaxon whose presence at Harwolfson's side was confirmed five months ago, surely past offenses and vendettas would be set aside, it being imperative Saxons unite. The Rebels of the Pale might not be great in number, but their fierce reputation had spread beyond this southeastern corner of Nottinghamshire where they vanquished Normans who trespassed, stole, maimed, and murdered. Hence, all these present would be welcomed by Harwolfson and, in turn, Jaxon.

"I have not decided where to place you, Em, though Vitalis concurs the patrol may be the best fit."

"But my lady—"

"'Tis not decided."

Em glanced past her to Eberhard who, having added more muscle and half a hand's height since his reunion with his sister, increasingly looked the warrior. "My little brother is of the sortie. Should I not be as well?"

"Enough, Em."

Once more it rose to mind Hawisa was as jealous of Eberhard's sister as his sister was jealous of the woman who had played his mother, but Em told herself, *I am grateful she kept him safe. Even if she knew.*

Hawisa stepped nearer and set a hand on her shoulder. "Patience is among the most difficult virtues a warrior must master. This is a good occasion to practice it."

"That I shall do," Em said with as little grudging as possible.

Hawisa gestured at Eberhard. "Your brother would like to engage you at spears."

Engage, meaning *instruct.* It was wrong to be offended that she who was grown should be taught by one who was not yet a man. True, he had more experience and skill, but it grated, especially as she was refused the sortie after successfully escaping Vitalis.

Lest anger make her sound a girl she should have been longer and never would be again, she strode toward Eberhard—long, unhampered strides, the advantage and protection of men

317

afforded her since she had flung off her gown and wrenched on chausses and tunic. Never again a man's plaything!

Isa stared after the young woman whose training had progressed poorly in the beginning, though not for lack of desire and courage. So affected was Em by close contact with men, it had been necessary to match her only with those of her sex. But no longer. If one looked closely, they could see she remained affected, but now she well enough tolerated contact that if still she shamed herself, she did so out of sight.

Seeing Em had reached her brother, Isa shifted her regard to Eberhard who had left behind the last of the boy when they fled Wulfen. He was a fine young man, now of an age near that of Wulf when she followed her son to Senlac and…

Isa's thoughts ran to the man who continued to administer Wulfen for Le Bâtard. When last she saw Guarin, she had declared all she had left to her was her tattered name and what remained of her followers, but she had Eberhard. She knew better than to love him, but it was hard to resist motherly feelings for one who loved her despite the loss of Wulfen, their dangerous and arduous existence, and his sister's disapproval that became most obvious when her brother defended Hawisa's decision to delay joining Harwolfson.

Restless Em. Resentful Em. Revenge-bent Em. Before long, she and others would go south—*if* it could be determined there was a greater chance of prevailing over being slaughtered. Should Isa add her numbers to those of Harwolfson, she hoped it would be after Guarin returned to Normandy. However, were he yet in England, it was possible they would not face each other across a battlefield since William had not summoned him earlier this spring to aid in relieving York of the rebel forces attacking that city.

Was it tragedy or blessing neither had Harwolfson and his followers been present with Edgar the Aetheling who had sought to assert his claim to the throne? Had they joined the northern rebels, perhaps they could have taken and held the city—even so thoroughly defeated the conquerors Le Bâtard would have abandoned England. Conversely, they could have fallen alongside their fellow Saxons, snuffing out the resistance's last great hope. Tragedy or blessing, it could not be known, but it was believed Harwolfson was weeks from challenging William for the heart and soul of England.

For naught? Isa pondered. As Guarin had warned, would it be better if her rebels remained here where they excelled at relieving the common folk of Norman oppression and violence?

"My lady?"

She had heard the one approaching and known it was Vitalis from the muscled weight grinding dirt underfoot, just as she knew for what he came.

"I am ready," she said and turned.

"Jonah! Edith!" he called to those who, unlike the others who had witnessed Em's victory, had not returned to their own training.

Together, the four strode to the crude structure that stabled horses nearly as numerous as rebels. The Normans who menaced the Saxons of this region might escape with their lives providing their injuries were not dire, but not their fine mounts—nor weapons, armor, and coin.

A quarter hour later, Anglicus beneath her, Isa charged Vitalis to demonstrate for Jonah and Edith one of many techniques for wielding weapons astride.

She shouted and swung her sword to meet her man's. As her blade slid up off his, she ducked and continued past, then reined around and urged her mount alongside Vitalis's—her side of strength with her right hand free to slash at her opponent, his side of vulnerability with his sword-wielding hand forced to cross over his mount to meet her steel.

"Ho!" Isa shouted and slapped the flat of her blade against his left shoulder.

He laughed and, as they slowed, said, "I have taught you well, my lady."

He teased. Though the techniques he began developing upon Wulfenshire were the foundation of their mounted combat, together they had perfected them to rival the Normans whose use of horses in battle had given William a great advantage at Hastings.

"So you have," Isa said, then they spurred to those who watched from atop their own mounts. Shortly, Edith charged Vitalis and Jonah charged Isa.

Until dusk, the lady and the housecarle instructed those born to earth and plow in the ways of the warrior in the hope united Saxons would conquer the conquerors.

"THEY AMASS!" Zedekiah shouted as he reined in, silencing all gathered for the evening meal—for a moment only, then they were on their feet, murmuring...chattering...shouting.

Now, Isa thought, heart pounding as she watched the burly man swing out of the saddle. Two and a half years after Hastings, it should not feel too soon. But surely better that than too late.

Lord God, let it not be too late, she prayed, then rose from the log she had settled on before the fire and commanded, "Be still!"

Likely as much for her authority as the need to learn details of the amassing, the scores of rebels quieted.

"Speak loud for all," she directed Zedekiah.

He halted alongside her. "Harwolfson and the usurper are to meet. The place—Darfield before Andredeswald. The day—five hence. The call—all able-bodied Saxons true to the blood, the bone, and the marrow are to rally to Harwolfson armed with whatever weapons can be brought to hand."

"At last we go!" someone cried.

"All they have done to us we shall do to them!" another shouted.

"We shall cast them into the pit, the dark, the bloody abyss," yet another kindled embers that would birth fire.

"Slit their throats, spill their innards!"

A roar of approval sounded. And there the fire.

Isa tensed at how quickly it rose through their ranks, but it was less disconcerting than the joy chasing it.

"Quiet!" she commanded thrice before being heeded. But even then, not all quieted—until Vitalis threatened to relieve them of their tongues.

"Hear me," Isa said. "I would have this be what we have long awaited, but lest we end the same as our men at Hastings and those at York, we cannot go blindly into this."

"Blindly?" Em cried where she stood on the opposite side of the fire. "We see all we need see—the place, the day, and the call for *true* Saxons to add their strength to those worthy of taking back our country."

"Aye!" the rebels chimed as Isa looked between the young woman and her brother.

Unlike his sister, Eberhard did not bristle with anticipation. At ten and two, he knew his limitations and those of the less seasoned among them.

"I do not say we will not go south, Em," Isa said. "I say first we look near on what we know and, as much as possible, learn what we do not."

"Five days!" exclaimed an aged Saxon whose fissured face appeared to have been mistakenly set atop the body of a fit young man. "That is all we have, and as most must be spent on the journey to Darfield, we can waste none looking for answers when we have one now. It is time our training benefit all of England."

"We will not risk our lives for naught," Isa snapped.

"Naught?" Em scoffed. "You think so little of our country?"

"I think much of England, but ahead of the land, I think of the lives—ours here and the people of the villages we protect. I would not see them end as did all those at York whom Le Bâtard let rot where they fell."

"For which we shall avenge them," Em countered.

Isa strode forward, and the young woman advanced to meet her.

"Do not!" Eberhard lunged between them, looked across his shoulder at his sister. "Lady Hawisa is our leader. She but wants what is best for us."

Em stepped alongside him. "Wanting and giving are two different things, and more right I have than many to question whether she knows the difference."

A chill went through Isa. *Not here,* she silently entreated. *Not now.*

"What say you, Em?" Eberhard demanded.

"Ask your beloved lady!"

"Ask her what?"

All but the three having gone silent, Isa said, "Let us speak in my tent."

"Nay, here." Em narrowed her eyes. "Or are you so ashamed you cannot bear others knowing the truth—that you knew?"

Vitalis stepped alongside Isa. "My lady?"

She glanced up at the one who knew what Em sought to unveil before all. "So be it," she whispered and nodded. "Aye, I knew, Em."

The young woman released her breath, in a quaking voice said, "How long?"

A grunt of frustration sounded from Eberhard. "Of what do you speak, Em?"

"I but ask Lady Hawisa how long she knew your sister was at Balduc, a slave to Campagnon—how long she kept you ignorant I was near."

"She did not know until the night you came to Wulfen."

"That is as she wished you to believe."

Eberhard opened his mouth as if to offer further defense, but Isa said, "Your sister is right."

He shook his head. "You could not have known long."

She swallowed. "As you are aware, I was at the auction. Unlike you who raged at being parted from your sister, I heard the name of the one who purchased her—the Norman rumored to have been awarded a portion of my lands." Though pierced by the disbelief on Eberhard's face shifting toward horror, she continued, "The rumor proved true the same as the expectation he would bring Em to Balduc."

His sister advanced another step. "And you made good use of me—persuading me to pass along information by assuring me Eberhard was safe among England's rebels."

"That was my doing," Vitalis said. "You were well placed to inform us of Campagnon's plans and vulnerabilities, and knowing my lady would not approve, I had the stable lad enlist your aid. For it, your anger is my due. But what was done was done, and rather than outraged, you should be proud of how much suffering you averted."

"I am, but—"

"You knew!" Eberhard stepped toward Isa. "You whom I came to love as a mother knew where she was—how she was abused—and said naught! Did naught!"

If I have not him, I am all emptiness, Isa silently bemoaned. "Forgive me, Eberhard. Forgive me, Em."

"Forgive you?" his sister scoffed. "You kept us apart."

"Enough!" Vitalis snarled. "She is not to blame. The laws of slavery—"

"As long I suffered beneath those laws," Em shrilled, "be assured I know them."

"It was of your own choosing," he retorted. "You and your brother sold yourselves into slavery—for a noble cause, aye, but it was your decision and you had to know what could happen to you."

Eberhard bared his teeth. "We were to be sold together so we could protect each other."

"As well you know, it was the auctioneer and lustful men who determined otherwise, not Lady Hawisa."

Some of the color drained from Em's face, but not her brother's.

"Now," Vitalis continued, "instead of being grateful what befell you was not as terrible as it would have been were Em sold to one who would have made a joy woman of her, and thankful you were given the protection of a noble life, you fling stones at the woman who made it possible for you to reunite."

Anger of a depth never before seen on Eberhard's face surfaced, and it took all Isa's will not to embrace him.

"And do you forget you were offered a means of escape, Em? At great risk to herself and those who would have done her bidding, my lady sought to free you from that devil, but you declined, determined to strike at Campagnon in the only way available to you."

The young woman looked nearly stricken. Nearly. Vitalis's arguments might be well founded, but fact and reasoning alone would not unwind to its good end the ball of anger she carried. She needed time, prayer, and only the Lord knew what else.

Isa's thoughts went to Dougray and his interest in this young woman—and veered away. Even if he could overlook she was Saxon the same as the warrior who had taken his arm, there was little hope Em could set aside he was Norman the same as the man who had abused her.

"I am sorry," Isa said. "Truly, I am."

"You should be," Eberhard said. "Even could you not aid her, you ought to have told me where she was."

"I wished to but feared..." She raised her palms in a gesture so helpless she was ashamed.

"Feared what?" Tears brightened Eberhard's eyes. "I would choose my sister over your failed attempt to keep hold of

Wulfen?" He nodded. "I would have. And had you refused to aid me, I would have myself freed her from that...ravisher!"

Em gasped.

"What?" he demanded. "You think the boy whose hand was torn from yours at auction reached to you only out of fear for himself? I knew what goes between husband and wife, and as we journeyed across England learned from the lament of many women those same things go between masters and slaves even if the slave is unwilling."

The young woman's face now the pale of the moon, she clapped a hand over her mouth, whether to hold in emotions or the contents of her belly.

Eberhard returned his gaze to Isa. "You knew what was happening to her—"

"Enough, boy!" Vitalis stepped before him. "Even with all your training, *this* day you could not stand against Campagnon, let alone all those it would be necessary to get past to reach him. You talk big, but your mind"—he jabbed a finger to the young man's forehead—"is small."

"Cease!" Isa cried a moment before Eberhard swung a fist.

Vitalis caught it in his palm, closed his fingers over it. "Even smaller than thought," he rumbled.

Isa gripped his arm. "He is upset, and rightly so."

"I am not a child in need of defending!" Firelight convulsed across Eberhard's contorted face. "And you are not my mother. You wished only to use me—never cared for me."

His declaration dropped her onto her heels.

"Vitalis," Em said softly. "Pray, release him."

He opened his hand, and the young man snatched his arm to his side.

His sister stepped in front of him. "'Twas not as bad as you think—as I make it sound. Vitalis is right. Had you come for me, Campagnon would have..." She set a hand on his jaw. "You were safe with Lady Hawisa, and I was where I needed to be."

He lurched backward. "I may not be a man, but neither am I a boy. I will kill Campagnon for what he did to you, and as many Normans as I can put through for what they have done to England."

Heavenly Father, Isa appealed, *he sounds like my Wulf.* She reached to him. "Let us speak, Eberhard."

"No more talking! 'Tis time we *do.* When all make for Darfield, dare not think to leave me behind. I shall go with you, even does my life end." He pivoted and strode toward the tents.

All stared after him, and when he went from sight, Em said, "I did not mean that to happen, Lady Hawisa, but there is so much tearing at my insides trying to get out." Momentarily, she closed her eyes. "Once he cools, I will make him see sense." She dropped her arms to her sides and strode after her brother.

Isa looked to her rebels whose fate must be determined—though not by her. "Let us gain our rest. On the morrow, we will speak of the great gathering in the South, but at the end of words, each man and woman decides their own way forward. As I shall decide mine."

Murmuring amongst themselves, the Rebels of the Pale began dispersing.

Isa looked to Vitalis. "'Twas deserved," she said. "As you urged, I should have told Eberhard and Em long ago." She shook her head. "I feared this, and I have made it more terrible by letting it happen now."

"You love the boy," he said as if that were all the excuse needed. "But you must not yield to him no matter how high he heaps guilt. He is twelve, and though great his skills, he is not ready to face warriors nor take lives."

"This I know, and that he will hate me all the more, especially if Em determines to go south."

"He may think he hates you, but he does not. You have been a mother to him as he has become a son to you. Given time, he will see that."

Wishing she could wrap her arms around his certainty, wishing she could feel for him what she felt for Guarin, she said, "I pray you are right."

"May the Lord grant you good rest, my lady."

He is Saxon, she told herself as he strode opposite. *He is here. His heart wishes to beat in time with mine. Instead, my heart beats out of time with another.*

She peered at the night sky flecked with light. Would she look upon this same sky at Darfield before the battle to be fought there? Would Guarin? Would next she see him on the side of her enemy?

"Pray not, Lord," she whispered, then lest she lose Eberhard as she had lost Wulf, went in search of him. But unlike her son, he did not lay plans nor await the right opportunity. The boy who was not a boy, but not yet a man, was gone.

CHAPTER THIRTY-FOUR

King William's Camp
Darfield, England

*S*he was not here. He had to believe it lest he compromise his ability to do his duty. His family's lands in Normandy and those here depended much on how well the D'Argents conducted themselves. Better than most of William's followers, better than Campagnon and his fellow mercenaries, they must make a good showing on the morrow when what was believed the Saxons' last great stand was toppled, the rebels' defeat paving the way for England to begin settling and healing.

"God willing," Guarin rasped.

"God willing," Cyr agreed.

Guarin looked to where his brother stood to one side of him on the ridge overlooking the unsuspecting meadow that was to become a battlefield. Guessing Dougray and Theriot on his other side also heard, he considered Cyr's face lit by moonlight and torches set around the immense camp.

Do I but imagine he looks a father? Guarin wondered. *Or are his eyes a brighter green? Have some of the creases of his face realigned, others deepened? Alongside joy and pride, surely that is greater concern now he lives not only for himself but his wife and the helpless babe presented him a fortnight past.*

"You fear the lady has come," Cyr said so low the others would have to strain to catch his words. "You fear she is in yon wood at the right hand of Harwolfson."

"I do. Though my scout brought word the day ere we rode from Wulfenshire she and her rebels remain encamped, that does not mean they did not depart thereafter."

"You must not dwell on it, Guarin. I like it no more than you that come the morrow once more we set ourselves at those who conquered this land before us, but William has our oaths. If we do not honor them in defense of our lives and the lives of others who now make England their home, it will be our blood more greatly feeding the streams carved into the battlefield. And the Saxons with whom we are becoming one, who depend on us for protection and stability, may find themselves beneath the heel of one like Campagnon—or worse."

"Campagnon," Dougray growled, evidencing if all other words had escaped him, that name had not. "He follows William around like a pup refusing to be weaned."

Guarin looked to the blond among them, saw his regard was on the wood where Harwolfson prepared for the day of judgment he believed would be in his favor. Was Dougray thinking of the slave, Em? Wondering if she was with Hawisa?

Someone approached, and as usual, Theriot detected it first. When the other brothers turned with him, they saw it was Maël. Whether he had avoided them earlier or been occupied with the king's business, at last he came.

Fatigue in the bow of his shoulders, he peeled off his gloves, tucked them beneath his belt, and halted before his cousins. "I apologize we could not meet sooner. Many are the preparations to ensure a quick end to Harwolfson's rebellion."

"Understandable," Guarin said.

329

Maël looked to Cyr. "How fares my mother?"

"Lady Chanson is well, though you would know if you visited more often."

Will Cyr deliver the tidings now? Guarin wondered.

Maël's eyebrows rose. "I am sure she understands."

"Understands? That you could not pause overnight following the victory at York?"

"I am the king's to command as he pleases, and he pleased to send me and my men the long way around Wulfenshire."

Cyr breathed deep. "Providing you can tear yourself from our liege's side long enough to attend your mother's wedding, I am sure she will forgive you."

All expression fell from Maël's face. When it returned, it was no disinterested, half-hooded eyes or slack mouth upon which the brothers looked.

"Whom does she think to wed?" he growled.

"My good friend, Father Fulbert. Though he wished to approach you himself and for that accompanied us here, I thought it best you hear it from me first."

"He is as much Saxon as Norman," Maël said. "More, he is of the Holy Church."

"So he is—of good benefit at this time in England and a portent of things to come, do we not hope?" Cyr nodded. "A fine, godly husband he will make Lady Chanson."

"The Church looks ill on married priests," Maël said. "For this, among other offenses, reform comes to England's church."

"Comes, but not yet here, Cousin. Hence, so what Chanson and Fulbert wish cannot be forbidden or undone, they shall speak vows within a fortnight. You will attend the wedding at Stern, oui?"

"She is a widow!"

"Indeed, and yet too young to spend the rest of her life thus when years of happiness, of which she has had few, are offered."

"Few?" Maël stepped nearer. "You say she was unhappy with my sire?"

Cyr advanced as well, tempting Guarin to pull him back lest they come to blows. Assuring himself he, Dougray, and Theriot could pull them apart before great damage was done, he resisted.

"All know the same as you, Hugh was undeserving of Chanson," Cyr said.

Maël's hands closed into fists.

"None would dispute your father was an outstanding warrior and trainer of knights, but that was his first love, perhaps his only love."

Maël swept his gaze over the other brothers. "Had I known I was to be berated for a poor son, my sire berated for a poor husband, I would have joined William and Campagnon at meal rather than *kin*." He dipped his chin. "'Til we meet again on the morrow and put finish to the rebels." He pivoted and strode back toward hundreds of lamp-lit tents, torches, and campfires that defied the darkness to warn rebels they had no hope of a night attack.

"Perhaps he will speak to me alone," Guarin said, though it was unlikely, having failed each time he tried during his recovery at Stern.

Theriot snorted. "Did you not hear? He would rather share a trencher with Campagnon than give account of what goes behind those scars."

Still, Guarin followed. Just inside the outermost ring of tents, he overtook his cousin.

"I thought you would come," Maël said. "A waste of much hope you would not."

"Will you share with no one what Hastings wrought in you, Maël? And do not say it wrought naught. You are much changed."

His cousin turned to him. "Are we to share now? You will tell what was done you while Lady Hawisa held you captive?" He thrust his face near. "Dare not say it was not she. Just as I am

331

certain, so is William it was because of her you were returned to your family half dead."

Guarin hesitated, said, "It *was* because of her, but—"

A group of soldiers veered toward them, not drunk in any obvious way, but of good cheer as evidenced by boisterous speech and coarse laughter.

"Pardon, Sir Maël!" one exclaimed and directed his companions opposite.

Maël grunted, demanded of Guarin, "How will you excuse what she did to you? Or perhaps the real question is why you would excuse it?"

"For now, it is enough to tell I live because she willed it—and for that made an enemy of her man, Jaxon. Now 'tis for you to give. What besides your sire's death and a blade to the face changed you?"

"You think that not enough?"

Guarin set a hand on his shoulder. "I believe it goes beyond that to whatever caused you to distance yourself from your family when we went into battle at Hastings."

Defiance grooving his face, Maël stared.

Movement ahead, so quick as to appear furtive, drew their attention to a hunched figure in profile dashing between two tents, a glint of silver at his side. Was this the prelude to an attack the Normans were certain would not befall their camp?

"I think that Wulfrith come spying," Maël rumbled.

It took Guarin a moment to realize he referred to the boy Rosa had said Jaxon wished to gain control of, Jaxon had let slip was an imposter, and Cyr had told Hawisa had presented as the twin of her son slain upon Senlac. Was the young man to be sacrificed, if necessary, to map the way in and out?

"Non," Guarin said, "it cannot be him. Lady Hawisa would not allow him to be used thus."

"And yet I am fairly certain it is him." Maël started forward. "This will greatly amuse William."

Guarin caught his arm. "At best, he is a very young man."

"Trained in the ways of Wulfrith, he is more than a young man, and he means us ill."

"For that, we will take him to ground."

"And?"

"I will ensure whatever his scheme, no Norman will be harmed. You have my word, Maël."

He did not agree nor disagree, and when once more they caught sight of the Saxon, Maël went left and Guarin right. There were opportunities to overtake the young man as he evaded other Normans, but in exercising patience, the cousins discovered his destination when he hunkered behind the tent of one of William's companions.

Tapping the tip of a dagger against the toe of his boot, he stared at the immense tent outside which a guard stood, while William and his dinner guests drew and drew again their shadowed figures against lit canvas.

Guarin looked to Maël twenty feet distant, and when his cousin inclined his head, started forward—and stilled at the appearance of a tall warrior striding toward William's tent.

"Baron Pendery," the guard greeted the younger of the two barons who had not only replaced his monk's robe with armor but wed the Saxon once betrothed to Edwin Harwolfson—a great beauty as seen this day when she accompanied the Bloodlust Warrior of Hastings to Darfield.

"I would speak with the king," Maxen Pendery said.

"A moment, my lord."

It was little more than that before he was ushered inside and William's voice rose above the others in greeting.

Another glance at Maël, another nod, then Guarin lunged toward the one who had taken the name of Hawisa's heir, clapped a hand over his mouth, and caught the wrist of the hand wielding a blade. But the youth had strength and skill—twisting, kicking, and jabbing so viciously it was difficult to keep his grunts and shouts from spilling.

As Guarin pinned him back against his chest, Maël appeared. "Almighty, he is a wiggly one," he muttered, then drew back a fist. "You may thank me for this later, Cousin."

The blow to the temple caused the young man to slacken and drop his dagger.

Rubbing his knuckles, Maël said with mock defensiveness, "It was that or rouse the guard. Now take him from here while I reinforce the sentries around the camp."

Guarin heaved the youth over his shoulder. "We are not done sharing, Maël. We will speak later."

His cousin's only response was a smile that told *later* might never come.

In a copse of trees well back from the ridge and distant from the sentries the trespasser had slipped past, Guarin bound his prey to a tree and gagged him. Two sharp slaps, and the young man snapped up his head.

"I am Sir Guarin D'Argent," Guarin said in Anglo-Saxon. "You know the name?"

The young man glared at the Norman crouched before him, bared his teeth above the gag.

"I think you do, and that I was Lady Hawisa's captive for nearly two years. Now you are at this Norman's mercy just as this Norman was at the Saxons' mercy. But I am not your enemy. If in seeking out the king you hoped to slit his throat, you would have failed and would now be in the hands of his guards. Else dead."

He strained to the side, surely testing the rope that would give only enough to snag his tunic against the bark.

"Do you wish your freedom, boy?"

His eyes narrowed.

"I shall remove the gag, but two things you should know. Do you call out, it will be to the king's sentries, and here they will find you trussed and ready to deliver to..." He shrugged. "Likely, they will not bother informing the king so unseasoned a rebel stole into camp. As for the other thing you should know from my every encounter with your lady, I mean her no harm. So nod if you will behave the young man rather than the boy who cries for help that is not here."

He jerked his chin, and Guarin tugged the pull knot and dropped the gag beneath his chin.

Shifting his jaw, the young man set his head back against the tree. "They called you the wolf."

Guarin raised his eyebrows. "The one this side. You were sent by the one on the other side?"

His nostrils flared. "Our wolf is more formidable than that of the Normans. When Harwolfson moves against you, he will succeed a thousand-fold where I failed."

"He did not send you?"

"He did not, nor Lady Hawisa."

No surprise the latter. "What did you hope to accomplish in drawing near the king, Wulfrith?"

"That is not my name!"

"Then give another."

"I am Eberhard."

"For what did you steal past our sentries, Eberhard?"

"I knew I could not get near enough Le Bâtard, but Raymond Campagnon? Possible."

Guarin frowned. "As he is no longer the Baron of Balduc, for what do you bear so great a grudge you risk your life to seek him in the midst of Normans?"

"For my sister, Em. Campagnon tore us apart at auction, bought her, abused her."

This surprised, though it fit. At that same auction, Hawisa had purchased Eberhard to play the half-Norman son lost upon Senlac to preserve as much of her lands as possible. "Unlike your sister, you were not made a slave, were you, Eberhard?"

He shook his head. "My lady burned my papers, and yet she

did naught to aid my sister though she knew Campagnon had her. For that, I cannot..." Tears sparkled in his eyes. "I do not know I can forgive her."

Guarin set a hand on his shoulder and felt him tense. "Slavery is wrong, but until it is abolished in your country as it has been in Normandy, it is no easy thing to take from another the one his coin has purchased."

"Because those who know it is wrong do not do the hard thing to make it right!"

A sound argument. "Your sister is free now. Think on that and how we are to return you to her." And here the means of discovering how near Hawisa was. "Em is with your lady in Harwolfson's camp?"

"I do not know. When I learned my lady did naught to aid Em, I left camp ere it was decided whether the Rebels of the Pale would come south, and I have been cautious moving amongst Harwolfson's followers lest I come to Jaxon's notice. He wanted to use me to hold Wulfen, and though I am of no use now, he is vengeful."

As was Guarin who feared he would find no rest until that villain was no longer capable of harming anyone.

"Eberhard, I am going to ask you to trust me as I believe your lady would trust me."

Suspicion flew across his face. "Trust a Norman?"

"*This* Norman who was captured twice for aiding your lady."

"Nay, I will not betray my people."

"I do not wish you to. What I ask is you trust me to return you to your sister and lady no matter where victory falls on the morrow."

"How?"

"You number only one and are barely a man. Accept Harwolfson has rebels aplenty to battle William, and I will take you to my tent where you will await the outcome."

"Cowering on the side of the enemy!"

"Not cowering—preparing to reunite with those you love so you may grow into a man to whom they can turn for protection."

"Nay."

At least he did not lie. "Then here you shall remain until I come for you."

"I will not!"

"So says the Saxon who thinks I seek permission." Giving him no time to cry out, Guarin wrenched the gag up between his teeth and secured it with a knot more easily cut than pulled free.

Eberhard kicked, dug his heels into the dirt to raise himself up the tree, and knocked the back of his head against the trunk when his boots skittered out from beneath him.

Guarin leaned near. "Save your efforts for when you are certain Saxons are near, not the Norman patrol who will pass close enough to investigate your sounds of struggle."

Though the words muffled by the gag were surely curses, the young man ceased struggling.

Guarin straightened. "I am guessing it will not be earlier than middle day ere I return." *And I will*, he assured himself, more certain William would win the day than Harwolfson.

But blood would tell...

CHAPTER THIRTY-FIVE

Harwolfson's Rebel Camp
Darfield, England

*J*sa had not expected to be granted an audience so soon. But of greater surprise was that the man before whom she was escorted was not entirely a stranger.

So jolted was she, it was as if it were just the two of them in a tent dominated by the table behind which Edwin Harwolfson and Jaxon stood. Even the latter, on whom her regard had first landed, could not return her gaze to him no matter how much his beckoned.

Did the rebel leader also recognize her? Certes, something had leapt in his eyes when first they fell upon her, and still he stared the same as she.

"Welcome, Dotter," he finally said in a voice as dense and coarse as wool. "It was not expected you would bring your Rebels of the Pale south to share in the glory of returning an Englishman to the throne."

Doubtless, a belief seeded and watered by Jaxon.

She cleared her throat. "My men and women are prepared and

honored to fight alongside yours." And it was true. So eager were all but a handful who remained behind, there had been no delay in departing the same night Eberhard left a scrap of parchment revealing he would wreak vengeance on Campagnon at Darfield. How Em had cried! And Isa had nearly crumbled…

Harwolfson shifted his regard to the man beside her. "You are Vitalis?"

"I am."

The rebel leader nodded at Jaxon. "I am told neither of you can be trusted—that you are Norman lovers."

Isa looked to the betrayer. As usual, his hair and beard were bound at the nape and beneath the chin, but both were lustrous rather than dull and matted. And his garments were hardly worn. The last time she had seen him so well groomed was when her sire lived and Jaxon was accorded much honor for being nearly as proficient as Wulfrith in training warriors. Though in this moment he appeared expressionless, the glint in his eyes evidenced he was pleased she was on the other side of the table.

"If by lovers you mean we do not kill indiscriminately," she said, "I must correct the bearer of…misinformation. We are not Norman lovers. We are Christians who, seeking to protect ourselves and our families, first give warning when feasible. When not feasible, we take up arms."

"And prefer humiliation of our oppressors over death," Harwolfson said. "Thus, some of those we must cut down on the morrow will be the same you could have cut down sooner, saving what might be scores of Saxons."

"Possible, but what I think more possible is such aggression would have lost a greater number of innocents upon Wulfenshire against whom the Normans would have retaliated. Perhaps even a harrying such as that threatened when the man who stands so smugly at your side condoned the murder of a Norman family, among them children."

A flicker in Harwolfson's eyes, a convulsing about the mouth.

Might he still possess a vestige of humanity? "I will speak to Lady Hawisa alone," he said.

"Edwin!" Jaxon protested.

"Alone!"

Stiffly, Jaxon came out from behind the table.

"I am safe, Vitalis," Isa said at his hesitation, "but you are not."

"Be assured, I will watch my back." He followed Jaxon from the tent ahead of the guards who positioned themselves on either side of the opening. When the flap fell, Harwolfson strode around the table.

Isa raised her chin, opening her face to scrutiny. So intense was it, it was as if his fingers moved over brow, eyes, nose, lips.

He nodded as if to himself, said, "I think 'twas you, Lady Hawisa."

"I think 'twas you, Edwin Harwolfson. Pray, give me your right hand."

He eyed the one she reached to him, and did as bid.

Cupping his hand in hers, she considered the calloused palm, then raised her other hand and drew a finger down the central crease. "Here I set my dagger so a royal housecarle who wished to end his misery could do what I could not." She folded his fingers over an imaginary hilt. "When he lost consciousness, I left behind my dagger so he would not be without recourse should he awaken." She felt a slight tremor. "And he is here now because neither could he do it."

He pulled free. "Do not think because you know mere minutes of my tale upon Senlac you know all. And if you hope gratitude will turn me from Jaxon, expect grave disappointment." He settled back against the table and curled his hands over its edge. "What do you want from me, Lady Hawisa?"

"I seek word of one who should not be here. Since our arrival, we have searched for a boy of twelve who departed our camp ahead of us to sooner join your army."

"He who played your half-Norman son."

340

What else had Jaxon told him about her? More, what lies? "Aye, to keep Le Bâtard from taking more of my lands."

"Your plan succeeded—for a time."

Stung by her failure, Isa continued, "I believe Eberhard—that is his given name—is near awaiting an opportunity to work vengeance on Normans, above all a mercenary named Raymond Campagnon who abused his sister."

"I know naught of the boy, my lady. My concerns are far greater than the whereabouts of a reckless child."

"Still, I would ask a boon of you."

His eyebrows rose. "Ask, and quickly. I have matters to attend to."

"While my rebels prepare for the morrow, I request an escort for myself, Vitalis, and the boy's sister so our search for Eberhard is not disrupted by those loyal to Jaxon who time and again thwart our efforts."

"With one such as Vitalis at your side, and considering your own skills which I am told are admirable, I wonder you should require aid."

"'Tis a matter of expediency and concern for your ranks. However, if you do not mind more of Jaxon's men suffering injury —perhaps so greatly incapacitated they cannot stand with you on the morrow—we can continue as before."

He laughed, and though that warm sound did not linger, something of a smile did. "I hardly knew your sire, but I believe he would be proud of one who is all that remains of his line— providing, she is loyal to her own."

"I am."

"Then you will be at my side on the morrow."

She hesitated. Though willing to fight, even if she had to face Guarin across the battlefield, she had hardly allowed herself to think there, focusing instead on delivering Eberhard from the encounter to come and hoping something would happen to avert bloodshed. The first was humanly possible, but the second...

Surely only by the Lord's hand.

"If you wish an escort, Lady Hawisa," Harwolfson said, "your word I require that not only your rebels shall fight alongside me on the morrow but you. Refuse me, and you add credence to Jaxon's charge you are a lover of Normans."

Only one Norman. The silent admission sped from her heart to her head. *And he asked me not to do what this one requires of me. But no matter how I wish to take Eberhard from here, that I can do only after leading my rebels.*

She set a hand on her sword hilt. "You have the word of a Wulfrith."

"Then you have your escort and another half dozen to send amongst the tents to aid in your inquiries. But only until the hour ere middle night. If the boy is not found, you and yours will gain your rest in preparation for ridding our lands of the tyrant. We are clear?"

"We are."

"Then let us see about finding this boy of yours."

Isa started to swing away, paused. "I do not try to turn you from Jaxon, for I know he is superior at training fighting men but, pray, be wary of disappointing him. He thinks mostly of achieving his end, little of the hearts and souls bridging the in-between."

"As he and I are mostly compatible, I foresee no difficulties."

"Unless you veer from his course as I did." She stepped nearer. "And for it lost Wulfen."

"We waste precious minutes, Lady." He stepped around her and tossed back the flap. "Come."

Hours later, past middle night, the stars shone bright against a sky of spilled ink. Gentle breezes kissed the trees and flirted among the tents. The leaves perched high on their branches whispered to one another of those who slept below and might never sleep again. And the smoke of the fires of warriors on one side and warriors on the other converged on a meadow where a woman knelt at prayer while one with drawn sword stood watch over her.

"Lord, Lord," Isa warmed her knees with beseeching, "if ever Eberhard was here, let him be making his way back to safety." She shuddered, pushed fingers into dirt, scraped it into her palms, and prayed harder for the many whose blood seemed destined to wet the earth when next the sun rose.

"Not again," she pleaded. "Not here. Not this boy."

She sat back on her heels, lifted her head, and opened damp eyes amid the smoke of Saxons and Normans that drifted, rose and fell, swirled and feinted. And became one.

CHAPTER THIRTY-SIX

Darfield
England

They came, the great host emerging from the wood promising to present nearly as formidable a presence as King Harold's upon Senlac though surely few of Harwolfson's men were born to the warrior class. Still, most of the rebels appeared well armed and armored, and unlike at the great battle, many were mounted. However, being astride and being proficient at fighting from atop a horse were different things.

Though they were yet too distant, Guarin was certain Harwolfson was the one at the fore of the cavalry. But of greater concern was whether Isa was among his ranks. Likely she was upon Darfield—hopefully only to retrieve Eberhard—but had her rebels come south to join Harwolfson, he had little doubt the daughter of Wulfrith would lead them. Hence, soon he might face her across a battlefield.

"Almighty," he entreated, that single name all that was left to him after a near sleepless night and pre-dawn visit to Eberhard.

The youth had been conciliatory, thanking him for the watered wine held to his lips, between mouthfuls of bread thanking him again, then promising he would immediately return to Nottinghamshire were he released.

Guarin had agreed, his lack of hesitation giving the youth no time to disguise the satisfaction streaking across his face. Thus, he was further surprised when Guarin once more bound his mouth and assured him *after* the battle he could return north. Another warning about the patrol had calmed Eberhard. But now that he could hear the gathering of armies?

Hopefully, he had enough control to suppress anger that could reveal him to the Norman patrol reinforced to ensure the enemy did not attack William's army from behind.

"Look how he comes!" the king snarled where he was mounted on his destrier ahead. Above him, the papal banner flown at Hastings once more shook itself out, while on his right sat both Penderys and on his left a favorite who, like the one Hawisa had slain at Senlac, held the esteemed position of *companion*. And alongside that one, Maël.

"See how he configures his army to mine!"

So Harwolfson did with three lines—archers, heavy infantry, cavalry.

"He mocks me!"

No mockery, Guarin mused as he fingered the string of the bow set over his shoulder and across his chest. Simply a lesson well learned and answered—identify the enemy's strength and make it your own. And as told by the Saxons continuing to emerge from the wood in such abundance they might exceed William's numbers—in great matters, bide your time.

Unlike others who led uprisings, Harwolfson had not moved against the king until he had amassed great numbers. Even so, his chance of success was hindered by those who comprised his army. No matter how good their training, most lacked the experience of warriors prepared to slaughter and die for their cause. Great damage the Saxons could inflict on William's men, but when the battle drew to a close, likely their blood would more vastly soak the ground.

"And weapons aplenty," William noted swords, spears, battle-axes, and bows glinting in sunlight. "I would not have believed it possible."

"We do battle?" asked the Bloodlust Warrior of Hastings, though not with the eagerness of one who sought blood. Had his two years in the monastery changed him? Or had a woman tamed the heart of so fierce a warrior, the same as Aelfled had done Cyr?

It was the elderly Pendery who answered the younger. "Of course we do battle! I fear not a Saxon dog whose greatest accomplishment is the ravishment of an innocent young woman."

Guarin's thoughts shifted to the two women who had accompanied Maxen Pendery to Darfield, the beautiful Saxon he had wed and a heavily pregnant woman rumored to be his sister, the child the latter would bear not of the man to whom she was recently betrothed.

Of a sudden, William's head swiveled. "Do you think to tell me what to do, Pendery?"

The old man stiffened. "I do not, my king. I but voice an opinion."

"Too loudly!"

"Pray, forgive me."

William returned his regard to the Saxons. Now the one who rode fore and center of the cavalry could be seen outfitted in the armor and finery of the royal housecarle he had been before Hastings. Proud. Determined. Formidable.

Would Darfield be the end of him? Guarin wondered as he searched beyond Harwolfson. More importantly, would it be the end of Saxon rebellion?

What his gaze swept over, and to which it immediately returned stopped his breath—grey strips on the sleeves of two score or more Saxons, and center of the mounted Rebels of the Pale, one whose hair and beard were of Vitalis. But it was the one beside him who wore the mail of a warrior, golden hair fastened close to her head, that made his heart test the strength of his breastbone.

~

"I SEE HIM." Isa stared at where he sat behind and to the right of Le Bâtard, his hair long, face lightly bearded, brothers on either side.

"The day has come, my lady," Vitalis voiced what she had feared—that they would face each other across a battlefield.

Drawing breath through her nose to clear moisture from her eyes, she said, "He is not the enemy."

"Yet this day he stands the side of one who is." Vitalis set a hand on her arm. "Regardless, I shall protect you with my life so if it is possible what was begun between the two of you can find a good end, it shall."

Kind words, the only falsity about them the hope she and Guarin had a future even should both survive. It was miracle enough Aelfled had her Cyr.

Isa moved her regard to that brother, and as she prayed the father of Aelfled's babe would return to his wife and child whole, felt something on the air that portended greater ill than the silence between two armies who awaited the command to engage.

Like evil, it slithered among those this side of the meadow, calling to mind the basilisk she had seen illuminated on a manuscript page when she was a girl. Her sire having been present, she had suppressed fear that nearly made her toss the book on the fire, but for weeks that serpent had trailed her dreams. And even now it visited when she was most vulnerable— as it had the one time fatigue closed her eyes last eve.

Seeking the source of the serpent in the Saxons' midst, Isa

looked around. It moved among some of her rebels, but more among the infantry, and perhaps the archers ahead.

Doubt. Worry. Dread. Fear. No matter how much the men and women more of the earth and plow than the blade and shield desired revenge, the prospect of failure and death threatened to root their feet and accept the yoke.

"'Tis the silence," Vitalis said. "It allows us to hear death walking amongst us, marking those it will take ere night falls."

"Walking?" She shook her head. "It slithers."

"I think you are right, my lady." He jutted his chin at Harwolfson. "And that he senses it as well."

The leader of the rebellion looked over those who wished to believe no matter the sacrifice, when next the sun rose it would be on an England ruled by the English. But it was no prideful eye that took in his army.

"Then this is for naught, Vitalis?"

"Tides can turn, my lady. Does God will it, we may—"

A high-pitched wail silenced Vitalis, and he looked to the ridge above the meadow where William had encamped on the night past. When another wail sounded, Isa was certain it was of a babe.

During her search for Eberhard, she had overheard talk of a woman large with child glimpsed in the company of the Penderys en route to Darfield. Might an innocent have been born here, its birth horrendously at odds with the butchery to come? If so, why would the Lord allow his newest creation to open its eyes upon so dark a day? There could be no good in it.

And yet what had been still moments earlier seemed a clamor compared to what settled over the meadow as the babe loosed lusty cry after lusty cry. Even when he quieted, the call to battle did not sound. It was as if Isa was not alone in pondering a babe born unto this.

Then all began to stir on the Norman side, causing her heart to race in anticipation she was moments from testing the warrior of her against men more tested than she would ever be, some of whom were not her enemy.

Lord, keep me distant from Guarin, she prayed. *Let neither of us see what our people do to the other.*

"God in heaven," Vitalis rumbled, "she made it past."

Isa lifted her lids and saw a woman with hair as golden as her own spurring her mount away from the Normans, a bundle in one arm.

Was this a ploy? If so, Edwin Harwolfson did not fear it. He urged his destrier forward, causing his men to step left and right to clear a path for him.

As she neared, he commanded his men to silence and shouted, "Come no nearer!"

More beautiful than the Lord ought to make a mortal, the woman slowed and turned her horse sideways.

"What have you come for?" Harwolfson demanded. "More trickery?"

With what seemed a smile of wonder, the woman plucked at the bundle she cradled, and the breath of many a rebel caught when a babe's face was revealed. "To present your son, Edwin," she said in Anglo-Saxon, no hint of the Norman across her tongue.

"Son?" He reined in several feet from her.

"Aye, yours."

Were that so, this woman could not be the mother, Isa thought.

Harwolfson peered at the child, then snapped his head up in response to the Norman spurring across the field.

"Edwin, pray, let him come!" the woman cried. "Surely you cannot fear one man with so many at your side?"

"More Pendery trickery," Harwolfson snarled.

Pendery—meaning it was the Bloodlust Warrior of Hastings who came?

"I vow he did not know I intended this," the woman said. "I hardly knew myself. He but seeks to protect me."

"What do you intend, Rhiannyn?"

Isa did not know the name, but she had heard that like Cyr D'Argent, Maxen Pendery was entranced with a Saxon, one he had taken captive with a great number of Harwolfson's rebels in retaliation for his brother's murder. Had the two become lovers?

"Peace," Rhiannyn answered.

"There can be no such thing between Saxon and Norman."

"But already there is. If you would just—"

The creak of wood and strain of strings being drawn flew her gaze to those intent on stopping Maxen Pendery.

"Edwin, order them to stand down!"

He considered the child again, then signaled to his men. "The babe is of Elan Pendery?" he asked.

Isa gasped. Then the inconstant young woman she had sought to avoid whilst at Trionne had conceived a child with Harwolfson?

"Aye," Rhiannyn said, "just born."

He went very still, then he said something too low to carry, and when the woman answered, neither could sense be made of her words.

What went between them? Isa wondered, feeling their angst across the distance, and more so with the arrival of Maxen Pendery.

"Almighty!" The warrior halted his horse alongside the woman's and gripped her arm. "What do you, Rhiannyn?"

"The woman who was first mine has presented me with a son." Harwolfson said bitterly.

Pendery looked between the rebel leader and the one who clearly belonged to him now, then he breathed deep and asked, "What think you of your son, Harwolfson?"

"As 'tis told he was born of ravishment, he cannot be mine."

Disbelief and resentment rippled through the rebels near

enough to attend to the exchange. They did not believe their leader had forced his attentions on Elan Pendery, but Isa knew so little of Harwolfson she could only hope he had not.

"It is not true he was got in that way," Rhiannyn said, "but it is true he is yours, Edwin."

He snorted. "How grand of you to believe me incapable of such behavior—believing me over the Pendery harlot."

She raised her chin. "Lady Elan recants."

"What?" both men demanded.

"As she was giving birth, she revealed the truth. She said she gave herself to you to hide her loss of virtue from her father."

Harwolfson appeared unmoved. "That may be, but do you count the months, you will see the babe comes too early to be mine."

"He was born young by a few weeks." Rhiannyn drew the blanket from the infant's feet. "But Harwolfson blood gave him life. Four toes on this one, as have you, Edwin."

He stared, then threw his arms wide. "This is your peace, Rhiannyn? A son in exchange for all of England?"

"England is William's," Maxen Pendery said.

"Not after this day!"

The Norman leaned in, said, "Even more so after this day if you fight a battle you cannot win."

Above the rebels' angry murmurings, Harwolfson declared, "My army outnumbers the usurper's."

Did it? Isa swept her gaze around. Were it greater, it was not by much.

"Numbers only," Pendery said. "Of more import is what each man brings to the battle. Can you say half yours are experienced in bloodletting? A quarter? If you stay the course, William will make but another example of you."

Jaw bulging, Harwolfson looked to the usurper's army, then once more lowered his voice. More unheard words, interrupted by scornful laughter, then what might be negotiation resumed.

Gaze drawn to Jaxon where he stood at the head of the infantry, Isa saw his color was so high it appeared he sat too near a fire. Just as she had threatened his plans, Harwolfson might, but would Jaxon retaliate?

As she had warned the rebel leader, it was possible. This could be Jaxon's last chance to slaughter Normans and send fleeing survivors back across the channel. Were he denied, what had he to live for?

Of a sudden, Harwolfson reined around. As he surveyed his rebels, Isa prayed he would also conclude that even with greater numbers, the Saxons faced further defeat. This time, however, nearly all the cost would be paid by common men and women and the battle of Darfield decided far sooner than that of Hastings.

Harwolfson's gaze lingered on Jaxon, moved to Isa, then he gave a slight nod and returned to Pendery. Shortly, the infant began to shriek, and Rhiannyn and his half-Norman son departed to allow the men to resume their discussion.

When Maxen Pendery himself put heels to his mount to deliver their words to the usurper, Jaxon commanded, "Speak, Edwin!"

Harwolfson turned his mount sideways and considered the one who approached on foot. "I have not summoned you, Jaxon. Return to your place and await my instructions."

The warrior continued forward, causing the murmurings of rebels to rise.

Vitalis leaned near Isa. "Now we shall better know the man this Harwolfson is."

Compatible with Jaxon, Isa recalled his claim. If so and a challenge was issued for authority over the army, who would prevail? Regardless, William would use it to his advantage—*if* it could be determined what transpired on this side of the field. For this, Harwolfson had turned sideways, blocking the enemy's view.

Jaxon halted and further defied his leader by gripping the

destrier's bridle. The only movement about Harwolfson an adjustment of shoulders and shift of hips, he looked down on the warrior whose usefulness may have come to an end.

Turning his profile to the ranks, Jaxon cast his voice wide. "We are here! We are battle ready! We thirst for the blood of those who bleed us! Tell, Harwolfson, why the greatest host of rebels our country has seen is not at arms!" As if for emphasis, he slammed his hand to the hilt of his sword. "Tell why we wait on the usurper! Surely not because of a misbegotten, Norman-stained babe. If that is it, the warrior of you is down around your ankles, and when the man made a woman trips over him, she will take the rest of us to ground with her."

Dear Lord, he does challenge Harwolfson, Isa lamented and looked to men and women near enough to hear every word of Jaxon's challenge. From their expressions, most feared a clash. Of those who appeared to welcome it, the majority were rebels who had chosen Jaxon over Vitalis and Isa.

"My lady?"

She looked down at the one who had come alongside and saw from Em's expression that just as the young woman's night into dawn search failed to uncover word or sight of Eberhard, neither had her perch in a tree this side of the field. From high above, she had watched the rebel army move out of the wood, hoping that vantage would confirm or refute the youth's presence.

Isa set a hand on her shoulder. "'Tis a good thing your brother is not here, as I would not have you—"

"He may be on that side." Em nodded at the Normans.

That he had gone there in search of Campagnon was a consideration from the beginning, but one about which nothing could be done.

Isa forced a smile. "I think were he ever here, he has returned north, and greater his need for you there than Harwolfson's need for another rebel here, Em."

Resentment brightened her eyes. "Only if Harwolfson fails us. Does he not, I shall stand with our people."

Knowing she could not argue her down, Isa looked to the mounted warrior and her sire's man who yet refused to accept horses had a place on the battlefield.

Silence prevailed, while beyond them Maxen Pendery continued to converse with his king, and Guarin—

She swept her gaze to Harwolfson and saw he had moved his regard from Jaxon to the infantry. A slight nod caused three men to step from the ranks and advance, while over a score slipped into the path earlier made for Harwolfson.

Whatever the old warrior had planned, he had not foreseen this—his followers' way forward barred and no apparent dissension from others.

"Traitor!" Jaxon swept his sword from its scabbard.

Before he could assume the proper stance to swing at one astride, the man he meant to supplant twisted in the saddle, unsheathing his own sword and arcing it downward. Harwolfson could have slashed Jaxon's neck, but he stopped the blade alongside the great vein and snarled, "Loose it!"

Jaxon held to the sword pointed heavenward, but when the rebel leader drew a line of crimson across his neck, opened his hand. That with which he had taught many a warrior dropped to the grass.

"You ask why we are not at arms?" Harwolfson shouted as his summoned men advanced on Jaxon. "'Tis because I, the leader of Saxons who look to me to aid in returning them to a life worth living, seek to do that."

"Leader!" Jaxon's throat muscles bulged. "You are too fearful to lead men, Edwin!"

Harwolfson's only response was to relinquish him to warriors of a size and strength to subdue him.

Vitalis leaned toward Isa. "He knew Jaxon would trouble him ere the woman brought the babe across the field. You warned him?"

"I did, though I do not think he required it. He understands Jaxon well."

As the old warrior was forced toward the wood—to put him from the rebels' minds and prevent dissension that would draw further attention from the Normans—Harwolfson urged his destrier down the front line.

"We are resolved!" he addressed his army. "We are courageous! We are mighty! And we are wise!" He swept an arm toward the enemy. "That is my son, she who birthed him Norman. It is true terms are sought with Le Bâtard, but terms favorable to all."

"What if they are not?" someone shouted.

"Then we proceed as planned. And regardless of whom God favors this day, many will die both sides, and those left behind will suffer—children, wives, husbands, mothers, fathers. Mayhap such great sacrifice will bring peace to our lands, mayhap not. But do we seek terms this day whilst we possess so great a power the usurper stands to lose much no matter who is victorious, there is hope for us beneath heaven."

Harwolfson turned his destrier and started back. "I am prepared to die here the same as you, and so we may if he who wears England's crown does not yield to our demands, but I ask you to trust me and let my decision be yours. Will you?"

As voices of what sounded mostly agreement rose, Em gripped Isa's knee. "He betrays us. Jaxon is right—all for a Norman-fouled babe."

Isa peered into her flushed face. "I know you think it so, and I do not doubt the child causes Harwolfson to reconsider as he might not otherwise, but surely you feel our people's relief." She jutted her chin at the Normans. "Such does not run rampant through them. If it treads there, it does so cautiously lest it step on anger rising from disappointment over having no blood to spill." She paused, struck by how distant these words from those that would have passed her lips two years ago. "Thus, do we not come to terms, likely Saxons will be worse for it."

Em pivoted and began shoving her way past the Rebels of the Pale.

"Em!" Isa started to dismount, but Vitalis gripped her arm.

"Let her go, my lady. Pendery returns."

She wavered, settled. Further reasoning with the young woman would have to wait until it was known whether Isa must lead her rebels into battle.

CHAPTER THIRTY-SEVEN

*T*erms were made. Though there were dissenters among the rebels, most went the way of Edwin Harwolfson.

All Saxons present would be pardoned for taking up arms against their king and allowed to return home. Harwolfson would be granted custody of his son whom the mother was either willing to relinquish or unable to prevent being taken from her. Of immense value, he would be awarded a sizable demesne. Of great contention, his lands would border those of Maxen Pendery, placing him under the watchful eye of the usurper's man. But it was done. Or nearly so...

Hostages were required to ensure the good behavior of Harwolfson and his followers.

What surprised that should not considering what had transpired this side of the field while Le Bâtard conversed with Pendery, was the first name on the list Harwolfson submitted to the conqueror—that of the last renowned trainer of warriors.

Long William had coveted Jaxon's knowledge in the hope those who defended England in his name would be more formidable. Hence, of the dozen offered up, among them rebel leaders that included Saxon nobles whose land had been confiscated, Jaxon was surely the most desirable. If he could not be persuaded to impart Wulfrith techniques, then for however long his life in captivity, no others who opposed Norman rule would have the advantage of that training.

Of those delivered to the center of the field, he was the only one who came bound, gagged, and prodded by the point of a sword. Several of the others who had filed past the Saxon army minutes earlier had exuded anger lest William choose them from amongst the offering to spend years, if not a lifetime, beneath the usurper's heel. If they behaved, they would be allowed to attend the king's court, but since they would be outsiders and never trusted, no life was that for a proud Saxon.

Once all were assembled facing the Norman army with Harwolfson mounted ahead, an armed rebel positioned behind each hostage, and in back of them a dozen rebels astride, Le Bâtard advanced. And among the dozen who accompanied him beneath a cloudless sun four hours higher than when first the armies amassed was Maxen Pendery, Maël D'Argent, and Guarin.

From where Isa remained among the Rebels of the Pale, she watched the latter draw nearer. When he reined in with the conqueror, she guessed it was as near as she would ever again be to him, his time in England drawing to a close.

My heart he shall take with him, she thought and told herself to be glad. Better it dwell across the sea than die here within her breast, even though never would he know it numbered among his possessions.

WILLIAM WAS PLEASED, though the Saxons would not know it from his expression, Guarin thought as he considered the king who sat to the right. By negotiation that cost little, a war had been averted whose victory would have cost the lives of numerous Normans.

There had been a moment Guarin sensed William's pride and

vengefulness would sacrifice those who fought for him, but sense had prevailed—better victory that did not reduce the number of warriors needed to keep control of England than victory that saw more Saxons than Normans dead. And sweeter the bargain made with Harwolfson that Jaxon was among the hostage offering.

William had been suspect, having thought he would have to press the rebel leader hard to see that one handed over, but Harwolfson was no fool to allow one made his enemy to move freely about England. And Guarin was grateful for his foresight that would ensure the warrior could do Hawisa no further harm.

As William considered the rebel leader mounted thirty feet ahead, Guarin looked to the bound Jaxon whose gaze awaited his. And felt satisfaction that all had come around, his tormentor now at the mercy of Normans. But unlike Guarin who was forced to bide his time to stay alive, he did not think Jaxon capable of passing so many days, weeks, and months as a captive. Perhaps not even this one day, so great the rage he exuded.

He becomes the mad wolf he sought to make me, Guarin thought. *If he is not already. And that is good. His days count themselves down.*

"Edwin Harwolfson," the king addressed his adversary, "Harold's housecarle."

"*King* Harold's *royal* housecarle," the man corrected, like many aware William objected to acknowledging his predecessor had worn the crown that now belonged to him.

William laughed, and even men who did not know him had to hear how false that gust of air. "Well, Edwin Harwolfson, no longer *King* Harold's *royal* housecarle—now *my* man—I am pleased no more of my subjects' blood had to be let this day, that you are a man of…reason."

"The same as you," Harwolfson said in Norman-French.

"Perhaps." William jutted his chin at the offering. "I am well with this selection of hostages. As you surely know, the trainer of Wulfrith warriors appeals most. I wonder, were I to take the bit from his mouth and bonds from his hands, what would he do?"

"As ever, seek to return an Englishman to the throne," Harwolfson said.

"Bring him near," William ordered.

The rebel leader peered over his shoulder and nodded at the one who held Jaxon at sword point. He and another gripped the warrior's arms and drew him forward. It took no effort, Jaxon averse to the humiliation of struggle.

When he was placed ten feet distant from the king, William said, "I am thinking there is no persuading you to train warriors for me."

Jaxon's upper lip curled.

"Remove the gag," the king ordered.

When it was done, the Saxon circled his tongue behind his lips and stared hatred at the one he could not defeat.

"You wish to kill me," William mused. "The same as you slew the Norman family passing over Wulfenshire, eh?"

Jaxon smiled the smile to which Guarin had become accustomed when the beatings had buckled his knees, giving his weight to manacled wrists.

Suppressing the impulse to touch those scars with their ridges and pits that extended from wrists up the backs of his hands and heels of his palms, Guarin ground his teeth.

As if sensing the control he exercised, Jaxon turned his smile on another he also wished to kill.

"Ah, that is right," the king said. "You know Guarin D'Argent. For—how long?—two years?" He put his head to the side. "That is a long time not to kill a man you detest. Unless it was not for you to decide his fate."

What was not tense about Guarin tightened. William hoped to fill the spaces left gaping in the tale of his vassal's captivity.

"Might my man be the reason you betrayed the daughter of Wulfrith—rather, *Dotter*? Did she forbid you to put an end to him?"

Maël leaned near Guarin. "And now I am glad you revealed so

little of your ordeal." He arched an eyebrow divided by the scar. "You might think I betrayed."

That Guarin would not believe of him. "I know you would not."

"William is not a man easily fooled, Cousin, and as his bloodlust has no battle upon which to vent it, I fear he intends to make much of you and the lady."

The same as Guarin feared.

"Where is she, Jaxon?" William demanded. "With her Rebels of the Pale? Those who defeated you at Wulfen Castle before fleeing to Nottinghamshire?"

Now Guarin was the one who wished to assure another he would not betray. But Hawisa had to know her rebels' bold exploits on that shire had become known to William following the castle folk's return to Wulfenshire.

The king raised his chin and surveyed the Saxon army that was too distant to hear what was spoken here.

He sees her, Guarin thought, *and surely not for the first time.* The pale worn by her mounted rebels marked them, as did her golden hair and place alongside Vitalis.

"Why is Hawisa Wulfrithdotter Fortier not among the hostage offerings, Harwolfson?" William asked.

Fingers clamped around Guarin's arm whose hand had gone to his sword hilt. "Be still!" Maël growled. "We are in the midst of warriors most loyal to William the Great."

We. Not *you.* The assurance Maël remained first a D'Argent was much needed in this moment.

"Have your men fetch her so I may better choose my hostages, Harwolfson."

"Quiet your face and body as my sire taught you," Maël rasped.

A lesson well learned. Much Hugh had liked angering his young pupils and dispensing punishment for their inability to hide what was in their minds and hearts.

"Harwolfson," William said, "our terms are dependent on

valuable assurance you will conduct yourself well henceforth—and I am thinking Dotter quite valuable."

The Saxon unlocked his jaw. "She is a woman."

"Indeed, but one who behaves a man, leads men, wields weapons alongside them, and plagues Normans."

"Only those who work ill upon *your* English subjects."

"So she may say, but who am I to believe? A defiant Saxon or a loyal Norman?"

Harwolfson's face darkened. "I do not think you wish me to answer that."

"You are right. Much I tire of Saxon lies, deceit, and argument. Now if you truly wish a bloodless end to this day and pardon for those who took up arms against me, deliver Lady Hawisa."

Reason, more than Maël's hand on him, prevailed over Guarin's desire to challenge William for making her a hostage. For a time—perhaps years—she would be the king's captive, but she would live as was unlikely should battle commence.

The rebel leader turned his destrier sideways and ordered two mounted rebels to escort Hawisa to the middle ground.

"Best she not be given warning of my reason for wishing to become acquainted," William made his command sound like advice.

She would come regardless, Guarin knew—sacrifice herself to save the many.

"Do as he wishes," Harwolfson said with grudging, and Guarin realized this was not the first time he had avoided respectful, formal address in speaking to or referring to the king. Though William might let it pass now, he would not always. As a vassal, Harwolfson would be required to show deference, beginning with properly titling William as his king and liege.

As the rebel leader's men reined around, the king returned his attention to Jaxon. "It occurs I shall be in possession of not one trainer of Wulfrith warriors but two. But how to choose between them—and choose I must since it would test the patience of your keepers to hold both, whether you are at each others' throats or joining forces to work your worst on them." William looked to Harwolfson's men who neared the Saxon army.

Guarin's heart doubled its beat, alternating between fear for Hawisa and anticipation of being near her again.

"A contest!" William exclaimed. "That will decide it. We shall, indeed, have a battle upon Darfield."

All that implied made Guarin's muscles cramp and his cousin's grip threaten the bones beneath.

The king's gaze landed on him. "Make no mistake, Guarin D'Argent, I know whom you would have be victorious and what tempts you to do what my vassal ought not. Your brother, Cyr, set me right on Hugh's failure to overcome the influence of his nephews' sire." His eyes shifted to Maël's hand on his cousin. "Oui, Sir Maël, I think you must, especially if you do not wish to earn your king's ire." He turned forward.

"Be still," Maël said as his cousin's breath poured in and out.

"Loose me," Guarin growled.

Maël complied. He did not wish to come to blows with his kin, but it would come to pass if Guarin did not heed the lessons taught him—not all of which applied to Hawisa.

"See here, Dotter comes as commanded," the king pronounced. "We shall yet tame this Wulfrith."

CHAPTER THIRTY-EIGHT

*W*ere it possible to make an enemy of Vitalis, she had done so in refusing to allow him to accompany her to the gathering of hostages, a summoning that portended ill.

Just as her man had seen it in the eyes of those who came for her, so had she. The harsh words she had spoken to keep Vitalis from following she heard again above the voices of the Saxon army who pondered aloud her place in the giving of hostages as she urged Anglicus past.

Words that cannot be unspoken, only forgiven, she told herself as she set a sedate pace between her escorts, then pushed Vitalis to a corner of her mind and acknowledged she was to be a hostage.

She had been relieved when earlier Harwolfson called forth notable rebels he believed Le Bâtard would accept and she was not among them—nor Vitalis who not only rivaled Jaxon but had youth to his credit. That she was summoned meant William had noted the absence of one who might prove as desirable a hostage as her sire's man.

She looked to Jaxon whose stance was defiant where he stood before the conqueror and thought how different his captivity would be from Guarin's. He would not be chained nor beaten without cause. Watched closely and never allowed too near the king, he would be permitted to move among his enemy— providing he presented no obvious threat. But would he be able to push his hatred deep enough to await an opportunity to wreak vengeance on the greatest number of Normans possible? She did not believe it.

And this lover of one Norman who shall likely dwell alongside Jaxon may find herself at his mercy.

The distance between the Saxon army and hostages closing, Isa shifted her regard to Le Bâtard. Sitting tall in the saddle, mail coif lowered to reveal brown hair and a hard-boned, clean-shaven face, he watched her.

Hoping her slow progress frustrated him, Isa looked to Guarin mounted alongside his cousin—on his other side Maxen Pendery who had not been there minutes earlier. Had Le Bâtard ordered him there, or had he himself sensed the need?

She could not read Guarin's eyes, but she knew his body, its tension further confirmation of her fate.

Control your emotions as I know you are capable of doing, she silently entreated. *I could not bear causing you to lose more than already I have taken. I dug this path deep and wide. It is mine to walk.*

She returned her attention to Le Bâtard, and when she and her escort halted behind the hostages, that one called, "Lady Hawisa Wulfrithdotter Fortier, we are pleased you deigned to answer our summons."

He thought to bait her. And she thought to bite. "'Twas no hardship," she said in her language, having heard his attempt to learn hers was proving more difficult than learning the lay of her country. "Already I was here and curious to look near on the one who confiscated the remainder of my lands though I paid the ransom—er, *tribute.*"

The hostages chuckled.

The usurper glowered. "You know my language, Lady. Use it!"

"Pardon," she said in Norman-French. "As king of the English

365

for nearly three years, I assumed you had conquered our language as long ago I conquered yours."

She vexed him, but what had she to lose that she had not already? Thinking her reasoning sound, she repeated in his language what she had spoken in hers and added, "And a most generous tribute it was."

"Sufficient for a loyal vassal, Lady Hawisa, but there is a cost for treason, and yours was forfeiture of Wulfen."

"But that is not the only cost, is it?" She swept her eyes over the hostages, lingered on Jaxon who had yet to look at her. But they would have time aplenty to face the other in the years to come.

"You do know your place, Lady Hawisa," Le Bâtard said. "That pleases me."

The last thing she wished to do. "For my people, I accept a hostage's yoke and assure you as long as you hold to the terms made with Edwin Harwolfson, I will give no cause to fear this Saxon amongst Normans."

"Hostage?" He smiled. "Perhaps."

Frowning, she nearly looked to Guarin, but too much it would reveal her. Instead, she shifted her regard to Harwolfson who sat before the hostages.

"Look to me to answer your questions, Lady Hawisa," William commanded. "He can only guess, though a good guess, I believe."

She sat straighter. "Am I or am I not to be your hostage?"

Some men shrugged their mouths as expressively as their shoulders. William was among them. "How can I know?" Before she could speak words she ought not, he said, "What do you think, Jaxon? Will you become my hostage or the lady you betrayed?"

No answer.

"And a dishonorable thing that, hmm? In betraying her, you betrayed her sire who surely entrusted her safety to you."

In the Norman-French he despised, Jaxon spat, "It was his *Saxon* daughter entrusted to me, not a traitor to her own."

William raised a hand. "Calm yourself. You shall have a chance to further betray." He returned his regard to Isa. "You lied to Sir Maël—hence to me—when you professed you knew naught of training up warriors. And yet see what you have made of scrabble —men and women my warriors take the long way around when they pass over that portion of Nottinghamshire."

There was no denying it now she sat before him in armor and wearing sword and dagger in place of psalter and keys that opened locks a lady required to keep her household in order. "Of course I lied. Would not your Matilda were Norman ladies capable of defending their homes and lives alongside their men?"

He ought to take offense, but he smiled. "Oh lady, I shall enjoy this contest. And you shall as well, Jaxon. Revenge, hmm?"

Isa blinked as the taunts and hints of what was to come slammed into place.

"That is correct, Lady Hawisa, much to the distress of Guarin D'Argent and Edwin Harwolfson, Jaxon and you shall meet at swords."

Her sire's man turned to her, and she saw no satisfaction on his face. But then, he did not believe in women possessing anything sharper than a meat knife. He might hate her for ending the Wulfrith line and finding good in some Normans, but great the shame of fighting a woman regardless of who won—and more so before an audience of Normans.

"I am as much aggrieved with Jaxon as he is with me," she said, "and just as I am certain he will decline to entertain you with the slaughter of a fellow Saxon, so shall I."

"I do not speak of a fight to the death." He shifted in the saddle. "I wish to see your skill against that of an esteemed warrior and Jaxon's against that of one born of Wulfrith. And as you are wont to deceive and he near withers at the prospect of proving himself against a woman, we require great incentive to gain your cooperation."

Though Isa felt Guarin's gaze, she held hers to the man who

367

was too pleased with himself. When he spoke no further word, she knew he required prompting. "What great incentive do you offer?"

"First, let me instruct my new subjects in something with which they are deficient—how to respectfully address *their* king."

"I know how to address *my* king!" proclaimed a hostage she had been told was a former thane who led two hundred rebels east to join Harwolfson. "That I would do were *King* Harold not in the ground."

Several concurred, but if William was angered, it did not show. "When you speak to me, regardless of whether I welcome your efforts to engage, you will begin or end with *My King, My Liege,* or *Your Majesty.* Even *My Lord* is acceptable though less preferred. Now ask me again, my lady."

Heavenly Father, I hate him, she silently appealed. *Give me strength.* "What great incentive do you offer, My Lord?" That last was low, most of her breath spent on the words come before.

"Freedom. Whichever of you betters the other to the extent you could take their life will go free, while the vanquished becomes my hostage—not as valuable, but useful in ensuring Harwolfson does as told."

Hope that had flickered through Isa flickered out. She was proficient at arms, but what chance had she of besting Jaxon? No matter his bones grew old and his speed suffered for it, surely his experience and greater strength would be impossible to overcome. And that was as Le Bâtard expected.

Hence, I shall be completely under my enemy's control, Isa thought, *just as Guarin was—*

Not the same, she admonished. *I may be confined for a lifetime, short though that of a caged bird, but what was done him will not be done me.*

She longed to look to him, but just as she dare not for fear Le Bâtard would glimpse her feelings for his vassal and wield them as a weapon against her, she dare not lest her disquiet move Guarin to act against his self interest.

As she stared at William, she considered all she would give to see amusement wiped from his face if she did best Jaxon. If *she* won her freedom.

Her heart beat faster, muscles twitched, palm longed for the sword.

I can best Jaxon, she told herself. *I am faster, lighter, a woman whose skill he underestimates. I am a Wulfrith.*

"But no matter how you may wish to slay your opponent, do not," William said, "for I require a hostage be made of one of you."

Then a wrong slice would see the victor's freedom disavowed. Le Bâtard was clever, easily overcoming their objections to entertaining him by offering liberty, playing the hand of benevolence in forbidding the death of the defeated, and ensuring no matter the outcome he possessed one knowledgeable in the ways of Wulfrith, even if that one refused to lend him that knowledge.

"'Twill not be me," she whispered. "I will gain my freedom."

For however long he permits you to keep it, a voice whispered.

Ignoring it, she said, "Your terms are acceptable...My Lord."

Le Bâtard laughed, that deep ripple more genuine than before, and as she gazed at the man peeking out from behind the devil, she saw he was not as old as first thought. Mayhap only a dozen years beyond Guarin.

"I am thinking you will be a welcome addition to my court, Lady Hawisa."

Further proof he believed her contest with Jaxon already lost.

"That is, if Jaxon prevails." He looked to the warrior. "Are my terms acceptable to *you?*"

He laughs at us both, Isa thought and steeled herself for Jaxon's gaze.

As she stared back, she wondered what he saw in looking upon her sire's only daughter who had been of little consequence born after so many sons. Might he remember the teetering child...the girl of middling years...the girl on the threshold of womanhood... the young woman who survived every one of her brothers? Or did he see only the woman she presented now who donned clothing and weapons he found offensive and whose hatred of the Normans was unequal to his own?

Her throat tightened. Never had he been one to show affection, but he had been kind to her during the best of times, tolerant during the worst as when she rejected marriage to his son and shortly thereafter bowed to her father's desire to wed her to a Norman of *good stock*—one who, following Wulfrith's death, Jaxon found himself serving. He had detested Roger but remained at Wulfen, though only because she birthed a son to continue her sire's line.

So much hope Jaxon had for Wulf. And so much anger when Isa's weakness caused the grandson of his beloved lord and friend to pass from this earth.

"You do not believe me, Jaxon?" the usurper prompted. "You think the word I give is the word I take away?"

Jaxon flexed muscled arms bound behind his back. "You give your word loosely, William of Normandy," he said in his enemy's language, eschewing the title Isa knew would never pass his lips. "Many are my countrymen who, fools they proved themselves, bent the knee for naught."

William's eyebrows rose. "As I have learned from your countrymen and women"—he nodded at Isa—"bending the knee once does not a loyal subject make. Ever too much weight on the back leg of a Saxon. But enough petty talk. Accept my terms as I speak them or do not and two hostages of Wulfen I shall have in my stable."

"I accept," Jaxon said. "Now unbind me and give me a sword."

"Non!" Guarin bellowed, and Isa's heart nearly fled her chest that it was for her he lost control of emotions he had kept leashed during all the days and months of his captivity.

Seeing his attempt to spur his destrier forward was thwarted by his cousin on one side, the Bloodlust Warrior of Hastings on the other, she whispered, "Hold him back. Save him from me."

He thrust with elbows and fists, drove a knee up into his cousin's gut.

Cease, Guarin! she silently beseeched. *This gives Le Bâtard power over you. Over me. Over us.*

He slammed the back of his head into Maxen Pendery's face, causing the horse beneath him to snap up one foreleg, next the other as if to rear. Then Guarin found his release and spurred toward her. But both Pendery and his cousin were fast after him, the former driving his destrier into Guarin's and turning him into the latter's path before veering away. A moment later, Maël D'Argent launched out of the saddle, slammed into his cousin, and carried him off the opposite side amidst a spray of arrows sprung from Guarin's quiver.

They hit the ground hard, and as the voices of their audience rose, the king's man who landed right side up thrust back and slammed a fist into Guarin's jaw. But if he thought to knock his cousin senseless he failed, possibly because many were the blows Isa's captive had sustained from vengeful rebels.

Guarin returned the favor of a fist, causing the one straddling him to lurch back, but as he wrenched at the hilt of his sword whose angled blade was pinned beneath him, his cousin drew a dagger. Its cross guard flashing blue, he swept it to Guarin's neck.

Still Guarin dragged at his hilt—until Maël D'Argent bent near and barked something. All that could be heard of their exchange was the rumble of their voices, then silence.

There seemed more pleasure about William's eyes and mouth than displeasure, and when he looked back at Isa, she knew he had verified Guarin's ties to her were far from rooted in revenge. This was not all about Jaxon and the lady he betrayed, nor the rebel leader and the hostages who would ensure Harwolfson kept the vassal's oath. This was also about Dotter and her Norman captive. Hence, though Guarin had satisfied much of William's curiosity, she would not herself—not out of stubborn pride but to deny the usurper greater power in knowing she returned Guarin's feelings.

But what will he do with what he has been given? she wondered. *Naught if I can beat Jaxon. And I shall.*

Maël D'Argent stood and offered a hand to his cousin.

Guarin clasped it and was heaved upright. He rolled his right shoulder, next his left above which the quiver on his back evidenced he retained few arrows. Then he drew his bow off, set its lower end in the dirt, and gripped the upper as if to support himself—support he did not need no matter how hard his fall.

Pray, do not, Isa silently appealed.

"I have set my cousin aright, Your Majesty," Maël D'Argent called and waved a dismissive hand at Maxen Pendery who walked his mount toward them. "Your loyal subject accepts it is for his king to determine who challenges Jaxon for the freedom of one or the other of these Saxons. However, he requests you consider he has a greater right for having been the knave's prisoner."

"You propose to fight in the name of Lady Hawisa, Sir Guarin?" William asked.

Isa sealed her lips against protest, certain no matter who had more right, Le Bâtard would see her and Jaxon at swords.

"I do, my liege! Jaxon and I have unfinished business."

"Ah, but if you prevail, your victory would earn the freedom of another of your jailers." He jerked his chin at Isa. "How do you reconcile that?"

Guarin stared, and she was glad he made no attempt to deny her involvement, certain it would delight William.

"Worry not for the lady, Sir Guarin," his king said. "Regardless the outcome, she shall live."

Maël D'Argent's hand was on his cousin again, and as more words were exchanged, Pendery looked to William.

His liege shrugged mouth and shoulder, jerked his head to direct him back to his side. "Ensure your cousin does not forget himself again, Sir Maël," he called. "Though this is all very interesting, my patience thins." He motioned two of his men toward Jaxon. "Unbind and arm him. And you, Lady Hawisa, dismount."

She touched the hilt of sword and dagger, looked to the sparkle of blue on her belt.

You are with me, Guarin, she thought, and seeing William had turned his attention to Jaxon, ventured a look at the man for whom she felt and found he watched her. *Is it possible you feel as much for me as I feel for you? Should I gain my freedom—*

Nay, he was of Normandy, and no matter what persecution she faced, ever she was of England. It would have to be enough to have loved a man as she had thought never to do. And to be loved in a way—no matter how small the measure—she had thought never to be.

She shook her head, entreating Guarin not to interfere, then swung out of the saddle and saw Harwolfson peered at her over his shoulder.

Regret and anger were in his eyes, doubtless at being helpless to stop the humiliation of a Saxon lady forced to battle one of her own.

She released her shield from the saddle, then strode between two hostages and past the man who no longer led England's greatest rebel army.

When she halted twenty feet distant from Le Bâtard, Jaxon said, "Dagger as well," causing the soldier who had passed him a sword to consult his king.

William shook his head. He might not know how swift and accurate the warrior's throw, but he had to know were Jaxon given a clear path, he would let the blade fly toward his greatest enemy.

The thought struck Isa she herself might seek such a means of putting finish to William's rule—and be justified in taking the life of the man responsible for her son's death—but even had she the skill, could she calculatedly slay another?

The answer making her soul shift toward darkness, she thought it good she had yet to master the throw of a blade so she might remain true to what was required of her rebels—*Take no life but in defense of your own and others.* By her hand, none would die this day. But one would bleed, even if he triumphed over her.

As Jaxon turned the sword side to side and peered down the blade's edges, the usurper said, "But do provide the old man a shield."

That *old man,* who was no more than ten years beyond William's age, snapped up his head and growled, "I require no shield, though the woman may keep hers."

Pride nearly made Isa cast hers aside, but she recalled her sire's admonition—*Be proud, but not so much pride raises your head to a height that exposes the great vein in your neck.* She slid her arm through the strap fastened to the inside of the shield, cinched it only tight enough to stabilize the movable wall, and curled her fingers around the center grip.

"Dotter is eager to begin your contest," William said as she drew her sword. "Proceed!"

Jaxon moved his gaze down her, on the return paused on her belt from which Guarin's dagger hung.

Let him come to you, she told herself. *Note his stride, the lay of his shoulders, the shift of his eyes, the grip on his sword. In the space between now and partnering in this deadly dance, firm your resolve, bolster your courage, accept death could be your end.*

Not her words, but her sire's spoken low shortly after the passing of his last male heir. In facing the skilled young man set at her—Jaxon's son who, unknown to her sire's man, Wulfrith had concurred was an unsuitable match—she had conformed to his instructions. And been beaten, though not soundly. Though her sire was pleased with her efforts, she had remained a womb for breeding warriors as evidenced by his decision to wed her to Roger.

"I have become more, Father," she whispered, and when Jaxon moved toward her, slid into the warrior.

Three strides distant, her sire's man halted. "Ever 'twas meant to be," he said.

"My sire would not agree. He would be appalled to find his heir betrayed by one he counted a rare friend."

"I knew him better than you, Hawisa Fortier, am certain he would accept what I do to one who once more proves unworthy of his name—a name that may never have been yours in truth."

And so begins the taunts meant to mangle my resolve, she thought, *but no matter where he thrusts the blade of falsehood, I shall turn it aside.*

He grinned. "Mayhap talk of your mother's cuckoldry was not all talk."

No such rumors. Her mother had passed before Isa could form memories of her beyond a haze of movement and sweetly crooning words, but Wulfrith's wife had been esteemed by all.

"Again, you betray my sire in dishonoring the memory of his wife," she said. "He would not know you at all, Jaxon, would himself set you out of Wulfen."

"More he would not know you! To ensure the Wulfrith line ends with him, I shall choke the earth with your blood."

Shoulders aching from bearing the weight of mail all these hours, Isa shifted her feet and set her sword's blade nearer the shield's edge, its point centered on Jaxon's chest. "In boasting of having known the mighty Wulfrith well," she said, "you forget freedom is forfeited should one of us slay the other."

He took a step forward, said low. "The word he gives *is* the word he takes away. Whether or not one or both of us live, neither of us goes free."

She feared that as well but more so that he believed it, meaning he might make good his threat to end the Wulfrith line.

"Come, Jaxon!" Le Bâtard shouted. "Do not be afeared. Beneath that mail she is all soft woman."

Not so, Isa silently disputed. She had her soft places, but all else that could be made muscular had been.

Of a sudden, Jaxon swept his sword back and rushed at her with a bellow that showed his teeth, the absence of many, and a humped tongue.

With so much thrust, weight, and width hurtling at her, defense was Isa's only option. Blessedly, she excelled at it, being lighter, shorter, and fleet of feet. Then there was timing, another skill to which she could lay claim.

At the moment before his blade came down on hers, she bent, leaned left, and let the force of his steel sweeping across hers spin her to the side. Her blade skittered down his, stuttered over the cross guard, then slid down his mail-clad arm and back as he continued past.

She turned on a toe and just missed the opportunity to slap her blade against his buttocks, a humiliation that could turn him reckless and render him vulnerable.

Or more dangerous, she allowed as she pushed off with her back foot and, raising her shield high, ran at him as he turned.

She had the advantage of being on the offensive, but quickly he set himself at her. Their swords met again, and his saliva sprayed her face as he cursed and thrust her back.

She stumbled, regained her balance, lunged. This time she shouted as she brought her blade down on his, shouted again as she knocked his sword to the side, then drove her shield up into his chin.

His head snapped back, but the impact was insufficient to knock him senseless. He found his balance and charged, driving her backward, striking from on high, the sides, and low. The last slice came off her sword into the gap between it and her shield, and the tip of his blade cut through her chausses and the inside of her calf.

Fear that Guarin would do what he ought not made her swallow a cry of pain. Then with her shield she deflected Jaxon's next blow, swept up her blade, and scored the back of his free hand. It was hardly blood for blood, but she was pleased to so soon take some of what he had taken from her. And from the rousing of Normans and Saxons, the contest between the renowned trainer of warriors and his lady held them captive.

Isa distanced herself from her opponent and came back around.

The hitch in Jaxon's advance reminded her of a lesson taught her rebels—exploit every known or perceived weakness your opponent presents. For Jaxon, that was his hip injured in his younger years when he was thrown from a horse.

It was more pronounced than ever she had seen it, but there was no time to determine how she had caused it.

Knowing he was slower to turn that side, she veered in that direction, with a ring of chain mail leapt up to match the height of his sword to hers, and slammed her blade against his. As she continued past, she landed the flat of her blade against his hip.

He lurched around and widened his stance. But before he could fully recover, Isa struck again with an upward cut he deflected mid-sword and a downward slice he evaded with a sidestep. Then, as if to gain time and space to recover, he pounded toward where the contest had begun near the usurper.

The Normans came to attention, and the ranks began to close around William, but when Jaxon had put twenty feet between him and his opponent, he turned back. As the Normans eased their guard, he beckoned, "Come, Norman lover! I would have my freedom."

More greatly she felt Guarin's gaze, but again suppressed the temptation to give her regard to one who could make her feet stick when movement counted for everything when blades sang.

Shifting her shoulders beneath mail that grew heavier, becoming aware of the scent and feel of perspiration that made tunic and chausses cling, she advanced slowly to give herself time to recover her own breath.

As she neared her sire's man, she glanced at William. She expected a smile of satisfaction, but no longer was there lightness about his mouth. Because he found this demonstration of Wulfrith training lacking?

One moment she was ashamed at not better representing her sire, the next glad. If he deemed the contest a poor showing and she lost, perhaps she would be passed over as a hostage.

CHAPTER THIRTY-NINE

*H*old! Guarin commanded himself. *This is what she desires and William requires. Leave it to her else you will undo any chance she has of gaining her freedom.*

Determined he would act only if it appeared Jaxon meant her mortal harm—better she find herself a hostage than dead—he tensed further as he inventoried the moves required to defend her.

"Patience!" Maël growled, referencing the bargain struck when Guarin was pinned and on the knife's edge between remembering and forgetting who kept him from Hawisa.

"I hold," he rumbled.

"By a frayed thread," his cousin bit.

And more frayed now Jaxon moved the fight back toward William, alarming the king's guard who were too quick to relax once the Saxon warrior swung around to face Hawisa. Though not certain Jaxon would put her through, Guarin had no doubt he would seize an opportunity to do what no other Saxon had accomplished—kill their Norman king.

Guarin looked between William and Jaxon. Though the king had refused the latter a dagger, he was no fool to believe a well-thrown sword could not prove his undoing, albeit the chance of that was thin. Eyes sharp upon the warrior, subtly William nudged the destrier left and right to ensure he presented as narrow a target as possible.

When Hawisa drew near enough to resume the contest, she halted, positioned body, feet, sword, and shield.

As Guarin had no hope of reaching her in time to give aid with his sword, he flexed his hand on the bow he made pretense of leaning on, and opened and closed his other hand in anticipation of snatching one of his remaining arrows from the quiver.

"Only if you must," Maël said, "and then make it look very good—though not my teeth, hmm?"

Gaze fixed on the combatants, Guarin said, "Only if I must. And not your teeth."

Isa had assured herself she could prevail against Jaxon, but this was more effortless than it should be, his increasingly pronounced hitch slowing him, over and again giving her the advantage.

She took blood from his lower leg, his side and shoulder, his cheek. He cut her as well, cursed her, spit in her face, and snatched at her hair to loose its vulnerable length, but ever she danced away before he could make minor victories great ones.

And so it went, his sword beating her back toward Guarin, hers beating him toward the conqueror—until her foot slipped in grass muddied by their combat and he landed a thrust to her forearm. Her mail stopped the blade from penetrating beyond its keen point, but the impact sent pain reverberating to her fingers.

She leapt back, ducked beneath his next swing, and sprang upright to slam her shield into his gut.

A great blur. Darkness. Rain the color of blood bursting across the black come down over her eyes. Then she was falling backward, memories flashing amid reeling consciousness—Jaxon's arm knocking aside her shield, his face coming toward hers, dropping her chin to deny him the soft landing of her nose, forehead striking forehead.

Isa's rear hit first, and as she fell onto her back, she felt the emptiness of her left hand that had worked the shield. Of greater detriment, no longer was her right hand intimate with the sword.

She struggled to bring Jaxon to focus, drew a sharp breath when she saw he was also bereft of sword and the step he took toward her evidenced he was dazed.

She flipped onto her hands and knees. Seeing black again, she crawled forward, blindly sweeping her hands in search of her weapon. As she did so, her vision cleared, but not sufficiently to point her toward her sword.

Hearing her name shouted in warning—was it Guarin?—she looked around and saw how near her opponent. Blessedly, neither had he recovered his sword.

She thrust upright, and as she whipped around nearly plunged back to earth.

Face bright with exertion and moist with perspiration, Jaxon took another step forward. As he did so, he lowered his gaze to her waist, and it lingered on the only weapon between them—freedom if she could set Guarin's dagger near enough her sire's man to prove herself the victor.

She snatched it from its scabbard, placed her back foot further behind, and glanced past Jaxon to Le Bâtard who leaned forward in the saddle. "'Tis over, Jaxon. Yield!"

"Not while still I can gain my freedom," he slurred loudly as she had only heard him do when he imbibed to excess.

As suspicion rose up around her, he blinked and gave his head a vicious shake. "Non, Hawisa, you are done playing at being worthy of your sire's name."

"No play this. It is all Wulfrith. Now yield!"

He peered over his shoulder, said in the language he detested,

"And disappoint the conqueror who has yet to have his fill of entertainment?"

This time, the dust of suspicion cast itself in her eyes. He wished the enemy to understand what was spoken between them, meaning he calculated more against the usurper than her.

I am exactly where he wishes me to be, she thought and tightened her grip on the dagger a moment before he lunged.

She swung the blade to the side and up, forward, down, slashed his exposed collarbone beneath gathered beard and above the unlaced neck of his mail tunic, saw red on the blade, then droplets on the air as momentum carried the dagger to her opposite side.

Intending to land a backward upper cut, she reversed her swing, but before the dagger began its ascent, his hand closed like steel over hers on the hilt.

Amid gasps of surprise, delight, and disappointment, he jerked her forward. Breath foul, yet soft on her face as if he hardly labored, he grinned. And increased the pressure on her hand when she tightened it on the hilt.

"Ah, unworthy one," he rasped in Anglo-Saxon, "who would have guessed you would share a sliver of my glory?"

He did mean to move against William, all this a farce to draw near, distract, and throw a dagger.

"Now struggle—curse, kick, scratch, bite—then loose the dagger and fall backward."

Would the blade land true, toppling William of Normandy, leaving him as dead as King Harold, England once more in the hands of—?

Nay, there hopelessness. It was not one man who had the English by the throat. Hundreds of his warrior nobles with their scores of castles would fill the void, and eventually one would rise above all. Thus, no quick end to this conquering—if an end at all. And those now upon Darfield...

In the frenzy sure to follow the death of a king, there would be great slaughter. And Guarin—

"Make your sire proud, Hawisa!"

Tears flooding her eyes, she said, "'Twill be for naught."

His mouth quivered, nostrils dilated as if to take in all the air in all the world, then he jammed her hand down and dropped her to her knees, nearly making her cry out as his fingers threatened her bones.

"I say she yields!" Jaxon shouted, then peered across his shoulder. "What do you think of your Wulfrith hostage, Le Bâtard?"

She could not see past him, but she did not doubt he made no friend of William in naming him that.

Isa wrenched at her hand, and feeling sharp pain from the heel of her palm to her wrist, feared he had snapped a bone.

"The contest is not over, old man," the usurper said. "Even does she yield, I require her life be in your hands, not her fingers."

Jaxon looked back at her, muttered, "Loose it, and I vow to put it in his eye the same as the Norman arrow in Harold's eye."

She squeezed the hilt tighter.

"Nithing!" he hissed. "Unworthy!" Then his other hand shot forward, closed around her throat, and squeezed. "In my hands!" he shouted.

AN ELBOW to Maël's nose, a reach over the shoulder, a shaft in hand, its end nocked, string drawn, missile flown.

The arrow was not meant to kill, though great the temptation. However, in the space between release and landing, Jaxon tore the dagger from Hawisa's hand and, shifting his weight around to do as Guarin suspected, moved the target from shoulder to chest.

The Saxon warrior screamed as his body twisted with the

arrow's penetration of his mail, then he fell onto his side atop the beaten grass.

Halfway to Hawisa who had dropped forward with one hand flat to the ground, the other at her neck, Guarin flung aside the bow and lengthened his stride.

As he neared, she stumbled upright and raised her face to William who, bâtard he was more by nature than birth, looked upon her with amusement and satisfaction—moments later what seemed curiosity when one of his guard urged his horse near and spoke in the king's ear.

As something dark replaced curiosity, Hawisa stepped forward, fell to her knees, and rolled Jaxon onto his back. Whatever she spoke to the warrior who gripped the shaft above a blood-stained beard and however he responded was masked by the din of their audience. But when Guarin lowered beside her, he heard her say, "'Twas all for naught."

Seeing Jaxon work his crimson tongue and lips as if to further stain her with blood, Guarin gripped her shoulder. "Come away."

She looked around, eyes moist searched his face as if to make sense of his presence, then said, "It was you. Your arrow. You—"

"D'Argent!" Jaxon rasped past frothing blood that wended down his jaw and pooled in the hollow of his neck. "Who wins, eh? Not she whom *you* made a hostage."

So it might appear. Though Guarin had resisted interfering when her opponent dropped her to her knees, once the warrior gave William what he required—proof he could end her life—in that moment Hawisa became the hostage. And the arrow had flown to ensure the vengeful Saxon did not snap her neck.

Jaxon moved his shuddering gaze to Hawisa. "I could have done it. If not the eye, the…great vein."

Confirmation the dagger she had not yielded was destined for William, a consideration secondary and distant to Guarin's need to save her.

"Traitor!" Jaxon gasped. Then his back arched, mouth worked like that of a fish plucked from water, and eyes rolled up.

Their audience quieted, and Guarin knew William had commanded it.

As death eased the warrior back to earth, emotions swelled through Guarin. Relief—indeed. Satisfaction—God help him. Regret—for the hostage Hawisa had become.

He looked to where she sat back on her heels, head down, golden hair a mussed halo of braids clinging to her crown.

"It was necessary," he said.

Her heavenward-facing hands resting atop her knees as if in submission curled inward.

"I could not risk him killing you, Hawisa. And already you—"

She slammed her hands to the ground, pushed upright, and turned to him as he rose beside her.

"You and your revenge!" she cried in his language, eyes bright with tears, throat muscles straining, skin flushed where bruises would soon appear. "You could not be satisfied with anything less than his death, could you? And though I kept you from the worst of him and you profess to feel for me, look what you have made of me!" She flung a hand toward the king. "A hostage to that devil!"

Guarin expected anger over her circumstances, but not directed at him alongside blame for what Jaxon and William had conspired to make her. "Hawisa—"

She swung the hand that had refused Jaxon the dagger.

He caught her wrist. And released it the moment he saw pain fly across her face. "Hear me, Hawisa!"

"Hear you? Non, hear me! I did not want nor need your aid. Now I have no hope because you could not resist vengeance." She drew a sharp breath. "Not only upon my sire's man but me, hmm?"

He delved her face, wondered what worked behind it. Had her feelings for him shifted so far? Or was she not thinking right? Did despair at her loss of freedom make her publicly cast words she would later regret? And one could not discount the effect of the contest. As with many a warrior who survived battle and the accompanying bloodlust, panic, desperation, and relief, it could be days before they came back to themselves—if ever.

"That is it!" She laughed bitterly. "Because I resisted your efforts to woo me—could not stand the thought of your Norman hands on me—you did this." She narrowed her eyes. "Leave my ruined country, return to your beloved Normandy, and think no more on the Saxon who rejects you."

I do not believe her, Guarin told himself. *This has to be for William's benefit, not mine.*

Or do you merely wish it to be? doubt suggested.

He unlocked his jaw. "We will speak later."

"Non! I wish never to see you again." She started to turn toward William, glanced past him. "Do not forget your dagger. If ever it was of use to me, it is no more." She gave him her back. "Providing you are sated, *My Lord,* this hostage requires a physician."

I do not believe her, Guarin more firmly asserted. *In sparing me no humiliation, she seeks to spare me worse.*

"Come, daughter of Wulfrith." William beckoned. "We shall see you properly tended and attired as befitting a guest of the king."

Guarin turned. He had no difficulty locating the dagger that made its bed amid grass, its gold and silver a sharp contrast—and more so, the sapphire in the throes of entertaining sunlight. He hesitated, then closed his hand around the hilt and wondered that it did not feel foreign after all this time.

He considered the initials that lacked evidence of an attempt at erasure. That Hawisa had not betrayed her keeping of the dagger beyond giving it to Vitalis did not surprise, but her man... That did surprise.

The D'Argent dagger returned to its rightful owner, no infamy for having slain a king, Guarin started back toward Maël. As he did so, he looked to Harwolfson who, his cause having brought

Hawisa south, bore nearly as much blame for her captivity as Jaxon.

Still, it was impossible to hate the man who had made the right decision for the Saxons and Normans who would have ended their days here, quite possibly among them D'Argents—and Hawisa.

Determining no matter the cost, he would speak with her, he continued forward and swept up his bow.

Now to retrieve the young man he had kept from William's clutches as he had not Hawisa.

~

King William's Camp
Darfield, England

NO CHAINS THESE, but still bondage.

Isa ran her gaze over the ermine-edged sleeves falling from her wrists and guessed the gown belonged to one of the Pendery ladies.

Lowering her arms, she looked down the bodice and skirts that were the blue of a sky passing from day into night—not as dark as the mantle given her captive, more the shade of the gem set in his dagger.

"Guarin," she breathed. Nearly yielding to emotions contained since William's physician tended her injuries hours past, she distracted herself by continuing to inventory her appearance.

Her boots of scuffed leather peeking from beneath the hem were no fit for the gown. The belt girding her waist was as plain as it was useless in the absence of keys, purse, and scabbard. And her hair... The best she had been able to do was unravel her braids, finger comb the tresses, and work a single plait that fell down her back.

She dragged it over her shoulder, stroked the crossings, shifted on the stool she had sat upon since accepting no relief could be had pacing the tent's confines while those posted outside talked and laughed.

Will I laugh again? she wondered. *Will Guarin?*

"How deeply did I wound you?" she whispered, hating it had been necessary to be cruel in denying Le Bâtard power over Guarin and her. But providing she was believed, threat to the man she loved could not be used to force her to give Norman troops the advantage of Wulfrith training. And should she escape—

She choked back a sob. As a guarantor for Harwolfson's conduct and that of the Saxons who remained with him, she could not seek her release.

"You will behave, Hawisa Wulfrithdotter," she said. "For however many years you are held, you will be silent and respectful, giving none cause to smile or laugh no matter how they taunt. Indeed, mayhap they will grow so bored you will be deemed a waste of time, clothing, and food, and they will set you out."

Or lock you away, reason snatched away hope.

"Not entirely silent," she amended. "Occasionally respectful, from time to time showing just enough Wulfrith to keep their interest the same as a...pet."

She pressed her lips to hold back another sob, and for the dozenth time since being left alone, moved her thoughts to Eberhard. How was she to discover if he was well? If he had, indeed, returned north? If he was able to reunite with Em?

Since she did not believe the young woman would join Harwolfson in making a new life beneath the watch of Maxen Pendery, would she unite with others to continue the fight? Would she drag Eberhard into what seemed hopelessness?

From outside the tent, a familiar voice amid the unfamiliar straightened Isa's spine. His next words, "Stand aside!" made her jump up. The snap of the tent flap made her set her chin high.

He straightened from ducking inside, and in two strides stood before her.

Noting a bruise on his clean-shaven jaw, she guessed Guarin had dealt it in order to come to her aid.

The chevalier's own eyes moved over her, paused on her bruised neck, then her bandaged hand and wrist the physician believed suffered no broken bones. "Lady Hawisa."

"Sir Maël."

"I am to deliver you to our king."

"Then it is time."

"It is."

Doubtless, a spectacle would be made of choosing hostages. Would Le Bâtard line them up and, as done by buyers at auction, inspect them as if those for sale were the beasts? Whatever the humiliation, already she was among the chosen ones, and yet still she would suffer degradation.

It is your lot, she told herself. *You must become accustomed to it.*

"I have no good regard for one who made my cousin suffer things unimaginable for a D'Argent," Sir Maël said, "and barely Christian tolerance after so worthy a man and warrior exposed himself to derision and punishment to preserve your life. But for Guarin who should not care what befalls you, I will do you a kindness."

She swallowed hard. "Much appreciated."

"You are to have a private audience with King William." His eyebrows rose, the scarred right not as far as the left. "Or nearly so."

It *was* kind of him to ease her angst over being humiliated far and wide, but that did not mean his king intended her any kindness. Perhaps her fate was to be worse than that of the other hostages and he wished to savor it alone.

"I thank you, Sir Maël. Lead and I shall follow."

The corners of his mouth rose. "Not an easy thing for a Wulfrith, I imagine."

"You imagine right, but you are wrong to imply such is exclusive to my family. None of my people, from the noblest to the least noble bows easily to brutes. Simply, some cannot resist as long as others. And I know it is the same with Normans as your cousin proved. And for that..." Momentarily, she closed her eyes. "...this is my due." She started past him.

He caught her arm. "Speak plainly, Lady."

"Of what?" she said though she knew she had led him this direction, albeit unintentionally.

"You were cruel in rebuking Guarin before all, and yet still my proud cousin cannot hate you. Why? And do not tell me he is a fool."

She could not name Guarin that. Though she longed to refuse the king's man further insight, perhaps if she unburdened some of what weighted her, she would be less vulnerable to William.

She looked to the chevalier's hand on her and, when he released her, said, "I fear Guarin did not believe me. Thus, I need your help. Not for me. For him."

Despite the distrust, perhaps revulsion on his face, it made the unmarred side no less handsome—unlike the other that was nearly sinister.

"If he did not believe me," she said, "and the bleeding of his pride was insufficient to make him cast off my confession, you must persuade him to leave England before he makes an enemy of William."

"What confession do you speak of?"

"I did succumb to Guarin's attempts to woo me, but it is more than desire I feel for him." She moistened her lips. "It is love. I know he cannot feel as much for me, but I fear he may be moved enough to lose more than he has since first he sought to protect me. Pray, Sir Maël, make him go home."

His eyes were like knives, slicing away her layers in search of a different truth, but finally he said, "He is his own man, but I shall do my utmost to see him reclaim his inheritance."

"I thank you." She smoothed her skirts. "I am ready for William."

He grunted. "No one is ready for William."

Not even Edwin Harwolfson and his great army, she thought. *But they live, and I am happy for it. Much praise, Lord.*

"Come." The chevalier started forward, then came back around. "What is it about the women of England that so ensnares, especially you with your warrior's ways that ought not appeal in the absence of soft and sweet?"

She peered into a face never before seen—almost childlike in his desperation to grasp what must be understood before another step forward could be taken. Though tempted to refuse him an answer, she said, "Perhaps the blood of long gone shield maidens yet courses our veins—the determined, hard, and fierce appearing when it is not enough for our men to defend family, home, and country. Perhaps you sense it. See it. Thrill to it." She nodded. "Very possible, but you are wrong to believe there is no soft and sweet when armor and weapons are shed, Sir Maël. For the right man."

"God's rood!" he muttered. "Does this not end with you, Saxon women may be the downfall of the D'Argents."

"Else salvation," she said, thinking of Aelfled who had tamed a merciless Norman and whose child born of their union had forged a stronger bond between conquered and conqueror.

"Salvation not needed," the chevalier scorned. "Hence, I shall guard against going where my cousins have gone."

She smiled. "Guard away, Sir Maël, but do you truly find the women of my country offensive, best you return to Normandy. If you do not, you may never leave."

He glowered, motioned her to follow.

CHAPTER FORTY

*B*end the knee."

Hawisa remained upright, eyes on the one who had made her wait long before turning from the table he bent over—his perusal of the map of Darfield not feigned but neither necessary now the battle was averted.

Upon entering the tent, other than a glance at Guarin where he stood in the back right corner, she had not acknowledged him. And so still had she gone, cradling her bandaged hand in the other, raised chin exposing bruises on her neck, one could almost believe her turned to stone.

"I know you heard me, Lady Hawisa," the king said. "Now let me witness with my own eyes you have become a loyal subject so I need waste no time verifying it should you betray again. Bend the knee—non, both knees."

Nearly all color except that of her bruises draining from her face, she remained unmoving. But as William's shoulders rose to give volume to displeasure, she dropped so hard the ground shivered.

"Both knees...*My Lord.*"

William strode forward and caught up her chin. "You can do better. Try *My Liege*."

"My Liege," she croaked.

"Now *Your Majesty*."

Her nostrils dilated. "Your Majesty."

"You will master it." He released her. "Assuming, of course, you have many an opportunity for practice."

Guarin stiffened, saw Hawisa also heard the threat. Whence did it come? Was she not to be a hostage? Deemed too divisive, imprisonment her fate? Exile? Surely not death, that a punishment William deemed barbarous—providing one was noble and had satisfactorily yielded to his superiority.

Guarin looked to Maël where he stood alongside the table.

His cousin shook his head, either at a loss or unable to offer insight at this time.

"Are hostages not given the same consideration in your court as they were in King Harold's and King Edward's before him?" Hawisa asked.

"They are, Lady. But I have learned something that may disqualify you from that comfortable life." He looked to the guard opposite Maël, the same who had drawn near the king on Darfield. "Pierre de Balliol, tell again what you witnessed on Senlac following the battle."

Inwardly, Guarin groaned. Here more cause for his summons —not only punishment for interfering with the contest between Jaxon and Hawisa, but for not revealing who slew William's companion.

"Your Majesty," the guard said, "upon the hill where the usurping Harold fell, I witnessed the murder of your companion."

Seeing Hawisa's gaze waver, her throat convulse, Guarin gripped his fingers in his palms.

"Though it was night and light was wanting, I saw a golden-haired woman stab your esteemed companion and a Norman warrior of an age to have silvered hair force her off the hill, onto a horse, and into the wood. This day, I thought it possible Lady Hawisa was that murderess, but when Sir Guarin came to her aid, I knew it was not the first time he safeguarded her."

The king returned to Hawisa. "Tell me it was not you."

Her chest rose with breath and she raised her eyebrows. "Why would I deny it? It is as true as it is what was done your esteemed companion was justified."

"How can murder be justified, Lady?"

"I came in search of my son, a child I did not yet know was slain by a Norman. Your companion attacked me, and you surely know what he sought. Thus, it was not murder that saw him slain but defense of my person."

William dropped to his haunches before her. "You say he violated you?"

Rather than fling denial in his face as she had when Guarin probed the extent of the assault, she stared. Might she confirm violation, even if only to gain grace?

"Lady Hawisa?"

Her tongue clicked off her palate. "Violation was his intent."

"That is not what I ask. Did he or did he not ravish you?"

"Does it matter?"

"It does!"

Another deep breath, then, "I do not know."

William shoved to his feet. "This your confession—you slew my man for doing something he may not have done?"

Now a sharp breath, and Hawisa thrust upright, so near the King of England that had she a blade he would be dead.

It surprised he did not knock her down. Was he as stunned as the others? Or did he sense the warrior at his back would not think well before once more defending her?

"You play with me, Lady Hawisa! How can you not know whether or not my companion violated you?"

"That day was a dark one for those who fell and those who fled, but it was a darker night with few to answer the calls of the dying who but wished not to be alone as they passed amid carnage." She swallowed. "That is what I walked through, my skirts so soaked in blood and gore I felt the weight in my shoulders as I prayed over and again none of it was my boy's."

A tear spilled onto her cheek. "How can I not know what was done me? Unlike you, I felt much for what happened on a meadow more ravished than ever I could be. Thus, perhaps God in His wisdom chose to spare me remembrance that might…" She muffled a sound of distress. "Though the loss of my son is so unspeakable I am no longer whole, I am not broken as my enemies wish me to be. What I am is justified in defending myself, whether to stop your companion from ravishment or continuing to ravish."

Chest tight, Guarin assured himself there was good in William's consideration of impassioned words that provided more to think on than rage against—hopefully, they would benefit Hawisa.

Not imprisonment, Lord, Guarin entreated. *A hostage, even an exile.*

Finally, William spoke. "Stand back, Lady. You offend." When she complied, he said, "You did not have permission to be on the battlefield. Why? Because warriors so soon out of the fray need time to cool their bloodlust lest it spill onto innocents. As a Wulfrith, you had to know that—and what you risked."

"A risk only a mother unworthy of the child God gifted her would not take. Of course I knew! But that does not excuse a man, especially one esteemed enough to be your companion, for being unable to control the animal within."

The king fell silent again, then with grudging, inclined his head. "You are fortunate the one slain was the least beloved of my companions and on occasion gave cause to question his integrity. For that and compassion for the loss of your son, I forgive you his death. But as for the rest…" He turned to the guard. "Go."

The man hastened from the tent, leaving Guarin, Maël, and Hawisa alone with the King of England.

"Still there is a price for your faithlessness, Lady."

"Which I have agreed to pay. For as long as required, an obedient hostage I shall be."

"As expected if I required that of you. I do not."

Her eyes widened. "Then what?"

"You know what I want."

"I will not better your troops with Wulfrith training so they may slaughter even more of my people!" she exclaimed. "If that means I am imprisoned the remainder of my life or this day marks the whole of my life, God will give me what is my due as He shall give you what is yours."

He chuckled. "How you thwart, Lady. And yet I cannot dislike you when you call to mind my beloved wife who, though I succeeded in wooing her where Guarin D'Argent failed with you, still thinks herself better than the son of a duke and a tanner's daughter."

He sounded genuine rather than mocking, and Guarin wondered if, like a handful of the many men who defied him, Hawisa had earned respect enough to be truly forgiven. Even so, there would be punishment. God willing, not so great it would break her.

"So how do I gain what I want?" William said. "Since you appear indifferent to Sir Guarin, threats against him for behavior nearly as treasonous as yours will not move you." He returned to the table and pushed back the map, sat sideways on the edge with one booted foot on the floor, the other hitched. "Even if your indifference is feigned, I believe you would choose your people over him. A sacrifice for the greater good, hmm?"

She kept her lips sealed.

"Tell, Lady, how do I move you from the rebel side to your king's side?" No sooner asked than he said, "Ah, already answered

—the greater good." He looked around. "Sir Guarin, stand beside the lady who so detests you she will not even acknowledge you."

I am drowning, Isa thought as she watched William who held the rope that, were he to toss it to her, would be slippery as if slathered in pig's fat.

Out of the corner of her eye seeing Guarin pass before his cousin, she commanded herself to maintain the pretense and to breathe when he drew alongside.

"I like this," Le Bâtard said. "One of Hugh D'Argent's most accomplished pupils and the last Wulfrith." He smiled. "Be assured, Lady, just as I know the son lost to you is the only one you bore your first Norman husband, I do not believe the slur you are ill-gotten. Had the reputation of your Rebels of the Pale upon Nottinghamshire not convinced me, your facility with weapons would. You are Wulfrith's daughter, and in your womb more Wulfriths."

Suppressing the impulse to cross her arms over her abdomen, she said, "You accuse others of games, but mayhap the feared conqueror is more a master of play than the sword."

He smiled. "The master of both, though I confess a fondness for play, it being among the best strategies of war whether the battle is between two men or too many to number. And then there are the battles between one man and one woman." He wagged a finger between Guarin and her. "If the contest can be won by neither side, one must play at a cessation of hostilities. Continuing one's line demands it."

Isa gasped.

"And now you understand *my* rules of play, Lady."

Dear Lord, he seeks to bind Guarin to me, to require of him greater sacrifice that, were I more selfish, I would wrap my arms around.

She ventured a look at Sir Maël, and seeing his indignation, silently entreated him to do something.

William stood from the table. "What I require of you is your mind, eyes, hands, and feet. Thus, your punishment is marriage to a Norman of my choosing."

She could no longer avoid looking at Guarin, but he kept his profile to her, a muscle in his jaw convulsing.

"And your punishment, Sir Guarin..." William thought on that. "Hardly punishment to give my liegeman the woman he desires, even if he did not want her for a wife, but there is his inheritance. As Lady Hawisa is of greatest use to me in England, your family's lands in Normandy shall pass to your brother, Cyr."

Pain gripped Isa. More sacrifice Guarin must make.

"Hence, Lady Hawisa, your Norman husband will be Baron of Wulfen, Stern, and..." He shook his head. "I think Balduc best awarded another—mayhap my slain companion's son, Estienne Lavonne."

Isa snapped her hands into fists. Who better to keep watch over those who had defied the usurper than one eager to avenge his sire's death?

William shrugged. "Until I decide, Theriot D'Argent shall continue to administer that barony. And you will have two of the three pieces of your demesne put back together. In return, warriors to defend my kingdom will once more receive training at Wulfen."

She shook her head and was ashamed she refused William more for Guarin's sake than her people's. "I will not give the benefit of Wulfrith training to men who would kill my people. Nor will I wed a man I do not want."

"For the greater good you shall."

"Were it for the greater good of *my* people, but you speak of *yours*."

"Non, I speak of the people of Wulfen. You have not forgotten Raymond Campagnon, have you?"

Surely he did not mean...

He did. If she did not yield, he would award her home to that villain. For a moment, fear for those of Wulfen moved her toward acceptance, but there was a greater good beyond those who named her their lady—that of England. Campagnon might make the people of Wulfen groan and hurt, but what of Normans who, their superior training bolstered by that of Wulfrith, did William's bidding? How many more Saxons would die?

"I do not see you have a choice," William said. "Accept my terms and once more don the mantle of Lady of Wulfen."

"Save hundreds of lives at the cost of what could be thousands? Non. Do you place the people of Wulfen under Campagnon, a man you ought to be ashamed to be associated with, I shall ache for their suffering but find comfort in knowing greater numbers do not suffer."

William's face began to darken, lips to thin.

Would he strike her? Worse, would the man to whom she had been cruel upon Darfield defend her again?

"Your Majesty."

She shivered as the breath of Guarin's voice made the fine hairs escaped from her plait dance against her cheek.

"An alteration to the terms might satisfy you as well as the lady."

"You assume I am open to alteration, D'Argent."

"More, I know you wish Wulfrith training to benefit those absent the unshakable hand of him who conquered this country and will himself stamp out the last of the rebellion."

Though what Guarin spoke was likely the truth, Isa's stomach turned at his flattery.

"I speak of your sons, grandsons, and all who carry your name across the ages," Guarin added.

"Though you have not my approval," William said, "you have my interest."

Guarin inclined his head. "I was not so isolated during my captivity among the rebels of Wulfenshire I was oblivious to their ways and training."

Isa prayed never would Le Bâtard learn he had aided in that training.

"Of my observations and tales overheard, I learned the greatest of those come out of Wulfen began their training at an early age—as few as five years."

Vitalis and Ordric beneath her sire and Jaxon beneath her grandsire, Isa recalled a conversation with Guarin when he asked what made those housecarles excel beyond others trained at Wulfen.

"As my Uncle Hugh knew the same as those who trained you at arms, the earlier the master places a sword in the hand of one destined to fight, the greater the warrior."

"I do not see where you go with this, D'Argent. Get there quickly so I may be done with Hawisa Wulfrithdotter."

Guarin looked to her, and there was something in his eyes that should have fled after she disparaged him before all. "I am thinking the lady would suffer marriage to me and aid in training up warriors were she assured they did so only after our two peoples become one."

Isa's knees nearly gave. She knew he had more than desired her, but it sounded even after this day he wanted her—enough to accept the loss of his inheritance.

William laughed. "Be it lust or love, you are a hound, the same as I in pursuing the King of France's niece. Neither did Matilda want me—and then she did." He shifted his regard to Isa. "If it is not a game *you* play, beware, Lady. The man you do not want may become the only one you desire. And a Norman at that." He nodded. "I understand what you propose, Sir Guarin. Rather than train men at Wulfen, it should be exclusive to those distant from earning sword and spurs."

"Boys, Your Majesty. By the time they are ready to fight for you and your heirs, the rebellion will be in the past."

Isa felt a fool for not sooner grasping that. Was it the solution? If Wulfen accepted none older than ten or twelve, it would be eight years or more before warriors were made of them. But would there truly be no sides to choose then?

"Do I send the young sons of my nobles to you, Lady Hawisa," William said, "will you give them the benefit of your family's training?"

Acceptance crept onto her tongue but was swallowed by the realization he excluded those who had more right to that training. "I have conditions."

"For what do you believe you are in a position to set conditions?" he demanded.

"Now Jaxon is dead, more than any I know the ways of Wulfrith." Not true, she silently amended. Vitalis excelled beyond her abilities, but she would not have the warrior who had escaped the usurper's notice become one of his conditions. Her man must be free to decide whether to continue opposing Norman rule or accept it. "Thus, I require equal numbers of Normans and Saxons receive training." Seeing refusal in his eyes, she added, "As my father told, no greater bonds are there between men than those forged in defense of one another's lives. If you truly intend us to become one, you cannot object."

"As your sovereign, I can object to anything. But continue."

"I shall have final..." She glanced at Guarin. "My husband and I shall have final approval of who is accepted at Wulfen."

His jaw shifted. "Continue."

"And women—"

"No women!"

"But many are capable of learning arms."

"Non, Lady! Wulfen is not a rebel camp. You will not be training desperate women and men. You will be training those dedicated to doing *my* will. Oui, some of your sex are skilled at wielding arms. You have proven that, but the benefit does not outweigh the danger of women in battle. Recall that of which you accuse my companion. Whatever his purpose in venturing to that hill, it was not ravishment." He stepped nearer. "Women are distraction, temptation, stirrers of bloodlust even hours after the battle—during a battle, chaos."

Nearly trembling with the strength of his words, her confidence wavered.

"Do I concede anything, it will not be that. If you require it, too highly you regard your worth and on the morrow your exile begins with transport to the coast where you will cross to Normandy and be imprisoned for as long as your king wills. Longer does he forget you as is often best with troublesome subjects."

Feeling her confidence creak and begin to crack, she was tempted to appeal to Guarin to assure her whatever he felt for her was worth the sacrifice of his inheritance. But any concessions to be gained would be forfeited if Le Bâtard knew the only hardship of wedding this man was guilt over his loss and that ever he might resent her for it.

"Decide, Lady Hawisa!"

"No women," she said and silently added, *Except those I instruct privately.*

"Very good," William said as if he had taught his pet a new trick.

She swallowed hard. "And my other conditions?"

"Whatever they were, I reject them."

As breath rushed from her, she felt a hand on her arm and knew Guarin sought to prevent her from giving his liege cause to do worse than imprison her.

Seeing William note the protection once more afforded her, she nearly pulled free, but she needed Guarin's strength— especially as it was the last time she would feel his touch now negotiation that had not been negotiation had failed. Hoping she would bear the greater blame, allowing Guarin to remain his sire's heir, she said, "Then it appears we—"

"But I have some thought on how best to utilize Wulfrith and D'Argent training," William spoke over her. "Boys only, none of an age greater than twelve, and drawn from Norman and Saxon families in equal measure."

He had resumed the game. Or perhaps he had not. Perhaps he saw great merit in Guarin's proposal and her conditions and but determined to make them his own. That was it, this usurpation as conscious an act as that of bringing war to England.

Spoiled child, she silently scorned and said, "Acceptable terms. But who is to determine which boys receive training?"

"I will send those I deem worthy. The others I shall trust your husband to cull from the best families of England."

An insult to her, and yet she felt as if she had won, especially as he did not stipulate the families be noble. As her sire and grandsire had known, a commoner with little to his name had greater incentive to excel than many a noble with much to his name.

"If Guarin D'Argent agrees," Isa said, "I agree."

"Agreed," Guarin said.

She had not realized her heart so clenched until she felt it begin to open. They were to be man and wife, would lie down every night together and awaken every morn to the face and arms of the other.

"I am pleased, though there is another matter," William said.

"Your Majesty?" Guarin said tautly.

Le Bâtard turned and once more dropped his muscular frame on the tabletop. "The name of Wulfrith is esteemed across England—less so on the continent though well enough regarded." He looked to Isa. "Hawisa Wulfrithdotter, next Hawisa Fortier, soon Hawisa D'Argent." His gaze shifted to Guarin. "Better Hawisa Wulfrith."

As Isa struggled to make sense of that, he continued, "You would not be the first of my nobles to wed a Saxon lady and take her sire's name."

Dear Lord, Isa entreated as Guarin's hand on her tightened, surely this time to hold himself back.

She looked to his cousin. His dark expression making his scars more sinister, she thought it possible he would soonest fail at containing his anger.

"Guarin Wulfrith." William nodded. "Your fellow Normans may think it humiliation, but it is good strategy that will sooner see you accepted by your wife's people. And since already you look the part, having shunned shears and razor, easier it shall be."

Though preservation of Isa's family name was desirable—indeed, she had scorned bearing children known by their Norman sire's name—already Guarin was accepted by Wulfen's people. This was further punishment of the warrior who had served his liege well that bloody day. But though she longed for Guarin to reject this term, not only would he be denied her lands but his inheritance. The one who had stolen England was too powerful. However, if she...

Nay, even if she claimed Guarin was unworthy of her name, she would not be believed. And whatever doubt William harbored about her indifference could move him to certainty it was no punishment she wed this man.

"Sir Guarin is displeased, Lady Hawisa," the usurper said. "Mayhap he is himself tempted to lock you away?"

"I will take the name of Wulfrith," Guarin said and released her.

William straightened from the table. "Then we shall see it done ere nightfall. Sir Maël, fetch the priest who accompanied your cousin."

He had to see the chevalier's anger, but he appeared unconcerned.

"A wedding ring," he said as Guarin's cousin exited, then eyed the one upon Isa's hand. "That of your departed husband?"

She touched the band worn to discourage Norman suitors. "It is."

"An ill wind to use it to bind you to my liegeman." William thrust a hand forward. "Remove it."

Quickly, she worked it off and dropped it in his palm.

"Methinks your Saxon bride more eager to wed you than thought, Guarin Wulfrith," he said and strode to a chest.

As he rummaged inside, Isa peered up at Guarin. "I am sorry."

He looked sidelong at her, returned his regard to his king—soon her king through marriage.

"I intended this for my Matilda." William strode forward. "I am told it belonged to King Edward's mother—my great aunt Emma —and was confiscated with many of her treasures when her political maneuverings displeased her son." He lifted the ring before Isa. "The metal is silver and plain, but the ruby is no small thing, and have you ever seen one so red?" He feigned a frown. "The color of Wulfrith, is it not?"

"It is, *My Lord.*"

"Perfect." He held it out to Guarin who, without a glance, closed his fingers around it.

William chuckled, demanded, "Now where is that priest?"

CHAPTER FORTY-ONE

*G*o to her, Baron Wulfrith. Make me Wulfriths mightier for their Norman blood."

I must be well with this, Guarin told himself as he exited the tent and lengthened his stride to sooner distance himself from William.

"Guarin!" Cyr called.

Equally resentful he was followed and relieved it was not also Maël and Theriot, Guarin did not break stride. But when his tent on the outskirts of camp came in sight and the footsteps quickened, he turned.

Cyr halted so abruptly a cloud of dust arose. Amid flecks shimmering in the last of day's light, he held up a hand. "Peace be with you, Brother."

"Peace?" Guarin said. "Brother?"

Cyr sighed. "Whether you are Guarin D'Argent or Guarin Wulfrith, ever we are brothers." He jutted his chin toward the tent. "Peace now she is yours as Aelfled is mine. True, at the expense of your pride, but I recall how great your concern for her after she and Vitalis freed you, just as I do not forget our conversation when you were installed at Wulfen."

Guarin ground his teeth.

"You made it sound a jest that England suited you and I remain our sire's heir, but she is what you want. Some will talk of what you yielded for such a woman, but that is just it—*such* a woman as they have never seen and can never have. And then there are her lands. Jealousy will fall from men like scales from a snake, but it is jealousy worthy of what you have gained. Break some teeth, break some ribs, break some limbs, and it will dry up."

Guarin wanted to accept the balm he offered, but he could not drag himself all the way down from the heights of anger to which a pride trampled one too many times had carried him.

Cyr set a hand on his arm. "Though it appears you are angry with Lady Hawisa and much it satisfies William, you are not. When I was told for what I was summoned, I was displeased, but throughout the ceremony I weighed her offenses against her losses and the return of my brother who lives because she willed it. When Father Fulbert led from the tent a woman so downcast one would think a cold cell and chains awaited her, I accepted the only thing for which I can fault your wife is blaming mine for the loss of her son when it was the boy's guile that led to his death."

Recalling his defense of Hawisa when Cyr had shared what Aelfled had withheld from her lady, grudgingly Guarin said, "More than your wife, she blames herself for the loss of her son."

"Regardless, when it is well between you, I ask the truth be revealed no matter how it hurts or angers her. Before I take my family to Normandy, I would have her and Aelfled further reconciled so my wife does not unpack that burden in the home we make with father and mother. Perhaps it will even lighten your wife's guilt."

"I will tell her, Cyr. But are you truly pleased to be our sire's heir?"

"Much I care for my wife's country, but I yearn for Normandy. As she is willing to go where I go, that is where we belong."

Guarin looked to the tent where his own Saxon bride awaited

him and knew *she* was where he belonged though she was not as biddable as Aelfled—or perhaps because she was not. Fire there, he had told Dougray, one only a man of foolish pride would seek to put out.

Lord, he silently beseeched, *more than ever, let not pride be my downfall.*

"And I believe Wulfenshire is where you belong," Cyr said.

Guarin nodded. "It seems I must set my mind to titling myself Baron Wulfrith without hesitation or resentment."

Cyr stepped near, clasped Guarin's arm. "Peace be with you, Brother."

"And you, Brother."

Cyr smiled. "Now release your bride from her prison."

"Providing she has not battled her way past Father Fulbert and fled, I shall," Guarin said, not entirely in jest.

Cyr chuckled and turned on his heel.

"She is what I want," Guarin said as he watched his brother go from sight. "What Baron Guarin Wulfrith wants."

❀

"He comes, my lady!"

Isa jumped up from the pallet, bent to retrieve the blanket sliding down around her calves.

"Leave it!" Father Fulbert sliced a hand where he stood alongside the tent flap. "You are modest enough."

She straightened. As she smoothed the bodice of her chemise, she caught the crunch of boots. Then Guarin tossed back the flap.

"Baron." The priest inclined his head, gestured at Isa. "Your lady wife and the bed—er, pallet—are blessed and blessed again. Be fruitful." He ducked outside, only the sound of the settling flap testament to him having been within.

Were she not so tense, Isa would smile at how different he was from the priest who had seen Roger and her put to bed, a task so solemn and lengthy she had nearly screamed.

As Guarin peered over his shoulder at where Father Fulbert no longer stood, she traveled her gaze from his long, silvered hair, to the dagger finally returned to him, to his boots. When she looked up, his eyes were on her.

"A peculiar priest," he murmured, then perused her—making her wish she had loosed her braid as the priest had suggested.

"Your hand?" he asked.

She followed his gaze to her bandaged fingers and palm. "Naught broken. All will heal."

He nodded. "I wished to tell you sooner, but there was no opportunity. The boy, Eberhard, has been in my keeping since last eve when Maël and I discovered him near the king's tent."

She gasped, and became so light of head she nearly lowered to the pallet. Her boy was safe. Here answered prayer, the Lord surely having set Guarin in Eberhard's path.

"Welcome tidings," the man now her husband said.

"Most welcome! When we could not find him in Harwolfson's camp, it was hoped he had returned to Nottinghamshire. Where is he?"

"When King William summoned me, I asked Dougray to keep watch over him. No harm will befall him."

"I thank you. Eberhard is vexed, not only with Campagnon for abusing his sister but me for not sooner reuniting them."

"He will come around."

Would he? she wondered, but in the next instant all wonder—and apprehension—was for the man striding toward her.

Though her chemise was of tightly-woven thread, she longed to cross her arms over her chest, a gesture that would make her appear painfully chaste though she was familiar with a husband's touch.

Guarin halted and raised a hand.

Reflexively, she stepped back, causing him to open his palm as if to assure her he would make no fist of it. Of course he would not. He was honorable. Worthy. A man as God intended him to be.

"I wish only to look," he said, then lifted her chin and examined the bruises on her neck whose colors she could only feel.

"They are unsightly?" she asked.

He met her gaze, and she saw the hard of his eyes had softened. "Unsightly only to one who was not quick enough to prevent them."

She moistened her lips. "Where is your anger, Guarin?"

"I make peace with it."

"I am grateful, but after all I caused you to lose and the humiliation you are made to bear, I would not begrudge you anger. Still, I would have you know the words I flung upon Darfield were not intended for you. Ere you slew Jaxon, I knew already I was in William's power as ever I was meant to be. I spoke them only to deny him more control over us after once more you proved you cared for me—and at the cost of relations with your cousin."

The corners of his mouth grooved. "I did not take Maël unawares. Lest I find myself removed by William's guard, we made it appear I yielded to reason. Lest my cousin incur the king's wrath, it was agreed were it necessary to defend you, I make it look I overpowered him."

Remembering what once he had told, she said, "First, in between, and in the end, you are D'Argents."

"So we are. As for the arrow, I flew it first for you, Hawisa, second for William."

"You knew what Jaxon intended?"

"It took no strain of the imagination, and neither for the king, I believe. But though William was wary, I think it possible Jaxon could have landed a blade. You knew it as well, did you not?"

"When he had me on my knees, he said that was his intent."

She glanced at her bandaged hand. "Though tempted to yield the dagger, I feared the meadow would become a battlefield if William fell."

"So you accepted your plight—to become his pawn."

"The same as you." She nipped her lip. "I am sorry for your lost inheritance and that you are forced to take my name."

"Wulfrith…" His shoulders rose with breath. "My pride suffers for it, so much it will be difficult to shake out its creases and mend its holes, but I know what my sire will say once he accepts his son is to be known by a name not his own—injury to hubris is a good thing in the eyes of the only one whose opinion ought to matter."

"The Lord," she said. "And yet still you have cause to be angry."

"Only over my pride."

Her hopeful heart swelled. "Truly?"

"Truly. As told, I make peace with it—much gratitude to Cyr."

She recalled Aelfled's husband standing between Sir Maël and Theriot D'Argent during the exchange of vows. A glance revealed one unhappily bearing witness, but when next she looked, Cyr had offered a sympathetic smile.

"What has he done, Guarin?"

He released her chin, caught up her hand, and considered the ring of the departed Queen Emma. "Wulfrith red," he murmured. "I would prefer D'Argent blue on your hand."

"The sapphire." She glanced at his dagger.

He nodded, then said, "Cyr reminded me you are what I have long wanted, so much I would wish to return to Normandy only were you denied me. There is a cost, as there should be for something precious, but now you are mine as Aelfled is his."

Her throat tightened. "Is it possible you love me as much as I love you?"

He set her hand on his chest, and she felt the thump of his heart. "Mayhap better the question—Might you love me as much as I love you, Hawisa Wulfrith?"

She loosed her breath and leaned in, as he gathered her close remembered how impossible this had been. "When you kissed me at the stream," she whispered, "I believed that was the most I would have of you."

"And now you find yourself wed to another Norman."

As she had wished never again to be, but the man she loved was far more than a Norman. "I feared that, but you have made good your claim to keep the Lady of Wulfen from William's wrath, and though you have brought me into the Norman fold, it does not feel a yoke."

He slid a hand up over her back, brushed fingers across her neck. "Never that for one who is to me what Matilda is to William, though I am determined to be more deserving of *my* wife."

She lifted her head. "The king does not regard Matilda as chattel?"

"I know it is difficult to believe, but she is so beloved none can carry tales he defiles the marriage bed, and so much he esteems her, he entrusts her to govern Normandy in his absence." He narrowed his lids. "I wonder if his regard for his wife's strength and determination saved you more than did his desire for Wulfrith training."

"Certes, not as much as you saved me." She frowned. "Do you think we have fooled him?"

"I think it possible we have as much as I think we have not. Regardless, he has the Wulfrith training he wants, but more on our terms than his."

"Because of you." She pushed onto her toes and considered his mouth. "I am wondering if my husband's kiss is as breathtaking as…"

"…your captive's," he said what she caught back, then, "I would live the past again to be here with you, Hawisa." He raised a hand, and the cuff of his sleeve fell back. "If ever you question how much I love you, look upon these scars and know I am glad for them."

Looking upon them now, remembering all he had suffered for her, she did not understand how he could forgive her—more, how he could love her. "Guarin," she breathed, then took his hand and pressed her lips to his wrist.

"Nay, Hawisa, here." He caught up her chin and moved her mouth to his. Then he kissed her so deeply the world with all its troubles and sorrows began to recede.

And now we shall become one, she thought as his hands explored the small of her back, curve of her hips, dips of her waist.

Strange his caresses were more unfamiliar than familiar. Roger had touched her the same, but she had not felt then as she did now.

Because this man I want. This man I love.

Breathing in his scent, she began her own exploration of the one with whom she would spend her life.

And then he set her back just as he had in the cave.

As she watched, he bent and reached past her, straightened and drew the blanket up over her shoulders. "Long I have waited for you, Wife. I can wait a while longer."

"Why?" At his hesitation, she said, "Because of what I am not certain William's companion did?"

He brushed the backs of his fingers down her cheek. "That and all you have endured this day. Just as I would give you time to prepare mind and body to lie with me, I would have you rest and heal."

She parted the blanket and reached a hand to his jaw. "It is almost three years since Senlac."

"And yet when you stood before William, I saw and felt the memory of it."

"Ever it will be with me, but less the assault on my person. That is mostly haze. What affects me is regret—rather, moments."

"Moments?"

"Moments I could have used to better defend myself had I more practice at arms. Moments Roger denied me by banning me from Wulfrith training though much counsel he required after my sire's passing. He said such is not for ladies, even those born of Wulfrith—that it is for men to protect them. But that night it was only I on the battlefield. Until there was you."

"And I came too late."

"You did not. I saw the others coming for me—of the same intent as William's companion. You appeared when you were needed most. And now you are needed again."

He searched her face.

"You for whom *I* have long waited, Guarin. You for whom I can wait no longer." She settled her body against his. "I would make love."

"You know not what that does to me," he growled.

She leaned up and brushed her lips over his. "I do know. That is why I do it. Now, pray, give answer, Husband."

Once more his arms came around her, once more he claimed her mouth, once more he learned her curves. Then he eased her onto the pallet, and as night drew curtains around the camps on both sides of Darfield, she drew the curtain of his silvered hair around her. And silently beseeched the Lord that were there Wulfriths in her womb, He would make D'Argents of them.

Worthy sons and daughters...

CHAPTER FORTY-TWO

*H*er feet atop his. Again. Her back to his front. Again.
But this time, the only chain between them was that
which bound hearts one to the other. And all the stronger it was
that it seemed not even a shadow of what had happened to her on
that hill cast itself across their nuptial night. In equal measure, his
wife had given and taken.

"Hawisa," he spoke into the dark lightened by the moon and
torches beyond their tent.

She curled her toes over his. "Husband?"

"Once you told our lives were entangled—and rued it."

"Because you were soon to learn a portion of my lands had
been awarded to Cyr, thus how very near your family whilst you
were my captive. But I do not believe our lives entangled now."

"What, then?"

"Intertwined, gently twisted together, yet stronger in the
absence of snarls and knots."

He slid his hand to her abdomen. "Strong, as will be our
children." Feeling her unease, he pushed onto an elbow. "You wish
children with me, do you not?"

She turned onto her back, and he saw the sparkle of her eyes. "I do, but 'tis only possible if God is done punishing me."

"Punishing you?"

"And my people—my loss of Wulf, the Saxons' loss of England..."

Guarin nearly chided her for thinking such but recalled his own struggle to believe otherwise during captivity. "You accept our Savior, do you not, Hawisa?"

Her breath caught. "Though your William further justifies his invasion by claiming Saxons are heathens in need of reform, I am Christian the same as you."

He cupped her jaw. "As thought, but you are mistaken to think God punishes us. As my sire impressed on me, because of our Lord's sacrifice, God corrects us as a father does a beloved child, allowing us to suffer consequences for our actions in the hope we return to Him and respond differently the next time."

"Still, it feels punishment," she said, "and cruelly unjust for the thousands of Saxons who have suffered for sins not their own."

"It does, but as also explained to me, we err in believing because we follow God He will keep us from trials and danger. I forget which scripture was given me, but it ends on sorrowful assurance that time and chance happen to all. Sinner and saint. Norman and Saxon."

"Then you never questioned God for what befell you for aiding me? The caging? The chaining? The beatings? You never rebuked Him?"

Guarin sighed. "You catch me out. Far easier to preach another back to God's grace than one's self. Aye, I questioned and rebuked Him, especially in the beginning when I was so angry it was with much grudging I acknowledged I suffered for the consequences of raising a sword against your countrymen—and later when, having confessed my sins, He made me wait on deliverance. But ever I knew He was not to blame, just as I know if we are not blessed with children, it will not be because He punishes us."

He sensed disbelief as she considered that, then she said, "I disappointed Roger in bearing only Wulf, and more greatly I would have disappointed my sire had he lived beyond learning I was with child. But more than them, I fear disappointing you."

Guarin brushed back the hair whose crossings he had savored loosening during their lovemaking. "If children do not come of our love, I will be disappointed, but not with you. My feelings for you will change only to grow."

"You are certain?"

"Once in anger, I taunted I would prove a good husband. Now, in love, it is my vow, Hawisa Wulfrith." He kissed her.

"Much you comfort," she whispered against his lips. "Much you heal. As I pray, I comfort and heal you."

"You do, Wife." He lowered to his side and drew her close.

When a quarter hour passed and it was obvious she was no nearer sleep than he, Guarin said, "I remain curious why your sire wed you to a Norman rather than one of your own."

"Ah, that is quite the tale." She drew back, raised her face to his. "And of great import."

"Even more curious."

She set a hand on his chest, traced the muscle up to his collarbone, slid her fingers over his neck. "When I was a girl and still my sire had male heirs, he considered matching me with Vitalis."

That did not surprise, nor a stab of jealousy. "You felt for him?"

"Only ever as a friend, but I would have preferred wedding him rather than Roger—and certainly Jaxon's son."

"Jaxon has a son?" Guarin did not temper his surprise.

"Had. He fell at Stamford Bridge."

First came relief vengeful kin could not set themselves at Hawisa, next greater understanding of Jaxon's hatred for invaders whether they were Norwegians or Normans.

"His son was a brute," Hawisa continued. "Fortunately, my sire agreed he was not a good match. And so...Roger. Not only did

King Edward wish our union, but my sire. He had no great love for your people but, more than most Saxons, cause to esteem them."

"For what?"

"As a young man, tragedy befell him, and it was men of Normandy who saved him. He thought them the most formidable warriors. And as Hastings proved and especially the D'Argents, he was right."

"Especially the D'Argents?"

"Excepting your uncle, all your kin survived the great battle. And though Cyr and you earned William's wrath, still you are well enough regarded to be placed in positions of authority."

"As with any ruler, one is either valuable or disposable, Hawisa. I came near to being the latter."

"Methinks that is as William wishes you to believe—his rules, aye?"

"His rules," Guarin murmured, then asked, "What tragedy brought your young sire into contact with Normans?"

"He did not heed his sire's warning as often his own sons—my brothers—did not heed his and my son did not..."

In the silence drawn around her was opportunity to keep his word to Cyr, but despite her concession Wulf was at least partially responsible for his downfall, Guarin let it pass. They would speak of it another night.

"Continue, Hawisa."

"My sire fled an argument with his father, recklessly riding unescorted from Wulfenshire into Lincolnshire. There he happened on slavers destined for the coast and determined to free one of the slaves—a beautiful young woman."

"Reckless, indeed."

"He was captured, beaten, and added to those destined for sale in the mediterranean. Had not a great storm grounded the ship on Normandy's shores, likely our line would have ended since he was my grandsire's only surviving heir." She sighed. "My sire had cause to believe we are not a hardy lot. For all my family's reputation, better we train up others to survive. We know what we ought not do and demand others learn self control, yet we yield to impulse. I fear we are reckless."

"If that is so," Guarin said, "methinks the D'Argent joined with the Wulfrith can set that aright. Now tell how your sire escaped."

"Normans patrolling the beach determined to confiscate the cargo, and though their numbers were small compared to the ship's crew and slavers, they were the victors. Upon discovering most of the cargo was human, the Normans slew the ones spared, naming it an offense against God to sell those made in His image, then freed the slaves. Thus, my sire gained the woman he desired and brought her home to wed—much to my grandsire's objections."

"Because she was a slave?"

"More because he thought her delicate. You recall when I spoke of the deaths of my brothers and told my sire feared our line weakened?"

"I do."

"Fearing the same, my grandsire wished to wed his son to a woman of strong stock—tall, large-boned, generous of hips. However, my sire ignored his warnings, and though his wife gave him many healthy sons, only his daughter survived. I think recklessness more our downfall, but with each loss of a son he became more convinced he should have heeded his sire, and when I was all that remained, he determined to wed me to one of those he deemed worthiest. A Norman."

"Then he regretted wedding your mother."

"Perhaps, though I know he loved her very much."

"I am guessing it is because of your parents' ordeal there are no slaves on Wulfenshire."

"You are right. Nevermore were slaves permitted on our lands. That is, until I purchased Eberhard, but I burned his papers and would have done so even had he not agreed to aid me in keeping Wulfen out of William's grasp."

"It served, and the boy is better for it."

"Still, I have wounded him."

"Such wounds heal, as you shall see when he goes home to Wulfen with us."

"Home," she drew out the word. "I did not know I could better like the sound of that, but you make it wondrous."

"As do you, my Wulfrith bride." Guarin turned her onto her back, lowered his head, and once more claimed her mouth. His wife tasted of salt and earth, of sweet and soft, of longing and loving—but more, of the impossible made possible by God's grace.

EPILOGUE

Wulfen Castle, England
Autumn, 1069

York had fallen. Though Edgar the Aetheling had failed last spring to take that city, he succeeded months later by joining forces with King Sweyn of Denmark when Harwolfson's aid was not forthcoming. A great victory over the Normans, but greater the price to be paid for it.

"More Saxon blood," Guarin acknowledged what those who continued to rebel refused to accept. William the Great and his army were coming. Had they not yet passed over Wulfenshire on their journey north, soon they would. Within days, the rebellion would be defeated.

"Non, decimated," he corrected. Had the king any patience left before York fell to the rebels, it was in ashes.

Gripping the missive whose seal he had yet to break though it could contain tidings of William's progression, Guarin rasped, "Lord, let it be swift and done, the king and his men soon returned south."

He rubbed his temples, drew his hand over his head to the leather thong binding his hair.

"Taken to ground!" called one whose voice soothed regardless were it whispered or shouted. "'Tis no more!"

He turned Anglicus toward the woman whose booted feet forged a path through the grass between castle and wood. Upon setting eyes on his beautifully disheveled wife who had cause to struggle more with the battle to come than he, he smiled as he would not have believed possible in this moment.

Within the donjon where she served as Lady of Wulfen, Hawisa wore gowns whose unlacing—at times gentle, other times fervent—pleased him. But upon the field where she personally aided in training those accepted at Wulfen, she wore tunics, chausses, and boots. There was pleasure in their removal as well, especially when they made the waterfall their bath following a long, arduous day.

"My lady is quite the sight," Guarin said as she neared, then looked past her to the boys and young men who had paused in their labors to watch the final strokes of her sword put finish to the wooden post whose only victory was that of dulling her blade.

The ranks of warriors in training were growing, now fifteen Normans to fourteen Saxons. And on the morrow, once more Hawisa would balance the scales with the addition of a youth from the village of Ravven.

Halting alongside Anglicus, she shaded her eyes against the sun at his back, denying him sight of the grey depths in which distress had resided these past days since word arrived of York's fall. She did not exalt in the rebels' triumph, accepting the same as he the lives lost on both sides would prove for naught. Bloody rumblings only.

"Now the pel is taken to ground, does my wife feel better?"

"I do," she said with unexpected lightness.

He leaned down and ran a thumb across her cheek, turned it to show the dark upon it. "You are a mess. At day's end, we should venture to the falls."

She raised her eyebrows. "Methinks I can be persuaded."

He wished to go there with her now, but there was much training to be done in the hours remaining of daylight.

Hawisa nodded at the missive delivered minutes earlier. "You have not opened it."

"'Tis from Cyr."

"You think it tidings of your brothers and cousin?"

Their whereabouts when York fell was unknown, but it was possible one or more was among the injured and slain Normans—just as some of her former Rebels of the Pale might be among the fallen and victorious Saxons. Even Vitalis.

"That or William's progress," he said.

She extended a hand. "May I?"

He wished he had opened the missive, but though tempted to refuse, the protection afforded her would not be appreciated. Unlike Roger—and no matter the king's disapproval—Guarin allowed her to be the Wulfrith she was born. There were limits, but he aspired they should never feel a yoke.

He passed her the missive, and as she broke its seal, returned his gaze to the fenced paddocks outside Wulfen's walls. He was not surprised their audience had not returned to their weapons and wrestling, Ordric and the other trainers having taken the older boys to practice in the wood—and with them Eberhard.

Hawisa was a distraction, a curiosity to the younger, an attraction to the older. Thus, much discipline was required to keep them on task when she was on the training field, and though Eberhard had yet to fully forgive her, usually he was the first to rebuke and thump on those who showed inappropriate interest in the lady he no longer named his mother.

Greater discipline being required as the boys grew nearer men, Guarin hoped when the blessing he and Hawisa quietly awaited was bestowed, she would be receptive to spending less time outside the hall.

"Resume your training!" he bellowed.

As pages and squires hastened to do as bid, Hawisa said, "There is no word of your brothers or cousin."

Guarin looked at where she bent her head to the unrolled parchment.

"Cyr but says once confirmation is received they are well, Aelfled and he will pass Stern into our keeping and cross to Normandy."

Though grateful his brother had not immediately departed England after Darfield, it was too soon to lose him. Much he would miss Cyr's companionship, but hopefully Dougray or Theriot would return to Wulfenshire to administer Stern. Until then, Aunt Chanson and her new husband would keep all in order —including their sister, Nicola, for whom a suitable husband had yet to be found.

"Regardless of their departure," Hawisa said, "they shall visit a sennight hence, and he asks that before then you keep your word to unburden his wife."

Guarin tensed amid the clang of swords, strike of pikes, grunts and shouts. Sooner he should have kept his word, but it was no easy thing to speak ill of the son of the woman he loved though she had acknowledged Wulf was not entirely innocent of his own death.

She raised her head. "Of what does he speak?"

He took the missive, read his brother's words. When he returned to his wife, her eyes were wary as though she were halfway to the answer. "That which Aelfled never revealed. Cyr believes it will unburden her—perhaps you as well—and better reconcile you."

"Wulf," she said and touched her abdomen as if remembering when he grew there. "Tell me, and do not spare me as Aelfled did."

He considered the boys at training, next the men-at-arms

patrolling the wall who would keep watch over them. Then he tucked the missive beneath his belt alongside the dagger that was no longer of D'Argent but of Wulfrith and reached to his wife.

She slid her hand in his, set a foot atop his in the stirrup, and settled in the saddle before him.

Drawing her back against him, Guarin nudged Anglicus toward the wood. As they entered the trees, he recalled the first time he had been thus with her on this horse. Had he known three years after that battle this would be his life, would he change anything? He would not.

When they reached the stream one had only to follow a short distance to gain the waterfall, Guarin said, "We shall speak here," and dismounted. As if it were a gown she wore and delicate slippers, she awaited his arms.

Guarin lifted her down, kissed her, and led her to the bank.

The words chosen during their walk were ready to speak, but when they lowered side by side, they gave him pause. "You know my every breath is yours, do you not, Hawisa?"

Though worry lined her brow, she smiled. "Just as my every breath is yours—no matter what you tell."

He took her hand and considered the ring on her heart finger, at its center the sapphire once set in his dagger. William would not like that his gift of the old queen's ruby was no longer on Hawisa's hand, but it had been put to better use, now set in the cross guard of the Wulfrith dagger. Just as Guarin was now a Wulfrith belonging to Hawisa, she was a D'Argent belonging to him.

"I am ready to know," she prompted.

He met her gaze. "What Aelfled did not tell was the promise Wulf made after you accepted her offer to keep watch over him."

He thought she stopped breathing, but she nodded for him to continue.

"He assured her if she did so from a distance, sparing him humiliation in front of his friends, he would behave. And so he did—until the day of the battle when he and four boys who also wished to play at warriors went out the back of the stables while Aelfled awaited them at the front."

Staring at her husband, desperately Isa tried to douse anger over what her former maid told of her beloved son—desperation because she knew it was instinct to protect the memory of her child by believing the best of him, even at the sacrifice of truth. But the truth was that anger over his sire's death, cunning, and recklessness were more responsible for his demise than Aelfled, and that even in the absence of Guarin keeping his word to his brother, long that truth awaited acceptance.

"She was not negligent in her duty, Hawisa. She was lulled into trusting one she loved too much to see what he planned."

"This I know," she said and saw Guarin's surprise. He knew her well enough to sense she was receptive to the revelation, but he had not expected her to so readily accept it. It surprised her as well, especially as once again the morn had begun with dread over Edgar the Aetheling's victory at York. However, God in His wisdom had chosen this day to impart another revelation of which her husband remained unaware.

Isa turned her hand up and squeezed his fingers. "Just as I know I should have given my son into the care of one more capable of ensuring he, a child, did not seek the revenge of men." Seeing argument in his eyes, she said, "Do not defend me. Aye, I grieved my son's loss of his father, but that does not relieve me of my responsibility as a mother."

Slowly, he nodded.

"Though I fear I would have rejected the truth had I learned it sooner, I believe Aelfled. And another truth I have come to accept after meeting William—it is not the Lord who moves us. We move ourselves, whether we step from one space to another or allow others to push us there. Sometimes our steps are wise, other times an affront to God. Sometimes a push is needed, other times 'tis our undoing." She angled her body nearer. "Hence, often

I go to my knees. And on days such as this, He makes it known my prayers are heard, gifting me with guidance—and forgiveness."

His frown deepened.

Isa drew his hand to her abdomen. "I have been entrusted with another, Guarin. Ours."

He drew a sharp breath, splayed his hand upon her. "Almighty, you are with child."

"Only just learned." She smiled at his confusion. "After felling the pel, I numbered how many I have taken to ground these months and, counting backward, recalled the one that bettered me because of the onset of my last menses. That was seven weeks past." She looked to her hand on his and the D'Argent blue on her finger. "Our child is too small to feel, but he—or she—is here. We are three, Guarin."

The release of his breath across her brow brought her chin up, and his smile she had not thought could be broader than those bestowed when he carried her to bed was breathtaking. And more so against her lips.

As his kiss deepened, she slid her arms around his neck.

"Blessed," he rasped and turned her in to him and lowered to his back.

Settled atop her husband, Isa made more of their kiss, then knowing where it would lead, raised her head. "Unseemly. We are too foul for such."

"There is a pond nearby," he suggested.

"Is there?"

Grinning, he scooped her up and set her atop Anglicus. At the falls, they bathed quickly, made love slowly, and afterward held each other in a world veiled from an England not yet tamed by the conqueror.

But William was never far and ever eager to assert his presence and power.

"I fear darker days ahead," Guarin said as he stroked Isa's damp hair where they lay atop their shed clothing, "that the fall of York will push the king past all mercy."

She ceased counting the beats of his heart. "If Vitalis is there..." She sighed over worry for him and other rebels who, having refused to go the way of Harwolfson, departed Darfield with Isa's former housecarle. No backward glance, not even from Em who had been delivered word Eberhard was safe and would return to Wulfen to resume his training.

"If he aided in taking the city, he is not so arrogant to believe the Saxons' victory is great enough to go unanswered," Guarin said. "He will protect his own, taking them back under to wait and watch whilst those alongside whom they fought boast and revel."

She smiled over how well her worthy husband regarded her worthy man, wished they could be as brothers. "If he would come to us, places could be made for him and his followers."

"Providing they did not draw attention. Unfortunately, what Harwolfson gained from the king is not likely to be granted another, especially if the ill York portends comes to pass." Guarin sighed. "When God wills, may the end be good. But I should not allow such talk. Let it be just the two of us."

He was right. Numerous were the hours ahead to ache over what was to come, not these that belonged to husband and wife only. Or nearly so...

She pushed up on an elbow. "Do you forget it is seven months ere there is any possibility we shall truly be alone again?"

He chuckled, swept aside the golden hair fallen between their faces, and tucked it behind her ear. "As told, our child is exceedingly small, but when the swell of my wife's belly provides further proof Norman and Saxon have become one, I shall need no reminding."

She lowered her head and touched her mouth to his. "I require no more proof. Already you and I are one. And many to come."

Dear Reader,

What a merry chase this tale led its writer, but despite hair pulling and nibbled nails, it was a wonderful journey—and such fun to seed the Age of Conquest series with heroes and heroines and their ancestors from my other medievals. Those who have blessed me with their readership throughout my romancing of the Middle Ages will recognize Maxen Pendery, Rhiannyn, Edwin Harwolfson, and others from LADY OF CONQUEST, and the names Lavonne and De Balliol from THE REDEEMING and THE LONGING. As for the lovelies who have championed Sir Guy Torquay as worthy of his own tale, I think that was him I glimpsed atop a destrier alongside King William in the next book in the series.

Thank you for spending time with Sir Guarin and Lady Hawisa. If you enjoyed the second Wulfrith origins tale, I would appreciate a review of FEARLESS at your online retailer—just a sentence or two, more if you have time.

For a peek at NAMELESS, the third book in the AGE OF CONQUEST series, an excerpt is included here and will soon be available on my website: www.TamaraLeigh.com. Now to finish that tale for its Autumn 2019 release.

Pen. Paper. Inspiration. Imagination. ~ Tamara

For new releases and special promotions, subscribe to Tamara Leigh's mailing list: www.TamaraLeigh.com

NAMELESS EXCERPT

THE WULFRITHS. IT ALL BEGAN WITH A WOMAN

From USA Today Bestselling author Tamara Leigh, the third book in a new series set in the 11th century during the Norman Conquest of England, revealing the origins of the Wulfrith family of the AGE OF FAITH series. Releasing Autumn 2019.

PROLOGUE

Normandy, France
Spring, 1067

*Y*ou are baseborn. Despite my every effort to remedy that beyond our walls, it cannot be undone. No matter how many masses a man attends, no matter how many prayers he prays, in the absence of much effort to change his heart, he will act in accord with that to which he is disposed." Baron D'Argent paused, sighed. "It is the same with women, Dougray."

"Non, Godfroi," his wife beseeched.

The man who possessed but a forelock of black hair to evidence he had ever been other than shockingly silvered, looked from her son before the dais to where she stood alongside the high seat in which he had been settled minutes earlier. "It must be told."

"Must it?" she whispered.

He took her white-knuckled hand in his and returned his regard to the one forced to his knees to prevent him from further injuring the men-at-arms. "It is not only Adela's sire who rejects you, Dougray. It is Adela."

His words did not surprise, but they were not to be believed. Dougray had not betrayed his conscience by aiding the Duke of Normandy in stealing England's crown and lost half an arm to a battle axe for this to be the reason the one for whom he had done those things stayed away. It was her sire who kept her from Dougray's side all these months while he fought infection that threatened to put him in the ground. Her sire who, as learned this morn from servants' gossip, meant to wed her to one of legitimate, noble birth and sizable lands. This very day.

Suppressing the impulse to resume his struggle against those who kept him from her, a slender thread of reason warning it would result in further humiliation, he growled, "You lie."

"It is a hard truth, but more true because it is hard, my son."

"*My son?* Non, as you say, I am baseborn. As you say, it cannot be undone."

"Dougray!" His mother stepped forward.

It was good the baron drew her back, though it would be better had he sent her away when her son was returned to the castle.

Despite the anger raking Dougray, he did not want his mother hurt more than already she had suffered these years of whisperings over the conception of her third child. Albeit an act of indiscretion, it had been forgivable under the circumstances—though few men other than Godfroi D'Argent would have pardoned her. And as Dougray needed none to put the question to him, would any other have given another man's child his name and raised him alongside legitimate sons?

Continuing to clasp his wife's hand, the baron leaned forward. "Even do you reject me as your sire, you *are* my son—another hard truth, though only hard in this moment of believing yourself betrayed."

Feeling ache in his knees against the stone floor, though not as great as that felt in his absent lower arm, Dougray said, "I *am* betrayed."

"Not by your mother or father."

"Am I not? You ordered me ridden to ground, bound, and returned here like a criminal. You speak lies of Adela. And unless you let me go to her, this day she will be wed to a man she does not love."

"But of whom her sire approves, as does she."

"Another lie."

"Non, Dougray. Do I let you go to her, all you will find there is humiliation at best when it is confirmed I speak true, grave injury at worst when her kin and betrothed retaliate for your offense. And think of what might be believed of Adela. If you succeed in stopping the wedding, it will be only until it is verified she is not your lover." The baron raised an eyebrow as if he himself questioned that.

That he thought it possible his *son* had dishonored her moved bubbling anger toward boiling. Here a reminder Lady Robine D'Argent had been tainted by a dishonorable man, as evidenced by Dougray's untimely birth that announced to all the babe was not of her husband. The sins of the father...

Longing to break free of those who held him, he glanced at the hand gripping his right arm. Bloodied, doubtless from being drawn across a broken nose, and the man-at-arms holding his left arm surely ached over fractured ribs. But though Dougray was tempted to accept those injuries as confirmation he could throw off these men, he knew he had landed those blows only because they had not expected them and, afterward, were loath to injure one who bore the name D'Argent.

The body and reflexes that had made Dougray a warrior capable of besting most opponents had suffered much wasting these months abed. Of a weight he had not been since his youth, he was at their mercy—rather, that of the man who sat in judgment of him.

"Adela is where she ought to be, Dougray."

He returned his gaze to the baron who but appeared the formidable warrior he no longer was. From the muscular breadth of his upper body, one would not know his legs were emaciated and immovable beneath the blanket. Though none witnessed the rigor to which he subjected his torso and arms, daily he exercised the muscles yet under his control.

"I know you wished to tell him when he is more fully recovered, Robine," the baron said, "but it must be done now, and I think it best heard from me."

"Non, I was there." She drew her hand from his, pressed her shoulders back. "It is for me to do."

Where had she been? Dougray questioned as she descended the dais. *And what was for her to do?*

"Release my son," she commanded the men-at-arms.

They hesitated, then receiving a nod from their lord, did as bid and took a single step backward.

Skirts gently billowing, Lady Robine sank to her knees before Dougray. The pain in her eyes and that lining her face was greater than he had seen since his brother, Cyr, returned her maimed son to Normandy and told no further word was had of her eldest son's fate. Though three of her four sons had survived the battle of Hastings, and she clutched at hope Guarin had as well, she mourned. And this day, she hurt more for whatever she meant to reveal.

For her, rather than take advantage of his release, he kept his knees to the floor.

Cupping his bearded face between her palms, she smiled sorrowfully. "Dearest Dougray, your father does not lie. Had you been awarded a sizable demesne in England the same as Cyr, it is possible Adela's sire would have relented and allowed you to wed, but even then she herself would not have you."

He curled his fingers into fists, felt the ache of both hands though one was absent. "She loves me, does not care I was born on the wrong side of the sheets."

"I do not question once she loved you, but I believe she does no longer. Hence, her love was not worthy of our son."

The strain of keeping his muscles unmoving causing them to tremble, Dougray said, "What lies would your husband have you tell?"

Her eyes flooded with tears, and the baron barked, "Dare not speak—"

"Non!" She twisted around, raised a hand. "Let me do this."

His face was so dark it appeared he was in the throes of apoplexy, but he acceded with a jerk of his chin.

She turned back. "The week after Christmas, while you were so senseless with infection we thought we would lose you, Adela came."

Dougray startled. "Why did you not say?"

"Because we needed you to have something to live for, and that day she snatched it away." She swallowed loudly. "When she saw you lying there, so thin and pale she could not conceal her distress, she…"

"What, Mother?"

"She cried out and turned away, but I told her there was hope you would recover and persuaded her to sit beside you, myself set her hand upon yours. But when you began to rouse and drew your left arm from beneath the cover as though to reach to her, she saw."

Dougray narrowed his lids. "You did not prepare her?"

"Tidings of your loss was not cast far and wide, but since she had stayed away, we assumed she knew and, like her mother…"

"Like her mother, what?"

"Ever beauty is the first consideration. Adela's mother could have wed any of a number of godly men, but she chose the most handsome—and the most ungodly."

"Adela is not the same."

"Is she not? As told your father, I was there. Upon her face I saw revulsion that could no longer disguise itself as shock as when first she looked upon you. I saw how quickly she loosed your hand and departed. And I heard tale of how horrid she thought your injury and what a pity you should be so unmanned—"

"Lies!" Dougray thrust to his feet, causing the men-at-arms to take back the step given. He pointed at the baron who was surely wishing legs beneath him so he could pummel the offender. "Lies he has you tell to keep me from her."

Lady Robine rose. "Were they lies, they would be mine alone. They are not, Dougray, and it feels a dagger to the breast to tell what I prayed I would not have to. Unfortunately, loose lips gave you false hope ere unbreakable vows could be spoken."

He did not want to believe it false hope. If he could get to Adela, she would go away with him, and he would make a life for them beyond Normandy.

"She is undeserving, Dougray," his mother said. "There will be one more true who does not first see your loss but, rather, first her gain in taking you to husband."

"Heed your mother," Baron D'Argent said. "If a wife you desire, when you are fully recovered, I shall make a match for you. A lady of constancy, kind heart, wit, beauty, and a good dowry—perhaps even lands."

As Dougray stared at him past his mother's shoulder, he ordered his face so it would not reveal he took stock of his chances of overwhelming the men-at-arms who were the only ones present capable of intercepting him. Make it past them and he had only to make it to one of the horses tethered in the inner bailey. Make it to the drawbridge before it was raised and he had only to make it to Adela's home. Make it to her side before his pursuers arrived and he had only to make it to the cover of the wood. Then they had only to decide whether to head north, south, east, or west.

Non, not west. Never again would he cross the channel. Never again would he set foot on English soil choked with the blood of thousands of his countrymen. And when Cyr returned from the pilgrimage undertaken to atone for those slain in the great battle, neither would he return to England. Providing still there was no word Guarin lived, he would assume his place as the D'Argent heir, and the lands awarded him in England...

Hopefully, the duke who was now its king would award them to one other than the brother who administered them for Cyr. Dougray did not wish the youngest denied lands of his own, but better Normandy lands acquired by way of marriage like that proposed for the baseborn one.

"Naught to say?" the baron said, and Dougray sensed he suspected what was behind this mask.

Lull him, he told himself. *Tell him what he desires, and the sooner you, Dougray not of the same silvered hair as your brothers and sister, will be away from here.*

He drew a deep breath, but before he could spend it on conciliatory words, the baron swept a hand in his direction. "Confine him. At peril of your positions, he is not to leave his chamber without my say."

Dougray was moving before those last words were spoken—as were the men who sought to seize him as he swung away from his mother who protested her husband's orders.

Though he had not mastered what was required to efficiently move a body whose one side was out of balance with the other, he made it to the doors. But as he reached to them, one swung wide with the entrance of a young woman.

"Dougray!" Nicola exclaimed, then shrieked when a man-at-arms slammed into her brother and carried him to the floor.

With fist, elbows, knees, and feet, Dougray fought his one assailant who quickly became two.

"They will hurt him, Godfroi!" his mother cried.

"Get off him!" Nicola screamed, and he glimpsed her dragging on the tunic of the man-at-arms who struggled to subdue Dougray's upper body, felt the one grappling with his legs jerk as if she kicked him hard.

Sanity prevailed. Though angered it must to ensure she was not harmed, Dougray went still and was pinned as thoroughly as when he fell at Hastings. Strange he had not been able to feel his lower left arm then, though still it had clung to the upper, but he could feel it now though it was long removed.

He did not resist when he was dragged upright, merely made a fist of the hand no longer visible and looked to his sister who was met halfway across the hall by their mother. Staring at the young woman who demanded to know the reason her brother was set upon and the older woman seeking to soothe her, Dougray made the baron wait on the regard of one who ought to be grateful first, repentant second.

He *was* grateful for all afforded the son of the man who cuckolded Godfroi D'Argent, but repentant? Not possible in this moment—if ever.

"Silence, Nicola!" the baron commanded, and when his daughter's impassioned words ended on a squeak, looked to Dougray. "I know you are not entirely healed. I know your loss makes it difficult to think right, but you offend—more than me, God."

Dougray stood taller. "God? Be assured, I but return the favor."

"Enough!"

"You say He knows what is in my heart," he disregarded the warning, "so what harm in letting *you* know it as well?"

The baron gripped the chair arms as if to keep himself from lunging out of his seat. As if *he* did not have cause to question God.

"I answered our liege's call to invade England," Dougray said, "salving my conscience over the longing for land with assurance the duke had the pope's blessing, and yet I lost the use of an arm to a heathen on whose side God should not have been. We lost an uncle and possibly a brother to more heathens on whose side God should not have been. Thousands of our people lost husbands, sons, and brothers to thousands of heathens on whose side God should not have been. And *I* offend?"

Red-faced, the baron said, "I feel those losses more than you, and more I shall feel them if Guarin *is* lost to us, but I hold to God. If you are determined to reject what I taught you, at least honor the memory of Hugh by remembering what he taught you."

Godfroi D'Argent's twin brother. More ungodly than godly, he had trained up his nephews, son, and scores of other young men in the ways of the warrior. Were it to be believed, he had suffered a less than honorable death on the same battlefield where Dougray fell.

"Were your uncle here," the baron continued, "he would say —*Let not your heart make a fool of you.*"

He would, after delivering a blow to impress those words on the offender.

"He would say—*Grind your failings and losses to rubble beneath your feet.*"

He would, after greatly shaming one who fell even slightly short of the mark set higher than most could reach.

"He would say—*Be a warrior, Dougray D'Argent.*"

He would, though never would he add his surname to his sister-in-law's baseborn son. Dougray had been treated nearly as well as those of legitimate birth, but ever Hugh left him nameless.

"He would say—*Be a man.*"

He would, but that last pushed too far, Godfroi D'Argent unmanning Dougray the same as it was said Adela thought him unmanned by his injury. Adela who would wed within hours and lie in another's arms this night.

Dougray struggled to keep reason intact, but that slender thread snapped.

He cursed, bellowed, threw off a man-at-arms. And was slammed to the floor by the other, straddled, his one and a half arms wrenched together behind his back. Then all the raised voices—angry and beseeching alike—were silenced by a fist to the temple.

Ever Dougray was quick to recover from such blows, whether they dazed or rendered him unconscious, and this was no exception. However, whatever slight hope remained for Adela and him was lost when he roused and found he was being bound to his bed.

When he was released two days later, the woman he loved was another man's wife and possibly soon to be the mother of another man's child. *That* Dougray would not trespass upon. Never would he be the same as the one who made him on his mother. Never would any child of his be nameless.

And never again would he darken the home of the family D'Argent.

Dear Reader,
I hope you enjoyed this excerpt of NAMELESS: Book Three in the Age of Conquest series. *Watch for its release in Autumn 2019.*

For new releases and special promotions, subscribe to Tamara Leigh's mailing list: *www.TamaraLeigh.com*

PRONUNCIATION GUIDE

Aelfled/Aelf: AYL-flehd
Aetheling: AATH-uhl-eeng
Alfrith: AAL-frihth
Balliol: BAY-lee-uhl
Bernia: BUHR-nee-uh
Boudica: BOO-dih-kuh
Campagnon: CAHM-paan-yah
Chanson: SHAHN-sahn
Cyr: SEE-uhr
D'Argent: DAR-zhahnt
Dougray: DOO-gray
Eberhard/Ebbe: EH-buh-hahrt/EH-buh
Em: EHM
Estienne: EHs-tee-ihn
Fortier: FOHR-tee-ay
Fulbert: FOO-behr
Guarin: GAA-rahn
Gytha: JIY-thuh
Hawisa/Isa: HAH-wee-suh/EE-suh
Hugh: HYOO
Jaxon: JAAK-suhn
Lavonne: LUH-vahn
Maël: MAY-luh
Mary Sarah: MAA-ree-SAA-ruh
Nicola: NEE-koh-luh
Ordric: OHR-drihk
Pierre: PEE-ehr
Ravven: RAY-vihn
Raymond: RAY-mohnd
Roger: ROH-zheh
Sigward: SEEG-wuhrd

Theriot: TEH-ree-oh
Wulf: WUULF
Wulfrith: WUUL-frihth
Vitalis: VEE-tah-lihs
Zedekiah: ZEH-duh-KIY-uh

∾

PRONUNCIATION KEY

VOWELS
aa: arrow, castle
ay: chain, lady
ah: fought, sod
aw: flaw, paw
eh: bet, leg
ee: king, league
ih: hilt, missive
iy: knight, write
oh: coat, noble
oi: boy, coin
oo: fool, rule
ow: cow, brown
uh: sun, up
uu: book, hood
y: yearn, yield

CONSONANTS
b: bailey, club
ch: charge, trencher
d: dagger, hard
f: first, staff
g: gauntlet, stag
h: heart, hilt

j: jest, siege
k: coffer, pike
l: lance, vassal
m: moat, pommel
n: noble, postern
ng: ring, song
p: pike, lip
r: rain, far
s: spur, pass
sh: chivalry, shield
t: tame, moat
th: thistle, death
t~h: that, feather
v: vassal, missive
w: water, wife
wh: where, whisper
z: zip, haze
zh: treasure, vision

GLOSSARY

AETHELING: term used to denote royal princes qualified for kinship

ANDREDESWALD: forest that covered areas of Sussex and Surrey in England

ANGLO-SAXON: people of the Angles (Denmark) and Saxons (northern Germany) of which the population of 11th century England was mostly comprised

BLIAUT: medieval gown

BRAIES: men's underwear

CASTELLAN: commander of a castle

CHAUSSES: men's close-fitting leg coverings

CHEMISE: loose-fitting undergarment or nightdress

CHEVALIER: a knight of France

COIF: hood-shaped cap made of cloth or chain mail

DEMESNE: home and adjoining lands held by a lord

DONJON: tower at center of a castle serving as a lord's living area

DOTTER: meaning "daughter"; attached to a woman's name to identify her by whose daughter she is

EMBRASURE: opening in a wall often used by archers

FEALTY: tenant or vassal's sworn loyalty to a lord

FORTNIGHT: two weeks

FREE MAN: person not a slave or serf

GARDEROBE: enclosed toilet

GIRDLE: belt worn upon which purses or weaponry might be attached

HILT: grip or handle of a sword or dagger

HOUSECARLE: elite warrior who was a lord's personal bodyguard

KNAVE: dishonest or unprincipled man

LEAGUE: equivalent to approximately three miles

LIEGE: superior or lord

MAIL: garments of armor made of linked metal rings

MISCREANT: badly behaving person

MISSIVE: letter

MOAT: defensive ditch, dry or filled with water

MORROW: tomorrow; the next day

MOTTE: mound of earth

NITHING: derogatory term for someone without honor

NOBLE: one of high birth

NORMAN: people whose origins lay in Normandy on the continent

NORMANDY: principality of northern France founded in the early tenth century by the viking Rollo

PARCHMENT: treated animal skin used for writing

PELL: used for combat training, a vertical post set in the ground against which a sword was beat

PIKE: long wooden shaft with a sharp steel or iron head

POLTROON: utter coward

POMMEL: counterbalance weight at the end of a sword hilt or a knob located at the fore of a saddle

PORTCULLIS: metal or wood gate lowered to block a passage

POSTERN GATE: rear door in a wall, often concealed to allow occupants to arrive and depart inconspicuously

QUINTAIN: post used for lance training to which a dummy and sandbag are attached; the latter swings around and hits the unsuccessful tilter

SALLY PORT: small hidden entrance and exit in a fortification

SAXON: Germanic people, many of whom conquered and settled in England in the 5th and 6th centuries

SENNIGHT: one week

SHIRE: division of land; England was divided into earldoms, next shires, then hundreds

THANE: in Anglo-Saxon England, a member of the nobility or

landed aristocracy who owed military and administrative duty to
an overlord, above all the king; owned at least five hides of land
TRENCHER: large piece of stale bread used as a bowl for food
VASSAL: one who holds land from a lord and owes fealty

ALSO BY TAMARA LEIGH

∾

CLEAN READ HISTORICAL ROMANCE

THE FEUD: A Medieval Romance Series
Baron Of Godsmere: Book One
Baron Of Emberly: Book Two
Baron of Blackwood: Book Three

LADY: A Medieval Romance Series
Lady At Arms: Book One
Lady Of Eve: Book Two

BEYOND TIME: A Medieval Time Travel Romance Series
Dreamspell: Book One
Lady Ever After: Book Two

STAND-ALONE Medieval Romance Novels
Lady Of Fire
Lady Of Conquest
Lady Undaunted
Lady Betrayed

∾

INSPIRATIONAL HISTORICAL ROMANCE

AGE OF FAITH: A Medieval Romance Series

The Unveiling: Book One

The Yielding: Book Two

The Redeeming: Book Three

The Kindling: Book Four

The Longing: Book Five

The Vexing: Book Six

The Awakening: Book Seven

The Raveling: Book Eight

AGE OF CONQUEST: A Medieval Romance Series

Merciless: Book One

Fearless: Book Two (Spring 2019)

Nameless: Book Three (Autumn 2019)

∾

INSPIRATIONAL CONTEMPORARY ROMANCE

HEAD OVER HEELS: Stand-Alone Romance Collection

Stealing Adda

Perfecting Kate

Splitting Harriet

Faking Grace

SOUTHERN DISCOMFORT: A Contemporary Romance Series

Leaving Carolina: Book One

Nowhere, Carolina: Book Two

Restless in Carolina: Book Three

∾

OUT-OF-PRINT GENERAL MARKET REWRITES

Warrior Bride 1994: Bantam Books (Lady At Arms)

*Virgin Bride 1994: Bantam Books (Lady Of Eve)

Pagan Bride 1995: Bantam Books (Lady Of Fire)

Saxon Bride 1995: Bantam Books (Lady Of Conquest)

Misbegotten 1996: HarperCollins (Lady Undaunted)

Unforgotten 1997: HarperCollins (Lady Ever After)

Blackheart 2001: Dorchester Leisure (Lady Betrayed)

*Virgin Bride is the sequel to *Warrior Bride; Pagan Pride* and *Saxon Bride* are stand-alone novels

For new releases and special promotions, subscribe to Tamara Leigh's mailing list: www.TamaraLeigh.com

ABOUT THE AUTHOR

Tamara Leigh signed a 4-book contract with Bantam Books in 1993, her debut medieval romance was nominated for a RITA award, and successive books with Bantam, HarperCollins, and Dorchester earned awards and places on national bestseller lists.

In 2006, the first of Tamara's inspirational contemporary romances was published, followed by six more with Multnomah and RandomHouse. Perfecting Kate was optioned for a movie, Splitting Harriet won an ACFW Book of the Year award, and Faking Grace was nominated for a RITA award.

In 2012, Tamara returned to the historical romance genre with the release of Dreamspell and the bestselling Age of Faith and The Feud series. Among her #1 bestsellers are her general market romances rewritten as clean and inspirational reads, including Lady at Arms, Lady of Eve, and Lady of Conquest. In late 2018, she released MERCILESS, the first book in the new AGE OF CONQUEST series unveiling the origins of the Wulfrith family. Psst!—It all began with a woman.

Tamara lives near Nashville with her husband, a German Shepherd who has never met a squeaky toy she can't destroy, and a feisty Morkie who keeps her company during long writing stints.

Connect with Tamara at her website www.tamaraleigh.com, Facebook, Twitter and tamaraleightenn@gmail.com.

For new releases and special promotions, subscribe to Tamara Leigh's mailing list: www.tamaraleigh.com